Two Novels
Apartheid
South Africa

~ ~ ~

I can hear them singing now

Hillbrow Heights: Immorality

HILTON HAMANN

ISBN: 9781519039552
INDEPENDENT REPRINT

DEDICATION

This book is dedicated to my wife, Joy, sons, Kevin and Bryan and to my parents, all of whom steadfastly supported my writing endeavors over the past 35 years.

CONTENTS

I can hear them singing now

Introduction

On 16 June 1976, black school pupils in Soweto – the huge black township located on the outskirts of Johannesburg in South Africa – staged a mass demonstration that quickly turned violent when police opened fire with live ammunition. Their protest was against being taught in Afrikaans in their schools and, although the unrest quickly spread to other parts of the country, the police and security forces were soon able to put a lid on it and bring it under control.

However, tensions continued to simmer and the banned African National Congress (ANC), the main organisation in the fight against the government, took note of how effective a mobilised population could be.

Using lessons it learned from North Korean and Vietnamese advisors, the organisation set about press-ganging communities in the black townships into the struggle against Pretoria. Terror and brutality was used to bring those who were reluctant to join, into line.

It was a terrible situation for thousands of ordinary black citizens, who found themselves between the government security forces on one hand and the ANC enforcers on the other.

By the mid 1980s South Africa was effectively involved in a low-level, civil war where black policemen, town councillors and perceived government-collaborators were targeted. Many were murdered and a large number saw their homes burnt down. In addition, a number of bombs were detonated in 'white' areas and rent and consumer boycotts were rigorously enforced by the instruments of the ANC.

The South African government responded by declaring a State of Emergency and cracked down harshly on activists and opponents. Military raids were launched against ANC targets in surrounding countries and the government hanged a number of political activists who were found guilty of murder.

In the 1980s, the purpose-built, gallows in Pretoria Central prison saw 1 123 people die at the end of the rope.

It is during this time that this story takes place.

The tale is completely fictional but some of the characters were real people and the underlying events and descriptions accurately portray the situation and what took place in the country at that time.

Chapter 1

News that your neighbours, people you've known for years, are burning down your home, can ruin your day.

But hearing it over the static-encrusted crackle of a Motorola police radio while crouching in the back of a Casspir, armoured police vehicle and not being able to do a damned thing about it, is even worse.

It was drizzling, not hard enough to be called rain, more like heavy mist, but still enough to invade the seams of their clothes and the cracks of their mood. The low cloud seemed to mix with the smoke of burning township houses and smouldering car tires, like cream swirled into coffee.

It was strange weather for that time of year. Normally there was no rain in May and the wet weather arrived only in October or occasionally in September if the country's farmers were lucky and then, most of the talk in the farming co-operatives, was about the promise of a good season.

But there was no talk of farming in the Casspir. Eight men, six black and two white, occupied a blue and yellow armoured police vehicle that displayed the scuffs and scars of previous battles. The days of the South African Police using soft-skinned vehicles to patrol in black townships were long-gone.

The faces of the men glistened as though oiled. Water droplets dripped from the peaks of their soft, navy blue caps and there was a water-sheen that glistened on the steel skin of the vehicle.

“Oscar Two, this is Oscar One...message over.”

“Send...over,” said the radio operator, a chunky, white sergeant with a bulbous gut that revealed his fondness for junk food, brandy and Coke. Secretly he was known as 'Fat Gut'. He pressed his lips against the microphone, as though he intended to swallow it.

The radio was silent for a moment other than a few static cracks and pops.

"Incident of arson at 21 Moroka Street. They say the house is going up in flames and there are barricades across the road. The fuckers aren't letting anyone through so there is probably no point if we call the fire brigade...in any case, it's probably too late."

The voice on the radio was high-pitched, tinged with both anxiety and excitement, standard radio procedures forbidding swearing were forgotten.

"Roger, Oscar One. Message received. We're on our way but it may take some time. The bastards seem to be burning down the whole township!"

'Fat Gut' replaced the handset. For a moment no-one spoke, the only sound, the engine of the Casspir and the hiss of the radio.

Then one of the black constables swore.

"Stinking sons of whores!" He spat the words out like a lump of phlegm expelled onto a pavement. He shivered and pulled the collar of his rain cape tight against his neck as the rain intensified.

No-one spoke. They all knew 21 Moroka Street was Warrant Officer, Templeton Ngubane's home.

Nobody knew what to say. What do you say to someone when you've just heard his home is being burned down? So they said nothing, preferring to simply sit and stare at the floor of the bowels of the steel vehicle.

Outside the sounds of a township war continued.

"I want to see!" said Ngubane suddenly. "By Christ, I want to see who is doing this to me!"

"Take it easy Temp," said Warrant Officer Eric Joubert, the other white cop in the Casspir. "Just leave it. There's nothing you can do."

He placed his hand on Ngubane's shoulder.

Warrant Officers Joubert and Templeton Ngubane had

come a long way together. They joined the South African Police Force 17 years earlier, just two months apart and, while they never socialised after hours, they respected each other and, in a strange sort of way, were friends. Each knew he could rely on the other to watch his back when the shit really hit the fan. Ngubane proved that the day he saved Joubert's life when the two of them were lured into an ambush, set up by Umkhonto we Sizwe operatives.

Ngubane's eyes narrowed and his brow creased. A vein throbbed in his temple. He was a large man who was once athletic, back in the days when he was an active amateur boxer. But over the years, middle-aged spread – the result of a keen fondness of the chocolate cakes his wife, Ellen, regularly baked – had crept up and won the battle, more by infiltration than direct, frontal attack. Nowadays, if he wanted a shirt to button comfortably across his midriff he had to get one with a neck size that was an inch or two too large.

He often joked with Ellen it wasn't his gut getting bigger but rather his neck getting smaller!

Templeton Ngubane knew he needed to get more exercise and to cut down on the chocolate cake and he was making an effort – he had started more Monday morning diets, that ended of Friday afternoons, than he could remember. It was a losing battle that he knew he was fighting in vain but he felt obliged to maintain token resistance against his slowly-increasing belt-size.

"Jesus! Don't tell me to relax, Jooba!" he snapped back. "It's not your fucking house they're burning down! I can't sit idly while my home and everything I worked for, for 17 years, is destroyed!

"Maybe it is too late and, maybe there is nothing I can do about it, but, by Christ, I want to see who is responsible!"

"Sure, Temp," said Joubert. "I understand. I'm sorry."

He turned to the driver.

"What are you waiting for? Let's get there!"

Chapter 2

Up ahead, a barricade constructed of burning tires piled in a heap, next to an over-turned bread delivery van, was erected across the potholed, unpaved street. Both the tires and the van burned fiercely and the thick, sticky smoke dirtied the limp drizzle.

The sign-writing on the side of the van could no longer be read, as the paint bubbled and peeled in the heat. Only an 'N' and an 'O' of the bakery's name remained unconsumed in a feeble protest against the firebrands.

The bread van driver was lucky. He was simply a target of opportunity for the band of youngsters who called themselves ANC Comrades. In the wrong place at the wrong time.

They stopped him at the barricade set across the road and swarmed around the vehicle, whooping and hollering.

“Get out!” yelled a youngster who wasn't much older than 14 and who held an unlit petrol-bomb in his right hand.

The driver did not hesitate for even a split-second. He did exactly as instructed and did it fast. He wasn't going to commit suicide for bread that wasn't even his!

“We are confiscating this bread in the name of the revolution and for the good of the people!” the youngster with the Molotov cocktail shrieked. His eyes were wild and crazed. Others began rocking the van from side to side, as they attempted to push it over.

The driver slid out of the van and when his feet touched the ground he started running and did not look back until he could no longer hear the shouts of the mob and was out of range of the stones thrown at him.

“Viva!” yelled another youngster, as someone snapped the padlock on the back doors of the van with a length of salvaged steel, water-pipe.

The double doors were flung open and the bread, destined for shops in the township, was quickly passed to outstretched hands. Then the howling mob toppled the van onto its left side. Petrol spilled from the fuel-cap and formed a little river that began to dam up.

"Stand back, Comrades!" instructed a youngster in a yellow T-shirt, so faded and ragged that it was impossible to read the slogan once printed on the chest.

"Give me newspaper."

A young woman in the crowd handed him a sheet of rolled up newspaper which he lit and, once the fire had taken hold, he held it up, like a participant in the Olympic Games torch-lighting ceremony. The crowd moved back and then he tossed the burning newspaper onto the puddle of spilled fuel. It exploded with a snapping 'poof' and quickly took hold in the rest of the tipped-over vehicle.

To outsiders and civilians, the roadblock would have looked impressive but a burning, light delivery vehicle and a pile of tires is nothing to an armoured vehicle that weighs more than five tons and is specially built to smash through such obstacles.

"Use the tear-gas and then go straight through!" ordered W/O Joubert as he peered over the top of the vehicle.

At the sight of the arriving Casspir, the youngsters at the makeshift roadblock dashed for cover between the box-shaped houses that lined both sides of the street. Many in the group were veterans of the township wars that had raged for months. This was not a retreat but rather a temporary withdrawal, so they could plan and launch an attack.

The Casspir drew to a standstill as the driver studied the roadblock, apparently unsure of what to do next.

"Here come the stones!" yelled a constable as a volley of thrown rocks was launched from between the houses on both sides of the street. This was followed by another salvo of missiles that rained down like giant hailstones, as youngsters darted out from between the houses to fling them at the police, then ducked back behind cover.

"Shit!" swore one of the cops as he crouched down behind the side-walls of the Casspir.

A large stone hit Joubert's chin and split it like a rotten tomato.

"Christ!" he blasphemed, his shirt already spattered with blood. "Where the fuck is the tear-gas?"

His voice was shrill and his colleagues detected a hint of panic in it.

There was chaos in the back of the Casspir. Policemen crouched frantically as stones rained down endlessly.

These kids were prepared, thought Ngubane. They knew we were coming and were waiting for us. He shivered, momentarily remembering the ambush he and Joubert had once survived.

A young constable, fresh out of the Police Training College at Hammanskraal struggled to clip the tear-gas grenade onto the front of his rifle. Twice he dropped it, as stones clattered like thunder against the sides of the blue and yellow vehicle. His hands were wet from a combination of clammy, fear-induced, sweat and rain.

"Give the damn thing to me!" roared Ngubane. He saw the youngster was getting nowhere. He snatched the rifle and the tear-gas grenade from the constable who was now trembling so badly it was impossible for him to deploy the grenade.

Ngubane, still crouched, clipped the canister onto the end of the rifle then stood up and prepared to fire over the side of the Casspir at the stone-throwing mob. As he did so, the youngster with the petrol bomb, now burning, ran out from of one of the yards on the right and, from a distance of about 30 metres, flung it at them.

"Fuck! Petrol bomb!" yelled Ngubane, instinctively ducking.

The fiery cocktail, contained in a green wine bottle, arced through the smoke-tainted air, spinning like a booted rugby ball, towards the men in the Casspir. It smashed onto the ground a few feet short of its intended target and shattered in a ball of fire.

"Shoot, damn it, shoot!" Joubert yelled.

Ngubane stood up and fired over the side of the Casspir in the general direction of the stone-throwers, making no attempt to aim at anyone specific.

The grenade-canister bounced once on the road before it hit a woman in the stomach and landed on the road, spinning and hissing like a snake doused in boiling water. It spewed plumes of angry, white gas into the air.

The crowd scattered immediately, running wildly in an attempt to escape the fumes that set their eyes on fire and made them retch so hard they felt they would puke up their own spleens.

"Come back and fight! Not so tough now 'eh?" Joubert yelled after the fleeing youngsters. Behind the houses some kids lit rolled-up sheets of newspaper and inhaled the smoke because this lessened the effects of the tear-gas.

Joubert held a blood-soaked handkerchief pressed tightly to his split chin.

"Go through! Go through, for God's sake!" Ngubane called to the driver.

Like a steel ramrod the Casspir lurched forward and crashed through the crude barricade. One hundred and fifty metres further on, it turned left into Moroka Street. All of the cops were standing up in the back of the Casspir now, scanning the road ahead and the houses that lined it. Two hundred metres ahead, just before the point where the road curved to the right, a crowd numbering about 100, was gathered outside the Ngubane house. A bonfire burned in the road in front of it.

The Casspir driver braked hard suddenly, causing the

men in the back to stumble forward.

"Why are you stopping?" Joubert bellowed. His eyes were red and watery – they'd had no time to fit their gas masks before firing the tear-gas that hung heavily in the air when they drove through it.

"We can't go any further," the driver said. He pointed to a freshly-dug trench that stretched across the road.

Like a grotesque, mocking mouth, it sliced across the untarred Moroka Street, four feet wide and three feet deep.

In the distance, outside the house, a 17 year-old schoolgirl tossed a framed photograph of Templeton and his family into the flames.

"What the fuck are you waiting for? Go!" W/O Ngubane snapped at the driver.

Joubert held his hand up, gesturing to the driver to wait.

"We can't, Temp," he said. "We'll be trapped in that ditch and be sitting ducks."

It would be suicide for eight men, armed only with one automatic rifle and some shotguns and pistols to try to cross with the Casspir. Outside, beyond the protection of the armoured vehicle, they stood no chance against a determined mob.

"There's nothing we can do here, Temp," his voice was soft and resigned as he scanned the crowd with a set of battered, police-issued, eight-power binoculars. The enhanced image allowed him to see how more of Templeton and Ellen's furniture was dragged from the house and committed to the fire.

"We might as well go," Joubert said.

"Give me those," said Ngubane in a harsh, raspy voice. He snatched the binoculars from the thin white man.

"I need to see this. This is a day I never want to forget. I want to burn into my mind the images of my own people turning against me!"

"Come on, Temp, let's just go," said Joubert. He gently

grasped the large black man's arm.

Ngubane shook him off roughly. Even without the help of the binoculars he could clearly see what was happening. The colour television set he bought only five months earlier with his Christmas bonus was carried out and dropped in the street.

Some of the Comrades wanted to take it and keep it for themselves but their leader, a 19 year-old school-dropout and veteran of the township struggle would not allow it. He wanted to make a point, a gesture the cop would not easily forget.

“Smash it!,” he tersely commanded.

A youth, armed with a metal pipe shattered the glass screen and then, with two vicious blows, broke the wooden cabinet in a shower of splinters.

“This is what we do to sell-out dogs!” yelled a kid who was still in primary school at the powerless Casspir.

“Viva!” he shouted. “Viva revolution! Viva ANC! Viva Nelson Mandela!”

The refrigerator was dragged from the house next and the food Ellen prepared for tonight's family meal was spilled onto the road like wino vomit. Then their clothes were brought out. One by one, suits Templeton purchased over the years for special occasions – birthdays, christenings and funerals – were thrown, like bad rubbish, into the fire.

When a woman waved a small yellow dress with lace around its collar Ngubane's heart sank. Nausea and anger welled up in him and he gagged, fighting an urge not to throw up. All the other things they had destroyed could be replaced, but this was personal and painful.

“Oh God, not that, please!” he whispered. The dress belonged to his five year-old daughter, Thandi. It was her birthday next week and the family planned a special party to celebrate the occasion. Part of her present was that she got to choose a new, special dress, for her party and, like any little girl, she could not contain her excitement when they went shopping for it two days ago.

"Please Mama, let me wear it now, it's so pretty!" she begged Ellen in the shop.

"No, you're going to have to wait until your party," replied her mother, trying to sound stern.

"Daddy, please speak to Mama! I can't wait that long. Please! Please!" she pleaded.

Templeton shook his head. "Sorry, Mama says 'no' and she's the boss." He smiled inwardly. Playing the role of good cop with his kids was something he enjoyed.

"Please Papa..." when she used the word 'Papa" rather than 'Daddy' and looked at him with wide, pleading eyes she always got her way. His heart melted.

"Come on, Ellen, let the child wear the dress...it can do no harm."

Thandi slipped her little hand into his. It was warm and soft as a puppy's breath. He looked down at her and smiled. Thandi had inherited her mother's fine, delicate, exquisite features and was definitely going to one day be a very beautiful woman.

"You big softie. It's no wonder the children get away with anything," Ellen chided him gently. She smiled. She loved it that he was such a good father. "I don't know how you're tough enough to catch those big, bad terrorists and gangsters that you're always locking up."

She stood on her tiptoes so she could kiss him on the point of his broad nose.

"But that's why I love you. Go on, put the dress on," she said, turning to Thandi, who whooped with delight.

The fine, silk fabric disappeared in a puff, as the flames swallowed it. Next, his son, Roger's books and Orlando Pirates posters went into the fire.

Oh God, please, not that, he thought. He clenched his fists and gritted his teeth. In the smoke, a comrade in a yellow COSAS T-shirt, held a white doll by its blonde hair.

He paused, as though contemplating its fate and then, with a shrug of his shoulders flipped it onto the burning pile.

How am I going to tell Thandi about this? Templeton thought. Tears welled in his eyes as he struggled to fight back his emotions and hold his composure in front of his colleagues.

That doll was part of their family. He bought it for Thandi when she turned three. He'd hunted for a black doll in all the toy shops he could find in the city but could find none.

"There's not much call for black dolls," a shop assistant told him. "Don't take this the wrong way, but in all honesty, I did not know blacks played with dolls."

And then, speaking more to herself than Templeton, she said: "Fancy that, you learn something new every day!"

Ngubane just smiled and bought the doll. The fact it was white didn't bother Thandi in the slightest. She named it Martha, after her grandmother and loved it like it was her sister.

How do I tell Thandi, Martha is dead? he asked himself again.

His growing anger suddenly burst like a popping balloon.

"You bastards!" he screamed, "You fucking bastards!"

His curse was met with waved, clenched fists and jeering political taunts and suddenly he felt drained. More tired than he had ever been in his life. His legs felt ropey and weak. He needed to sit before he collapsed.

"Let's get out of here, I've seen enough," he gasped.

Jesus, I can't breathe, he thought. I think I am having a heart attack.

The Casspir reversed, did a three-point turn and headed back up Moroka Street. Behind them flames were beginning to lick through the windows at number 21.

Chapter 3

The rain had stopped and, with it, the township battles. Reinforcements consisting of additional policemen as well as a contingent of 100 soldiers arrived and the area was locked down tightly.

An uneasy calm settled in, as security forces stepped up patrols and began clearing away the roadblocks and obstacles erected by township youngsters.

House-to-house searches were planned but right now the priority was to properly secure the area. Damage and situation reports were radioed in and logged and recorded at the police station. In just three hours the homes of eight black policemen had been burned to the ground. Three municipal councillors' homes suffered the same fate and four delivery vehicles were either completely destroyed or badly damaged. Eighteen people were in hospital being treated for injuries, mostly the result of rubber bullets but, so far, there were no reported deaths. Two policemen, one of them Eric Joubert, required treatment after being struck by rocks thrown by protesters.

It was obvious to the security force commanders that this was no spontaneous uprising, it was too well-planned and co-ordinated.

Overhead an air force helicopter circled. The occupants scanned the smoking ground below them, ready to report the gathering of any groups. The thumpa-thumpa beat of it's engine reverberated through the alleyways of the township and caused people to hide.

But, for the moment, it appeared the anger on the ground was satiated and most people had retreated into their houses, where they waited and prepared for the inevitable police searches and raids to come.

In the command room at the police station, a police

colonel was on the phone to head-quarters in Pretoria. He was put through to a Brigadier in charge of members' welfare.

"We've got eight members and their families who need to be housed somewhere today," he said, speaking in Afrikaans. "They can't stay in the township. Can you sort something out?"

***

"Drink this coffee, Temp." Eric Joubert handed his colleague a chipped, floral-patterned mug of steaming coffee.

Ngubane was a big man who cut an imposing figure but, right now, to Jooba Joubert, he appeared much smaller. He took the steaming beverage without saying anything and held the mug in both hands so it could warm his fingers.

Joubert had three stitches on the point of his chin. He was a small man, thin and wiry with a whipcord body. Every day he forced himself to complete a weight-training regimen at home that kept him as strong and supple as he was when, fresh out of the police college, he was a member of the SAP Greco-Roman wrestling team.

His features were sharp and pointy, rat-like in many ways and, unlike Ngubane whose hairline was receding, Joubert sported a full head of blue-black hair that he kept short and held in place by daily applications of *Vitalis* hair oil. A thin dark moustache underlined his nose.

Templeton sat on a bench against a wall in the courtyard at the police station. The grey paint on top of the bench was long-since worn away and its surface was rough-scarred, the result of countless people over the years scraping their initials into the wood while they waited to be attended to.

A small, delicately-featured woman dressed in jeans and a black wind-breaker sat beside Templeton. She wore no shoes and her feet were cut.

"Are you cold, Mrs Ngubane?" Joubert asked. Many times before she'd asked him to call her 'Ellen' but he steadfastly resisted. The last thing Joubert wanted was to become too familiar and matey.

"I see you're shivering, I can get you a blanket."

She shook her head. "No thanks. I'm fine it's probably just the tension and reaction to what happened today."

"Bring a blanket anyway," he said to a constable standing nearby.

"You were lucky to escape with your lives," said Joubert.

"Yes," sighed Ellen Ngubane. "I saw them coming down the road and knew they were on the way to our house. I grabbed Thandi and we climbed over the back fence and were able to escape without them seeing us. I didn't even have time to put on my shoes."

She looked tired.

"What I don't get, Temp, is why you waited until this morning to get out. For the past week we heard policemen and councillors were going to be targeted," said Joubert.

"Why didn't you move your stuff out earlier?"

Ngubane took a sip of the coffee and shrugged his shoulders.

"I suppose I preferred not to believe it. I've lived with and served these people for years. I watched those kids grow up. I probably lied to myself, by choosing to believe they wouldn't turn on me."

He turned to Ellen and put his arms around her.

"My arrogance in believing that, nearly cost you and Thandi your lives," he said. "I am so sorry!"

Ellen softly pressed her forefinger to his lips to stop him talking.

"Hush, This is not your fault."

Templeton crushed her to his chest and held her.

"Thank you," he whispered.

"Where is Thandi now?" he asked, finally releasing Ellen.

"She's fine. She's with a female police officer who has managed to find a few toys for her."

"How is she?"

"She's okay. I don't think she really understands what happened."

Ngubane took another mouthful of coffee.

"Find me a cigarette please," he said to the constable.

Ellen looked sharply at him then changed her mind and kept quiet. Templeton gave up smoking three months earlier when, at his annual physical exam, the police doctor told him he was fast heading for a heart attack. But at this moment, the possibility of a heart attack seemed insignificant.

The constable handed him a half-empty pack of Gunston plain cigarettes. Ngubane took one and tapped the ends against the side of the matchbox to tamp down loose strands of tobacco. He licked one end, put it in the corner of his mouth and lit it.

"I just didn't believe it would happen to me," he said, drawing smoke into the depths of his lungs. "Other policemen maybe...but not me."

Chapter 3

The rain had stopped and, with it, the township battles. Reinforcements consisting of additional policemen as well as a contingent of 100 soldiers arrived and the area was locked down tightly.

An uneasy calm settled in, as security forces stepped up patrols and began clearing away the roadblocks and obstacles erected by township youngsters.

House-to-house searches were planned but right now the priority was to properly secure the area. Damage and situation reports were radioed in and logged and recorded at the police station. In just three hours the homes of eight black policemen had been burned to the ground. Three municipal councillors' homes suffered the same fate and four delivery vehicles were either completely destroyed or badly damaged. Eighteen people were in hospital being treated for injuries, mostly the result of rubber bullets but, so far, there were no reported deaths. Two policemen, one of them Eric Joubert, required treatment after being struck by rocks thrown by protesters.

It was obvious to the security force commanders that this was no spontaneous uprising, it was too well-planned and co-ordinated.

Overhead an air force helicopter circled. The occupants scanned the smoking ground below them, ready to report the gathering of any groups. The thumpa-thumpa beat of it's engine reverberated through the alleyways of the township and caused people to hide.

But, for the moment, it appeared the anger on the ground was satiated and most people had retreated into their houses, where they waited and prepared for the inevitable police searches and raids to come.

In the command room at the police station, a police

colonel was on the phone to head-quarters in Pretoria. He was put through to a Brigadier in charge of members' welfare.

"We've got eight members and their families who need to be housed somewhere today," he said, speaking in Afrikaans. "They can't stay in the township. Can you sort something out?"

***

"Drink this coffee, Temp." Eric Joubert handed his colleague a chipped, floral-patterned mug of steaming coffee.

Ngubane was a big man who cut an imposing figure but, right now, to Jooba Joubert, he appeared much smaller. He took the steaming beverage without saying anything and held the mug in both hands so it could warm his fingers.

Joubert had three stitches on the point of his chin. He was a small man, thin and wiry with a whipcord body. Every day he forced himself to complete a weight-training regimen at home that kept him as strong and supple as he was when, fresh out of the police college, he was a member of the SAP Greco-Roman wrestling team.

His features were sharp and pointy, rat-like in many ways and, unlike Ngubane whose hairline was receding, Joubert sported a full head of blue-black hair that he kept short and held in place by daily applications of *Vitalis* hair oil. A thin dark moustache underlined his nose.

Templeton sat on a bench against a wall in the courtyard at the police station. The grey paint on top of the bench was long-since worn away and its surface was rough-scarred, the result of countless people over the years scraping their initials into the wood while they waited to be attended to.

A small, delicately-featured woman dressed in jeans and a black wind-breaker sat beside Templeton. She wore no shoes and her feet were cut.

"Are you cold, Mrs Ngubane?" Joubert asked. Many times before she'd asked him to call her 'Ellen' but he steadfastly resisted. The last thing Joubert wanted was to become too familiar and matey.

"I see you're shivering, I can get you a blanket."

She shook her head. "No thanks. I'm fine it's probably just the tension and reaction to what happened today."

"Bring a blanket anyway," he said to a constable standing nearby.

"You were lucky to escape with your lives," said Joubert.

"Yes," sighed Ellen Ngubane. "I saw them coming down the road and knew they were on the way to our house. I grabbed Thandi and we climbed over the back fence and were able to escape without them seeing us. I didn't even have time to put on my shoes."

She looked tired.

"What I don't get, Temp, is why you waited until this morning to get out. For the past week we heard policemen and councillors were going to be targeted," said Joubert.

"Why didn't you move your stuff out earlier?"

Ngubane took a sip of the coffee and shrugged his shoulders.

"I suppose I preferred not to believe it. I've lived with and served these people for years. I watched those kids grow up. I probably lied to myself, by choosing to believe they wouldn't turn on me."

He turned to Ellen and put his arms around her.

"My arrogance in believing that, nearly cost you and Thandi your lives," he said. "I am so sorry!"

Ellen softly pressed her forefinger to his lips to stop him talking.

"Hush, This is not your fault."

Templeton crushed her to his chest and held her.

"Thank you," he whispered.

"Where is Thandi now?" he asked, finally releasing Ellen.

“She's fine. She's with a female police officer who has managed to find a few toys for her.”

“How is she?”

“She's okay. I don't think she really understands what happened.”

Ngubane took another mouthful of coffee.

“Find me a cigarette please,” he said to the constable.

Ellen looked sharply at him then changed her mind and kept quiet. Templeton gave up smoking three months earlier when, at his annual physical exam, the police doctor told him he was fast heading for a heart attack. But at this moment, the possibility of a heart attack seemed insignificant.

The constable handed him a half-empty pack of Gunston plain cigarettes. Ngubane took one and tapped the ends against the side of the matchbox to tamp down loose strands of tobacco. He licked one end, put it in the corner of his mouth and lit it.

“I just didn't believe it would happen to me,” he said, drawing smoke into the depths of his lungs. “Other policemen maybe...but not me.”

Chapter 4

"What will happen to us now, Papa?"

Thandi slipped her hand into his. Her eyes were red and swollen from crying for Martha.

"Martha's gone to heaven," said Ellen gently. "You remember what they taught you at Sunday School about heaven don't you?" The little girl nodded. "Well that's where Martha is. She is safe and happy there and you'll see her one day."

Templeton took a white handkerchief from his pocket and used it to dab the tears running down his daughter's cheeks.

"Don't cry any more. I'll get you another doll."

"But it won't be Martha," she said softly and sniffed. "But what's going to happen to us, Papa?"

Templeton shrugged his shoulders. "I don't know exactly. I suppose the police will make some arrangement. They'll make a plan and find us somewhere to live."

He picked Thandi up and held her to him.

"Don't you worry. They won't let us down. Everything is going to be fine...I promise."

"The army is going to put up tents behind the station," said Eric Joubert. "You'll stay there until other accommodation is found. Some members of the Top Brass are on their way from Pretoria with press and television people. They'll probably tell you exactly what's going to happen then.

"The press will most likely want to interview you as well."

"Jooba, they can go to hell!" snapped Ngubane. Like all policemen who operated in the field, he deeply disliked and distrusted the press. "I'm not going to be a performer in some media circus!...bloody pack of vultures! I don't want them picking over my problems."

"Hey, I understand exactly how you feel," said Joubert.

"If I were in your shoes I'd feel exactly the same but I'll write you a letter now, that you won't have a choice. Opportunities like this don't come often for the police and the PR boys are going to milk it for all it's worth.

"You and your family are going to become the poster children of the SAP, the symbols of injustice perpetrated by the ANC against the police. Mark my words about that!"

They were sitting in an unoccupied office at the rear of the police station. Joubert poured himself a second cup of coffee from a blue flask.

"Want some?"

Templeton shook his head.

Joubert's carefully combed and oiled hair shone in the light cast by the single, overhead, bare bulb. The open stitches on his chin gave him a slightly ghoulish look. He put three heaped teaspoons of brown sugar into his coffee, stirred vigorously and took a sip of the lukewarm beverage.

"The broader South African public is going to know that the lot of a policeman is not a happy one...oh yes!...bet your bottom dollar on that."

Chapter 5

Warrant Office Templeton Ngubane squinted into the harsh television light aimed at his face. He couldn't clearly see the people behind them.

Jooba was right. He didn't have a choice. His bosses deemed the Ngubane family's appearance before the press was in the greater interests of the SAP and they ordered him to do it. Fuck how he felt!

Ellen handled the ordeal – and it was an ordeal – well but for Thandi, it was an absolutely terrifying experience. She clung to her mother and refused to answer questions or even look at the cameras. She buried her face against her mother's breast and was soon crying.

The PR guys loved it. They couldn't have scripted it better themselves, as photographers and cameramen tried to capture the pitiful moment.

Eventually, when they were sure the shots were in the can, they took pity on the little girl and a white female lieutenant took her from Ellen and away from the members of the media.

"How do you feel now?" asked a journalist with a British accent. Ngubane later learned he was from the News of the World, a London-based tabloid and was their local correspondent.

What a stupid, fucking question, Templeton thought. My house and possessions have been destroyed and I put the lives of my wife and daughter at risk...how the fuck does he think I feel?

"I've felt better," he said tersely.

"What will happen now?"

"I don't know."

A newsman wearing a khaki shirt with an embroidered logo of one of the country's top game lodges on the breast pocket, thrust a microphone into Templeton's face.

"Warrant Officer Ngubane – John Carlisle, ABC Morning News – you lost your home and your family barely escaped death. In addition, all your possessions are gone and all for one reason – the fact that you are a policeman. Has this made you bitter towards the SAP?"

"I'm still trying to process and come to terms with what happened. I don't know how I feel right now."

He looked straight ahead, now and then using his hand to shield his eyes from the bright lights but still he could not see the face of anyone clearly.

Photographers jostled with each other, bumping and pushing, in an effort to gain the optimum position for their shots.

"Another cluster-fuck!" said one, as he pushed forward.

Strobe-lights flashed like artillery batteries firing salvoes into the night-sky.

"How do you, as a black man, feel about enforcing laws most black people find unjust and repugnant?"

"I just try to do my job to the best of my ability," said Ngubane. "There are some laws I don't agree with or like but then..."

"What laws in particular are you referring to?" shot the man from ABC Morning News.

The PR men moved fast.

"I think Warrant Officer Ngubane has more than answered your questions," said a Captain dressed in a smart civilian suit. He stepped in front or Templeton to block him from the view and cameras of the press corps.

"I am sure you understand what a traumatic experience this has been for him and his family and won't begrudge him a break, so he can spend some time with his little girl."

"As a spokesman for the South African Police let me say, we deplore the acts of wanton violence being perpetrated against our members, who are just doing their jobs and attempting to ensure their communities are safe. They are just trying to keep this country safe for all citizens."

He paused while he swept his eyes over the gathered media people. He saw the red active recording lights glowed on every television camera.

The kids are going to see their old man on TV again tonight, he thought.

"With regard to these brave policemen and their families," he swept his arm in an arc to direct the attention of the press people to Ngubane and his colleagues, "these brave members who have lost so much simply for doing their duty, let me state categorically that the SA Police Force will fully compensate and reimburse them for their loss.

"As for their housing we already have plans in place to address that issue. It is our expressed policy to take care of our members.

"Thank you, Ladies and Gentlemen, that is all."

He turned and briskly walked out of the room ignoring the questions shouted after him. The remaining PR minders quickly chaperoned Ngubane, Ellen and his similarly-affected colleagues from the room, making sure they spoke to no one.

In a back office, away from the glare of the TV lights, Templeton relaxed. He put his arms around Ellen's shoulders.

"There you are. You've heard it from the horse's mouth. There is nothing to worry about. They're going to take care of us."

She slid her slender arms around his waist and held him tightly.

"Oh God, Templeton. I was so afraid."

He looked down at her. She was crying for the first time today.

"Don't be afraid," he whispered. "We'll be okay, I promise!"

Chapter 6

"You know," said Templeton, "this has its bright side."

They were busy packing up their things in the tent behind the police station. Their new, prefabricated house, built by the Army's Engineering Corps was complete and it was time for them to move there.

"Look at it this way...there's so much less to pack!"

Ellen picked up a pillow and threw it at him. "Yeah, that's a big consolation!"

She carefully folded a jersey and meticulously placed it in a gaudy suitcase that looked at though it was covered in blue and red, cheap linoleum floor covering.

"This suitcase is too terrible for words," she said, turning up her nose and pulling a face. "How is it possible anyone would actually buy one of these?"

Templeton lit a cigarette. He promised Ellen he would once again stop smoking when their lives were back to normal but he knew that wasn't going to happen.

He studied the suitcase and scowled. "I suppose it is pretty...uh...third world."

"That look is supposedly very big amongst the jet-set travellers of deep, Kwa Zulu," she said, smiling broadly.

"At least they are travellers and not just goat-herders, sitting on their backsides all day in the Transkei hills," retorted Templeton.

Templeton was a Zulu whose ancestors had lived in Natal for generations. Ellen was a Xhosa and her people originated from the Transkei and Eastern Cape. For centuries the two tribes had been opponents, every now and then locking horns in fierce skirmishes.

Ellen and Templeton liked to tease each other about their roots. Just innocent banter and fun, like family members who happen to support different football teams.

When Templeton proposed marriage to Ellen and had to

go and ask her father's permission, he was afraid their tribal backgrounds might pose a problem to the parents. But it was no issue at all. They liked the burly, ex-school-teacher-turned-cop from the moment they met him and Templeton's parent's adored Ellen.

Ellen carefully folded a pretty blue and white dress sent for Thandi by a white woman in Sandton. A lot of people had sent things after the television interview as there was great sympathy for the policemen whose homes were torched.

At first the Ngubanes were deeply moved by the out-pouring of generosity, especially from whites but with time, each arriving donation simply served to emphasise the predicament in which they found themselves.

"I am not some object, some down-and-out to be pitied by whites," said Templeton one day when a parcel of dirty, second hand clothes arrived for them. "I am not going to pretend any longer to be grateful when someone sends me their old rubbish."

"Okay, that's it, all packed!" said Ellen. "Let's get out of here."

They spent three weeks in the army tent and she was glad to go. It was cold, they had to wash in a basin in one of the toilets at the back of the police station and there was little privacy. There was always someone staring at them.

"I'll be glad to be in the new place where you and I can finally have a little alone time," said Templeton. In the tent there had been no intimacy between them and he missed it. He longed to lie beside her in the same bed. To feel her warmth, to savour how fresh she smelled when she came out of the shower and to feel her heart beat while she slept.

"I know the new house is not going to be as nice as our old house," he said. "They say those prefab houses are very cold in winter and hot in summer but it's a start on the path to getting our lives back together and being a proper family again."

She kissed him on the lips. "It's okay," she said, "I know it's only temporary. I don't want to live in an army base forever."

The Engineering Corps erected the temporary houses for the affected cops on a piece of unused land below the rugby fields at the Doornkop Military base as, it was decided, it was not safe for the members to go back to the townships. Situated near the southern fence, the front of the houses looked out at the massive Johannesburg prison, called Sun City by inmates, that was located almost directly across the road.

The military authorities positioned the houses in that spot deliberately. They did not want them to be near the white residents of the base.

"They can come and go through the bottom gate and no-one will ever see them," an Engineering Major explained to the Base Commander.

The commander, a Colonel with a bushy moustache and a year to go before retirement, nodded and pursed his lips.

"Good plan," he said. "No need to ruffle any feathers."

Chapter 7

The white constable looked up sleepily from his aimless doodling on a government notepad, the cigarette he placed on the edge of the polyurethaned reception desk was beginning to burn the wood. It didn't really matter – just another mark amongst the many others left by constables of the past who also had no ashtrays.

He stubbed the cigarette out against one of the table's legs and dropped the butt into a waste-paper basket and peered at Templeton, making no attempt to hide his obvious boredom.

Ngubane was dressed in a conservative grey suit with turn-ups in the trousers, cut at exactly the right height, over a pair of dark brown Crockett and Jones shoes.

The middle button of the jacket was buttoned over a blue shirt with fine white stripes and, around his neck, he wore a red paisley tie.

"Yes?" asked the constable. "What do you want?" His voice was disinterested and he idly pushed a spilled sugar grain along the desk with the tip of a ballpoint pen.

"I'm here to see Captain van Rooyen."

The constable looked up from his sugar-pushing activity and studied the black man standing before him. He immediately concluded he must be a businessman of some sort. But why would a businessman want to see van Rooyen in the SAP Welfare department?

"And who are you?" His voice was insolent.

Templeton felt a little vein in his left temple begin to throb, a warning sign that he was dangerously close to losing his temper. He clenched his fists then relaxed them and took a deep breath before he replied:

"I am Warrant Officer Ngubane." His voice was laced with contempt. He drew his police identification card from his wallet and flipped it onto the table in front of the constable.

If the constable was fazed by Templeton's actions or voice he did not show it. After all, everyone knew black ranks were really only for the benefit of black policemen and a white skin out-ranked any black rank. He picked up Ngubane's ID card and made a great show of carefully examining it. He painstakingly studied the photo on the ID card then looked carefully at Templeton, as though he were making absolutely sure it was the same person, then he slid it back across the table to him.

Without saying a word he lifted the hand-set of a grubby telephone that was once ivory-white and punched two digits, with a nicotine-stained forefinger.

A few moments later he said in Afrikaans: Captain, there is a Warrant Officer Ngubane here to see you."

Templeton was still seething. Being treated with disrespect by snotty white kids fresh out of the police training college went with the job, he supposed, but it still burned his arse.

He took a slow, deep breath. "Calm down," he told himself, "you'll need all your wits for this interview."

The generous promises of full compensation made during the television media interview by the Public Relations people had come to naught. Templeton's claim appeared to be bogged down in a quagmire of bureaucracy and red tape. This was the fourth time he'd driven through to Pretoria to be interviewed about his claim and each time, he left with promises and hope that it would soon be settled, only for nothing to happen.

The interviewing officer always expressed sympathy at his predicament and faithfully promised everything possible was being done to get it sorted out speedily.

I'm so sick of hearing the words: 'but you must understand, things take time in the police force,' thought Templeton. How much fucking time?

It was always the same. He answered their questions and

they scribbled notes and comments in his case-file next to the items listed on his claim.

"Thank you for coming in Warrant Officer Ngubane. I will send this through and we will see what we can do. We'll be in contact."

Thank you very much, shake hands, smile, don't call us, we'll call you, fuck off and stop bothering us you black bastard.

"First floor, second office on the right," said the constable, cutting into Templeton's thoughts.

Chapter 8

In his younger days Captain Wikus van Rooyen was a fairly good amateur boxer and had even held the SAP middle-weight title for almost a year, before losing it to a sergeant who later turned pro. The battle scars from those days still showed and the operation to straighten a nose, broken half a dozen times, could not be considered a complete success.

But the days of being lean, mean and keen were long gone and his once athletic body was replaced by a sagging waist and jowled cheeks. Little broken veins that spider-webbed across his shiny nose were evidence of just how much he enjoyed his daily, after-work trip to the Police Officer's Club for a glass or six of his favourite drink, Klipdrift® Brandy and Coke. Most nights he left the club legally unable to drive and, in fact, was once stopped and charged for driving under the influence. But a couple of phone calls the following day, saw the charge dropped.

Van Rooyen hated his job as Welfare Officer. It was not what he signed up for as it kept him out of the field where the real police work was done, where he believed he was called. He was convinced his job was the main reason he was so physically out of shape and, every time he looked in the mirror, he was reminded of that and he hated himself just that little bit more – but not as much as he hated the cops who were out there doing what he should be doing.

Only three more years and then I go on pension, he consoled himself. Then I can move to the farm and forever forget about this bullshit, the nurse-maiding and all the bleeding-heart stories I have to listen to!

He glanced at the old Rotary watch on his wrist. Three fifteen. Forty five minutes to go before he could have his first drink of the day. But before that, he had to listen to another bleeding-heart story!

He took the last Texan® plain from a packet that he crushed before tossing it into a waste-paper basket and fished in his upper tunic pocket for his Bic® lighter.

As he drew the first puff of smoke into his lungs Ngubane entered his office.

"Captain van Rooyen, I am Warrant Officer Ngubane. I have an appointment."

"Yes, sit down Ngubane." he pointed to a chair covered in blue vinyl that was starting to crack.

Ngubane sat down. For a few moments they regarded each other warily across the table, each trying to sum up the other.

This wasn't the first time Templeton had encountered an officer like this.

You're going to try to screw me, he thought, holding van Rooyen's stare, and you know there's probably not a damned thing I can do about it.

This was the fourth occasion he had come to Pretoria to try to get his claim sorted out and each time it was a different officer who interviewed him.

Eventually van Rooyen broke eye-contact.

"Okay Ngubane," he said, "let's see what we've got here."

He rummaged around in a pile of brown, soft-covered files with the SAP crest of arms emblazoned on the front and all stamped Confidential.

"Yes, here we are. Ngubane Templeton, Warrant Officer," he read out loud pointing to the folder.

He opened the file and paged through the contents. He seemed to be making a show of how thorough his examination of the contained information was.

"Hmm...interesting," he said without looking up and continuing to read. "Okay...worth bearing in mind..."

When he finished his reading he scribbled a few notes that Templeton could not read on a pad beside him, then he looked up, leaned forward with both forearms on the desk and interlocked his fingers.

For a few moments he was quiet, as though carefully considering what he was about to say.

“Let's cut the bullshit, Ngubane!” he said suddenly. “You are trying to rob the police force!

His voice was menacing and took Templeton aback, even though he was expecting the accusation as it was made at the three previous interviews. But on those occasions it was skirted around initially. He had expected van Rooyen to engage in small talk and niceties for a short while, not to launch an immediate, sudden, full-frontal attack. In truth, if were earlier in the day and not so close to Officers' Club time, Captain van Rooyen probably would have done just that. But now he was impatient...and thirsty!

Keep calm, Templeton told himself, frantically trying to calm his racing mind and rising temper.

“With respect, Captain, what exactly do you mean?” his voice was chilly as a frozen Popsicle.

“By God man Ngubane, look at this claim. Video recorder, Crockett and Jones shoes, colour television, camel-hair coat, Sony Hi-Fi. It looks to me as though you're trying to become wealthy out of this thing. I mean why are you not covered by your normal insurance?”

The vein in Ngubane's left temple began to pulse. He took two deep breaths hoping an infusion of oxygen would somehow calm his boiling temper. In his lap, out of view from van Rooyen, his fists were so tightly balled that his knuckles had turned white.

Get a hold of yourself! he thought. This white bastard holds all the cards. Don't blow it!

“Captain!” he spat, unable to keep his tone civil, “If you are accusing me of trying to defraud the SAP, I would advise you to tread carefully, because, if that is what you are doing, I WILL take this matter further! Every single item on that list was bought and owned by me, I am not, as you put it, trying to get rich out of this!

"In addition, as a Welfare Officer, you should know insurance companies will not pay in cases of civil unrest – or is that something you simply never took the time to learn!"

Templeton was about to explode.

van Rooyen was taken aback. He was not used to cheeky blacks and it seemed this one could cause him a lot of trouble if he set his mind to it.

He stared across the desk at Templeton considering what he would say next. He ignored the urge to look at his watch and thought of how tough things were at home, now that he was paying for his daughter's university education.

For the van Rooyens there were no video recorders, Crockett and Jones shoes or camel-hair coats. No, for them, good white Afrikaner stock, whose forefathers had taken this hostile land by the throat and turned it into a paradise, there was barely enough money to survive each month.

If he had not been left the family farm, his upcoming retirement would be a miserable affair.

He stared at Templeton who was clearly furious and thought, it's not possible he could afford that stuff. I'm a captain and he's only a warrant officer!

"That came out wrong, Ngubane," he said. "I am not accusing you of anything. I'm just trying to establish the facts.

"I understand what it must be like to see your home go up in flames. I know how you must feel..."

Templeton cut in: "Again, with all due respect, Sir, (the Sir was said in a tone that made it a sneer) you have absolutely no fucking idea. You don't have to go home at night to a little prefab house in the back of an army base. You don't have to sit on borrowed furniture or see your kids dressed in donated clothes. You don't have to lie to your daughter and tell her everything is fine when it fucking well is not!

"And in addition, you don't have to force yourself to face the truth that the organisation you believed in and served faithfully appears to have turned its back on you."

He paused, took a deep breath and relaxed his fists before continuing. "But most of all Captain you don't have to sit in front of someone like you who has the power to decide on his future.

"So again, Captain van Rooyen, with all due respect...you have no fucking idea!"

Ngubane's words stung van Rooyen like a slap in the face with a wet dish-rag. He felt no sympathy for him, just anger.

Just who does this cheeky *kaffir** think he is? He thought.

"Now you listen to me, Warrant," he hissed, his thin lips drawn back in a snarl. "Watch how you speak to me! I can hold this claim up for ever if I choose to and there won't be a thing you can do about it. Fuck with me and you'll regret it. Do I make myself clear?"

He stabbed a finger in Templeton's direction.

"Yes Sir, perfectly clear." He knew the white prick was right and that his outburst had likely made him an enemy.

"I am sorry, Sir, I'm sure you'll understand I've been under a lot of strain but I realise that's no excuse."

That's right, grovel you son-of-a-black-bitch, thought van Rooyen.

"The crux of the matter, Ngubane, is that we need proof. We need receipts to show you did indeed own those items."

Templeton sighed. He'd gone through this three times before.

"As I explained to the other officers, on three previous occasions, the receipts were burned in the fire...Sir," he added as an afterthought.

Van Rooyen frowned and rubbed his chin before making a note in the file. He felt in his pocket for his cigarettes then remembered he'd smoked the last one just before Ngubane arrived. He cursed silently under his breath and glanced at his watch. Fifteen minutes before official knock-off time. Just enough time to clear his desk and be at the Officers' Club when it opens.

He snapped the file shut, making it quite clear the meeting was over.

"Okay, Ngubane," he said, "I'll get back to you."

* *kaffir – derogatory term for a black person.*

Chapter 9

Roger Ngubane was a lot bigger than other 15 year-old boys. He had inherited his father's size but, at the same time, had his mother's fairer complexion. His shoulders were broad and he was starting to lose the puppy fat of his pre-teen years.

He was a big lad with a gentle nature who preferred to avoid confrontations. But at the same time he possessed a stubborn streak and determination that often surprised his parents and when he set his mind to something, or adopted a moral position, almost nothing would cause him to deviate.

He attended a private, multi-racial boarding school in the Kwa Zulu – Natal Midlands, paid for by Ellen's parents, who owned two supermarkets and a bottle-store in Butterworth and Umtata in the Transkei.

Templeton knew Roger was infinitely better off at the private school than he would be at a township school but he still did not like taking gifts from his parents-in-law. It is a man's job to take care of his own family, he believed.

"Do not think of this as me helping you," explained Ellen's father. "I'm doing this for my grandson. It is my gift to him. This country is going to change one day and will need educated young black people to take up leadership roles, Roger will be one of those people, if we help him."

He had a point, thought Templeton, I shouldn't let my pride disadvantage my son and so he agreed to the arrangement.

Roger blossomed at the school. Academically he was only average, but, because of his size, he excelled at sport. He not only won but also set new records in the shot-put, javelin and discus events in his age-group at the Natal Midlands Inter-schools Championships and he played left back for the school's first soccer team. He was a keen Orlando Pirates supporter and aimed to win a try-out with them one day.

The news of the attack on his home in Johannesburg was given to him by Mr Carrington, the headmaster, after he was summoned to the head's office during soccer practise one afternoon.

"Sit down, Roger," said the old man. He had thick bushy eye-brows and grey hair that seemed to possess a mind of its own. Strict and a stickler for rules and tradition, he was nonetheless a kind man who embraced the role of away-from-home-father to the boys. He believed it his duty and calling to guide them along a path that would allow each scholar to reach his full potential.

Roger instantly knew something was wrong. The headmaster never called pupils by their first names – it was always Mr Ngubane, Mr Thomson, Mr Naude...

He sat down on a leather chair, polished by the backsides of generations of schoolboys who'd sat on it before.

Carrington removed his tortoise-shell-framed glasses, breathed moisture on them and vigorously polished the lenses on the tip of his tie, while he peered at Roger from beneath his bushy eye-brows.

"Something has happened at home, Sir, hasn't it?" Roger's voice trembled slightly. This was the day he had always feared. The day they called to tell him something terrible had happened to his father. It was a fear he carried with him daily, from the moment he realised Templeton was a policeman and understood the dangers of his father's job, like a stone permanently glued inside his shoe,.

He felt his stomach knot and his chest tighten.

"Is it my Dad?"

"It's okay. No-one is hurt, everyone is fine at home," Carrington said. His voice was gentle.

He told Roger what had happened and how his home was

burned down. The boy sat quietly, stunned while he listened but he could feel tears damming in the corner of his eyes. He wiped them away with the back of his hand.

It was all so unreal and remote here in the rolling green hills of the Natal Midlands. News of riots, burnings and killings were like scenes from a bad movie.

"Your father wants you to come home for a while. Quite understandably, he and your mother believe the family needs to be together at this time.

"I have made arrangements for you to catch the train tomorrow. Your father will meet you at Johannesburg station."

He stood up and came around the desk to Roger who stood up.

"We'll see you back here soon and I'll arrange extra lessons so you can catch up, but right now you need to be with your family.

"Go back to your dormitory now and pack your things. Good luck to you, Son. We'll be thinking of you and praying for the Ngubane family."

He held out his hand which Roger shook with a firm grip.

"Thank you, Sir," he said.

Chapter 10

"I know it's probably not the right decision but I need my family here!" said Ellen.

Her eyes burned like glowing charcoal. She and Templeton had just had a blazing row.

"By Christ! Be reasonable and think about it, Ellen. Roger needs to get back to school and it's not safe for him to go to a township school. You know damn well that we are targets. Let's just be rational about this!

"I understand how you feel but you can't let your emotions get in the way of making the correct decision!"

"Are you so arrogant that you think I have not thought about this?" she snapped back. "I have thought of nothing else! It is all I have thought about! But I don't believe Roger is in danger. He knows the kids in the township. He's not the one they're angry with – it's you! You are the cause of this!"

She knew her words would be like a pike in his heart. He already blamed himself for their situation. She saw him grit his teeth and noticed his bottom lip tremble.

"You didn't complain when things were good," he said. "You ate the food I supplied and sheltered under the roof I provided."

Suddenly she felt ashamed.

"I'm sorry," she said. "I didn't mean it like that. I understand your concerns...I share them. I too am tormented but I need my family with me now, they are all I have."

Templeton could see her anguish. In truth, he felt the same.

Ellen was dressed in a yellow dressing gown and was aware that the children who slept on makeshift beds in the lounge could likely hear every word they said to each other through the paper-thin walls of the prefab house.

She'd tried to keep her voice down but as her anger and exasperation rose so did the volume of her voice.

Their situation was starting get her down and cracks were slowing developing in their marriage. Since moving to the army base there'd been precious little emotional intimacy and they'd only been able to make love once when the children were out and even then it appeared Templeton was more interested in burning off anger and frustration than experiencing tenderness and emotional connection with her.

Now she spurned the advances he made because she resented the way he was on that occasion and also because she was afraid the children would hear. This annoyed Templeton and left him feeling frustrated and rejected.

In addition their compensation claim seemed permanently bogged down. Ngubane was sure the Welfare Officer, Captain van Rooyen, was deliberately screwing him over, which he was. When Templeton left his office after their meeting, van Rooyen had decided there and then he would teach the cheeky *kaffir** a lesson.

Their emotional stress was made worse as they continued to lie, both to themselves and, to each other. They knew the system was going to screw them but neither actually wanted to come out and say so openly, as that would destroy the final strand of hope that they clung to.

"For Christ sake! How many times must I tell you, they're working on it! I don't know when they will settle the claim!" he snapped whenever she asked of its progress.

"You were there when they told the reporters they would take care of us. But these things take a long time. We're not the only people in the world!"

On one occasion she said: "My parents will help us if I ask them. We don't have to live like this."

Templeton refused and despite her compelling

arguments as to why they should accept help, he refused to budge.

So they maintained the facade, both pretending that things would come right but neither believing it. It was just easier that way.

Roger's return home from boarding school was a blessing to Ellen. He provided the comfort and emotional support that Templeton did not. His gentle manner was both soothing for both her and Thandi. She knew he should go back to school and resume his studies before he missed too much and had to repeat the year but, at the same time, she did not know how she would cope without him.

Templeton was growing increasingly moody and difficult to live with and Roger had a way of calming his father. He seemed to be the only one Templeton would listen to and displayed a calmness and wisdom beyond his years.

But he too was feeling the strain in the household and was, after all, still just a 15 year-old teenager trying to grow up in a world turned upside down.

It was all very well for Templeton to say the children would be better off away from home, Ellen thought. He is at work all day – and getting home later and later each evening – but I have to sit here alone in a place where I have no friends.

It was true, Ngubane was spending more time at work. It diverted his mind and kept him away from seeing the predicament in which he had landed his family. It was a shield that he used against his pain.

She didn't want to fight. She just wanted her family with her and her life back to normal.

"Temp," she said, wrapping her arms around him and nuzzling up against him, "I don't want to fight.

"I understand what you are saying and your concerns. My head tells me you are right but I need my children here. Please, I'm begging you, can't we think about getting Roger into a school here, even if it's just until the end of the year?

"By then things will probably have settled and he can go back to boarding school."

When he felt her warm arms around him and her soft breath on his neck it extinguished his anger .

"Please Temp," she whispered softly, "I need this."

He was silent as he considered what she said. His mind swirled like stirred coffee with conflicting thoughts. As the children of a policeman, he knew his kids were at risk at a township school but Ellen had a point. She too had lost a lot and now he was asking her to give up her kids and maybe that was just too much to ask! He could shut off his mind with his work but she couldn't and the house in which they lived was a constant reminder to her of what had happened and the fact she was married to someone considered a pariah in her community.

"Okay, just until the end of the year and then he goes back to boarding school. As your father says: he is going to be needed when the new country comes one day."

"Thank you," she said softly. Her cheek was wet from tears rolling down it. She held him close, pressing her warm body against hers, she turned his face towards hers and kissed him on the lips. It was the most passionate and urgent kiss they'd shared in weeks and he began to stir.

* *kaffir – a racist term for a black person. Same as "nigger".*

Chapter 11

"Warrant, there's a message for you to call a Captain van Rooyen in Pretoria," said a white constable as Ngubane breezed into his office one afternoon.

He handed Templeton a slip of paper with a Pretoria phone number written on it.

"He said you'd know what it's about and to please call him."

Templeton examined the note. All that was on it was van Rooyen's name and the telephone number written in an untidy hand with a ball-point pen.

"Did he say anything else?"

"No, that's all."

"What time did he call?"

"Let's see, what time is it now," said the constable. He looked at his watch. "Two fifty. It must have been about quarter to two."

Chapter 12

The telephone number given to Templeton put him through to the same surly constable he'd seen at the reception desk during his last visit to Pretoria.

"This is Warrant Officer Ngubane," he said, "I'd like to speak to Captain van Rooyen."

The line clicked and went dead. Templeton wondered if he had been cut off or if the constable had even heard him. Then a voice spoke from the other end.

"van Rooyen."

Captain van Rooyen, good afternoon, it's Warrant Officer Ngubane. I have a message to call you."

Then, in customary black fashion when greeting someone, he added: "how are you?"

"Aah, yes, Ngubane. The man whose house was burned down. I have an answer to your claim. Just let me find it, it's somewhere in here."

Ngubane waited. He could hear the welfare officer rifling through what sounded like a mountain of papers. He held his breath, silently praying and hoping for a good outcome.

"Here it is. Let me see what they have to say."

Who is 'they'? Templeton thought.

"Okay," said van Rooyen. "This is what they say: the total value of your claim is a little under R30 000. Let me read exactly what head quarters has written here:

"After fully investigating this member's claim resulting from damages he suffered as a result of a riotous gathering, the following settlement will be paid out by the Treasury: R11 263.93 being full and final settlement.

"The assessing officers are of the opinion that, as proof of ownership of many of the items being claimed for was not presented in the form of purchase receipts, the settlement is in their opinion fair and equitable.

"It must also be borne in mind that the State, at its own cost, has provided alternative housing for the member and his dependants.

"A cheque for the above amount will be forwarded to the claimant upon receipt of the signed, enclosed, Acceptance of Settlement form.

"That's it Ngubane. It's signed by Major P.J. Theron on behalf of General Wiese."

For a long time neither man spoke. Templeton felt as though he had been kicked in the balls. He felt sick and thought he might vomit. R11 000! that wouldn't even cover the outstanding amounts owed on the hire-purchase agreements. He reached for a cigarette, his hands trembling as he tried to strike a match. He drew the smoke deeply into his lungs and held it there in an effort to stop himself hyper-ventilating.

"Are you there, Ngubane?"

"Yes I am here. Now let me see if I understand this properly. Am I right? You say they are going to pay me R11 000 and something to settle my claim in full?"

"That's correct. R11 263.93."

"Jesus fuck man! What about the promises those fucking assholes made on television when they told the world we would be compensated in full?" Ngubane was shouting now and everyone in the office stopped doing what they were doing to watch and listen.

In the opinion of the assessors the settlement is fair and in full," said van Rooyen. He was enjoying this.

Teach you to fuck with me, he thought.

"I told you and everyone else the receipts were burned in the fire along with everything else I owned!" roared Templeton. "How am I supposed to produce receipts that are burned in the fire that is the cause of the claim? Jesus! Don't you people have any fucking brains? Is the concept too hard for you idiot paper-pushers to grasp!"

He was seething. Every muscle in his body seemed

knotted.

"Let me tell you something Captain van Rooyen, and you'd better believe it, there is no way I am going to accept this. I will take you, the general, the SAP, the minister and even fucking PW Botha to court if I have to!

"I will fight you bastards every step of the way and I promise you, you will not get away with this!" His voice was laced with icy fury.

"Don't waste you time or money, Ngubane," said van Rooyen. "Go and take a look at your employment contract. I think you'll soon see that avenue is closed to you and, in any case, even if you could, do you really think you have the money to go the distance?

"Use your head man, take what they're giving you and call it quits. Shall I send the Acceptance of Settlement form to you or do you want to come through and sign it?"

"Go and fuck yourself!" said Ngubane and slammed the phone down. The walls of the room were closing in on him. He felt nauseous and needed air. He rushed out of the office and threw up in the corridor.

Chapter 13

The Ngubane family was quiet as they sat around the Formica® kitchen table eating their supper. Roger and Thandi ate without looking up from their plates. They were used to the black moods that followed their father around, like a starving stray dog that refused to go, no matter how often you threw stones at it.

Roger wanted nothing more than to go back to school in Kwa Zulu – Natal where he could escape the cloud hanging over their lives but he knew his mother and Thandi needed him. At night he prayed for a miracle that somehow, when they awoke, the dog would be gone but it never was.

Templeton was angry. The slightest thing could trigger a fierce rage that burned brightly then continued to smoulder until the next trigger-event. He knew the effect he was having on his family and hated himself for it but seemed powerless to do anything about it.

He thought about visiting a police shrink but was afraid it would be logged on his personnel file and hinder any chances he had of future promotion.

So he woke up angry and went to bed angry.

Ellen tried to speak to him but the invisible barrier he'd erected was impenetrable. He believed this was an inner-struggle no-one could help him with. It was a battle he alone could win, the problem was, he had not idea how.

It consumed him, occupied every thought of every moment of every day.

He could not come to terms with the fact that one of his core beliefs – something he built his life on – was shattered. He knew it, but could not admit it, even to himself. It was as though he subconsciously believed that, if he refused to acknowledge that the organisation to which he had devoted his life had betrayed him, that truth would somehow disappear.

He felt cornered, out of control, events dictating his life, rather than the other way around.

Life was so easy and ordered before. His community respected him. He believed he was a valuable member of society who, in a small way, provided protection and safety. He once was a good father and husband...a provider but in just one day everything had collapsed about him. And he was the cause of it because of his naïve, stupid beliefs.

He was trapped and there was no way out.

I can't resign, he thought. What else will I do? The community has made it clear they don't want me there so there is no way I can go back to teaching.

And van Rooyen was right. He had no chance of winning a claim against his employers. The bastards have me over a barrel and there is fuck all I can do about it, he thought.

"When are we going to hear about the claim, Dad?" asked Roger, who shook his head when Ellen offered him a second helping of mashed potatoes and green peas.

The question penetrated Templeton's deep, private thoughts. He'd said nothing about his conversation with the Captain van Rooyen preferring to wait for the appropriate moment to tell his family.

He put down his knife and fork and pushed his plate away from him.

"I finally got an answer," he said.

"Oh good!" said Thandi, her eyes shone with excitement. "When can we get a colour TV so I can watch my shows again?"

"Can we get it before the weekend so we can watch the knock-out rounds?" asked Roger. He looked expectantly at his father.

"It'll be nice to have a decent television again," said Ellen, "and to get some new furniture. When do you think we'll be able to start looking for a house of our own?"

Templeton sighed. “There won't be any new TV, or furniture or a new house,” he said. “I am not even sure how we're going to pay off the debts that we owe.”

“What do you mean?” asked Ellen, her voice anxious. “You said you'd finally heard about the claim!”

“Those bastards have rejected it, They're only going to pay a third of what we claimed.”

“What does that mean, Papa?” Thandi. Her eyes had tears in them.

“It means they aren't going to pay us for everything we lost in the fire, Sweetie,” he replied. He reached across the table, took her tiny right hand and held it between his.

“Jesus, Temp! Why. They promised we'd be compensated in full!”

“I don't know, I really don't know,” he replied, his voice tired and resigned, his shoulders stooped. “They say they can't pay everything because we can't prove we owned some of the stuff. They won't believe me that the receipts were burned in the fire.”

He felt exhausted. His body ached.

“That's ridiculous! You're going to fight it aren't you?” snapped Ellen. The colour had drained from her face and he couldn't help noticing that she somehow looked older.

“There's nothing to fight. We have no option and just have to accept what they offer us.”

“But they promised!” said Roger.

“You promised!” wailed Thandi.

“Surely we can take them to court. There must be something we can do. We can't just sit here and do nothing!” said Ellen, her voice strident and accusing.

Templeton felt the cracks in the calm he'd been trying so hard to maintain strain and then split.

“Damn it! Listen to me all of you! I am not an idiot. If I say there is nothing we can do then there is nothing we can do. I've looked at our options and right now there are none. They've got us stuffed! Get that into your thick skulls! Stuffed!”

The room fell silent apart from Thandi's quiet sobbing.

“If you're going to cry, go to your bedroom,” snapped Templeton.

“I don't have a bedroom any more,” sniffed Thandi.

“Don't shout at her!” said Roger. His voice was raised, something that took Templeton aback.

“This is not her fault! It's yours! You and the police lied to us! You said the police always look after their own, but they don't, do they?”

The words were a dagger in his guts. The battle in his mind raged again. The instinct to defend the organisation he had faithfully served for so long versus the truth of the words spoken by his son.

“The police do look after their own but there are procedures and policies in place that they have to follow. I am sure they did everything they could but no doubt their hands were tied.”

He knew he did not sound convincing. They wouldn't believe him. Fuck, he couldn't even convince himself!

Roger's eyes filled with tears, the final disappointment lay heavily upon him.

“If you weren't a policeman this would never have happened!” he snapped, his voice childish and angry.

Templeton looked at his son. Tears streamed down the boy's cheeks.

“Roger,” he said gently, “the SAP has looked after us for the past 17 years. If it weren't for it we wouldn't be where we are today.”

The boy's eyes flashed. “You're damn right about that! Just look where we are today and it's all because of the bloody police!

“We have nothing! People view us as dogs. They sneer and spit when they see us in the road. In truth, I sometimes think we deserved to have our house burned down because you are in fact an oppressor. You are one of the apartheid regime's dogs!"

Templeton hit him. His back-handed slap with his right hand smashed into Roger's lips and nose and the force of the blow knocked him off his chair. In a second Templeton was up and out of his chair, standing over his son, his hand cocked to hit him again.

"No!" screamed Ellen. She grabbed his arm and pulled him away. Thandi began to sob. Roger scrambled to get up and once on his feet backed away. His face was a mess of blood, snot and tears. "That's right!" he sneered at his father. "That's all you oppressors know!"

Templeton tried to jerk free from Ellen's grasp but she held him tightly.

"Get the hell out of here you little prick!" said Templeton. His voice was cold as death. "Get out of my fucking sight before I give you a proper beating!"

"You don't have to ask again! I'm going but believe me you'll hear from me!"

Roger turned on his heels, left the kitchen and went to the lounge where he scooped up a black tog-bag made of webbing. In it he kept his wallet and most of the things that were important to him.

He slammed the front door so hard that the plates on the kitchen table rattled. Then he disappeared into the night.

Ellen held Thandi in her lap. Both sobbed so hard that their bodies jerked in irregular spasms.

"Please Templeton, go after him!" she begged. "I don't want anything to happen to him!"

"Nothing will happen to him. He'll soon come crawling back like a dog with its tail tucked between its legs," said Templeton as he resumed his eating. The explosion of anger and violence had caused his inner tension to subside.

"Now let me eat. I don't want to hear any more about this."

Chapter 14

Roger took off out of the house running. He went through the bottom gate of the Doornkop Military Base where he was not challenged by the gate guards, as they all knew about the black police families living on the base.

On Old Potchefstroom Road, still running, he turned right as that route led to Soweto. That was where he planned to go. He had friends there and hoped one of them would put him up until he figured out what to do.

About two kilometres from the Doornkop Base he finally stopped and sat down beside the road. He made no attempt to move out of sight as, deep down, he hoped his father would come to find him.

He was exhausted and so thirsty his tongue and throat felt as though they were coated in scratchy steel-wool. Suddenly he realised he was just a 15 year-old boy, alone and away from home and he began to sob.

He shivered as the sweat began to dry on his body. It was not all that cold yet but, on a clear, starlit night like tonight it would get down near freezing sometime after midnight.

He knew his father wanted him to come crawling back and honestly, he wanted to go back. He wished he could somehow turn back time so they could return to a period when they were all happy. How he wished his father would come and look for him and apologise, so he could forgive him and they could try to be normal.

He imagined how his mother and Thandi felt. But he was not going to go back and beg forgiveness when he had done nothing wrong. Everything he said was true and if his father wanted him back then Templeton would have to make the first move!

He wiped his nose on the cuff of the blue cardigan he wore and gingerly touched his lip where it was split by

Templeton's blow. It was swollen and he winced as his fingers grazed it.

What do I do now? he thought. He knew he needed to find somewhere to sleep or at least somewhere to shelter from the cold, until he could figure out what to do tomorrow when the sun was up. One thing that he was sure of was he would not go home until his father came and asked him to.

I'm sure Simon will let me stay with him, he thought. Simon was his best friend at the new school he attended in Soweto. He lived with his single-parent mother who had met Roger and who liked him.

Roger got to his feet, dusted off the seat of his jeans, picked up his tog-bag and began walking south down Old Potchefstroom Road. He knew a few blocks further on he would likely find a minibus taxi that was going to Soweto.

Jesus but he was thirsty!

Chapter 15

When Roger knocked on the door the two scrawny dogs tethered to a pole with a long chain in the back yard, began wildly barking. That set off the other nearby township dogs.

A light went on in the house across the road and Roger saw a curtain drawn back slightly as one of the occupants looked to see what it was that was upsetting the dogs.

Simon Malazi's house remained dark and the more the dogs barked the more anxious Roger became. He was afraid the neighbours would mistake him for a thief and he knew township justice was harsh.

He knocked on the door again. This time harder and louder.

A few moments later the frightened voice of a woman spoke from inside.

"Go away and leave us alone! My son is not here!"

She believed it was the Comrades here to summon her son to street committee meeting or to get him to take part in some or other freedom activity held in the name of the struggle.

It was a fear the majority of black township parents lived with daily. The night when the Comrades knocked on your door and demanded the children come out to join in battle against the apartheid forces or be part of the group that burned down the home of a collaborator. Young children were used as the liberation struggle's cannon-fodder and often forced to carry out brutal crimes.

And there was nothing a parent could do about it. Reluctance or resistance immediately brought accusations of being against the struggle, of being a collaborator – and collaborators' homes were burned down, sometimes with the occupants still in them.

She panicked when she heard the urgent knocking on

the door and the baying of the dogs.

Oh God! They've come, she thought. Blind terror swept over her.

She would have to open the door. What else could she do, a woman against a mob? She had no telephone, so calling the police for help was impossible.

There was no-one to help her – Simon's father left one night before his son was born and never returned and the father of Miriam, her eight year-old daughter was murdered two years earlier by *tsotsis** while they robbed him of his pay-packet.

All she could do was pray that Simon had slipped out through the back and got away.

How different life was in the white suburbs of South Africa. How little they understood about the lives of their fellow citizens.

"But Betty why do you let the children push you around?" her 'madam' once asked her. She cleaned house and did washing and ironing for her, three days a week. Her children faced no such problems. "Why don't you people give these kids causing all the trouble a good hiding?"

They lived barely ten kilometres apart but could just as well have been on different planets. Her madam would never hear the screams of an 80 year-old almost-blind, granny and five children, one of them only three years old, scream and beg as they struggled to open the doors and windows of their burning house – torched by the Comrades because the old woman refused to let the kids be press-ganged for their struggle activities.

When the old woman refused to open the door to send the children out, the mob of youngsters, bound the front and rear doors with wire they stripped from the front fence. Then they roused the neighbours and the other residents on the block and herded them into the street so they could witness justice being applied.

Their leader was a 17 year-old known as Comrade Nylon, a name he earned because he had proved so slippery to the police. When he was satisfied a large enough audience was gathered, he lit a petrol bomb, walked right up to the house, broke the lounge window with a brick and flung the petrol bomb into the building.

Betty Malazi, who had been rounded up with the rest of the people who lived in the area, remembered how at first it looked like Christmas lights flickering inside the house but then they became brighter and flames could be seen. Inside there were screams both of pain and terror. The occupants smashed the windows in a desperate attempt to save their lives but burglar bars, designed to keep thieves out now imprisoned them.

Betty Malazi's impression, just before she turned away as she could no longer look, was of the old lady reaching through the window and screaming to the onlookers – people who had known her for years – and screaming to them to save her and the children. Like Betty, many turned and looked the other way. The vision was burned into her brain and she knew it would remain with her for the rest of her life.

And now that horror was at her front door. It was ironic. In the past it was the police and municipal Black Jacks who came knocking on the doors in the deep of night when they carried out passbook raids or came searching for white men sleeping with black women and breaking the Immorality Act. Those laws were gone but now the night-time raids came from her own people.

Her daughter, Miriam, who had been asleep on a mattress next to her bed came into the lounge and said: "Mama, who is it?"

She clamped her hand over the child's mouth.

"Ssshh! Not a word!" she whispered urgently. "Go and hide under the bed and don't come out until I call you! Do you understand?"

The little girl nodded then went back to the main bedroom and slithered under the bed.

"What do you want?" Betty Malazi asked again, her mouth held close to the keyhole. She could not disguise the terror in her voice and her heart pounded so hard in her chest that she was sure it could be heard outside.

"Just leave us alone!"

"I want to see Simon," said the voice from outside.

"I told you he's not here," she said, silently praying that her son had somehow escaped through the back door.

"Please," pleaded Roger. He was tired and very cold. "I'm not here to cause trouble, I just need to see Simon!"

"That's Roger, I know him, open up, it's okay!" said Simon standing in the doorway to the lounge.

He had just woken up.

* *tsotsis – township thugs or criminals.*

Chapter 16

"I want you to meet some friends of mine," Simon said to Roger one morning. The young Ngubane had been at the Malazi home for the past five days.

Roger was sure his father would have come to fetch him, in truth, it was something he hoped for. Despite the anger and accusations of that horrible evening, he missed his family and longed to be back with them. He knew all it would take for them to be reunited was a single phone call from him or hopping on a taxi and going home but his youthful pride would not allow it.

In fact, on the third day Templeton had come knocking on Simon's door looking for his son but Roger was in the backyard at the time and Betty was away at work.

"I am sorry, Sir. I have not seen Roger at all. We were all wondering why he has not been at school," Simon lied to Templeton. "But if I do see him I will be sure to tell him you were looking for him."

That night Simon told Betty that if Templeton or any other policeman ever came asking about Roger she must say she has never seen him.

"There is very bad blood between those two," he told her. "If his father finds him he will beat him or maybe even kill him!"

Mrs Malazi was worried. "But he is the police! What happens if he finds out his son was here and that we lied to him. He will lock us up!

"I am afraid, Simon. Ever since you started hanging around with some of those Comrades I have been worried that something terrible will happen. And now we are lying to the police."

Simon saw the worry deeply engraved in her brow. He put his arm around her shoulders.

"Don't worry, Ma. Nothing will happen to us exactly

because I have friends amongst the Comrades. Think about it, they have caused us no trouble at all. They have not come and knocked on our door.

What Betty did not know was just how deeply Simon was involved.

"Don't worry at all. I promise you we will be fine. This afternoon I will take him to meet some people who can make arrangements to take care of him so his father won't come looking here again.

"By the end of the week I am sure he will be gone."

Betty Malazi did not like the situation at all but there was nothing she could do. Things were so different nowadays. The kids were in control of the parents now and there was something different about Simon. Something sinister and evil about the little boy she had not so-long-ago bounced on her knee.

She started to see it when he started associating with that band of thugs who called themselves, Comrades.

She shuddered involuntarily.

The sooner Roger Ngubane is out of my house the happier I'll be, she thought!

Chapter 17

Roger knew some of the youngsters sitting in a circle on up-turned boxes, kitchen chairs and the back seat of a scrapped Chevy Impala, drinking beer. Around their feet a few scrawny chickens pecked at the dirt and a mangy dog of dubious parentage lay curled up against the back wall in a hollow it had scraped for itself in the sand.

Those he knew he had seen at school, the others he had not seen before. He was nervous. He knew just what these guys were capable of. He had no desire to be involved with or even meet with the street committees and Comrades who ran the township. All he wanted to do was go home.

Why didn't you come and fetch me, Dad? he thought. When he discussed it with his friend, Simon told him his father had not shown up because he obviously did not care but Roger knew Templeton. He hadn't come because his pride wouldn't allow him to, just as his foolishness had landed him here. He was in a situation in which events appeared to have gathered a momentum that swept him along – and there didn't seem to be a thing he could do about it.

"This is the man I told you about," said Simon to the beer-drinking group. He shook each of their hands in turn while they studied Roger.

Roger lifted his hand in a hesitant greeting, not sure what else to do or what to say. No-one made any effort to return the greeting but their animosity and suspicion was obvious.

There were eight youngsters in total, the youngest thirteen, the oldest twenty. No-one spoke for a few moments then the leader, the 20 year-old who went by the name of Comrade Jack, pointed at a spot on the ground between a chair and an overturned beer-crate and said: “Sit down!”

His voice was terse and unfriendly.

Comrade Jack considered himself a 'war veteran'. Although only eight years-old at the time of the 1976 student uprisings, he had watched how his brother, then a member of the Soweto Students' Association, became a political activist. He stood on the sidelines and watched his brother engage in battles with the police and saw how he was constantly on the run, sleeping in different houses, always just one step ahead of the security forces.

He clearly remembered the day his brother was shot. A march was organised to protest the arrest of black student leaders and to demand their immediate release. It started peacefully but when the police blocked their way a confrontation started. Stones were thrown at the cops who replied by firing tear-gas then a petrol bomb was thrown and the police opened fire with shotguns and FN assault rifles firing live ammunition. Five protesters died and 33 were wounded. One of the wounded was Comrade Jack's brother.

A bullet smashed his left thigh – an injury that resulted in his walking with a limp for the rest of his life and earned him the nickname: Comrade Crutch. He was arrested and admitted to Baragwanath Hospital where he was kept handcuffed to his bed for the duration of his recovery and then brought to trial and charged with public violence. He was sentenced to serve three years in prison but was paroled after two.

If the authorities believed a stint in jail would cool his political ardour they were sorely mistaken. Comrade Crutch came out hating the *boers** more than ever and was even more committed to being involved in the struggle.

At the first opportunity, he made contact with the ANC underground and told them he wanted to fight and one night they smuggled him across the Botswana border.

From Gaborone he was taken to Zambia then sent to a training camp in Angola known as Base 32, about 120 kilometres south east of Angola's capital, Luanda.

To Comrade Jack, his big brother was a source of inspiration and a true hero and it was therefore perfectly natural that he too should also become involved in the black consciousness struggle.

At school he joined the Congress of South African Students, COSAS, who in effect were the local, overt, youth wing of the banned African National Congress. They saw their primary function as mobilising students in the struggle against the government.

"So you're Ngubane," said Comrade Jack, more a charge than a question. He was considerably darker in complexion than Roger and suffered from bad acne.

Roger nodded.

"Why have you come to see us?"

"Simon said I should meet you."

Comrade Jack's eyes narrowed.

"When you speak to anyone here you will address them as 'comrade'. We are not your chums from that fancy school you went to in Kwa Zulu. It is Comrade Simon and I am Comrade Jack! Do you understand?" His voice was menacing.

"Yes."

"Yes who?" he bellowed. The others were all watching intently now.

"Yes, Comrade Jack. I am sorry."

"Comrade Simon says your father is a policeman, is that correct?" He spat the word 'policeman' as though it were a chunk of phlegm.

"Yes, Comrade Jack."

"How then do we know you are not a spy. An *impimpi** sent by your father?"

Everyone was carefully scrutinising his face now, studying his body language.

Roger was expecting the question. He'd thought long and hard how he would answer it but still did not know.

"Comrades, I am not," he said softly. "I left my father's house and cannot return there."

He told them of the fight he had with his father. Of his doubts about his father enforcing laws that discriminate against blacks. He spoke clearly and lucidly, holding the attention of the small gathering. They listened carefully, interrupting only briefly to open more quarts of beer.

"So why do you want to come to us?" asked Comrade Jack when Roger finished speaking.

"I have nowhere else to go, Comrade," he answered softly.

"Take him and go and wait in the kitchen," Comrade Jack said to Simon. "We need to discuss this. Close the door."

Through the closed kitchen window Roger and Simon could hear them speaking but could not make out any of the words. One thing, however, was very obvious, not all were in agreement. There was animated arguing and gesticulating. At one point two youngsters stood up and pointed accusing fingers at each other. Another comrade shook his head violently and waved his hands in the air.

"What do you think, Simon," Roger asked. He was anxious. His life was in the hands of a bunch of beer-drinking kids, sitting in a dusty backyard.

"I don't know. They're afraid you might be an impimpi but at the same time I think they were impressed with the case you made." He too was anxious. If they decided Roger was indeed a spy there would be consequences for Simon.

"What will happen if they don't accept me? If they decide I am a police spy?"

Simon shuddered.

"They will order you executed and I'll have to do it to prove my loyalty."

A wave of terror and panic swept over Roger. He

contemplated making a dash for the front door but he would never get out of the township alive and flight would just serve to confirm their suspicions of his guilt.

"Jesus!" he said, visibly trembling. "I am your friend, would you do it?"

"I would have no choice. If I didn't they would kill me as well."

Outside the comrades' discussions were becoming increasingly heated.

"If you believe in God, now would be a good time to pray that they believe your story," said Simon.

* *boers – white Afrikaners. A generic, slightly derogatory term used by blacks.*

* *impimpi – spy or police informant.*

Chapter 18

Ellen was absolutely frantic. She and Templeton had searched for Roger for the past five days with no success. It was almost as though he had disappeared off the face of the earth.

He had not been at school and no-one seemed to have seen him.

"How is that possible, Templeton?" asked Ellen. "How can my son just disappear?"

Things were more strained than ever between her and Templeton.

"Someone has seen him," said Templeton, "but you know what the township underground is like – they know where he is but they're not saying!"

He was surprised by Roger's actions. He really thought the youngster would come crawling back.

The boy has some guts, thought Templeton. Deep inside, hidden from the world he held some admiration for his son.

Ellen was crying again. It's all she seemed to do nowadays. She carried a weight on her shoulders that she simply could not shake off. Her sobs caused her entire body to tremble.

"Why didn't he come back? He belongs here, where we love him." She sniffed then dabbed her eyes with a damp tissue.

Templeton looked at his wife and his heart sank. She seemed older and smaller. He put his arms around her and held her tightly.

"We'll find him," he said softly. "We are going to start putting pressure on his friends. They know where he is, that's for sure and they're going to tell me even if I have to beat it out of them!"

Ellen pushed him away, suddenly angry. She'd lost

almost everything she cared about and it was all because of the organisation her husband so blindly served.

"That's your way of solving everything – dishing out a beating. It's how you chased our son away. This is all your fault!"

Her accusations stung him. Ever since Roger walked out his feelings of guilt had grown and festered. At night he lay awake, wondering where his son was and what he was doing. Was he safe? Was he hungry or cold? Ellen was right, he often beat the solutions out of his problems. He constantly prayed that Roger was safe and would soon be back.

"I'm sorry," he said, avoiding her gaze. He went to her wanting to wrap his arms around her but she pushed him away angrily.

"Just find my son, Templeton and bring him back safely or you will have destroyed a part of me that can never be restored!"

Chapter 19

The liquid seared Roger's throat, causing his eyes to water. He fought back the urge to gag, trying hard not to display any signs of weakness. He wiped his mouth with the back of his hand and passed the bottle of J&B Whisky® along to the next youngster.

Around him, still sitting in the same circle were the Comrades. The bottle of whisky they passed along had been 'liberated' from a shebeen. Roger swallowed a few times, trying to rid his mouth of the foul taste.

Jesus! What did people see in alcohol? he thought.

Roger waited. His stomach felt as though it had tied itself into a tight coil and then crawled into his chest, causing his breathing to be shallow and rapid. After their deliberations were done, the Comrades called Simon and Roger back and told them to sit. The whisky bottle was produced and passed around clockwise. The fact they were included in the drinking meant nothing – certainly not necessarily an act of acceptance or friendship as, in many cases, booze was offered to someone before pronouncing a death sentence on him.

Little sweat ball-bearings popped out under the hairline on the back of Roger's neck and strangely, at a time like this, he was acutely aware of them as they gathered volume to the point where they were heavy enough to roll down beneath his shirt collar.

His hands were clammy and he was terrified that when he spoke his voice would be high-pitched and pinched.

The Comrades could smell Roger and Simon's unease but made no attempt to placate it. This was a moment they enjoyed and savoured when they could experience and bask in their own power.

When the whisky bottle reached Comrade Jack he took a healthy swig then spoke.

"You were brought here by Comrade Simon to join the struggle." He spoke softly enough to require them to lean forward and tilt their heads.

"Your father is a policeman so there is the possibility that you are an impimpi, a police plant..."

"I am not..." Simon put his hand on Roger's arm to shush him. And Comrade Jack waved his hand at him in a warning to shut up.

Comrade Jack paused while he gulped down the last dregs of the whisky. Then he dropped the empty bottle at his feet.

"We have spoken about this and not all agree you are who you say you are. Some say you are genuine, others believe you are a spy and should be dealt with as a spy and collaborator."

All eyes were on him.

"You know how we deal with impimpi?"

Roger nodded. He couldn't speak, his mouth was dry and his tongue felt as though it was glued to the roof of his mouth.

Jesus! How could this be happening? A week ago his biggest concern was whether Orlando Pirates would get through to the finals and if they would have a television set to watch the game. Now he was sitting in a dusty backyard with chickens, a bony mongrel and a bunch of youngsters – some of them from the same school he attended – and those youngsters would decide whether he lived or died!

"We could not decide what to do with you so we voted, we are, after all democratic."

The others laughed at Comrade Jack's joke.

"The result, and it was only by one vote, is...," he paused for effect like a television game-show host milking the moment for maximum dramatic effect, "...you live!"

Roger thought he was going to faint. His body felt like bundles of over-cooked spaghetti. His relief was so tangible he could taste it – and it was the sweetest taste ever.

"Thank you," he said meekly.

For the first time since sitting down he studied the members of the circle carefully. He held each person's gaze, contemplating who had voted for his death. But their faces were inscrutable and cold gazes held his.

Comrade Jack continued: "However we have decided you will need to prove yourself and your loyalty before you can be fully accepted and you will be tested. We will soon discuss and decide what that test will be but it will prove, with certainty, whether you truly support the struggle or are just a filthy impimpi.

"If you pass you will be one of us. If you fail..." his voice tailed off and he shrugged his shoulders before lifting and placing an imaginary tire around Roger's neck.

Chapter 20

"Ellen! Ellen!" Templeton yelled, bursting through the front door with such violence that the windows rattled.

"We've found Roger!"

She almost dropped the clothes-iron she was using to press Templeton's trousers.

"Where?" she asked, her voice choked. Oh, Jesus, thank you, my son is found!

"Is he okay? Templeton have you spoken to him? When is he coming home?" She fired her questions like a machine gunner repelling an advance.

He chuckled, ecstatic that he was able to make her happy. He swept her up in his arms and spun her around.

"Whoa! Slow down! One question at a time. The answer is, yes he is fine I am told, no I haven't spoken to him and I don't know when he is coming home – just as soon as we go and fetch him I guess."

He put her down and she sat down, weak with relief. She beamed with joy and her face glowed. Oh dear God, her son was okay! She had been so afraid. At night, in restless sleep, she often dreamed he was dead or lying injured and calling to her where she reached out to help him but her feet seemed chained to the ground and she could not help. But now, everything was going to be okay, her boy was found! They'd be back together as a family. Happy again.

We'll just forget the past and start again. We'll build the life we want, she thought.

Ellen knew Templeton felt deep remorse for the way he acted. She reached out and clasped his chunky right hand between hers.

"Where did you find him?" she asked, squeezing his hand.

"I told you we were going to start putting pressure on his

friends," Templeton replied, "and you probably won't be happy about this, but Msibi hauled in a guy who is at school with Roger. Apparently he took the youngster to the toilets at the back of the station for a little chat and when they came out, amazingly the kid had remembered where Roger is.

"Msibi can be very persuasive..." he paused but Ellen said nothing. When it came to finding Roger she didn't care how they got the information.

"He's living at the far end of Soweto with a youngster and his grandmother. I have the address. We didn't go and pick him up because I thought you might want to come with. We go as soon as you are ready.

"I'm ready. Let's go now. Thandi is playing next door I'll quickly go and ask them to keep an eye on her."

She got up to leave then stopped as though she had suddenly thought of something she wanted to say.

"Temp, please can we go all go and eat at a restaurant tonight? A family reunion and celebration?"

"Sure!" he said. "Now hurry up, let's go and fetch our son!"

Chapter 21

Templeton knocked loudly on the door. From inside they could hear music belting out with a raw, monotonous beat.

"I wonder if they heard," said Ellen, "that music is very loud."

Templeton knocked again, this time using the bottom of his fist to hammer on the door.

"I'll give it a moment then go 'round the back, " he said.

Just then they heard the scrape of a safety-chain as someone inside threaded it. The two dead-bolts were drawn back and the door opened to a thin crack. An old woman, her hair beginning to grey peered at them.

"Yes?" she asked, "What do you want?" Most of her front teeth were missing, those remaining were yellowed with age and decaying.

"Good afternoon, Grandmother, I'd like to see your grandson, please Ma," said Templeton, addressing her in the old, customary style to show his respect.

"Wait here."

The old hag shut the door in their faces and shuffled away.

"Do you think she's going to call her grandson?" asked Ellen.

"I hope so."

A little while later the door once again opened a few inches, stopped by the security chain, and a youngster about Roger's age looked out at them.

"What do you want?"

"I'm looking for my son, Roger Ngubane. I believe he's staying here."

The youngster's lips compressed.

"I've never heard of him. He's not here!"

He tried to slam the door shut but Templeton had firmly

wedged his foot against it.

"I told you, he's not here! Get off our property!" snapped the youngster, his eyes flashing.

The Security Cop's left hand moved faster than a striking puff adder. Before the kid knew what was happening Ngubane had his thumb in the youngster's mouth and under his tongue. It was an old police trick, designed to subdue and opponent and worked every time if done fast enough. With his forefinger wedged firmly under the boy's chin, Templeton drove his thumb into the soft part of the kid's mouth. At the same time he dragged him forward and smashed his face against the door-frame. The pain was excruciating and the boy's eyes stretched wide.

"You've got two chances, little boy," said Templeton in a volume only just above that of a whisper, his voice smeared with menace.

"You can open this door and co-operate or I can rip your face off and then kick the front door down and still come in, except then, very pissed off!

"What's it going to be?"

The youngster's eyes were glazed from the pain being inflicted. His legs were wobbly and he was about to collapse. Weakly he indicated surrender.

Templeton released him and a moment later the door was opened.

"Where is Roger?"

The boy held his mouth, both hands pressed over his lips, unable to speak.

"Tell me where he is, before I get really rough."

"There'll be no need for that," said a voice from the lounge doorway. "I'm here."

Standing framed in the doorway and lit by the late afternoon sun that streamed through a back window was Roger.

"I wondered how long it would take for you to find me."

"Roger!" Ellen gasped. She rushed to him and wrapped

him in her arms with the warmth that is found only in a mother's embrace.

"Oh my God! It is so good to see you. You can't imagine how much I've prayed for this moment!"

"It's good to see you too, Mother." His voice trembled somewhat but lacked emotion. His kept his arms by his side and did not return her embrace.

Ellen stepped back and held him at arm's length. She studied him carefully.

"You look as though you have lost some weight," she said.

Templeton put a meaty hand on Roger's shoulder.

"How are you, my son?" he asked.

"Fine," replied Roger, his voice still emotionless.

The other youngster, still holding his jaw, stood quietly watching the family re-union. Templeton suddenly became aware of him. He pointed to the front door that was still ajar.

"Get out! Leave us alone with our son!"

The youngster took off like a feral cat with a pack 'o dogs behind it. But he stood in the yard in a position from where he could continue to watch.

"Get your stuff, Roger. Thandi is waiting for you and we'll all go out to dinner to celebrate. I want to put things right between us."

He pulled his son roughly against his chest and hugged him.

Roger pushed him away. Out of the corner of his eye he could see the youngster in the yard watching them.

"I am not going home!" His eyes were filled with tears but his voice was resolved.

"Do you think you can just arrive here and say: 'come home Roger, everything's okay now?' Well you can't.

"You can beat me and drag me home but you'll have to keep me locked up for the rest of my life because the moment you turn your back I'll be gone!"

Tears streamed down his cheeks. He had been expecting this meeting with his parents and dreaded it. On one hand he wanted more than ever to go home and see his little sister again. He longed to have a normal life. To lie on the couch when he got home from school. To talk about soccer and to make plans to go back to Kwa Zulu – Natal.

He was trapped in a situation he wanted no part of – he was no political activist but now he had no option but to be one.

If he walked out with his parents now, he would effectively be signing Simon's death warrant and he, himself, would never be safe.

"You can't mean that, Roger!" said Ellen, her voice anxious. "You can't just turn your back on us – we love you!" The last part of the sentence emphasised her desperation and rising fear.

She reached out to her son, desperately praying the physical contact would bring down the invisible barrier.

Inwardly Roger felt as if his heart was about to burst. He wanted to be enveloped in her arms, to lay his head on her shoulder and weep. He wanted to be free of this gutting emotion that clawed at his innards like some barbed, steel octopus. He swallowed and fought back his tears. Now was definitely not the time to display weakness.

"Please go. I am no longer part of your family." He paused then quickly embraced her. "I'll come when I can," he whispered, then pushed her away.

Templeton felt like he'd been kicked in the groin. A sick, hollow feeling welled up in the pit of his stomach then spread through the rest of his body, nauseating him. It was his fault they had lost their son.

"My God, Roger! Please don't do this to your mother and me, I'm begging you. I am so sorry for what I did to you and I promise you I will make it up to you." He pleaded, his voice desperate, like a drowning man screaming for a rope that would never be thrown.

"Please Roger, we love you! Your mother, Thandi and I love you dearly."

"Just go," said Roger. Then he turned and fled from the room, silently weeping.

Through the open front door, the youngster, still nursing his jaw, stood and watched.

Chapter 22

"Give it some time, Temp, he'll come back." Eric Joubert lit a cigarette and then, as an after thought, offered the pack to Ngubane. "Sorry, I keep forgetting you've started again."

Templeton tapped the packet with a meaty finger.

"Jesus, why Jooba? I mean all parents have problems with their kids along the way. I'm sure you've had to give your kids a hiding or two but then you sort it out and carry on with your lives!"

Joubert got up to close the window. The racket from the construction site across from the courtyard made it difficult to hear each other speak. It also resulted in a thin layer of dust that covered everything in the office.

"I wish they would finish building those damned single-quarters," he said. "It's impossible to get any work done in here!"

He fished in his pocket for a handkerchief so he could wipe the sticky dust from his fingers, acquired when he parted blades of the grimy Venetian blinds to get to the window.

"Ja, I've given my kids hidings – plenty."

"So what the fuck did I do wrong, Jooba? Why is Roger acting the way he is?"

Joubert leaned back in his chair, balancing it on its two rear legs. He sucked in a lung-full of smoke while considering Templeton's question.

They had worked together for just a fraction under five years now. In a way they were partners – not in the American-cop-television-series kind of way – rather they worked on many cases together and shared the same office. Beyond that there was little personal interaction. They knew the cursory details about each other's lives – the names of their children and wives, where the other went on holiday, that sort of thing – but there was no social contact outside of business. After work, when cops got together in the mess for a few drinks, white members went to their facility and black members to another. The only occasions Joubert and Ngubane ever ate or drank together was when, out in the field, they bought greasy takeaways and ate them in the car.

But Joubert liked Templeton. He had a bond with him that ran deep and was quite prepared to put his life on the line for his black colleague. It was the respect that men developed when they had faced danger together. In another life, political system or different society, they probably would have been close, after-hours friends but now they lived in times where the white race was under threat and some things just couldn't be.

It's funny, thought Joubert, here we are discussing the raising of children, drinking coffee and smoking together, thought Joubert. Me and a black man. He couldn't help smiling. A moment of irony.

Joubert was behind a petition against a local restaurant that recently announced it was opening its doors to all races and would serves non-whites.

He also left the NG Church after its proclamation that apartheid was not in accordance with the teachings of the Bible and was in fact a sin. He remembered the day the church's Moderator, Professor Johan Heyns said that. What a crock of shit! Separate Development was completely in line with the Bible, did not Jesus himself say water and wine do not mix?

Heyns will get himself killed talking kak like that, he thought.

The Immorality Act was gone. Now *meid-naai** was legal and he'd heard there were some blacks and whites living together in places like Hillbrow. Jesus this world was changing and he didn't like it but what else could you expect with a liberal like PW Botha in charge?

Yet here he found himself genuinely drawn to this man sitting across from him. A black man. Fuck it! Things are complicated nowadays.

"Youngsters are different today," Joubert said. "They don't respect their elders any more. But from what you've told me Roger is a good kid. He'll be back. He probably just needs time to think."

Templeton stubbed out his cigarette. He pinched in his lips and sucked air through his nostrils.

"I hope you're right, Jooba, because this is killing Ellen."

Another sign of change, thought Joubert. Ten years ago no black would have dared use a white police officer's nickname.

But actually, I don't really mind, he thought.

**meid-naai – derogatory term for a white man having sex with a black woman, a practice that was once a criminal offence in South Africa.*

Chapter 23

"Come on! Come on! Wake up! They want to see you!"

Roger sat up immediately but didn't know exactly what was going on or where he was. He blinked and rubbed his eyes, as he struggled to brush away the cobwebs that clogged his thinking.

"What is it? What's happening?" he asked. He shook his head trying to shake loose the fog.

It was early afternoon and the sun shone brightly. His memory slowly started to creep back, like a guilty dog. There was drinking he remembered. Ma Moroka's Tavern. That was it. He went there with Simon and a few other youngsters. In his skull a demolition crew started up their equipment and cranked the volume up high.

Jesus! What a headache! He felt ill.

They must have drunk a lot because the last thing he could remember was a drunken argument...about a girl? His head hurt just trying to think. He was lying on the floor where he must have slept. He turned his head slowly taking in his surroundings, none of which was familiar. He had absolutely no idea where he was.

"Get up," said Simon, who was a little better than Roger but only a little. "Comrade Jack and the others want to see you, now!"

Roger stood up. Fuck what was that smell? He sniffed then wrinkled his nose in disgust. It was him. At some point he had vomited and must have slept in the puke that was now dried and made his shirt and the front of his trousers crusty.

"Oh God!" he said. "I need to change my clothes."

"No time for that now," said Simon. "We have to go, they're waiting."

"Where are we going?"

"To the bus and taxi depot."

"Do you know why?"

"Do you know about the boycott of white shops?"

Roger did.

The leadership of the exiled ANC in Lusaka believed that a fundamental component in their eventual success was to cause disruption in the lives of, and injury to, ordinary white South Africans who supported the current government. Doing so would cause whites to become disillusioned and dissatisfied, as their normally comfortable lives were increasingly disrupted. The organisation hoped that, as the situation become more untenable, whites would pressurise the Government to negotiate with the ANC.

Already they enjoyed international successes, as an increasing number of countries instituted sanctions against Pretoria. But they wanted to hit white businessmen, farmers, factories and suppliers where it most hurt – in their pockets. The sheer number of black people in South Africa meant, when it came to buying power, they formed a very significant component of the economy.

It was a fact the ANC leadership understood very well and they issued instructions that no black people were to make any purchases from white businesses or shopkeepers and the activated youth – the comrades – were tasked with ensuring the boycott was enforced.

It was a simple, very effective tactic. White business soon felt the effects of black economic muscle. Shareholders and business-owners watched profits decline and what to do about it was discussed in detail over good scotch and G&Ts at the Rand and Inanda clubs in Johannesburg and other, similar fine gentlemen's' establishments throughout the country.

Suddenly the captains of industry were prepared to talk to township leaders, leaders they previously dismissed as 'rabble-rousers' and 'cheeky trouble-makers'. They made urgent representations to Government in letters and widely publicised meetings where they urged the authorities to 'make significant and meaningful changes.'

In the townships and Lusaka the effect was electric. They had no idea the tactic would be so effective and produce results so quickly. At ANC headquarters the National Executive Committee decided now was the time to the tighten the screws to ensure the consumer boycott had maximum impact.

Once again they issued the order that no-one was to buy any goods of any sort from a white-owned store. Purchases could only be made from black *spaza** shops in the townships. It was of little concern to the Lusaka exiles that many of those township shops were burnt down or looted during the periodic rioting or that those that remained, charged more than the shops outside the townships, sometimes up to four times as much for the same item.

They also chose to ignore the fact that people could often not buy bread from township shops as bakeries, worried about their vehicles and personnel, refused to make deliveries there.

Hunger and sacrifice were apparently just part of the price township residents were expected to pay.

The comrades took to their role of enforcers with gusto and enthusiasm. They patrolled the streets, bus depots, taxi-ranks and train stations like packs of feral dogs. People were stopped and had their parcels and bags searched. When someone was found with a forbidden item, the youngsters sometimes confiscated the goods (which they kept for themselves or resold) and let the guilty person proceed or sometimes administered a beating before destroying the contraband. What they chose to do, depended entirely upon how they felt at that particular moment.

There were also occasions when people were forced to

eat what they had purchased and there were many tales of a guilty shopper having to drink a bottle of cooking oil or fabric softener.

"We're going to check on boycott-breakers," said Simon. "Comrade Jack will give you your instructions. This will be your test."

***

Comrade Jack and three of his lieutenants were waiting at the combined bus and taxi-rank.

He looked Roger up and down and it was clear he found the youngster's appearance and smell offensive but he said nothing about it.

"We have received instructions from our Comrade leaders," he said, moving so that he stood down-wind of Roger. "They want the consumer boycott to be applied more strictly. It is starting to weaken the resolve of the boers but there are still traitors undermining the struggle by buying from white shops. When they do so they support our enemy and must be rooted out and dealt with."

Roger's head was still fuzzy and he struggled to make complete sense of what was being said.

He heard something about these being direct instructions from Comrade *Alfred Nzo**. He had heard the name before and knew Nzo was an ANC leader but had no idea what position he held in the banned organisation.

"Comrade Nzo has instructed that these traitors and collaborators be found and brought before a Peoples' Court, given a fair trial and if found guilty eliminated," continued Comrade Jack. "There is no room in our struggle for puppets!"

Roger gasped. "You can't be serious! Surely you wouldn't kill someone just because they bought food at the wrong shop."

Comrade Jack's eyes narrowed as he gave Roger a withering look.

"What are a few lives if they further the struggle?" he said, his voice like a mid-winter icicle spike.

** spaza shops – small township shops often run from residents' homes.*

** Alfred Nzo was the ANC's longest serving Secretary General.*

Chapter 24

The Street lights burned dimly in the quickly-darkening evening when they reached Dieprivier bus depot. Streams of blue PUTCO commuter buses came and went and, from afar, the hundreds of disembarking passengers all hurriedly scurrying homewards, made the place look like an overturned ants' nest.

They seemed to have adopted a faceless shuffle, avoiding eye-contact and looking at the ground as they made their way home. There was a dark mood that blanketed the area, oppressive and burdensome. It had been there since the start of the consumer boycott and, like police tear-gas, it made everyone uncomfortable and afraid and once in the air there was no escaping it.

People no longer talked to each other the way they used to. Now they just wanted to get home as quickly as possible where they could lock their doors and hope there would be no night-time knock.

They tried to blend into the shadows, hoping the comrade enforcers would not see them. Nowadays even the township vendors left early. Although the boycott brought them more business they preferred not to become haphazard targets of a roving comrade or criminal group. All it took was one accusation that they themselves were selling goods purchased at white shops and they could be forced to hand over the day's takings or forfeit their stock.

It wasn't too long ago that the informal traders arrived long before dawn and set up their shop counters that they constructed with planks laid across paraffin drums. From those quickly-erected stalls, they vied with each other as they tried to persuade commuters to purchase their hard-boiled eggs, roasted *mielies**, *braaied nyama** and boerewors or just peanuts, potato crisps and cigarettes, that they sold either either individually or in packs.

They would stay until the last evening bus was gone but now they packed up before dark, driven away by the all-embracing fear that dusted the area.

Roger watched the many commuters queueing for mini-bus taxis. Those vehicles were the backbone of the transport system in the black townships. Every year they carried millions of passengers into the cities and to and from bus and railway stations into the heart of the townships. For a long time the government tried to regulate and control them but in the end gave up as 'pirate' taxis overwhelmed their law-enforcement capabilities.

“What do we have to do?” asked Roger. He was assigned to partner Simon and another youngster whose name he could not remember and who said very little. Comrade Jack was also there. As a Street Commander he needed to keep an eye on things but mostly he was there to test Roger.

According to a plan to control townships, reportedly devised by Nelson Mandela and known as the 'M Plan', the ANC divided them up into Regions, Zones, Blocks, Streets and Cells. Street Commanders were put in charge of residents living on a particular street and reported to a Block Commander in charge of a number of blocks within a suburb who in turn reported to a Zone Commander in charge of a number of blocks and so on.

It was a simple and brilliant method that allowed the ANC to control and identify people, right down to the lowest of grass-root levels.

Its effectiveness was proved in Port Elizabeth when, on one occasion, the ANC was able to mobilise 20 000 people in less than an hour.

The M Plan made life very difficult for the Security Police.

On the walls of the Dieprivier bus-depot many slogans were painted: Viva ANC, UDF Lives, Free Mandela.

Comrade Jack issued final instructions.

"Stop anyone with a parcel or bag. Make them empty out the contents. If anything looks like it is a violation of the consumer boycott, bring that person to me. When we're done questioning everyone, I will question those people and decide if they must appear before a Peoples' Court or not."

He stood with his thumbs clipped in the belt of his jeans and felt like a cowboy, as he watched the returning commuters who did their best to avoid his gaze and hurry on their way.

"Don't listen to excuses or sob-stories. It's not your job to decide what happens to traitors!"

* *mielies – corn ears*

* *braaied nyama – barbecued meat*

Chapter 25

"I'm sorry, Mama, but I must check your bags, please," said Roger. He stopped an old woman who was hurrying along, trying to avoid him.

"Please, I must go," she pleaded. Her aged eyes were watery and she reminded him of his own *gogo**. "The children are at home on their own. I must get back to them. They'll be worried if I am late."

Roger hesitated. The old lady was frail and frightened and he wondered how she even able to carry her bags. He guessed she must be about seventy years-old and she wore the lines of a hard life on her face.

"I...I...don't know," he stammered, unsure what to do. He wanted let her pass.

"Please," she said, pleading, "let me go."

"I...I..."

"What is the problem?" snapped a voice from nearby. It was Comrade Jack. He looked at the bags the old woman held and then fixed his gaze on Roger.

"Nothing, there is no problem," said Roger. His voice was a pitch higher and his mouth was dry. He ran his tongue over his lips then swallowed and said:

"I'm sorry, Mama but I am going to have to insist you show me what's in those bags. Please empty them out."

The old woman began to tremble. She looked around, twisting her head in different directions in the hope she would see someone who would help her. She was like a frightened rabbit cornered by a pack of hounds and there was no-one who could, or would help.

Roger tipped the contents of the bags onto the road.

"I didn't buy any of this. I promise you I didn't buy it!" Her voice was spider-webbed with rising panic.

At Roger's feet was a loaf of bread, a tin of condensed milk, a can of instant coffee and chicory mix and a tin of

Portuguese pilchards in olive oil.

"I promise you I did not buy any of this in town!" Her voice was urgent. "My Madam gave them to me. It's for the children. We have to eat! Please, you must understand, we have to eat!" She was gasping like a beached mackerel as she tried to speak and her words came out in breathy puffs. "What else must we do?"

Roger glanced furtively to his right where Comrade Jack stood. The Street Commander watched him carefully but showed no emotion, rather a just kind of expectant curiosity.

Roger swallowed again. His hands began to tremble.

"I'm sorry, Mama," he said, his trembles creeping into his voice, "you are going to have wait over there."

He pointed to a spot beside Comrade Jack who now lounged against one of the bus-depot walls.

"What is going to happen to me?" she asked. Her dark eyes darted from side to side, reflecting her growing dread.

"I don't know but I'm sure everything will be fine," said Roger but he knew he was trying to convince himself as much as he was her. "I'm sure they'll understand when you explain."

** Gogo – Granny*

Chapter 26

The 'peoples' court' was convened on an open lot, not very far from the bus-depot. It was littered with garbage dumped there by township residents.

At the extremities of the side that faced the road, were two high, multi-light, street lights that lit up a large surrounding area. The light-clusters were purposely built on tall concrete pylons to keep the powerful halogen globes out of the range of thrown stones.

They dragged the old woman along towards the court site and as they did so youngsters rounded up people in the houses they passed along the way so they could come and witness justice being done.

“Please,” she begged. “I have done nothing wrong. I have children at home that I must care for!”

They ignored her pleas and shoved her forward. In the middle of the growing march, Comrade Jack had a hand on Roger's shoulder and firmly guided him along the course.

At the back, a youngster, in a green jersey and a tatty, red, woollen knitted cap, carried two tires and a blue, plastic bottle filled with gasoline.

Chapter 27

The crowd sat mostly in ranks facing Comrade Jack and an older man who was probably around thirty years old. He wore a once-white sweat-shirt with an image of Bob Marley's face printed on the chest.

He had the hood pulled forward over his head making it difficult to see his face but, in the flickering light from a fire burning in a drum before them, his eyes glistened and flashed.

Both he and Comrade Jack warmed their hands over the fire while they waited for the 150-strong crowd of bemused, older, residents and a group of ululating youngsters to settle down.

On the left of the two men who were standing by the fire, three of Comrade Jack's lieutenants sat on a wrecked and stripped Chrysler Valiant car body.

The man in the white sweat-shirt went by the name of Comrade Rambo. He was an active member of the ANC's military wing, Umkhonto we Sizwe (MK) and had received military training in Angola and Tanzania and took part in a number of military-style operations, including a sabotage attempt on a fuel-storage depot in Durban.

But Lusaka recently decided to deploy him in a different role. His task was now to activate the people and to increase the intensity of the struggle in the townships, in and around Johannesburg.

From his political education in the training camps, where some of the lecturers were North Korean and Vietnamese, he quickly learned that terror was an effective tool to motivate and bring people into line.

“In a revolution if the people are more afraid of the insurgent than the government forces they will support the insurgent,” he was taught.

“To be properly effective the application of terror should

be so decisive and have such impact on the people that it does not have to be repeated often."

They were lessons Comrade Rambo learned well.

He tossed a plank from a broken box onto the fire in the drum causing sparks to spiral into the air like dancing fire flies. From under his sweat-shirt hood he eyed the crowd. The powerful street-lights made the individual members easy to see and he could see their unease. They didn't want to be there but were too terrified to leave.

Comrade Rambo smiled. Terror was indeed a very effective tool!

He had chosen his own township name and as he looked out at the people and could actually feel their fear tingle on his skin, he truly felt like Rambo. Fuck! It felt so damned good!

I wish I had a machine gun and a couple of grenades, he thought, then I'd give them a real lesson in terror.

He held up his right hand to quiet the crowd and to indicate the proceedings were about to begin. The hum that was soft talk stopped immediately.

Comrade Jack indicated to his lieutenants, with a flick of his head, to bring the old woman.

She struggled feebly as they roughly dragged her in front of Comrade Rambo. She looked at him, softly sobbing.

"What is the charge against this woman?" Comrade Rambo asked.

Comrade Jack stepped forward.

"She broke the consumer boycott and by doing so has proved she is a traitor and a collaborator," he said in a clear voice.

"No! No! I didn't!" screamed the old woman. She tried to shake herself loose from the hands that held her arms.

"Be quiet, old woman!" rebuked Comrade Rambo. "You will have the opportunity to state your case."

He motioned to Comrade Jack to continue.

"Present your case."

Comrade Jack stepped up onto a pile of building rubble so that the crowd could see him more clearly.

He paused, giving the assembly the opportunity to contemplate the gravity of what he was about to say.

"In accordance with your instructions, as well as the directive issued by our wise leaders in Lusaka, especially, Comrade Nzo, this afternoon we carried out checks on people returning to the township to see if any were breaking the consumer boycott and supporting the aims and objectives of our enemies."

He paused to clear his throat, then continued.

"This old hag, a traitor and collaborator was found in possession of this." He held up the bag the old woman had with her when stopped by Roger. He began removing the items contained in it, holding each up to show it to the people. First the bread, then the condensed milk, then the pilchards.

"There can be no doubt, if it were not for our vigilance, this..." he searched for the right word, "this traitor..." he spat at his feet, "would continue to support the Apartheid regime."

There was murmuring in the crowd. Many knew the old woman and knew the charges were ridiculous. She was seventy two years-old and had spent almost every waking moment of her life just trying to eke out a living. She had no time to think about, much less support, a political philosophy. In an attempt to earn a bit of extra cash, over the years, she baby-sat the children of quite a few of the people gathered there. Heck she'd baby-sat some of the adults there.

"Who caught her?" Comrade Rambo snapped, interrupting the monologue of Comrade Jack and instantly quieting the murmuring.

Comrade Jack pointed a spear-like finger at Roger who immediately felt the gaze of the crowd pierce his heart.

"You did well," said Comrade Rambo.

Roger lowered his head. He thought the weight of his guilt might crush him.

Rambo stood up and faced the old woman.

"Let her go," he ordered the two youths who detained her.

"Come forward, accused and present your defence."

When they released their grip on her arms the old woman stumbled and fell onto one knee. She got up, dust on her dress and stepped over a chunk of concrete so she could face Comrade Rambo and address the people. These people who were her friends many of whom had grown up in front of her.

If she told the truth and appealed to them, surely they would not let a group of youngsters kill her, she thought. I am going to be all right. For a moment she thought about her grandchildren waiting for her back home. They would be worried but she would soon be home.

Comrade Rambo once again held up both hands to ensure the crowd remained silent.

"You have heard the charges, old woman, what do you have to say?"

Her voice was steady and clear when she spoke and everyone could hear.

"Please, I am an old woman. I have never caused anyone any harm..." she passed her gaze over the watching people. Many looked away. "All I have ever wanted to do is live my life in peace. For the past three years I have cared for my two grandchildren after their parents were robbed and killed by tsotsis. You all know that to be true."

She paused while she swallowed. Her mouth felt dusty. She prayed God would help her get through to the people. Surely they would not kill her just because she had a parcel of food for her grandchildren. Food that she was given, that she hadn't bought from a white store. The stories she'd heard about people being killed for such things surely couldn't be true.

I know these people, they won't have lost their humanity. The ANC said they were coming to liberate people, they wouldn't harm an old lady for taking care of her grandchildren!

"It is true, I had food in my bag," she continued. "But I did not buy it. I work for a very kind woman doing ironing and cleaning for her. When she heard how we are suffering she gave me some food to bring home."

She looked at Comrade Rambo to see if what she said had any impact on him. She searched for a glimmer of emotion but he just stared back at her with cold, black, emotionless eyes and she became afraid again.

"Please, you've got to believe me!" she pleaded. "Ask these people, they know me." She turned to the crowd.

"They will speak for me."

"Very well," said Comrade Rambo. "I will ask them."

He took a few steps forward so that he stood almost amongst the first row of people seated on the ground and raised the volume of his voice when he spoke.

"Is there anyone here who wishes to speak in the defence of this woman?"

No-one spoke up. Most preferred to look away or to look at the ground in front of them. At a time like this, saying anything could bring repercussions later.

The old woman struggled to breathe. She could feel a noose tightening around her neck.

"You know me!" she screamed at the crowd. She pointed an accusing finger at a woman sitting on the hull of a discarded refrigerator to the side of the main gathering.

"Nomsane, you know me. Have I not looked after your children before? Did I not come to help when your boy was sick and you were afraid he might die? I beg you now, speak for me!"

She began to sob, her old, wrinkled body heaving as spasms ran through it.

"Nomsane, what will happen to my grandchildren if you

do not speak for me now?"

The woman she addressed bowed her head, then got up, turned her back and pushed her way through the crowd. Not once did she look back but she did clamp her hands over her ears to block out the pleas of the grandmother.

"Nomsane!" she screamed. "Come back! Speak for me!" But she was gone, running up the road as fast as she could.

No one said a thing. The only sound for a few moments was the crackle of the fire and the sobs of the old woman. Then someone in the crowd sniffed and began to softly weep.

The old woman drew in breathe, as though about to speak again but before she could Comrade Rambo snapped: "Be quiet old woman! You have had your say."

He called the two youths who previously detained her.

"Take her over there and keep her until we have decided our verdict." He pointed to a spot behind the Chrysler Valiant carcass.

Rambo, Jack and the three lieutenants drew together and squatted on their haunches, their heads close together. Roger, who stood a little way away, towards the side of the crowd, could clearly see them talking but could hear nothing they said. They spoke in low, muted tones and once, both Comrade Jack and Comrade Rambo turned around and looked at him before returning to their deliberations.

Finally after some gesticulations and affirmative head-noddings they stood up. Rambo and Jack took their places at the fire and the three lieutenants resumed their spots on the Valiant.

The crowd began to once again murmur. They were restless and uneasy and Comrade Rambo held up his hand to still them.

"We have reached a verdict," he said speaking so that everyone on the lot could hear. "We find the accused guilty of breaking the consumer boycott and therefore a traitor and collaborator."

There was a collective gasp. Everyone knew what the sentence would be.

"No!" the old woman screamed, struggling desperately to break free.

"Be quiet while Comrade Rambo speaks," hissed one of the youngsters holding her. He slapped her hard against the side of her head. The effect of the blow was as though the tendons in her legs were slashed with a *panga**. She simply folded into a heap and lay whimpering.

"In accordance with the instructions issued by Comrade Nzo," continued Comrade Rambo, "examples are to be made of collaborators so that other potential traitors will not be tempted to follow the same path.

"I therefore have no option but to do my duty and have no choice but to order that the necklace be applied."

A wave of shock swept over the crowd. Some people voiced their dissent and horror to each other but no-one had the courage speak out directly against the sentence to the comrades.

"Quiet!" bellowed Comrade Jack.

Comrade Rambo continued. "As this is a Peoples' Court and because the ANC is a democratic liberation movement, you, as the people, now have the opportunity and right to speak before the sentence is carried out."

No-one spoke. They chose to rather avoid the aggressive stare of Comrade Rambo and kept their mouths firmly shut.

So easy to scare and control, thought Comrade Rambo.

"It is settled then. The decision of the people is unanimous and the sentence will be carried out immediately."

He turned to Roger who was still standing on the sidelines and pointed at him.

"You came to us but you are the son of a policeman.

Some believe you are an impimpi but tonight you will have the chance to prove you are not. We will give you the opportunity to show your commitment to the freedom struggle and your loyalty to your comrades."

He paused briefly, considering what he would next say. He wanted it to be profound and important for he believed his contribution would one day be taught in history classes at schools.

He kept his gaze firmly fixed on Roger.

"Comrade Winnie Mandela recently said: 'with our tires and boxes of matches we will liberate this country' and tonight you will make a contribution to the liberation of our country. You will have the honour of executing the traitor."

Roger gagged. He felt as though he had been kicked in the guts. Nausea welled up in him and he could taste raw bile in his mouth.

"No..." he choked, starting to protest but he stopped when he felt a hand clamp his arm tightly. It was Simon.

"Shut up!" hissed his friend, speaking quietly under his breath. "They've brought two tires, one for you if you refuse. You can't save the old woman, they are going to kill her, whatever you do, but you can save yourself...and me."

I can't kill someone because they had food in a bag for their grandchildren, thought Roger.

"Do it," said Simon softly as though reading Roger's thoughts. "You can't save her."

He pushed Roger forward and the policeman's son stepped up to the fire, dazed and uncertain.

The old woman lay on the ground, whimpering the names of her grandchildren and praying softly. Beside her stood the youngster with the tire and plastic container of gasoline. Her eyes were wide as she looked into the hideous face of death.

Roger knelt beside her. Tears streamed down his face.

"I am sorry, Mama. God forgive me. I am truly sorry but there is nothing I can do."

She held out a bony hand and softly touched his cheek. It was a gesture that would haunt Roger for the rest of his life. Was it the touch of forgiveness or a pathetic attempt to stop him? He held her hand against his cheek clasped both of his hands but the youngster with the tire and the gasoline kicked her forearm with all the might he could muster.

"Get on with it," he said. He was was about thirteen years old.

Comrade Jack handed Roger a brick.

"Break her hands so she can't throw the the tire off her neck," he instructed.

Roger held the brick in his right hand but seemed dazed and confused.

Comrade Jack snatched it back from him. "Like this!" he said, his voice filled with contempt.

He grasped the old woman's left arm by the wrist, jerked it violently forward until it lay flat on the ground then jammed his foot onto her forearm in order to keep it trapped. With the brick held in his right hand he held it high above his head before smashing it down onto her crooked, old fingers.

She screamed as the flesh split and and the bones broke and mangled. The old woman lay sobbing as she clutched her broken hand to her chest when Comrade Jack stood up and handed the brick to Roger.

In a daze, as though he were separated from his own body, Roger followed Comrade Jack's example. His mind registered only how strange the old granny's hand looked. Her fingers were bent, the result of long-term suffering with arthritis. It was bizarre how vividly aware he was that they straightened when the blood-stained brick he held in his hand, smashed down on them.

As though in a trance and completely detached from

reality Roger took the tire from the youngster and placed it around the old woman's neck, who now, had mercifully fainted from the pain.

"Wait!" said Comrade Rambo, his voice stern. "Wake her up! A traitor must experience his or her punishment. Piss on her face to wake her up."

Roger stared at him blankly.

"What don't you understand?" Comrade Rambo screamed. "Get your fucking prick out and piss on her."

Slowly Roger unzipped his fly of his jeans and urinated on the unconscious woman's face. As the warm liquid splashed onto her she stirred.

"Wake up you old bitch," Rambo said, his face close to hers. "I want you to know what it's like to stand in the way of the struggle."

"Pour the petrol on," he ordered Roger.

Roger closed his eyes tightly and gritted his teeth as he held the bottle over her head then turned the mouth upside down so that its contents spilled on her. Strangely he was aware of the vibrating jerk of the container as the fluid gurgled and glugged out. A large pool of it dammed in the base of the tire hung around her neck, the rest saturated her grey hair, face and clothes.

"God forgive me, please," he said out loud.

Comrade Rambo handed him a box of matches. He took it but, for a few moments stood and did nothing.

"Do it!" said Rambo in a firm voice.

As though in a dream, from which he hoped he would wake and find himself back at home with his parents and Thandi, Roger slid the box open and withdrew a match. His eyes were drawn to it hypnotically. He lit it. There was no wind and the flame burned easily. He looked down at the old woman, her mouth open, her hands bleeding and her eyes blood-shot from the gasoline poured on her face.

For what felt like an eternity these two unlikely people gazed at each other. The one a teenager and about to become a murderer, the other seventy two and about to be murdered. Her countenance was changed. The fear he previously observed gone as though she could see life beyond the grave and it no longer frightened her.

As the match burned down the flame burnt Roger's fingers and he tossed it onto the old woman.

Instantly there was the familiar exploding poof of igniting petrol and she was engulfed in flames.

She screamed in excruciating agony as first her hair twisted and scorched, then melted to her scalp, then her skin began to blister and peel.

"Jesus! No!" screamed Roger. He picked up the brick he used to break her hand. "Let me end it quickly for her!"

One of Comrade Jack's lieutenants pulled him back and restrained him.

"She must die the death chosen for her," he said. "You must not interfere."

Roger tried to block out her screams of agony. They seemed to go on forever but really only lasted less than a minute before the burning fumes destroyed her tongue and larynx so she could not longer scream. The smell of burning flesh was so strong that it clawed at and clung to Roger. He ran his tongue over his dry, cracked lips and could actually taste it.

He turned away, vomiting and crying all at the same time.

"Well done," said Comrade Jack. He put his hand on the boy's bent-over back. "You passed the test."

Roger retched again.

He straightened up and wiped his mouth with the back of his hand making sure he did not look at the burning woman. The smell of her death hung heavily in the air.

He looked at the crowd. In the light thrown by the street-lights and the two fires their faces looked like those of the living dead.

Comrade Rambo observed them too.

A lesson well-taught, he thought.

* *panga - machete*

Chapter 28

"We've got a nasty one here, Temp."

Warrant Officer Eric Joubert replaced the telephone handset back in its cradle. He hated Mondays, it was the day they had to clear up the weekend's shit.

"That was Detective Branch. Seems a couple of nights ago an old woman was murdered in a vacant piece of veld near the Dieprivier bus and taxi rank."

Templeton lit a cigarette then tossed the packet to the thin, blue-black-haired man standing by the office window. Mercifully the excavations for the single quarters were now complete and with the foundations thrown and the commencement of bricking, things were much quieter.

They could at least damn well think now and Templeton had done a lot of thinking lately. Roger hadn't changed his mind and come home as Joubert predicted and he and Ellen decided decisive action needed to be taken.

They would go and fetch him and take him back to school in Kwa Zulu - Natal. They believed that would restore stability and happiness to his life. Ellen hated the thought of not having her son around - but he wasn't now in any case - and she knew it was the best they could do for him. All necessary arrangements were in place. The school awaited his return. His clothes and uniform were packed and all that was left to do was to collect Roger.

"What if he doesn't want to come?" asked Ellen.

"I'll damn well handcuff him, if I have to," said Templeton.

The plan was to collect him on Friday so he could spend the weekend settling in at the school.

Joubert took a cigarette and tossed the pack back to Templeton who caught it with one hand and put it in his shirt pocket.

"What's it got to do with us?" asked Templeton,

shrugging his broad shoulders.

"Let the detectives handle their own murder case without trying to palm their workload off onto us."

"Uh uh, 'fraid not," said Joubert, shaking his head from side to side. He flicked cigarette ash through the open window.

"Tire 'round the neck, hands broken...you know the scene. This one's political."

"Shit!" Templeton swore. "Necklace!"

"Precisely! And you know what that means."

Ngubane sighed. "Yes, it means the detectives want us involved and holding their hands every step of the way. It means they'll want us to twist a few arms and crack a few heads to get information they can't and it means drop everything for them, solve the case and in the end those fuckers will walk away with the glory.

"It also means no bloody sleep until we nail the bastards."

As the violence in the townships had increased, so the line that divided the functions of the Security Police and the Criminal Investigation Department, the detectives, became increasingly blurred.

The brass at Wachthuis, headquarters of the South African Police, believed much of the crime committed in the black townships was directed by the ANC or organisations aligned to it. This meant Security Policemen increasingly found themselves involved in cases that normally would be the domain of the Detective Branch. Their role was to interrogate suspects to establish what links they had to banned organisations and institutions that were considered a risk to South Africa's security. Information they gathered was collated and passed up the chain-of-command and had resulted in the arrests of a number of terrorists and some pre-emptive special forces military operations in Swaziland, Lesotho and Mozambique.

But this invariably led to their becoming fully involved in the criminal investigations, as they chased-down leads supplied by interrogated suspects.

It was a situation that neither the CID or Security Branches liked. Both believed the other was intruding on their territory and they distrusted each other.

"We do the bloody work and they get the glory," growled Ngubane. He stubbed out his cigarette and flicked the butt out of the window.

"I hate working with those bastards!"

He was still prickly as a three-pointed dubbeltjie thorn but since making the decision to fetch Roger, in general, his mood had improved. The oppressive weight of guilt that weighed him down was lifted and he looked forward to putting his family's life back together. His improved disposition was also a welcome relief to all in his section and everyone's spirits had improved.

"I can't say that I am too keen on working with the detectives either, " said Joubert. "But ours is not to question why..." he couldn't remember the rest of the line he'd learned so may years ago at school. "But there's nothing we can do so I suppose we should just get to it and get things rolling. First stop, CID."

"I guess you're right," said Templeton. He pulled his cloth, camouflage-pattern, field cap on. His voice showed no enthusiasm for the task at hand.

I wish it was Friday already, he thought.

"I'll meet you down at the car, I need to take a leak first."

Chapter 29

No matter how much alcohol he drank, Roger could not get the smell of burning flesh out of his nostrils or the screams of pain and death out of his ears.

Every time he shut his eyes the old woman was there looking at him, begging for her life or accusing him with liquid eyes. He still felt her touch on his cheek and still saw her dry, bent, fingers straighten as he smashed them with the brick. Nothing he did would free him of her tormenting and mocking. She was there when he was awake. She was there when he was asleep, she was there when he was drunk and, every now and then, when he somehow was able to forget for a few moments, she reached out and touched his cheek to remind him she was still there.

Roger believed he was destined for hell and he had seen, first-hand, what the fires awaiting his arrival looked like.

This was not the way it was supposed to be. In just a few short weeks he was robbed of his childhood.

When he walked out of his parent's home it was just a childish gesture of defiance and petulance. They were supposed to come running after him, apologise and bring him back. But his father and his fucking pride...

Tears of frustration and anger stung his eyes.

You bastards! He thought. Why did it take you five days to come to me? If you'd come earlier I could have gone home and none of this would have happened and an innocent, old woman would still be alive!

But taking five days to come to him meant it was too late. By then he was already introduced to Comrade Jack and the others and if he had left then with his parents he would have effectively sentenced Simon to death. People accused of bringing in spies didn't live very long.

But Roger was either too young or naïve to see the irony

of the situation. If the shoe were on the other foot, Simon would sacrifice his friend's life in the blink of an eye and think nothing further of it. When it came to survival in the township, you did what you had to.

"Come on man! Why so down in the mouth? This is a party and there are girls here who will make you very happy now that you are a freedom fighter!"

A youngster swaying to the blaring beat of the white Zulu, Johnny Clegg and his band, Juluka, slapped him on the back and pushed him towards the dance floor where a few girls older than he were dancing together. He had a bottle of vodka in his hand that he shoved towards Roger who took a swig.

On the day after the necklacing of the old woman, Comrades Jack and Rambo met to discuss Roger. Whatever he was in the past, he was no longer. There was no going back, he was now one of them.

To celebrate they carried Roger into Mama Moroka's Tavern on their shoulders and plied him with liquor as though he were a conquering general returning from a bitterly-fought campaign.

"Now you are a soldier!" declared Comrade Jack and he raised his glass in a toast to their newest member.

But Roger did not feel like a soldier. No matter how hard he tried, he could not convince himself that an old woman , aged 72, with a shopping bag, containing a loaf of bread and tin of pilchards, was somehow the enemy.

There was no escaping the fact - he was a murderer, plain and simple, someone the police would hunt down the way a pack of dogs hunts a jackal. Maybe it would even be his father who hunted him down.

But even if they failed to catch him and he escaped them, there would be no escaping the old woman. She would always be there, touching his face and examining his soul.

He gulped down another mouthful of vodka and closed

his eyes, silently praying the old woman would not be there. This time she wasn't. She'd sent someone else to continue with his torment. In her place was Thandi, tightly hugging her doll and smiling at him.

Chapter 30

"Sit down," said Detective Sergeant Collins. He indicated to Ngubane and Joubert to take a seat on two maroon vinyl chairs opposite his desk.

He was dressed in a mint-green safari suit that bulged at the back where it covered a Czechoslovakian CZ 75 9mm pistol tucked into an inside-pants holster. He carried his private firearm because he was more comfortable with it and it was slightly smaller than the SAP-issued Beretta 92.

"I presume you're here about the killing at Dieprivier?"

Joubert nodded. "What have you got?"

"Just give me a second, the docket is in here somewhere."

He lifted a large file of brown, manilla, folders from the pending tray on the right-hand corner of his desk, flicked through them and drew one from near the bottom of the pile.

"This is it." He opened it and skimmed through the contained documents. "Not too much at the moment, I'm afraid. We are seriously snowed under."

He pointed to the pile of other cases awaiting his attention. "Haven't really had a chance to even take a look at this one."

Templeton leaned back and crossed his legs. He took a handkerchief from his pocket and dabbed his brow where he felt beads of sweat forming. The room was uncomfortably hot with the heaters on and the windows closed.

"Do you know anything at all?" he asked. "Victim's name? Any witnesses? Have you got anything at all?"

Collins leafed through the docket.

"Yes, they've ID'd the victim," he said, frowning irritably when Joubert lit a cigarette. He'd given up smoking two years ago and since then had become something of an anti-smoking zealot. For a moment he thought of asking Joubert not to smoke but decided not to. But he still couldn't help himself saying: "You should try to give that up Warrant, it's not doing your health any favours."

Joubert ignored the advice and said nothing but he thought: does he think he's my fucking doctor or mother or something?

"The victim was Lena Mhlangu," said Collins, reading from the details recorded in the docket. "Her grandchildren confirmed she was seventy two."

He read dispassionately as though reciting a grocery list.

"The body was found in a vacant lot in Dieprivier, badly burnt with the remains of a tire around the neck and shoulders.

"Sorry, we can't give you a make on the tire but, for her, it couldn't have been a Goodyear, more likely a Firestone."

He looked up laughing at his own joke but continued reading when he saw Ngubane and Joubert were not amused.

"Death was as a result of the burns." he paused and pursed his lips while he continued reading. "What do you make of this? The autopsy report says both hands were broken, presumably as a result of a blow or blows with a blunt object."

"That's common practice," said Templeton. "In a necklacing the victim's hands are usually broken before the tire is place around the neck. It's done to stop them throwing the tire off."

Collins grimaced. "Jesus that's horrible! We've come up with no witnesses yet but that's probably because people are too afraid to talk."

Joubert nodded in agreement.

Collins continued reading. "The grandchildren say she left for work on Thursday and when she was not back on Friday they reported it at the police station. At that stage the body had already been discovered."

"How was she identified?" asked Joubert.

"Seems she had her ID book and purse stuffed in her panties. Only the top half of her body, but especially her head was badly burned."

Templeton nodded. Township residents had many ways they hid the valuables in the hope the tsotsis would not find them.

"Was there any money in the purse?"

Collins leafed through the folder again.

"Yes, R35 in notes and silver."

"Okay, Sergeant, thank you for your trouble," said Joubert. He stood up to leave. "We'll need to take the file with us, if you don't mind."

Collins did not mind. It meant one fewer case in the pile for him to investigate.

"Sure, no problem at all," he said. "So you agree this isn't just an ordinary murder?"

"Absolutely," said Templeton. "This was a public execution designed to make a point and be a warning to as many people as people as possible.

"That is why it was so horrible – and a gruesome brutal death. The message they sent was 'if we can do this to her, think what we can do to you if you step out of line'.

"No, Sergeant, this was no common or garden township crime."

Chapter 31

"When that idiot detective said they haven't done much with this case, he certainly wasn't kidding," said Templeton, leafing through the docket.

"All they've done is talk to the grandchildren and log the autopsy report."

Joubert nosed the white Toyota Corolla® onto the pavement outside a row of houses, not far from the Dieprivier bus-depot.

"Okay, we start from scratch, it won't be the first time," said Joubert.

They got out of the police car and made sure it was locked – not even police cars were safe these days – before walking to the vacant lot where Lena Mhlangu was murdered.

The drum in which the fire was made, where Comrade Jack and Comrade Rambo stood and warmed themselves, was still there. A couple of metres away was the spot on which the old woman was necklaced.

The ground was scorched and the charred remains of the tire's shell lay on the spot. There was still a faint smell of roasted flesh when Templeton squatted and, using his pen, began scraping through the ashes. Some of the bits of what appeared to be charcoal were no doubt once human flesh.

"Anything interesting?" asked Joubert. He searched other areas of the open piece of veld.

"Nothing unexpected, a few burnt fragments of cloth. Probably the clothes she wore. You?"

"Nope, except, if you look at how the grass has been flattened and trampled, a lot of people witnessed this."

Templeton stood up and wiped the pen on his trousers before returning it to his shirt pocket.

"Let's go and ask some questions," he said.

As they crossed the road and walked to the houses where they left their car, they had the distinct feeling they were being watched.

The homes all looked similar. Small square boxes built with large, unplastered, concrete blocks. Some owners, where they could afford to, added personal touches by painting doors and window-frames in other colours. Here and there was a house that was added to – mostly an extra bedroom.

There were few gardens as, when the government housing authorities constructed the houses, they provided no outside taps.

"Blacks aren't interested in gardening," the town planner declared and by omitting the taps his statement became a self-fulfilling prophesy.

Yet, in a few of the front yards, flowers and lawns were planted and, relying on the Highveld summer rains and buckets of water carried from inside, those residents cheered-up their homes.

But those properties were the exception. Over all, the area, was dusty, bleak, miserable and dirty.

Three houses up from where their car was parked, a group of young men sat outside on Formica kitchen chairs, playing cards at a rickety table. They saw the cops approaching but studiously ignored them and continued with their card game.

"Let's start with those guys," said Joubert, using his chin to point at the card-players.

Not one of the four bothered to even look up when Ngubane and Joubert approached and stood, quietly, watching the proceedings.

"Jesus! What's that terrible stink?" said one of the card players dressed in a red and blue, checked cotton shirt. He continued to deal cards from a dog-eared, battle-scarred deck, without looking up.

"Smells like dog-shit," said another in a faded wind-breaker and knitted woollen cap.

One by one, each player picked up his cards, fanned them out in his hand, arranged them and then held them close to his chest.

"I can also smell it," said the player sitting opposite the dealer. He closed his hand and, with a great flourish, as though the unwanted cards were living things and he wanted to punish them, he slapped one of them down onto the centre of the table.

"But I don't think it's dog-shit, actually. It smells worse. I think it's a pig or two."

"You probably right," said the dealer. "Most likely a pig."

Still no-one even glanced in the direction of the two policemen. They continued their game without any acknowledgement of their presence.

Templeton took a deep breath and promised himself he would not rise to their bait.

"Okay, boys, let's cut the crap, we want to speak to you."

"Did you guys also hear that?" asked the dealer. "Sounded like a pig squealing and that shit-smell is even worse now."

Ngubane sighed and then turned to Joubert as though he was about to walk away. Why did it always have to come to this?

"Bye bye, Piggy," sneered the dealer.

Joubert stood directly behind him at that moment and, with his right foot, kicked him in the small of the back, just where his right kidney was located. The power and viciousness of the kick knocked him sideways off the chair and caused him to upset the table at the same time.

Before he knew what had happened Templeton was on him. He clamped the man's right arm behind his back and, with his knee on the back of the dealer's head, he drove his face into the ground and made him eat dirt. Still holding the man trapped, Templeton turned to the other card-players.

"Anyone else got any jokes they want to tell?" He twisted the dealer's arm violently and the man yelped in pain. Joubert's kick would have him pissing blood for the next few days.

No-one spoke as Joubert, filled with menace, loomed over them.

"Get up you puss-filled pimple," growled Ngubane in Zulu. He yanked the man to his feet then pushed him roughly onto a chair.

"Sit there and shut the fuck up until I speak to you!" His eyes blazed as he scanned the youngsters.

"A couple of nights ago, in that piece of veld over there," he pointed at the vacant lot, "an old woman was killed with a necklace.

"You pieces of shit know who did it and you're going to tell me!"

They avoided eye-contact and remained silent.

"Perhaps you didn't hear," said Joubert. His voice sounded like a sword being drawn from a steel scabbard.

"Maybe it is your ears that are at fault." He paused. The calm before the breaking storm.

He stood behind the dealer, who was still doubled over as a result of the kick. "Maybe this will help open them."

With his hands cupped, he belted him on both sides of the head. Joubert was a master of the technique. The blow had enough force to cause excruciating pain but not enough to burst the ear-drums. The man gasped and collapsed sideways off the chair. He curled himself into a foetal position and lay whimpering, mucous running out of his nose.

"Okay, boys," said Templeton, his tone condescending, "now that we have your attention, let me ask again, who killed the old woman?"

Templeton nudged the dealer in the ribs with the tip of his shoe.

"Speak to me my friend and save yourself a world of

pain."

He looked up at Templeton with watery eyes and a snot-glazed face.

"I don't know who did it. I only hear things in the township."

Templeton squatted next to him, his backside against his heels. He rocked to and fro slightly.

"Tell me what you heard."

"She was killed because she was a collaborator."

"Who did she collaborate with?" asked Joubert.

The dealer turned so he could see the white cop. He sat up, leaning on one elbow.

"They say she broke the boycott."

"The consumer boycott?"

"Yes."

"Did you see it happen?"

He nervously ran his tongue over his lips before answering.

"No I was at the shebeen."

"Which one?" asked Templeton. He adopted the tone of a professional interrogator.

"Mluzi's."

"You know I am going to check up and if I find out you're lying I'm going to come back and make you pay – big time!"

He nodded.

"Who is the Street Commander here?" snapped Joubert suddenly.

The dealer was startled.

"W...wh...wh...what do you mean?" he stammered. "I don't even know what a street commander is." He turned his gaze away from Joubert and touched his nose and mouth.

Joubert took hold of the front of his shirt and pulled his face so close to his they could smell each others' breaths. Joubert breathed heavily onto the man and spoke slowly and deliberately.

"Have you heard of the water-bag?"

The sharp intake of breath by the dealer told him he had. He knew exactly what the security policeman was talking about.

It was a torture technique reportedly carried out by the police but which had never been proven in court.

The water-bag has two variations and the choice depends upon the whim of the torturer.

One method was to take a tractor-tire, inner-tube, cut in such a way that it forms a cylinder that is open at both ends. This is pulled – like rolling on a condom – over the victim's head. The bottom of the tube is then tied tightly around the neck, beneath the chin, so that it is secure but not so tight as to cause choking or marks on the neck.

With the victim's hands handcuffed behind his back, the rubber tube is filled with water from the top, until the enclosed head is completely submerged. Only at the point where the person being tortured is on the point of becoming unconscious, is the rope that holds the bottom of the tube sealed, released to allow the water to escape.

By then the person being interrogated is so desperate for air that, when the water gushes out, he takes such great gulps of air that the rubber is sucked against his face and nose, once again restricting the air-flow to his screaming lungs.

The process is repeated until the interrogator gets the answer he wants.

The alternative water-bag version is similar, except in this instance, a soaked canvas bag is pulled over the victim's head before an electric shock is applied. The effect, when gasping for air, is the same as that experienced with the rubber tube.

The dealer shuddered and began to tremble. He knew these men were serious and would think nothing of hauling him away for interrogation. "You are never completely right after the water-bag," people said. "You will never be able to sleep again properly."

But on the other hand, if he told them the name of the street commander...

Joubert smacked him on the side of the head again.

"Talk to me now or talk to me at the station. It doesn't matter to me, but talk you will. That I guarantee you." He prodded him between the eyes with his index finger.

The dealer swallowed twice and had to clear his throat before he could speak. His voice wavered.

"I don't know but I think if you speak to Whitby Tsitseng, he may know." He had probably just signed his own death warrant.

"Where do I find him?" This time Joubert prodded him in the chest with his hand held as though it were a pistol.

"Around the corner in Leshebi Street. It's the first house next to the park."

"If you're lying..." Joubert didn't bother to complete the sentence. He drew his index finger across the dealer's throat.

"Okay, Temp. Let's go. It's been a pleasure chatting to you boys. I'm sure we'll meet again."

Chapter 32

"They'll come for me," said Roger. "It's just a matter of time."

He looked dreadful. His eyes were bloodshot, he had barely slept and the ever-haunting images of the old woman and his family grew worse all the time.

When he did manage to sleep it was only for short periods and was never restful and he woke feeling more tired than before he went to sleep.

His skin, normally shiny and healthy was sallow and dry. His eyes were sunken back into their sockets and appeared lifeless most of the time. His clothes were dirty and he had a sour, unwashed, smell about him.

They were on the move constantly, sleeping in different township houses every night, to keep a step ahead of the police who must surely be hunting them. It wasn't the murder of the old lady that particularly worried them – the constant relocating was a way of life, to prevent the organisation's leaders being captured and falling into the hands of the government's security forces.

Comrade Jack had assigned Roger to a cadre called Comrade Disaster. The plan was to get Roger out of the country and to one of the ANC's training camps. But that took time, so in the meantime they kept moving.

"Who will come?" asked Comrade Disaster.

"The police." His voice was without emotion, resigned. He wasn't afraid (truth be told he was too tired to be afraid). It was just something that would take pace. Like day follows night. He wasn't worried about what would happen to him, just the shame he would bring to his family. He was going to hell anyway, and maybe that would be a relief!

"They'll never find you. We move too much and soon you'll be out of the country," said Comrade Disaster.

"You're an idiot if you think they'll find us."

Roger smiled a humourless smile.

"They'll come," said, more to himself than his companion."I know them, they'll be here soon."

Chapter 33

It took some effort for Ngubane and Joubert to change Whitby Tsitseng from township freedom fighter to singing choirboy.

They picked him up as he left his house on his way to a meeting with a few friends. With little ceremony or struggle they pulled a canvas bag over his head and cuffed his hands behind his back before bundling him into the boot of the Toyota. It all happened so fast he only managed to catch the shortest of glimpses of his abductors.

They drove to the back of the police station, to a building far from view of the public. When they opened the boot and dragged him out him out, he began to yell but Templeton punched him hard in the stomach.

"Shut up!" snarled Joubert, speaking Zulu.

Templeton unlocked a steel door on the outside of the building and they shoved Whitby into the room. Still blindfolded by the bag over his head, he fell heavily. Ngubane took him by the scruff of the neck, dragged him upright and plonked him onto a straight-backed, heavy, metal, chair situated in the middle of the room. He handcuffed his prisoner's hands to the back of the chair – tightly enough to be uncomfortable but not so tight as to present evidence to a district surgeon or human rights lawyer.

The room was large and empty, other than a scarred table in front of the chair, upon which Whitby sat. On it, was a breadloaf-sized field telephone, with a hand-crank on the side and a pair of electric wires running from two brass, screw-on connection point. On top, but was a recess into which a telephone handset once fitted.

Against the far wall – painted in battleship grey enamel paint – were two chairs, next to which was a light-stand fitted with castors. A 500W photographic light was attached to the top of it. The light could be adjusted be either a floodlight or spotlight.

The single window on the same wall as the door through which they had entered was blacked out with a dark blind that was pulled down and taped around the edges to prevent light seepage and outside prying eyes.

On the back of the steel door and the ceiling, cardboard egg-boxes were glued as do-it-yourself sound-proofing that was crude but very effective.

There was a basin on the wall opposite the window and beside it was a mop and a plastic bucket.

The floor was covered in light-grey linoleum that bizarrely colour co-ordinated with the walls. Its function, however, was practical rather than decorative. Linoleum was easy to clean.

Next to the chair on which Whitby sat handcuffed was a London Trolley-Bus-red, bucket with the word Fire painted on the front. It was filled with water upon which specks of dust floated.

This was a room that, over the years, had seen much and been a taste of hell for many.

Chapter 34

In his own way Whitby was a brave man but by the time the car drew up at the back of the police station his courage was beginning to waver.

Now he sat, God-knew-where, shackled and blindfolded. He had only caught a quick glimpse of his abductors but figured they must be Apartheid agents. Someone must have betrayed him. He began to experience the first inklings of terror.

He went through the scenario many times before in his mind, imagining what he would do if the police came. He always pictured himself stoically resisting their questions, a hero in the finest of struggle traditions. But now his resolve was beginning to crumble.

Were these guys even the police? he thought. What if they were right-wing vigilantes? If that was the case then he was as good as dead. Think man! Think!

No, they can't be right-wingers. One of the guys who grabbed me was black.

He felt a surge of relief. It must be cops. With the cops he would probably come out of this alive. Oh sure, there were plenty of cases of people dying at the hands of the police but his odds of survival were a lot better than with those right-wing, AWB madmen!

Someone in the room spoke.

"Can you take care of this on your own, Jooba? I've got a few things I need to sort out for Roger before we take him back to school on Friday. Ellen wants me to help pick out some new clothes for him."

"No problem," said Joubert. "Go and do what you need to. I can handle this..." A wry smile creased the corners of his mouth.

"It's not like I haven't done it before!"

Whitby heard someone rack a dead-bolt back on the

steel door that creaked as it was opened. A few moments later the door slammed shut and he heard the dead-bolt rack home.

Even with the canvas bag still over his head he was suddenly aware of an intensely bright light being shone on him. Someone standing behind him yanked the bag off his head and he blinked as he tried to turn away from the light but whoever was behind him hit him when he did so.

"Look straight ahead, you piece of shit," said a voice speaking next to his right ear.

"Tell me about the necklacing of the old woman in Dieprivier. I know you know about it."

Whitby shut his eyes but the light still burned through his eyelids. His head shook as he was hit from behind again. In the sealed room the clap of the blow sounded like a pistol-shot.

Joubert spoke softly, his cheek almost touching Whitby's. "We can do this the easy way or the hard way but either way you will tell me what I need to know. It's your call."

"I know nothing. I wasn't around on Thursday."

"If you know nothing, how do you know it was Thursday." Joubert knew he'd asked a dumb question but it was a technique he often employed to get the person being interrogated to start talking – a sort of priming of the pump.

Whitby snorted derisively. "Everybody knows when a collaborator is killed in the township. That's the point; that everybody knows!"

Joubert said nothing. He stood leaning against the back of the chair.

"I'm not saying anything more," said Whitby. "I want a lawyer."

Bam! Joubert hit him again.

"A lawyer is not going to help you. Nobody knows you are here."

He pulled the canvas bag over Whitby's head again then

went around and stood in front of him.

"I'm tired of playing games with you. It's been a rough day and I want to get home so I am not going to waste any more time speaking to you nicely."

He undid Whitby's belt and then in a single, swift and decisive movement, yanked his grey flannel pants and his underpants down to his ankles, living him naked from the waist down.

"Jesus! What are you doing?" Whitby yelled, squirming in the chair. He began to kick, hoping to somehow protect himself from his tormentor.

Joubert stepped to one side then punched him powerfully in the solar plexus, winding him and stopping his struggles. Moving to the table located in front of the chair to which Whitby was secured, Joubert uncoiled two electrical wires attached to the field telephone on the table. The ends of both wires were stripped bare of their plastic insulation so that the last 30 cm displayed the bare, inner, copper core.

He wrapped the exposed copper end of one the electrical wires around Whitby's left leg in the crease behind his knee. Then he wrapped four or five twists of the exposed part of the other wire around his prisoner's penis.

Whitby began to whimper.

"Last chance to tell me what I want to know," said Joubert.

Whitby shook his head defiantly, still whimpering.

Joubert dumped the contents of the fire-bucket into Whitby's lap, soaking his genitals and legs.

"Okay, don't say I never gave you the chance," said Joubert. He spun the crank-handle on the side of the telephone and kept turning the generator as fast as he could for about 15 seconds.

Whitby's body straightened, his back arched as though he was having an orgasm. He tried to scream but the sound was trapped in his throat.

"That's just a little taste of what's to come," said Joubert. "I can keep this going for hours, so save yourself the trouble and tell me what I need to know now. You will in the end."

Whitby gasped violently inside the canvas bag.

Joubert cranked the handle again and kept going for longer this time. When he stopped Whitby slumped back, with his head limply bowed on his chest. He retched in the bag and while the electric shock was applied had pissed himself.

"I tell you what," said Joubert. "I'm not an unkind man. You probably just need a bit of time to think about it. So I am going to get a cup of coffee and maybe buy a doughnut. Perhaps I'll read the newspaper. That should give you some time to consider your options."

Whitby heard the dead-bolt on the door being slid back.

"We'll continue our chat when I get back."

The steel door slammed shut and Whitby Tsitseng was left shackled, snivelling and semi-naked.

This wasn't at all how he imagined it would be.

Chapter 35

"Water! Please!" gasped Whitby as Templeton undid the cuffs that kept him restrained to the chair.

"I am going to remove the hood but if you make any attempt to see my face, I promise you, you will regret it."

"I won't," said Whitby weakly.

Ngubane removed the canvas bag. A white crust had formed around the young man's face and he had flecks of vomit on his chin and chest. His throat was parched and raw.

Still, standing behind him, Templeton handed him a mug of water. He gulped it down.

"Can I have some more please?"

"Look down and keep your eyes closed," said Templeton. "Remember what I said about looking at me."

Whitby lowered his head and closed his eyes tightly. Templeton filled the mug at the basin and handed it to his prisoner.

"Thank you."

"Do you want a cigarette?"

"Yes...please."

Templeton passed the packet over Whitby's shoulder.

"Keep the packet," he said. "Hide it in your pocket and don't tell the other guy I gave it to you."

Although there was no-one else in the room, Templeton spoke softly, almost in a whisper, as though he was part of a conspiracy.

Whitby started to pull up his trousers but Templeton stopped him.

"Don't do that. My partner is going to be back soon to continue with his questioning and he will wonder why I removed your handcuffs."

"Oh Jesus!" groaned Whitby. He could feel a new seed of terror starting to sprout in his gut. "Why are you doing this to me?"

"I am really sorry," said Templeton. He had his mouth close to Whitby's left ear and spoke in barely a whisper. "If there was anything I could do to stop it, I would. But I am powerless.

"I hate seeing this happen to my people – we are both black and understand each other. But that white bastard...he's different. He enjoys hurting people and he will kill you, just because he enjoys killing people."

Whitby sucked in his breath. Joubert had worked him over for an hour and he knew he couldn't take much more of the excruciating pain.

"You're going to have to help me here. I can't stop him. I'm just one black man."

"What do I have to do?" Whitby stammered.

"Just tell me who killed that old woman. If you tell me, I will be able to keep him away from you and you can go home."

Whitby hesitated. He was deeply conflicted.

"I don't know anything. I promise you, I don't know anything. You've got to believe me!"

"Whitby," said Templeton, speaking gently as a father would to his son, "I told you, I can't help you unless you help me. You've got to trust me."

"I...I...don't know anything." His voice was desperate.

Just then someone banged on the door and Templeton recognised the voice of one of the constables in his department.

"Telephone, Warrant. They say it's urgent!"

Chapter 36

There was in fact no telephone call. It was simply a ruse employed to get Templeton out of the room so that Whitby could stew for a while and have time to consider the proposals the 'good' cop made.

"How did it go?" Joubert asked, heaping two spoons of sugar into a mug of coffee. "The pot's fresh, pour yourself some."

"I think he'll crack soon. If he doesn't before, then just one more session." Templeton poured himself a cup of coffee, sat down and sighed deeply.

"You know I hate this sort of thing, it twists my guts."

"Yeah, I understand," said Joubert. He leaned back in his chair and put his feet up on the desk. "I don't like it much either but sometimes for the greater good you have to do things you don't like.

"What's that they say about breaking eggs to make omelettes? If we played this by the rules that guy in there would have a human rights lawyer in here faster than you can say 'kiss my black arse' and he would be out on the street and gone before we knew it."

"I know, Jooba," said Templeton, "of course you are right but I still wonder if what we are doing isn't going to come back and bite us in a big way somewhere down the road."

"You think too much. What I think about it that old woman and how she must have felt while she burnt to death. I can think of no worse way to die. I think about how that piece of shit knows about it, may well have been involved in it and how many other people will die the same way if we don't get him to co-operate."

Templeton shrugged his shoulders in defeat. "Like I said, I know you are right but I still don't like it."

Joubert fished a pack of Lucky Strikes from his shirt pocket. He lit one then passed the pack to Templeton.

For a few minutes they sat and smoked together in silence. Then Joubert stubbed out his cigarette in a white, porcelain ashtray that needed emptying.

"Okay, back to work, I guess," he said, pushing back his chair and standing up.

"I'm sure after our next chat, he's going to be yelling for you, his new best buddy to come and take his statement."

Chapter 37

Twenty minutes later, Joubert returned.

"He's all yours. He is ready to talk to you and I suggest you take a notebook along, because he is going to be singing opera to you."

"Did you give him much of a workout?"

"Naah," said Joubert. "After two cranks of the handle he started screaming at the top of his lungs that he was ready to talk but only to you." He smiled wryly. "Seems he actually believed your bullshit that you're a good guy.

"He's waiting for you. See, I was right, sometimes you do have to break some eggs."

Templeton sighed and nodded.

"I know. You coming?"

"No. I've done my bit for the day. Let me get home a bit early. Maybe I'll earn a few brownie points with the wife...know what I mean? And besides, he'll only talk to you. I'll see you in the morning, you can fill me in on the details then."

He took his jacket, hanging on a wire coat-hanger behind the door and slipped it on.

"With any luck we can have this thing wrapped up and tucked away by the end of the week. When you're done questioning him, get them to hold him for at least another 72 hours. I am sure he's going to have a lot more to tell us in addition to what we want to know about this case.

"See you in the morning," he said and left.

Chapter 38

Templeton uncuffed Whitby. His head hung limply on his chest and he looked a broken man.

He held out much longer than I imagined, thought Ngubane, but in the end they all talk...or die. He yanked the telephone wire off the prisoner and removed the canvas hood.

“Pull up you pants and put this on,” he said. He tossed a white t-shirt onto Whitby's lap because the one he wore was caked in vomit.

Slowly Whitby raised his head and saw Templeton's face for the first time. With bloodshot eyes he stared at the large black man's face. Both knew it no longer mattered that he was now able to identify the cop. He was going to tell him what he wanted to know and they would end up bringing charges against him. The price of belonging to a banned organisation was jail. It was as simple as that. And right now, prison was a better option than going back to the townships where people would wonder just what he told the cops. And besides, being a political prisoner brought with it a lot of credibility in the community.

He tried to stand up but his legs were wobbly and he had to sit down again.

“Relax for a moment and gather your strength first, then I'll help you,” said Templeton.

Whitby sat for a few moments taking deep breaths, then he tried to stand up again while Templeton held his shoulders to support his efforts. He swayed a bit at first but his strength and balance began to return and when he was steady, Ngubane released him.

He pulled up his trousers and shakily buckled his belt. Then he pulled off his soiled t-shirt and replaced it with the white one brought for him.

Templeton pushed the chair on which Whitby was cuffed

up to the table and indicated that he sit.

When Whitby was seated, Templeton angled the photographic light towards the ceiling so it no longer shone in the prisoner's eyes but still provided enough light to brightly illuminate the room.

He left the field telephone on the the table, aware of the effect it would likely have on Whitby.

He pulled up a chair and sat directly opposite Whitby and placed a foolscap-sized, official, South African Police notepad in front of him. He removed a pen from his top pocket and was ready to take Whitby's statement.

Whitby's eyes carefully studied Templeton's face then flicked towards the field telephone. He swallowed nervously and blinked a number of times.

"Tell me what you know about the murder of Lena Mhlangu in your own way, your own words and your own time," said Templeton.

Whitby took a deep breath and closed his eyes. He was silent for a few moments. He knew once he spoke there was no going back.

He opened his eyes and stared squarely at Templeton's face and when he spoke, his voice was remarkably calm and even.

"She was a collaborator and was tried and found guilty by a People's Court convened on the spot where her body was found."

"How did she collaborate?"

"She broke the consumer boycott and was found at the bus stop with groceries she bought at white shops, although she said she did not and that the items were given to her. But the court did not believe her and she was condemned."

"Who convened the court?"

"Comrade Jack and Comrade Rambo?"

Templeton made notes while Whitby spoke. He nodded when he heard the names. He knew who they were.

Whitby's statement was going to put a big dent in the township underground, he thought.

"How many people were there?"

"A lot. I don't know. People were called from their houses." He shrugged his shoulders. "A hundred...maybe more."

"Who were the other people involved in running the court?"

Whitby told him the names of Comrade Jack's lieutenants and some of the others.

Templeton noted them as well as the number of the people Whitby thought were there.

"Did Comrade Jack or Comrade Rambo do the actual killing?" he asked without looking up.

"No they just ordered it."

"So who was it who struck the match?"

"It was the guy who caught the old woman at the bus stop. He is new and they wanted to test him."

"Uh huh," said Templeton, still writing. "Why was that?

"They were worried he might be an impimpi. I was told he is the son of a policeman."

Templeton sat up straight so quickly it appeared he was being shocked with the field telephone.

"Name!...Give me his name!" he snapped.

"I don't know...Roger something or other."

Chapter 39

"Oh my God!" screamed Ellen. "What are we going to do?"

Templeton sat on the couch with his head in his hands. He still could not believe what Whitby had told him. He did not know what to say to Ellen. What could he say? What could he do?"

"You had better fucking well do something!" she screamed. Then she jumped up and began to punch him on the back of his head and shoulders, with both hands, over and over and over.

"This is your fault! You made him go!"

He made no attempt to stop her blows and simply allowed her to punch until she could not longer do so and collapsed, sobbing, in a heap at his feet.

Neither did he try to defend himself against her accusation that this was all his fault as he thought so too.

From the moment Whitby said Roger's name, Templeton had been in a daze.

I turned my son into a murderer because of my pride and arrogance, he thought. Oh my God! What have I done?

When he left the police station he wasn't really even aware of what he was doing and he certainly had no idea what he would or could do. He couldn't even remember driving his car.

Eventually he parked under a tree next to a dam where he wrestled with the problem or more correctly, it wrestled with him. He considered every option he could think of but, no matter how he sliced or diced it, there was no way out. He couldn't keep Roger's name hidden. It would come out. And now that Whitby was in the holding cells and booked into the system he could not engineer an 'escape attempt' in which he had no option but to shoot and kill him. Jesus, why had he not killed him in the interrogation room. It would have been so easy to claim the prisoner lunged for his gun and he killed him in the struggle but he was too shaken to think clearly and when the fog faded in his head that fucking constable was there to clean the room. And then it was too late. FUCK! FUCK! FUCK!

Tomorrow Joubert would ask him what Whitby said and to see his notes. He too would question Whitby who would sing like a pop star – once the dam of confession cracked it was not long before it burst and a deluge followed.

There was just no way out that he could see.

Eventually he went home. The moment he walked through the front door Ellen could see something terrible had happened.

"It's Roger, something has happened to him, hasn't it?" Her voice reflected her feeling of dread.

Templeton's bottom lip and jaw began to tremble and there were tears in his eyes. He said nothing but just wrapped his arms around Ellen and held her close. Pressed tightly against his chest she could feel his heart beating in his chest and he could feel her shiver.

"What has happened? Tell me," she screamed, loudly enough that Thandi heard and came to see what was distressing her mother.

He sat them down and told them and they all wept. Thandi did not really understand but instinctively she knew something was terribly wrong and they weren't going to see Roger on Friday.

For a while they just sat holding each other then Ellen sent Thandi outside.

"What are we going to do?" she asked through tear-swollen eyes when Thandi was gone.

"I don't know, I really don't know." His voice was tired, robotic. "Nobody knows about it but me, so far."

A flicker of hope flared up within her.

"But then you can keep it quiet...lead Joubert in a

different direction."

He shook his head. "It's too late. Tomorrow, Joubert and probably others, will question the guy who told me and he will tell them the same. Then they'll go and pick up Roger."

"There must be something you can do. Can't you make this person disappear or have an accident? Those sort of things happen all the time."

He was momentarily taken aback. A mother will do anything to protect her young.

Templeton shook his head. "It's too late. I should have done something when I had him alone but now it's impossible."

She dabbed her eyes with a tissue then blew her nose.

"Will they hang him?" she asked simply.

"No I am sure they won't. He's too young. He'll probably go to jail for a few years. They may hang the people who gave the orders."

Later that evening she turned on him and pushed him away when he snuggled up to her and wanted to hold her but she refused to help lift the weight of his guilt.

"Don't touch me!" she snapped, before swinging her legs out of bed and getting up.

She pulled on her dressing gown.

"This is your fault! You condemned my son when you drove him away with your pig-headedness! I will NEVER forgive you!"

When she scooped up her pillows and a blanket so that she could go and sleep in Roger's bed, she was once again weeping softly.

Chapter 40

"Jesus, Templeton! You can't be serious!"

Joubert was visibly shocked. Templeton nodded, his lips clenched as he struggled to keep his emotions in check.

He looked terrible. His skin was ashen, his eyes, bloodshot and baggy. They seemed to be set back further into his skull. His shirt looked as though he had slept in it which, in fact, he had.

When Ellen left their bed he got up, got dressed then took the car and drove back to the spot by the dam where he once again tried to figure out what to do.

Perhaps the only way out was to put the barrel of his service pistol in his mouth and pull the trigger. The cold, black weapon lay in his lap, the butt held firmly in his right hand. Maybe that was best. He lifted the pistol and caressed it with his left hand, like a shy seducer timidly stroking a young girl's thighs. It felt cold and reassuring under his finger-tips.

It would be so quick. Punishment and absolution from the pain at the same time.

But then he thought of Thandi and what she would have to carry with her for the rest of her life. He couldn't leave her with that shame.

For a second he even considered going back home to shoot them both, so their suffering would be over but he quickly pushed that dreadful thought away and berated himself for entertaining it at all.

At dawn, just as the rising sun began to set the horizon on fire, he fell into a restless sleep. He dreamed he was playing soccer with Roger in the front yard of their old house. Ellen stood in the doorway, with Thandi, just a baby in her arms, watching them kick the ball to one another. But when he turned to wave to her the house was on fire and she was surrounded by flames. In his dream he tried to help her but the ground turned to molasses and sucked at his feet and legs and no matter how hard he tried, he could not free himself.

When he woke, about an hour later, his neck was stiff and his throat was dry.

"I'm really sorry, Temp," said Joubert. "You know we're going to have to pick him and the other others up. You understand that, don't you? This thing has gone too far to make it go away."

Templeton nodded, a sheen of tears glistened his eyes.

"Let me do it," he said in a shaky voice. "Please!"

He looked firmly into Joubert's face and held his gaze.

"This is something I must do."

Joubert was hesitant and unsure.

"You owe me at least this," said Templeton.

Joubert nodded. He did owe Templeton. He put an arm around Templeton's shoulder. His partner's pain was palpable.

"You've got to have a back-up, Temp. You know what the regulations say."

"Screw the fucking regulations," spat Ngubane. "For Christ's sake, this is my son we're talking about here. Can't you fucking well understand that?"

His large body began to shake as he tried to suppress his rising emotions.

"Please, Jooba, this is something I have to do," he said weakly.

"Okay, Temp, I can understand that," said Joubert softly as he took Templeton's right hand in both of his and squeezed it.

Chapter 41

Roger and his comrade colleagues did not see Templeton until he was already standing in the lounge. They were all sitting around listening to music blaring from a radiogram that had seen better days.

The doors to the house were not locked and the youngsters had no pickets posted outside, so Templeton was able to simply walk right in.

When they realised he was there, he already had his Beretta 9mm pistol in his hand and was pointing it at them. They got such a fright they almost shat their pants.

"Get the fuck out of here!" he growled gesturing with his pistol where they should go. "I want to speak to my son."

They didn't need to be asked twice and scrambled and tripped over the furniture in their haste to get out and away.

Once outside they split up and fled in different directions. Only Roger remained. He sat on the floor and made no attempt to get up.

"Hello, Dad," he said simply. "I knew you would come. I told them it was just a matter of time."

Templeton holstered his pistol and stood looking down, long and hard at his son. His eyes filled with tears.

Jesus, the boy looked as bad as he felt. His clothes were dirty and he stank. He'd certainly lost weight, his skin looked almost transparent, as though he were dehydrated. His lips were cracked and his eyes had a vacant look about them.

"Oh my God, Roger, what have I done to you?" He reached down and helped his son to his feet.

"You've come to arrest me," said Roger. "I knew you would. Let's get it over with, I'm ready to go."

He held his arms out in front of him so that his father could attach the handcuffs.

Templeton pushed his arms down and then pulled Roger to him and held him to his chest. Tears streamed down his face.

"Did you kill the old woman?" he asked. Roger was trembling but his voice remained even and detached.

"Yes."

He felt a sudden surge of relief. It was out there in the open now and soon everything would be over. Acceptance brought its own peace.

"Why?"

"They would have killed me if I didn't. It was a test to see if I was spying for you."

Templeton's blood turned to ice and suddenly he was angry, really almost uncontrollably angry. It always came down to the same damn thing, the police. The police, always the police. Both his and his family's lives were in disarray because of the God-damned police.

His mind flashed back to the events that landed them in this situation. The burning down of his house because he was a policeman and the meeting with Captain van Rooyen when he tried to get his claim settled and how that white bastard sat there, hands clasped over his belly.

How he said: "It seems you're trying to become rich from this thing."

Fuck you! Templeton thought. Fuck you all! Because of you, we've lost everything!

"My God, son, why didn't you come home before things got out of hand?"

Roger shrugged his shoulders.

"I didn't think you would take me back. You were so angry when I left."

"Oh Jesus, Roger, I am so sorry."

They clung to each other and both wept. Sobs racked their bodies.

"What is going to happen, Dad?" Roger asked between gulpy sobs.

Before he could answer they heard a car screech to a halt outside. Templeton released Roger and quickly went to the window where he pulled the curtain back.

"Fuck, it's them!" he swore. Eric Joubert and two black constables were getting out the car. They promised they would wait a few blocks away and give him half an hour alone with his son.

When he spoke there was panic in his voice.

"Listen to me carefully and don't argue. Go out through the back and make your way to *Bophutatswana**. You'll find it easy to cross the border into Botswana without being caught. Go to Gaborone and find the other South African exiles and refugees there. They will help you. And whatever you do, don't ever come back they will always be looking for you."

Joubert and the two constables were out of the car. After Joubert locked it they turned and started walking down the driveway.

"Take this and go," said Templeton. He pressed the cash he had in his wallet into Roger's hand.

"Go!" he said, his voice urgent. "And remember, I'll always love you."

Roger hesitated.

"Get out of here!" urged Templeton. "I screwed up, now give me a chance to put it right."

Roger touched Templeton's hand and dashed to the back door. He turned and looked back at his father. Tears slicked his face.

"I'm sorry, Son. I messed up all our lives," said Templeton.

For a moment it looked as though Roger would return to his father's side.

"Go!" shouted Templeton and the boy ran out of his father's life.

** Bophutatswana was an "independent" black homeland*

created by the South African government in line with its apartheid policies.

Chapter 42

As Joubert and the two constables approached the front door Templeton drew the Beretta from its holster.

He sat in a scruffy armchair located against the wall opposite the front door and slightly to one side. He raised the pistol and took careful, deliberate aim at the centre of the door.

"Fuck you all," he said out loud. "You've taken everything else, you're not having my son."

***

Constable Thomas Sibanda never knew what hit him. As he opened the door and stepped into the lounge of the small, block-like house in Phaka street, a 9mm, full-metal-jacketed bullet traveling at a fraction under 1 200 feet per second, slammed into the centre of his chest. It shattered his sternum but was deflected to the right where it passed through his heart.

The element of surprise was complete. Before any of them could react, Templeton fired a shot at the constable who was directly behind Sibanda. The bullet hit him in the stomach and he collapsed. It was not a fatal wound and he recovered after emergency surgery.

When the second shot was fired, Joubert reacted quickly. He flung himself onto the ground outside the firing line and crawled as quickly as he could where, after fumbling about for the keys, he managed to get the door open and radio for reinforcements.

Inside the house Templeton knew exactly what would happen. There was no escape, he would either be captured or killed but none of that mattered – all he wanted to do was give Roger enough time to get away and to divert attention from his son's escape. He fired a shot through the lounge window that shattered the glass. Joubert ducked down behind the car and fired two shots back. Not for a single second did he think that the person shooting at them was anything other than an MK operative that they'd accidentally stumbled upon. The possibility that it was his partner was so ridiculous it never entered his mind.

In the 15 minutes it took for the SAP Task Force to arrive Templeton and Joubert exchanged sporadic shots, more just to let each other know they were still there, than to cause injury.

When the Task Force arrived they quickly took up positions around the house. Snipers were put in place and the street was blocked off. Overhead a police helicopter circled so that surveillance information could be passed to the ground crew.

"You in there!" boomed the Task Force Commanding Officer, a white lieutenant colonel with a bushy ginger moustache over a megaphone. He wore a beige bullet-proof jacket and had a Beretta 9mm pistol strapped to his leg in a nylon webbing holster.

"The house is surrounded. You cannot escape. Throw your weapon out and come out with your hands up."

There was no response.

He repeated the instructions. Still no response.

Twenty seven minutes later he gave the order to storm the house. Two tear-gas canisters were fired through the lounge window. As they landed and began spewing their contents, a team of gas-mask-wearing policemen flung stun-grenades into the house and burst through both the front of rear doors.

Three shots were fired rapidly at a figure sitting on a chair in the lounge.

When the fog of the tear-gas settled they found Templeton, seriously wounded and unconscious – and just barely alive.

Chapter 43

The media absolutely loved it. It had all the ingredients that were needed to sell newspapers or gain viewers. A black policeman on trial for murder as well as additional charges of furthering the aims of the ANC, aiding and abetting a suspected criminal, obstruction of justice and a few others as well.

The hierarchy of the South African Police Force was determined to go all out on this case. They wanted an example to be made of Ngubane and were determined to show the public that, when one of their own crossed the line, no mercy was shown.

The public couldn't get enough of the story. Newspapers flew off the stands and record numbers of radio listeners tuned into lunchtime and afternoon news broadcasts.

Additional advertising spots were booked, to be flighted during the evening news transmissions to take advantage of the increased television viewership.

Every day the public gallery in the Rand Supreme Court in Johannesburg was packed to capacity as people queued for a place from early in the morning. Police with dogs and dressed in riot gear were called to help control the crowds that were gathered in Pritchard Street, as people mulled about waiting for any snippets of news about the proceedings taking place inside the court building.

So great was the interest that the Johannesburg Star newspaper took the decision to bring out an additional, daily edition.

The Department of Justice had no option but limit the numbers of members of the general public present in the public gallery, in order to accommodate the increased number of media representatives. And even then, there were not enough seats for the press and, on occasion, scuffles broke out.

It was not just local journalists who covered the case, there was a large international contingent reporting on it as well.

For many blacks, Templeton had become something of a folk hero, a man who saw the light and turned against an oppressive, unjust, system, to help bring about liberation.

He became a Robin Hood figure and a symbol of the struggle. Large groups of people from Soweto and Alexandra Township travelled into the Johannesburg city centre by train and bus to demonstrate their solidarity.

They gathered in crowds on the pavement in Pritchard Street and on the steps of the court buildings, where they chanted, sang liberation songs and *toyi-toyied**. On one occasion, the group became so large that it spilled off the pavements and into the streets, bringing traffic to a standstill and the police had to use dogs and tear-gas to restore order.

Ellen suddenly occupied a special place in the community as she had given a son and a husband to the cause. It was a position she did not want to occupy.

Winnie Mandela, wife of jailed ANC leader, Nelson Mandela, put in a number of appearances at court where she spoke to local and international press members and praised Templeton's actions.

“He's like a prodigal son returned,” she told an interviewer from NBC.

“Whenever a lost sheep returns to the fold, we rejoice.”

**toyi-toyi – a sort of war and protest dance.*

Chapter 44

Ellen was steadfast. She refused to be interviewed by the press and declined to answer any questions put by the media.

For her, the daily arrival at court was harrowing and a nightmare and she was forced to run the gauntlet of journalists and photographers firing questions and camera flashes at her as though they were wielding machine guns. Most days she was in tears when she took her spot in the courtroom and seeing her like that, disturbed and upset Templeton.

In the end she could take it no more and appealed to Eric Joubert for help. He called in a few markers he had with the security department of the court building and it was arranged that she be brought in through the back entrance that was inaccessible to the public.

She had little opportunity to speak to Templeton while the trial took place. They allowed her to hug him when he was brought up from the holding cells in the morning and then again before he was taken back down at the end of proceedings. She was also permitted to visit him for an hour in the evenings.

And she spent some time with him on occasion when he consulted with his lawyer. She was to be called as a witness to present her version of the events that led up to the shooting of Sibanda.

Her testimony, it was hoped, would convince the judges that, because Templeton was a member of the police force, a chain of events, over which he had no control and that was unstoppable, was set in motion.

Templeton was aloof and distant during her visits, as though he had erected an invisible wall that neither of them could penetrate. When she asked a prison social worker why, she was told it was something prisoners often did and was a technique they used to try to shield their loved ones from the emotional pain they suffered.

On the first two days she brought Thandi to see her father but, when he saw her, he broke down and then instructed Ellen never to bring her again.

"This is not how she must remember me," he said. "I want you to send her to your parents until this is all over. I don't want her to be a part of this."

For almost three months Ellen had sat by Templeton's hospital bed while he recovered from the gunshot wounds received when the Task Force stormed the house.

At first it was believed he was held hostage in the house but forensic investigations clearly proved the fatal shot was fired by his pistol.

And even then no-one wanted to believe Templeton could be the trigger-man.

"It's simple," said Joubert. "They took his gun off him and used it."

But only Templeton's finger-prints were found on the Beretta and tests for gunshot residue showed he had fired a gun.

Not even Joubert could deny the evidence.

The investigating officers came to see Templeton in hospital when he was sufficiently recovered to answer their questions.

"I'll save us all wasted time," he said, grimacing in pain, as he struggled to sit up. "I pulled the trigger."

"Why?" asked Colonel 'Snake Bite' Vosloo, one of the county's most renowned detectives. The authorities wanted Templeton hung out to dry and accordingly assigned their best team to the investigation. Vosloo was brought in from Pretoria as, it was feared, investigators in Johannesburg, many of whom knew or knew of Ngubane, may be tempted to lose crucial evidence.

"They took everything from me. I wasn't going to let them take my son as well – especially when it was not his fault.

Ellen and his attorney begged him not to plead 'guilty' but he maintained his position.

"I waited for them and then pulled the trigger," he said. "I chose to take Roger's place."

Chapter 45

The weight of guilt Templeton carried on his soul was now shared by Ellen. It weighed heavily upon her how she had rejected Templeton and gone to sleep in son's empty bed, the night he came home with the terrible news about Roger.

That single act had caused Templeton to take desperate action in order to reclaim some honour in his life. Honour she now believed, she had stripped away.

She didn't know how to answer Thandi's daily question: "Where is Pappa? When is he coming back? I miss him and Roger."

It was with enormous relief that she waved goodbye to Thandi when her parents came to fetch their granddaughter. She missed her desperately but knew, in the meantime, the child was better off far away.

"What will happen?" she asked Eric Joubert on the first morning of the trial when he came to fetch her.

He didn't really know how to answer her.

"I think they'll understand what he...and you... went through and take that into account," he replied.

He had grown closer to the Ngubane family since the shooting, although he deeply resented Templeton's actions. But their pain and anguish was clear and he felt it.

So much so that, after Thandi left, he insisted that Ellen come and stay in the guest room at his house.

"It'll be much more convenient than having to travel so far out of the way to pick her up for court in the morning," he explained to his wife. "And besides, imagine what it must be like for her to sit at home, alone, with just her thoughts for company."

Joubert's wife wanted none of it.

"No, Eric!" she said firmly. "That is just taking kindness

too far. It's fine for you to work with blacks and coloureds and Indians but I draw the line at having them in my house, eating at my table, off our plates, with our knives and forks.

"I mean do you even know if she knows how to use a knife and fork? What if she uses her fingers? What kind of example will that be to our children?

"What will people in the bible-study group think when they hear we have a *meid** living in our house?"

"Jesus, Marie!" he snapped. "She completed more school than you did. The Ngubane's are just ordinary people, like you and I, who are going through hell.

"This is my house and you damn well will do as I say. You WILL treat her decently and you will look as though you enjoy having her here."

She could hardly believe what she heard. Nor could he. This was so out of character.

Joubert's wife muttered and complained as she cleared the dinner dishes from the table. "I just praise the good Lord that my father is dead and not around to see this. Blacks sitting and eating with us at our dining-room table!"

Two days later Ellen moved into the Joubert guest-room and despite their misgivings, the awkwardness and issue of different skin colour quickly became a non-issue.

"I have to eat my words," said Marie Joubert to her husband one evening, when they lay in bed. "She's just like us. She feels pain just like a white person and she's so clean!"

"Will they hang him if he's found guilty?" Ellen asked one evening as they drove back after visiting Templeton in the holding cells?

Joubert was tired. He too felt the strain of the court case.

"I think the prosecutor will ask for the death sentence," replied Joubert as he waved away a street beggar.

"I don't think they'll get it though. If he's found guilty I think he'll get life, which is basically 20 to 25 years. There's an automatic reduction of a quarter of the sentence and then he'll get time off for good behaviour so he'll be out in fifteen or less."

"My God, Eric, that'll make him sixty!"

"Yes, but at least he'll be alive."

* *derogatory Afrikaans term for a black woman.*

Chapter 46

Right from the start of the trial it was obvious things were not going to be easy for Templeton. His back was firmly against the wall and it was quickly apparent he was fighting for his life.

Both he and his advocate, Pat Naidoo, an Indian with a legal practice in Fordsburg, who had defended many people charged under South Africa's State Security legislation, knew there was no chance of his being found not guilty. The best they could hope for was to avoid a date with the hangman.

"It won't be easy," Naidoo warned Templeton, when he took the case, "but I don't believe they will hang you.

"I am also confident we can beat the add-on charges like 'furthering the aims of the ANC' and probably also 'aiding and abetting a suspected criminal' but I think you must prepare yourself that, unless there is some sort of miracle, you will be found guilty on the 'murder' and 'attempted murder' charges.

"That said, however, I am pretty certain we can show extenuating circumstances and diminished responsibility. You will end up with a prison sentence."

Templeton nodded. He'd been involved in enough court cases to know how things worked.

"It doesn't really matter one way or the other," he said, shrugging his shoulders. "I don't have a lot left to live for in any case."

"That's up to you," said Naidoo. "My job is to try to save your skin."

Chapter 47

(Report in The Star – Johannesburg newspaper.)

SENSATIONAL START TO 'ANC-COP' TRIAL

By

Gerald Levin

Johannesburg – The trial of Security Policeman, Templeton Ngubane began in dramatic fashion this morning when the presiding judge, Justice Peter Thornton, ordered an early recess after onlookers became unruly.

Police arrested three people after a scuffle broke out between members of the public attempting to gain access to the public gallery.

The State alleges Warrant Officer Ngubane is guilty of murder and attempted murder. He is also charged with furthering the aims of a banned organisation, the African National Congress and of aiding and abetting a suspected criminal.

The case arises from an incident on April 23, last year, when Constable Thomas Sibanda, a black policeman, was fatally wounded during a shooting incident. Another black policeman, Constable Amos Molefe, was also wounded during the shoot-out.

The State contends Ngubane, wilfully and with pre-meditation, opened fire on his colleagues in order to allow his son and a group of ANC members and sympathisers to escape arrest.

Appearing for the prosecution, the Attorney General of the *Transvaal**, Mr Tielman Theron said he would present evidence that would conclusively prove Ngubane is an ANC supporter.

Despite being advised to the contrary by his Defence Counsel, Advocate Pat Naidoo, Warrant Officer Ngubane pleaded guilty to the murder and attempted murder charges but not guilty to the other charges.

Outside the court buildings, police and traffic authorities struggled to control large crowds as hundreds of blacks gathered and sang and chanted freedom songs.

At one stage traffic in Pritchard Street was brought to a complete standstill.

The crowd dispersed when two Police Casspirs arrived on the scene.

In terms of the Government State of Emergency restrictions on media coverage about security force actions, what followed may not be reported.

The crowd dispersed but windows of nearby shops were reported smashed and some parked cars were damaged.

The hearing continues tomorrow.

** Transvaal – was one of the four original provinces of South Africa.*

Chapter 48

"I'm sorry, Temp," said Ellen. Her voice was distorted by the crackly handset attached to the intercom through which prisoners and visitors had to speak. Tears ran like baby, summer streams down her cheeks.

"When you needed me I wasn't there for you."

They were in the Visitors' Room at the Johannesburg Prison at Doornkop, virtually across the road from the temporary accommodation in which they lived on the army base. He couldn't see their home when he was out in the exercise yard but could see other parts of the base and was constantly reminded of a life that seemed so long ago.

Along with a few hundred other inmates, Templeton spent his evenings and weekends in Block A, where prisoners who were awaiting trial were kept at Sun City, the name given the Johannesburg Prison, by locals and former inmates.

It was a Saturday morning and she had gone through the humiliating experience of signing in at the Visitor's Reception area and then sitting with dozens of other people, all waiting to visit with incarcerated friends or family members.

Only when they called her name was she allowed to pass through a metal detector that did not work and board a bus that stopped at Blocks A,B,C and D.

No physical contact was allowed and they peered at each other through an inch-thick, sheet of glass. They spoke to each other using an intercom.

In court Templeton's advocate applied for bail but the application was strongly opposed by the prosecution.

Advocate Tielman Theron argued that, in light of the seriousness of the charges and the possible outcome, if Ngubane were granted bail, he would likely skip the country – just as his son had done.

"Your honour," he appealed, "if this man leaves the country and joins the ANC, as we believe he will, it will cause incalculable harm to this country and result in countless innocent people being killed or harmed.

"He was, after all, privy to sensitive information about security force operations that would be of great value to the enemy."

Naidoo argued that Templeton faithfully served the police for seventeen years, had displayed immense loyalty and bravery and was therefore not a flight-risk at all.

Justice Thornton agreed with Theron and bail was refused.

Ellen placed her hand against the sheet of glass. It felt sticky and greasy from all who had touched it before. More than anything she wanted to take Templeton in her arms and hold him.

"I am sorry, Temp," she said speaking into the mouthpiece. "I can't get over the guilt and shame I feel for abandoning you and going to Roger's bed when you needed me to comfort you.

"Can you ever forgive me?"

Even through the greasy, scratched glass he could see the pain she bore by the lines etched on her face. In a year she'd aged ten. He felt as though his heart would break. God, how he loved her and how he had fucked up! He put his hand onto the glass against hers.

When he spoke his voice was choked with emotion.

"Of course I forgive you," he swallowed and clenched his lips. "None of this is your fault. I am the one who drove Roger away and caused this."

"No!" she spoke gently but her lower lip quivered. She sucked in her breath doing all she could to not to break down. It was too late for tears now. They did nothing but increase Templeton's anguish.

"It was both of us. All we could see and think about was

what we lost. We never paused to consider what we had was all we needed – each other and our children. None of the other stuff was important."

He gritted his teeth. "You must teach our children that."

He took a handkerchief from his pocket and blew his nose.

"How is Thandi?"

"She is fine. I speak to her on the telephone often. She is happy there but misses her Papa. Can't I make a plan to bring her to see you?"

"No!" said Templeton firmly. "Absolutely not! I won't have her seeing me like this."

He pointed at the glass separating them and the guards seated nearby.

"I understand," said Ellen.

"And Roger, have you heard anything about Roger?"

"Eric said the intelligence he has, is Roger arrived in Botswana and appears to have been taken to Tanzania. He is safe."

Templeton sighed. "Thank God."

With their hands still held together on the glass, Ellen's gaze fell softly upon Templeton's face.

"Temp, I want you to hear this and to understand it. I blamed you for all that has happened and for Roger's leaving. But I don't any more. I don't deserve to say this, because it is me that needs your forgiveness, but I unreservedly forgive you."

She dabbed her eyes with a white tissue.

"We still have all that is important in the world. Let's put that behind us and get through this upcoming phase so we can be a family again. We can start over one day."

A great weight suddenly fell off Templeton's being and his spirits soared. He felt as light as a soap bubble, as though he could surely float on a gentle breeze.

"We can beat a prison sentence," he said. "With a bit of luck I'll be out in 15 years – and who knows, maybe there'll be another amnesty and it is sooner."

Fifteen years was a small price to pay for saving his son. So what if he went to jail, Roger was, after all, just starting out in life.

"Please stick with me, Ellen. Together, we'll make it."

She stared into his face, wishing she could take it in her hands. For the first time in a very long time she felt a warm blanket of inner peace drawn around her.

"I will," she said. "I promise you I will."

Chapter 49

Eric Joubert poured his third Castle Lager® of the day into a fresh, chilled beer glass.

It was almost five thirty in the afternoon and the Club, as members of the force called it, was filling up as cops pulled in at their favoured watering hole before heading home.

Summer was fast approaching and the evenings were starting to turn sticky. Ceiling fans, turned ivory from years of cigarette smoke, slowly rotated as though gasping for air themselves.

The room smelled of stale beer and dusty dartboards and the once-green carpet was worn and musty with holes where the countless darts players had stood over the years.

Near the windows that overlooked the car-park was a snooker table that had long-since ceased to run true and was the cause of many a visitor losing large sums of money when the white ball suddenly changed direction for no apparent reason.

Yet, for all its seediness, the Club, as it was affectionately known, provided a sanctuary and a place where the cops who visited it were shielded from the outside world.

It was a place a man could get drunk, raise hell, debate politics, lie about women he slept with and sort out his differences with his fists. Like Las Vegas, whatever happened in the Club, stayed in the the Club.

It was a place to unwind and Eric Joubert needed to unwind. He sat on a high bar-stool, his elbows resting on the bar counter and his feet hooked under the brass rail that surrounded the bottom of the counter.

He quietly sipped his drink and, in between mouthfuls, drew patterns on the counter-top in the moisture that dripped off his glass with his index finger. He avoided conversation with the other patrons.

Nearby a game of darts was under way and every now and then there was a loud cheer when someone successfully hit the number he aimed at.

The bar counter was long and L-shaped and just at the bend sat five policeman. Two were dressed in uniform. They appeared to be attempting to set a new world record for getting smashed in the shortest possible time. Periodically they roared with laughter as one or other told a joke that seemed to get funnier the more drunk they became.

The court case had taken its toll on Joubert. He was tired and irritable and welcomed the opportunity to relax and enjoy a few beers. He had become increasingly involved with the Ngubane family and Ellen in particular. His wife, Marie, was now firm friends with Templeton's wife.

“You know, Eric,” she said one night as they lay in bed with the lights off, “I must admit, in the beginning, I wasn't very happy about having Ellen stay in our house. But now that I've got to know her, it has been a very rewarding experience. I've learnt so many things from her but, perhaps the most important lesson I've learned is we are far more alike than different.

“It's funny how we live in the same country but, until we meet and get to know each other, we actually live in different worlds!”

Joubert took her hand and squeezed it. They had both come a long way and so had Ellen. All of them had had prejudices and fears wiped away and felt humbled.

Joubert took a large mouthful of beer and swirled the cool liquid around his palate while he closed his eyes and rubbed them. He thought of Templeton and what he would have done, faced with the same situation and same choices. He concluded he would probably have done exactly the same.

Next to him the party with the five cops was building up

a head of steam.

“Hey Eric, man, come and have a drink with us, man,” called one of the men. His voice was loud and thick, his tongue and lips swollen by the alcohol he had consumed.

Joubert opened his eyes and looked at them. Their eyes were bloodshot and they looked back at him with blank stares and their mouths hung slightly open. He could only imaging how bad their breath must be.

He was in no mood for a drunken piss-up and badly-told jokes. He just wanted to be left alone.

He held up his hand and waved them away.

“No thanks, I'm happy here,” he said and took another sip of beer. He was going to leave after he finished this drink anyway.

“What's wrong?” slurred on of the men. “Aren't your white mates good enough for you any more?”

Joubert felt a flame of anger flare deep within his belly but he quickly extinguished it.

“Ja,” said one of the uniformed policeman, a sergeant, “I've heard Ngubane's wife has moved in with you.”

In Monty Python-style he nudged his mates.

“When the cat's away, hey Eric! Nudge! Nudge! Wink! Wink!”

They all roared in amusement.

“Ja it's okay now. The law's changed so it's legal to fuck a coon now. Just make sure you don't end up with a *Hotnot** kid, 'eh Eric?

The quip was really funny. They laughed and laughed and laughed. They were still laughing when Joubert smashed a beer bottle on the uniformed sergeant's head and cracked his skull.

** Hotnot – derogatory Afrikaans term for a mixed-race person.*

Chapter 50

(Report in the Beeld Newspaper. Translated into English)

POLICE REFUTE ALLEGATIONS IN NGUBANE CASE

By

Louwra Potgieter – Court Reporter

JOHANNESBURG – A senior police officer yesterday denied claims by the Ngubane defence team that they had abandoned one of their own and, as a result, the SA Police had to bear some of the responsibility for Ngubane's actions.

In answering questions put to him under cross-examination, Captain Gerrie van Rooyen said, a claim for the replacement of household good and other items owned by Warrant Officer Ngubane and his family that were destroyed during township rioting, was handled strictly according to regulations.

Captain van Rooyen dismissed charges by Advocate Pat Naidoo that his client was not fairly treated by the South African Police.

The defence contended that Ngubane lost everything he held dear, simply because he was a policeman. The Police Force's failure to live up to promises made on television that it would fully compensate members for all their losses sustained during the rioting on that day, had left his client bitter and disillusioned.

This in turn effectively led to the break-up of his family and the final desperate act to save his son.

In response to Advocate Naidoo's contentions, Captain van Rooyen said the police handled Ngubane's claim in exactly the same way any insurance company would have. He said because Warrant Officer Ngubane could not produce receipts for some of the items for which he was claiming compensation and therefore could not prove he in fact ever owned them and it was unreasonable to expect the Treasury to pay for them.

Captain van Rooyen did however concede it was possible the receipts in question were destroyed in the fire that burnt W/O Ngubane's house to the ground.

Throughout the day's proceedings, Warrant Officer Ngubane, dressed in a neat grey suit with a blue tie, sat quietly listening and occasionally taking notes.

As has been the case since the start of the trial, his wife, Mrs Ellen Ngubane, sat two rows back. She was dressed in a stylish yellow suit with a black blazer and wore a black hat. She was accompanied to court by Mrs Marie Joubert, wife of Warrant Officer Eric Joubert, Ngubane's erstwhile partner.

During the proceedings Mrs Ngubane and the accused exchanged glances and, on one occasion, he gave her a 'thumbs up' sign.

Warrant Officer Ngubane looked much more relaxed yesterday than he did at the start of the trial.

The case continues tomorrow.

Chapter 51

"Please state your name for the record," said the prosecutor, Tielman Theron.

"Warrant Officer Eric Joubert. I am a member of the South African Police, Security Branch."

Theron removed his horn-rimmed spectacles and polished them vigorously on his tie before continuing. He was not a large man but his presence and bearing commanded respect and the way he used his reading glasses to engineer dramatic pauses or emphasise a point was his trademark. He used them like a music conductor uses a baton to direct an orchestra and influence an audience.

"Would it be fair to say, Warrant Officer Joubert," he said, fixing a steely gaze on Joubert over the top of his glasses, "that you would prefer not to be in the witness box right now and that in many ways you could be considered a hostile prosecution witness?"

Joubert nodded.

"You have to speak," said Theron so we have an audio record. "We can't hear you nodding your head."

"Yes I would rather be somewhere else. Yes I am reluctant to give evidence. Yes you threatened to subpoena me if I refused to testify," said Joubert testily.

"Good, I'm glad we've got that out of the way," said Theron.

"Do you know the accused?"

"Yes?"

"In what capacity?"

"We worked together in the police for the past five years. You could describe us as partners."

"Would you please tell the court what happened on April 23rd last year?"

Joubert took a deep breath. He was in an untenable

position. They were going to use him to skin Templeton and if he refused to give evidence, or committed perjury, they would lock him up.

He exhaled deeply, aware of a fluttering in his chest.

"Warrant Officer Ngubane had questioned a suspect in a murder case involving the death of an old woman."

"How was she murdered?" Theron cut in.

"Her wrists were broken, then a tire was placed around her neck, filled with petrol and set alight. It is called necklacing."

"Is...er...necklacing, as you call it, a method of murder popularised by the African National Congress." Theron knew it was. The apparent hesitation and uncertainty was just part of his courtroom choreography.

Joubert hesitated. He could see where the prosecutor's questioning was going.

"Please answer the question, Warrant Officer!" snapped Theron.

"Yes."

"Yes what?"

"Yes, it is a method designed by the ANC."

"If it please Your Honour, please note that." Oh how Theron wished for a Jury to play to rather than a judge and two assessors.

Advocate Naidoo started to rise as though to object but Thornton waved him away and he sat down again.

"Please continue telling us what transpired on April 23rd."

"The suspect, that Temp...I mean Warrant Officer Ngubane was questioning told him he knew who killed the old woman and knew where the killer could be found."

Theron removed his spectacles and turned towards the public gallery. When he spoke it was more to them than to Joubert.

"Who did the person, Warrant Office Ngubane was questioning say was the murderer?" He used the last word deliberately as he understood how carefully-selected words that meant the same as other words could alter perceptions.

Joubert swallowed. His mouth was dry. He poured water from a ribbed, glass bottle with a hard, black, plastic, screw-on, cap into a thick, similarly-ribbed glass tumbler and took a gulp. The water was warm but it still lubricated his throat.

"He said it was a youngster by the name of Roger Ngubane."

There was a collective gasp in the courtroom.

Judge Thornton called for order.

Theron patiently waited for the hubbub to settle, milking the moment.

He turned on his heel and cast a penetrating gaze over Joubert.

"What is the name of the accused's son?"

Joubert knew Theron was leading him into a trap he would soon shut, and there was nothing he could do about it. All he could do was wait for the moment the prosecutor made him pull the trigger on Templeton.

"Roger Ngubane."

"Were you present when Warrant Officer Ngubane questioned the suspect?" asked Theron suddenly changing tack.

"No, he was alone."

"So it was Warrant Officer Ngubane who told you the suspect said the killer of the old woman was his son?"

"What happened then?"

"He was was very upset," said Joubert, clearly remembering that horrible day.

"Go on."

"I told him we would have to go and arrest his son. He begged me to let him do it..."

"Arrest his son?"

"Yes. What could I do? I would have asked him to do the

same if I were in that position."

"Then what happened?" Theron cut in, not wanting to give Joubert the chance to become emotional.

"I told him I couldn't allow him to go on his own but would give him thirty minutes to be alone with his boy."

He looked at Templeton sitting across the room, beside his defence team with two uniformed policemen seated just behind him. The two men locked eyes for a moment then Ngubane mouthed: it's okay to Joubert.

I'm sorry, old Buddy, Joubert thought.

"A little while later two constables and I went to the house where his son was reported to be to make the arrest."

"What happened then?" asked Theron after pouring himself a glass of water.

Joubert hesitated.

"Please answer the question, Warrant Officer."

"As we entered the house shots were fired from inside and the two constables who were ahead of me were hit. I ran back to the car, radioed for help and a short while later the special anti-terrorist task force arrived and took over control of the operations."

"Did you have any warning that you were going to be fired upon?

"No."

"So even though Warrant Officer Ngubane is your partner and knew both of the other policeman, he gave you no warning but simply fired upon you?"

"Yes."

"Would you agree then that his actions were premeditated?"

Advocate Naidoo leapt up.

"Objection, Your Honour. That calls for the witness to speculate. In any case, as my learned friend well knows, my client has entered a plea of guilty on the charge of murder and attempted murder."

"Your Honour," said Theron, in a tone like that of a teacher attempting to explain a simple concept to a particularly slow student, "the defence maintains the accused carried out his actions in a state of mind that was not normal and that his judgement was clouded by emotions that caused him to act in a completely irrational manner.

"I am simply trying to point out that Warrant Officer Ngubane did no such thing and that he acted in a cold, rational and premeditated fashion."

"I'll allow it," ruled Thornton. He turned to face Joubert. "Answer the question."

"Yes, I believe his actions were premeditated."

Theron smiled. He loved being the courtroom chess grand-master.

"Where was the accused's son when the shooting was over and the police entered the house?"

"I don't know," said Joubert. "he wasn't there."

Theron, who for the past few moments sat on the corner of his desk, stood up and crossed the floor to the bench where the judge and his two assessors sat. He turned and faced the court.

"Your Honour," he said, speaking mainly in the direction of the press contingent in the gallery, many of whom were busy jotting notes in Croxley flip notebooks, "the prosecution will present witnesses who will testify they saw a youngster who looked like Roger Ngubane leave the house in question BEFORE the shooting took place. I would also remind the court that the accused has already admitted helping his son escape."

He turned back to Joubert.

"Warrant Officer Joubert, earlier you told the court the necklace method of murder is an ANC-designed system of execution. Is that correct?"

Joubert sensed Theron was about to snap the trap shut.

"Yes."

"So in your professional judgement," he looked at Naidoo as he continued, " as someone whose job it is to study and investigate these sorts of political crimes, it would be reasonable to assume that someone committing a necklace murder is a member of the ANC?"

"Yes, that is what we would assume," replied Joubert. "But in this case it is ludicrous to say Roger was a member of the ANC. He was just a youngster trapped by circumst..."

Theron cut in.

"Warrant Officer Joubert, is it or is it not true that the security branch has intelligence reports that Roger Ngubane made contact with the ANC in Botswana and has now left that country, presumably for Tanzania where the most likely scenario is he will undergo military training and will come back to perpetrate acts of violence against the people of South Africa?

"Answer the question and remember, you are under oath."

"Yes, it's true." The trap slammed shut. All Theron had to do now was ram the dead-bolt home.

Theron smiled. Like taking candy from a baby, he thought.

"You promised the accused thirty minutes alone with his son, is that correct?"

"Yes, I already told you that."

"That's right, you did and it was very humane of you. Now you've been a policeman for a long time...er..." he rifled through the pile of papers in a folder although he well knew the answer but stating it would spoil his carefully-crafted dance-routine. "Seventeen years, I believe."

"That is correct."

"So it is safe to assume, with that much experience you probably are quite knowledgeable when it comes to the question of murder."

"I suppose so." Joubert felt a rivulet of perspiration trickle down the back of his neck and his face felt clammy. He drew a handkerchief from his trousers' pocket and dabbed the back of his neck, then his brow.

"In your expert opinion then, from all your years of experience, would you say half an hour was more than enough time for a man of Warrant Officer Ngubane's ability, skill and knowledge of police procedures, to plan and execute a murder?"

Theron rammed the dead-bolt home.

Naidoo leapt to his feet.

"Your Honour, I must protest!" he said, his voice sharp and urgent. The prosecution is once again asking the witness to speculate and pass an opinion."

Theron sighed and gazed at Naidoo with a hint of contempt.

"Your Honour," he said, looking at the judge over his glasses that were perched right on the tip of his nose, "we have established the witness's credentials as an expert in the field. Obviously my learned friend is not familiar with the term expert opinion.

"The crux of the matter here is whether the accused pulled the trigger as a result of a fit of passion or whether it was a cold, calculated, premeditated action. The witness, considering his background and experience is certainly qualified to voice an opinion on that issue."

Justice Thornton pondered the matter for a few moments then cleared his throat and said: "The objection is overruled. The witness will answer the question.

Joubert looked first at Templeton then at Ellen. For the first time in a few days he saw fear reflected in their eyes.

"I prefer not to answer that question," he said.

Thornton sat up straight and glowered down at Joubert from his lofty position on the bench. His voice was laced with irritation and menace.

"Warrant Officer Joubert, I will hold you in contempt and

lock you up!"

"You must do what you must do, Your Honour," said Joubert, holding the judge's gaze.

"Just answer the question, Jooba!" said Templeton in a loud voice. He stood up so suddenly and unexpectedly that the uniformed policemen behind him had no time to restrain him. "I doesn't matter. Don't throw your career away for someone you can't help anyway!"

The cops put their hands on his shoulders and pushed him back down onto his chair.

Thornton turned towards Naidoo. "If you can't restrain your client I will have him taken back to the cells and we'll proceed without him!" he said.

"I'm sorry, Your Honour, said Templeton. I apologise. It won't happen again."

Thornton addressed Eric Joubert: "Are you prepared to answer the question, Warrant Officer?"

Joubert looked at Templeton then nodded his head.

"Yes, Your Honour."

He looked squarely in the eyes of Tielman Theron and said in a firm even voice: "Yes, half an hour would have been enough time to plan and commit this murder."

As the words left his mouth he felt as though he were plunging a knife into the hearts of both Ellen and Templeton and he suddenly knew what it must have been like for Roger just before he struck that fatal match.

Pandemonium broke out in the court and it took almost a minute of banging with his gavel before Judge Thornton was able to restore order.

He immediately called an early recess.

"This court will adjourn until after lunch," he said, "and I warn you, if there are any similar outbursts I will order the court cleared!"

Chapter 52

(Report in The Star – Johannesburg newspaper.)

PARTNER DENIES ANC CONNECTIONS
By
Gerald Levin

A Security Policeman today dismissed suggestions that Warrant Officer Templeton Ngubane could in any way have connections with or ties to the banned African National Congress.

Answering questions put during cross examination by defence counsel, Advocate Pat Naidoo, Warrant Officer Eric Joubert said, in his opinion it was ludicrous to suggest the accused had any connections with the ANC.

He said he had worked with Ngubane for five years and during that time, Ngubane was commended for bravery for saving his (Joubert's) life during a shoot out with the terrorist organisation.

During the proceedings, Joubert painted a vivid picture of Ngubane's humanity and kindness and said 'he was one of the best policemen he had ever had the privilege of serving with.'

He said he firmly believed circumstances beyond Ngubane's control had driven him to take the drastic action he had and any father who found himself in a similar situation would do exactly the same.

Earlier in the day, during questioning by the State, Warrant Officer Joubert conceded the accused could have had the time to purposely plan and execute the murder of Constable Thomas Sibanda.

Throughout the proceedings Ngubane sat quietly, occasionally passing a hand-written note to his wife sitting a few rows back, except for a single instance when he interjected and urged his former partner to answer a question so that he would not be charged with Contempt of Court.

Mrs Ngubane has attended the trial every day but has refused to speak to the press or to comment in any way.

An interesting aspect of today's proceedings was the appearance of Mrs Winnie Mandela, wife of jailed ANC leader, Nelson Mandela.

At an impromptu press conference held on the steps of the Rand Supreme Court building, Mrs Mandela described Warrant Officer Ngubane as a hero of the people. She called on other policemen to follow his example and warned that 'the people of South Africa would remember those who were not part of the struggle.'

“You are either with the liberation struggle or against it,” she told the mainly foreign press corps.

The hearing continues on Monday.

Chapter 53

"I spoke to Naidoo," said Ellen, speaking into the intercom hand-set and gazing at Templeton through the glass partition in the prison visiting room. They touched hands against the glass, just as they did during every visit.

"He says things aren't going too badly. Eric's testimony during his cross-examination did us a lot of good, as did your record with the police. He says he thinks the circumstances of the case will win you a lot of sympathy."

Templeton regarded her through the misty glass.

"I know. I spoke to him earlier, before you got here. He says things are turning our way but I am not getting my hopes up. Theron was pretty impressive this morning and it's going to take a lot to undermine the gains he made."

He was quiet for a moment then he said: "Let's not talk about that now. We'll cross those bridges if and when we get to them.

"How are you? How are you and Thandi doing?" he asked gently.

The sadness in her voice was obvious. "We're okay. I speak to Thandi on the phone every night, Marie insists I call and won't take any money for the calls. Thandi asks about you but I don't think she really understands. But Jesus, I am missing you."

Her voice was uneven but she was determined to hold her composure for his sake. She needed to present a strong front but inside she felt anything but strong. Her eyes had the sheen of moisture.

Even through the murky glass Templeton could see that and he too began to feel tears trickle down his cheeks. His tears were a mixture of regret and anger. Anger at the situation and intense frustration that he could not take her in his arms and comfort her when she so needed it.

"Don't," he said, wanting more than anything else in the world to be able to touch her. "Don't cry. We'll make it. It's all going to be okay, I promise!"

"I'm sorry," she said sniffing and searching in her handbag for a Kleenex. "I promised myself I would be strong but sometimes... Oh Templeton, I know we're going to all be together again as a family. A lot of people are praying for us and God answers prayers."

She dabbed her eyes and wiped her nose.

"I know I shouldn't cry. I know it upsets you."

He smiled. "Don't worry about me," he said. "Now tell me how you really are."

"I'm fine. I have good and bad days but overall I am doing okay. I don't think I could have coped without the support and love of Marie and Eric. They truly have been good friends and provided immense comfort."

"I am pleased. I will thank Eric when I see him."

Their conversation was awkward tonight. Sometimes it was like that when they thought about the gravity of the situation.

A prison official dressed in a smart khaki uniform with green epaulettes approached Templeton.

"I'm sorry Templeton, but time is up." His voice was soft and sympathetic. There was no doubt, just as Naidoo said, a lot of people had sympathy for him.

"I love you," said Templeton to Ellen. Their fingertips touched again against the glass barrier.

"I love you too, my Darling. Please be strong. We're waiting for you to come home."

When she turned and left he could not see she was crying.

Chapter 54

(Report in The Star – Johannesburg newspaper.)

VERDICT IN NGUBANE CASE TOMORROW

By

Gerald Levin

Johannesburg – The defence counsel in the controversial Templeton Ngubane trial, today concluded its case, eighteen days after the State commenced its arguments.

Today's proceedings were largely occupied by summing up of the evidence that was presented by both the Prosecution and the Defence.

The Attorney General of the Transvaal, Advocate Tielman Theron, acting for the prosecution, called on the Judge Peter Thornton and his two assessors to find the former security policeman guilty of murder, attempted murder as well as furthering the aims of the banned African National Congress (ANC).

He urged the court to impose the death sentence and said Ngubane was a menace to society who had admitted to committing the most heinous of crimes and was a threat to the safety and security of the State.

Advocate Pat Naidoo, counsel for the defence, said his client had never denied shooting and killing Constable Thomas Sibanda but contended there were mitigating circumstances and the incident was a crime of passion.

Naidoo reminded the court of the evidence presented by Professor Karel Trichardt, Head of Psychiatry at the Johannesburg Hospital who said, given the circumstances in which Ngubane found himself, it was reasonable to assume his mental capacity and powers of reasoning were impaired.

"It is quite understandable for a father who found his son

in dire trouble to react passionately and beyond what would be considered normal and rational behaviour," he said. "In those circumstances the abnormal become normal."

Naidoo also charged that the South African Police must bear a large part of the responsibility for Warrant Officer Ngubane's actions, as none of this would happened had they honoured the promises they made to compensate him for the losses he suffered when his home was burnt down during township unrest.

He pointed out that Ngubane and his family were targeted by the community solely because he was a policeman.

"As regards the charge that Templeton Ngubane is an ANC sympathiser, a quick examination of his police service record will show how ridiculous and ludicrous that assertion is," said Naidoo.

Judgement and sentence will be passed tomorrow.

Chapter 55

"The newspapers are generally sympathetic, so that's a very good sign," Naidoo said to Templeton.

He paced ceaselessly up and down the consultation room, reserved for lawyers and their clients. Before they started speaking Naidoo carried out a quick examination of the room to make sure no-one was listening in. There were plenty of rumours about the room being bugged and police and prosecutors listening in to privileged conversations between attorneys and their clients, especially in political and security cases.

He found nothing. But then he didn't really know what to look for in the first place. Templeton, who had some experience in this area, also checked the room and found nothing.

Physically, Naidoo was not a commanding figure. He appeared older than his forty six years and perhaps the most lasting impression he left with people he met for the first time, was his limp, clammy handshake that was like squeezing a damp sock.

Naidoo's political awareness took flame in the mid 1950s when the new Group Areas Act forced him and his family out of the home they had owned for over forty years. From as long ago as he could remember, he wanted to be a Civil Rights advocate.

And there was no doubt he was a very good one. On many occasions he snatched victory when it appeared there was no hope and while Tielman Theron respected him, he disliked the Indian intensely. Theron more than anything wanted to see Templeton found guilty and the harshest possible sentence imposed.

That would be as good as kicking that *coolie** in the nuts, he thought.

"If public sentiment is on your side, I think the judge will have to take that into account," Naidoo said.

"I hope you're right," said Templeton. "Suddenly I don't feel as confident as I did. To be honest, I don't share your confidence."

"I'm not saying you're going to walk out of the court a free man tomorrow but I honestly don't believe you'll get too heavy a sentence. My bet is you'll get fifteen years."

"That's on the murder charge. What about the other charges? The attempted murder and the ANC side of things. I was involved in a case where a guy got three years just because he drew the ANC logo on his coffee cup."

Naidoo kept up his pacing. It made Templeton nervous and began to irritate him.

"They'll probably let the attempted murder sentence run concurrently with the fifteen and there's not a chance they'll get you on furthering the aims of the ANC – there's simply too much evidence against that. I don't think you should worry."

He glanced at his watch. Eight twenty three.

"Get some sleep. I want you looking fresh in court and don't worry, everything is going to be just fine."

* *coolie – derogatory term for an Indian from India.*

Chapter 56

It was the lead story in every newspaper, radio and television news broadcast!

Templeton Ngubane, former security policeman, was found guilty on all charges!

In passing judgement, Justice Peter Thornton and two assessors concluded that Ngubane, with malice and premeditation, fired on members of the South African Police so that his son could escape arrest and ultimately join the armed wing of the ANC.

"This court therefore concludes," he told a stunned public gallery, "that as a result of the accused's training and knowledge of firearms and police procedures, he knew, full well, the probability of fatally injuring the people at whom he fired."

Templeton sat silently. Somehow he appeared paler. Inwardly he trembled but showed no signs of nervousness on the outside.

Ellen held her right hand to her mouth and bit on her forefinger in an effort to keep her emotions in check. In her left hand she held a tightly scrunched-up tissue.

The judge continued.

"This court has carefully considered all of the evidence presented and can come to no other conclusion than the shooting and killing of Constable Thomas Sibanda and wounding of Constable Amos Molefe was premeditated, deliberate and cold-blooded."

The courtroom was dead silent aside from the voice of the judge and soft whirring of three ceiling-fans. It was as though everyone was holding their breath.

"The court therefore finds you guilty of murder and attempted murder."

"Amandla!" suddenly shrieked a shrill voice from the gallery.

Thornton fell silent. He removed his reading glasses and carefully and deliberately glowered at the person who caused the disturbance.

It was a young, white man, wearing an End Conscription Campaign t-shirt. He sported a scraggly blonde beard with matching, equally-unkempt hair and was most likely a student.

"Eject that man from my courtroom!" ordered Thornton in a calm, determined voice.

He sat with his elbows on his bench and his chin resting against his balled fists, as two policemen cornered the youngster and began frog-marching him from the gallery.

"We shall overcome! Viva!" he yelled as they pushed him out of the room and hustled him down the passage.

When all was once again settled Thornton continued.

"Referring to the matter of the charge of aiding and abetting a banned organisation the court believes the fact that the accused arrived at a house containing a number of known ANC members and made no attempt to apprehend them – in fact instructed them to leave – clearly proves his guilt. He is therefore found guilty on this charge."

There was a collective gasp from the members of the public and Thornton raised his gavel but they settled down and he did not have to rap it.

He turned towards Templeton, Naidoo and the defence team.

"Stand please."

They stood up. This was the moment of truth, the moment the sentence was passed. Templeton's legs felt rubbery and he had to put his hands on the desk in front of him to steady himself. Naidoo put a hand on Templeton's shoulder and was aware of the big man's trembling. In his left temple, Ngubane could both feel and hear the pulsing of a blood-vessel.

At the desk, to their right, the prosecution team also

stood.

"Templeton Zolini Ngubane, " said Justice Thornton. His voice was clear and steady and could be heard clearly at the furthest reaches of the room.

"You have been found guilty on a charge of murder, one charge of attempted murder and a charge of furthering the aims of a terrorist organisation.

"This court has carefully considered the evidence presented in mitigation. However we do not believe there is sufficient evidence to suggest this was a crime of passion committed during a period of diminished responsibility.

"On the charge of furthering the aims of a terrorist organisation you are sentenced to a prison term for ten years."

Naidoo squeezed Templeton's shoulder.

"On the charge of attempted murder you are also sentenced to a prison-term of ten years."

He peered over his reading glasses at Templeton.

"On the charge of murder you are sentenced to death. You will be taken from here to a place of safety where, at a time determined by the State, you will be hanged by the neck until you are dead."

Templeton's legs buckled. He was sure he would faint. He stumbled so that Naidoo had to catch and hold him with both of his arms. He was sure his head was about to explode.

Surely he was dreaming. This wasn't possible! The death sentence! Naidoo said that would never happen! Soon he would awake and find this was all just a nightmare and he was home with Ellen, Roger and Thandi.

"No!" he wanted to scream but no sound would emit from his throat.

Ellen, however, did scream.

"No you can't! You can't kill my husband! He was just trying to protect my baby!"

She broke down, sobbing uncontrollably. Eric Joubert and his wife, Marie, put their arms around her and held her tightly.

Pandemonium broke out in the public gallery and it took almost five minutes for order to be restored.

Templeton turned around to look at Ellen. He called her name softly and she looked up.

"It's not over," he said, trying to keep his voice steady. Even at this time he knew he had to be strong for her. He prayed he had successfully hidden the fear growing within him. "There is an automatic appeal. Don't give up hope."

She went to him and they held each other for a few minutes.

"It's going to be all right," he said as he held her trembling body to his. "This will be overturned on appeal."

She tried to speak but could not.

"I'm sorry, Warrant," said a white, uniformed, police sergeant. "It's time to go."

Templeton nodded. He tenderly kissed Ellen on her forehead and released her. He turned around with his hands behind his back so the sergeant could attach the handcuffs.

"We'll talk soon. It's going to be okay," he said to Ellen as he looked over his shoulder through watery eyes while they led him away.

Chapter 57

Templeton knew exactly how Death Row at Pretoria Central looked. The entrance was not through the gates the public sees when driving down Potgieter Street towards the city centre. It was set around the back and was a place he had visited on three occasions to question inmates at the facility.

The entrance doors were solid wood with polished brass hinges and a brass postbox set in the centre of the left hand door. Beyond those doors were three sets of thick solid bars and gates that reached from floor to ceiling and barred entrance or exit to a bland, typically, government-designed building topped by zinc water tanks.

This was Death Row and the site of the gallows where, since 1967, all judicial executions in South Africa took place.

When Templeton arrived there, 1 937 prisoners had been hanged since the commissioning of the purpose-built death-facility.

In a small reception room, he was booked in by a white Warrant Officer from the prisons department.

"Undress and put your clothes and personal possessions in this bag," he said, handing a large, transparent plastic bag to Templeton. "Then put these on, they should fit."

He held out a neatly folded, green, prison uniform. Templeton took it and shuddered involuntarily.

He knew those trousers and shirts were worn by someone who was executed, maybe even worn on the gallows. It was the way things were done. Executed prisoners were stripped naked, hosed down and then placed, still undressed in cheap chip-board coffins before being sent for burial at cemeteries around Pretoria. Their prison uniforms were washed and used by other prisoners awaiting the same fate.

As though in a trance, Templeton did as instructed. When he was done and the paper-work completed, he was given an additional uniform, four rough, grey, blankets, a towel and a small bar of soap.

The Warrant Officer, who booked in Ngubane then called to a white, warder standing in the passage.

“Koertzen,” he's ready, “take him to his cell.”

The youngster who took charge of Templeton had just turned twenty three but had already worked on Death Row for four years.

Johannes Koertzen joined the Prison Services straight from school in Stilbaai because it paid better than a position in the army as a conscript and, he figured, he needed a stable job offering some security and prospects.

When he completed his basic training in Kroonstad he was transferred to Pretoria and posted to Death Row.

“I had absolutely no idea what was going on, Pa,” he told his father on his first trip back home since his posting, while they sat by a barbecue fire, drinking beer.

“We arrived at Pretoria Central and fell in for a parade. The commander welcomed us, said he hoped we'd be happy and explained our duties and responsibilities. Then we were taken on a tour of the prison.

“I saw a group of civilians outside the chapel in the prison grounds and asked what they were doing. We were told there were executions that morning.

“Pa, of course I had heard of executions but I didn't know they happened there, where I was going to be working. When we saw the black coffins in the chapel it was all so unreal.”

A week later, aged only 19, Koertzen escorted his first prisoner to the gallows. Since then his was the last face that 184 people ever saw.

Templeton, carrying his blankets, towel and soap, followed Koertzen down a long passage, brightly-lit with fluorescent lights past a number of cells. The cell doors were unlocked and open. In some, an inmate lay on the bed, in others two or three sat on the bed talking or playing cards.

As he passed one of the cells Templeton saw its occupant sitting on the edge of his bed at a fold-down, TV-tray sized desk, writing something.

The inmates regarded the new arrival with detached curiosity.

Three quarters of the way down the passage, Koertzen stopped in front of a locked cell with the number 73 painted above the door frame. He unlocked the heavy steel door with a key he took from a large bunch that was attached to his belt with a chain and swung the door open.

“You'll sleep here,” he said to Templeton. “Make yourself at home,” he said with a smile.

Templeton stood in the doorway trying to take in his new accommodations. He could touch the opposite battleship-grey walls at the same time if he stretched out both arms. Metal struts attached to the right-hand-side wall supported a wooden board on which was a thin foam-rubber mattress with a blue and white cover that convicts and warders called a pis-vel (foreskin). There was no pillow.

Above the bed was a small shelf and in a corner, against the opposite wall, was a stainless-steel toilet with no liftable seat and above it a small wash-basin.

Bolted to the same wall, near the door was a fold-down 'desk', just large enough to hold a single book. There was no chair. When a cell-occupant wanted to make use of the desk, he sat on the bed.

There was no window and attached to the high, steel-reinforced, concrete, ceiling was a light bulb that burned brightly.

“That stays on all the time,” said Koertzen when he saw Templeton look at it. High up, in the front, left hand corner of the room, a steel radio speaker was attached that constantly broadcast Radio Pulpit, a dour, fire-and-brimstone radio station that broadcast only a religious message and no news, from Pretoria.

Templeton tossed his blankets, spare uniform and towel onto the bed and turned to face Koertzen.

"This is how it works here," said the youngster. "Roll call and cell inspection is at 07h00 and 20h00 every day. After morning roll call the cells are unlocked and you are free to interact with other prisoners. Lock-down is at 20h00.

"You have a one-hour exercise period every day and are allowed fifteen minutes to bath every day. No books other than the Bible and those you borrow from the prison library are permitted. The library cart comes around every Tuesday afternoon.

"Once a month you will be able to buy provisions, sweets, toothpaste etc. from a warder who operates a small tuck shop.

"We are not inhuman here so play by the rules and I will do what I can to make things as comfortable as possible."

Templeton nodded blankly. None of this was real. How was it possible to go from admired policeman to...to...THIS?

After Koertzen left he sat on the bed, his head in his hands staring at his feet and the canvas, slip-on shoes he was issued.

No shoelaces! They want the pleasure of hanging you, he sardonically thought.

"Hey, it's not so bad, Bra," said a voice from his cell, doorway.

He looked up and saw a heavily tattooed black man and two Indian men standing in the passage looking in at him.

"You'll get used to this shit as long as you don't let them get you down," said the black man, stepping into the cell with his right-hand thrust out towards Templeton.

"My name's Clubber and these two *Charas** are the

Govender brothers."

Involuntarily Templeton recoiled. These were the kind of people he'd spent most of his working life trying to put away – the dregs of humanity – and the thought of being cloistered with them filled him with horror.

Clubber Nthwele got his nickname as a result of his particular brand of robbery. He loved robbing and raping women – any women, young, old, fat, thin, it didn't much matter to him – and then beating them to death with an axe-handle.

He was 32 years-old but but had spent 18 of those locked up in reformatories or prison and managed to collect an impressive array of prison-gang tattoos along the way. When Clubber finished working-over a woman she could not be recognised as one and was little more than a lump of tenderised meat.

The Govender brothers, Manilal and Reggie, from Richmond in Kwa Zulu – Natal, killed two security guards when they robbed an armoured cash-in-transit vehicle. They simply waited at a shopping centre where they knew a cash-collection was due to be made and, when the driver and his partner got out and opened the rear doors, they killed them in a hail of gunfire.

Templeton shook each of their hands in turn.

Reggie took a packet of Chesterfield cigarettes from his shirt pocket .

"Have a cigarette," he said, offering the pack to Ngubane.

Templeton took one and accepted the light offered. He drew the smoke deeply into his lungs and held it for a few moments before exhaling.

"I thought they only allowed you one cigarette in the morning and another in the evening," he said.

"That's how it's supposed to be," said Clubber, "but the warders aren't bad. They turn a blind eye in return for the occasional "gift"," he made two air-speech inverted commas with his fingers, “from our visitors.”

“It's the same on the inside as it is on the outside, money greases the wheels.” He smiled revealing gaps in his teeth.

* *Charas – once a derogatory terms for Indians.*

Chapter 58

Ellen really tried hard but just could not hold back her tears. She visited Templeton every Saturday and Sunday, driving the 47 kilometres from Johannesburg to Pretoria.

Visiting regulations were more lenient on Death Row and she was able to spend two hours with Templeton on each day. But, as was the situation at Johannesburg Prison, prisoners and visitors had no physical contact. A 50mm-thick armoured glass panel separated them and they had to speak to each other through a metal voice-tube. A warder monitored all conversations.

Death Row inmates were only allowed newspapers censored by the prison staff, so news of the outside world was patchy, at best. There were no televisions and the only radio broadcast they ever heard was that of Radio Pulpit. Letters coming in or going out were also censored.

They placed their hands together against the glass.

My God, thought Templeton, it's been four and a half months since I last touched her.

He could hardly remember when he last saw Thandi but every day he studied the last photograph taken of them when they were a complete family.

"You're looking good," lied Ellen. "You've lost some weight but it looks good on you."

He smiled wryly. You were never going to get fat on the food they fed you on Death Row.

Breakfast, served at 8 am, was *mielie-pap*,* complete with plastic utensils and a mug of tea or coffee. Lunch was at 11am and was always four slices of bread, two with syrup or jam and a mug of synthetic fruit juice. Dinner was served at three in the afternoon and was normally soya mince on rice with a vegetable. Sometimes there was an apple or a banana.

"Thanks," he said. "How is Thandi?"

"She's fine. She says she has some new friends. I brought a photograph that my parents sent."

She took a Polaroid® photograph from her handbag and held it to the glass pane. The attending warder stood up to see what it was and after seeing it was just a photograph, sat down again.

Templeton looked at the picture of the smiling face of his daughter and felt as though his heart would break.

"She is so beautiful," he whispered. The pain was almost more than he could bear. "Have you heard anything about Roger."

She shook her head. "Eric says that's a good thing and that they have heard nothing more.

"I'll leave the photo with the warder so he can give it to you. There is also a letter from Thandi that I will leave with him, as well as R100 for you and I have a bottle of his favourite brandy to keep things running smoothly in here for you."

"Thank you," he choked, trying to keep his feelings in check.

"Have you been able to buy some sweets and chocolates?"

"Yes, Koertzen gets me stuff if I ask him to and every two weeks one of the warders brings in stuff that he sells. It's weird but he sets up shop on the steps that lead to the gallows and in the cell right by their entrance is this crazy old white man who keeps screaming about a tape worm that made him do it. When I asked about him, they told me he is Dimitri Tsafendas, the guy who killed *Verwoerd**.

"He's been in here for over 20 years. He sees the guys going to the gallows and he can hear the clap of the steel trap-doors. It makes him more insane every the day!"

Ellen shivered. Jesus! Was that the fate that awaited her husband?

Templeton saw how what he said upset her, so he changed the subject.

"How are things in the new house?" he asked.

"It's okay. It's not like our old house but it is kind of the Silumas to let me stay there while they're overseas.

Ellen had to vacate the temporary police house at Doornkop Military Base after the conclusion of the trial. The Jouberts offered to let her continue living at their home but Ellen decided against it.

Despite the removal of the Group Areas Act, the Immorality Act and other discriminatory laws, middle-class conservative, white, South Africa was not yet ready to accept a black woman living in the home of an Afrikaner family. The servant's room, maybe, but certainly the not in the same house as the family.

She saw how her presence made life uncomfortable for Eric and Marie and the disapproving looks they got from neighbours and how people whispered and cast furtive glances in their direction.

"Naidoo says the appeal will only be heard after Christmas. The court is apparently seriously backlogged."

He was glad about that. Even though he was locked up, away from his family and had lost all, he still wanted to continue living. Every day he dreamed of what he would do when he got out. He planned to go back to teaching. Maybe move to somewhere in the countryside where he could keep some livestock and grow some vegetables for his family. Perhaps Thandi would be married by then and he could teach and help raise his grandchildren. Maybe the country would be changed enough that Roger would be back home.

As long as he was alive, even it it had to be on Death Row, there was hope.

"We're going to make it. The appeal will succeed," she said. "There is no way God cannot hear my prayers and, if he will not hear mine, surely he will listen to Thandi's!"

** Hendrik Verwoerd – Prime Minister of South Africa from*

1958 until his assassination in 1966. He is remembered as the man behind the conception and implementation of apartheid, a system of racial segregation dividing ethnic groups in the country.

**mielie-pap – a porridge made from ground maize.*

Chapter 59

Johannes Koertzen, or Joe, as his colleagues called him, came into Templeton's cell just after dinner one afternoon.

Templeton lay on his back on his bed with his hands under his head and his eyes closed. He felt Koertzen's presence rather than heard his approach and opened one eye.

“I've got a letter that arrived for you in the post from your wife, Ngubane,” he said and handed an A4-sized brown, manilla, envelope to Templeton.

Koertzen was a kind man. For that matter, all the warders working on Death Row were kind. The young prison official was busy undertaking a correspondence course in religious studies and hoped to become a full-time pastor, when he completed it. This was a particularly stressful week for him as 11 executions had taken place. It seemed, when the end of the year approached, the Justice Department wanted to tie up as many loose ends as possible, before staff left for their Christmas holidays.

A dark cloud descended over the inmates whenever executions took place, as each prisoner realised his turn drew nearer. No-one slept on the night before an execution because prisoners sang through the night. But at 7 am the cells became deathly silent and everyone listened for the clap of the one and a half ton, steel trap-doors as they opened.

Templeton tipped out the contents of the envelope of which the top was already torn off by the censor, onto his lap. There was new photograph of Thandi and, in a pink envelope, a letter from his daughter. His hands shook as he removed the correspondence from the envelope and began reading.

My Dear Papa

Gogo is helping me write this because I am too small to

write properly yet. I am telling her what to say and she is writing it.

How are you? I am fine except I am missing you and Mommy and Roger. I am being good and helping Gogo as much as I can.

I help to clean the house when I get home from school. I like school and my teacher and my friends.

I am missing you and Roger very much but I am trying not to cry as I have asked Dear Lord Jesus to fix everything and Mommy says if we believe, then Jesus will always hear us.

I wish I could come and see you but Gogo says they will not allow me to, so I will just have to wait until you get home. I know you will come home because I know you are a good man.

I love you.

Lots of love and kisses.

Your daughter,

Thandi

XXXXXX

Included in the envelope was a drawing she had done on a sheet of paper torn from a school exercise book. It was of four people walking in a field with flowers and a square house with a chimney emitting tendrils of smoke. In the sky, flying near fluffy clouds were birds that looked like slightly flattened Ms.

Tears streamed down Templeton's face as he read and he did not care that Koertzen still stood in the doorway.

He turned onto his stomach, buried his face in the mattress and wept.

Chapter 60

Templeton sat in the Clubber's cell, one morning, shortly after breakfast, playing cards. It was one of the ways they killed time, while waiting for their daily exercise turn.

Exercise hour was the major highlight of every inmate's day. It was the only time they saw natural light and could look up at the sky and see the sun, birds and clouds. It took place in a grassed courtyard surrounded by high walls and covered by high, criss-crossing, security bars. There were no exercise facilities or weights, as commonly shown in movies about American prisons. If inmates wanted to flex their muscles they were free to do push-ups, sit-ups or to run around the perimeter of the courtyard. Most chose to just lie on their backs and feel the grass beneath them, while they gulped great lungs full of fresh air, watched the clouds float by overhead and imagined themselves also drifting away. Some took off their shoes and pressed their toes into the turf and remembered times long ago.

At the end of the passage the heavy steel cell-block door opened.

"*Baadjie en adres*!*" A warder yelled as he moved down the passage. "Baadjie en adres!"

Oh, Jesus! thought Templeton as a surge of terror rushed through his veins, even though he knew it could not be his turn because his appeal was still to be heard.

Baadjie en adres, the three words that terrified Death Row inmates more than anything else.

Seven days before a condemned prisoner was due to be executed he was told to put out his spare clothes and possessions and to supply an address where they should be sent after his execution.

When the dreadful call came, all prisoners were required to immediately return to their cells where they were locked in and had to prepare their possessions. Once done the Sheriff visited the cells of those whose execution-date was set and informed them they would be executed in seven days time. No-one knew whose time had come until the Sheriff stopped outside that particular cell door. As soon as the prisoner was informed of his fate he was handcuffed and moved to a group of cells known as the 'Pot' situated in a separate area, right by the entrance to the gallows.

Baadjie and adres prisoners were kept locked in their cells until they took the final trip to the scaffold but that did not prevent them from having loud conversations through the metal grille of their cell doors.

Most still clung to the belief they would somehow still be reprieved and many believed an often proclaimed myth that prisoners were not really hanged but were sent to work as slaves in a great mine located deep beneath the prison. With nothing to live for, they still hung onto life.

Templeton sat in his locked cell with his head in his hands, his palms tightly clamped over his ears. Though he knew it was not him, he still wanted to block out the voice of the Sheriff and the groans of disbelief and horror from those to whom he had brought the bad news.

Two weeks ago the Govender brothers and three others were moved to the Pot and a week later dispatched. There were no formal goodbyes. The condemned inmate was immediately taken from his cell, while the others remained locked in theirs, and marched down the passage to the Pot. As they walked down the long corridor messages were sometimes yelled but there was not time for anything more. The prison authorities wanted them out of there as quickly as possible, to avoid escalating the already high stress levels.

Today they stopped at six cells including that of Clubber.

“Take care of yourself, Policeman,” called Clubber as he passed Templeton's cell.

"You too!" called back Templeton.
He didn't know what else to say.

* *Baadjie en adres – Jacket and address*

Chapter 61

Christmas was a time when the mood on Death Row lifts. A kind of calm falls over the place.

The courts were closed, the Sheriff stopped calling around and the Pot was empty. Every inmate knew he would be alive until at least the middle of January and they felt almost as though they've been given a reprieve. For about six weeks there were no executions, there was no night time singing and prisoners finally got some hours of continuous sleep.

But it was also a sad time because they were most acutely aware of being separated from their families and the spectre of what lay ahead, still hung heavily over them. Most did their best to wake up each day and focus just on the fact that they were still alive.

As Christmas approached Templeton's spirits lifted considerably. Clubber's execution had hit him hard and he lapsed into a dark mood.

How strange life on Death Row is, he thought. Clubber is the last person in the world I would ever imagine would become a friend.

A few days before he was called Baadjies en adres, Clubber told Templeton he really was truly sorry for the things he had done. He hadn't got religion or anything like that but he wanted to write to the families of his victims and tell them he was sorry.

“I'm not trying to work an angle here,” he said. “The truth is, from the day I was born I knew my life would probably end this way, if I wasn't shot before. But writing letters and apologising is just something I think I should do.”

Templeton wondered if he did indeed write those letters while he was in the Pot.

“I don't feel that confident about the appeal any more,”

he told Pat Naidoo, one afternoon in December. "Since I have been in here I have not seen a single appeal succeed but I have seen 33 men go to the Pot and never return."

"Each of their situations was completely different to yours," said Naidoo. "I am very confident your appeal will be successful."

Templeton wondered why he used the word 'confident' rather 'sure' as he'd always said in the past but he said nothing.

"Do we have an appeal date yet?" he asked.

"Yes, I got confirmation yesterday. It is set down for the third week in February."

Templeton nodded while he did mental calculations.

"Good." He offered a cigarette to the Indian advocate who shook his head in refusal. "At least I know I'll be alive until March, maybe even April or May."

Chapter 62

"Eric and Marie have gone on holiday to the seaside," said Ellen during a visit a week before Christmas. "They invited Thandi and me but I didn't want to go, I wanted to be with you and I didn't want to upset Thandi's routine, as she seems to be coping a bit better nowadays."

She held her nose close to the glass panel and he touched it through the barrier that separated them. She had aged since the start of this bad business but he still regarded her as the most exquisite creature he'd ever set eyes upon.

"You should have gone. You both need a holiday."

"I wanted to be with you over Christmas."

"Thank you," he said softly. He still could not completely conceive the extent of her dedication and love.

"Eric says news has filtered through from a source in Botswana that Roger was seen in Gaborone.

He sighed in relief. At last news about his son – and he was safe!

"Tell Eric to somehow get news to him that he must not come back. If he does and gets caught," he paused and used his right hand in a sweeping gesture around the room, "if he gets caught all of this will have been for nothing."

Chapter 63

The prison cooks outdid themselves on Christmas Day. They sent fifteen large fruit cakes to Death Row. In addition lunch consisted of roast chicken, roast potatoes, rice and vegetables, followed by jelly and custard.

Some of the food was supplied by the Department of Correctional Services, the rest was bought by warders with money given to them by the inmates and their families.

Although completely contrary to regulations, the section Head Warder, Piet van Zyl allowed the inmates to decorate their cells - just for that day - with pictures from newspapers and magazines.

One prisoner made Christmas hats from sheets of newspaper. Many, including Templeton, had visits from family members that morning and, before lunch was served, Joe Koertzen delivered a religious message.

They drank Fanta Grape®, toasted each other, their families and the reprieves they said would be granted in the new year.

Some even, almost believed it would happen.

Chapter 64

Early in February, Joubert came to visit Templeton. He had wanted to come and see him before but somehow could not pluck up the courage, as he was not sure what he would say to his colleague. He hoped Templeton would understand and judge him by his kindness to Ellen.

They sat in the Visitors' Room and spoke through the metal, speaking-tube, separated by the glass partition.

Joubert had a lump in his throat when he saw his former partner for the first time since the trial.

"You're looking good," he said, trying to keep his voice light. "You've lost weight and it suits you."

Why does everyone begin a conversation with a comment about my weight? thought Templeton.

Templeton pulled the front of his green prison shirt forward to show Joubert just how baggy it was.

"Yes I have," he said. "It's the first time in ten years. I can highly recommend this place for anyone who wants to shed a few pounds but, as health spas go, the recreation facilities leave a lot to be desired."

Joubert smiled wryly.

"I suppose they want to avoid hanging fat people in case they break the rope," said Templeton.

The atmosphere was strained. Neither really knew what to say to the other. Secretly they both wished this meeting was not taking place at all.

Templeton was uneasy because he knew, if Eric had been the first through the door of the house in Phaka street, it would have been him whom he shot and killed. But at the same time this was the man who, despite that, showed Templeton's wife incredible support and kindness.

The Afrikaner had always been a mystery to Ngubane. He seemed to believe he was somehow superior to all non-Afrikaners in the country and readily enforced his authority with unspeakable brutality. Yet, on the other hand, he was capable of surprising acts of kindness.

Templeton had heard tales of Afrikaner farmers driving great distances in the middle of the night to get a sick, black child to a doctor or a hospital but then just a few weeks later giving that same child a severe thrashing when he was caught stealing chickens. That was the paradox of South Africa, he guessed.

But, one thing a black man could always be sure of was, he would always know where he stood with an Afrikaner.

Joubert was ill at ease. What does someone say to a friend sitting in the shadow of the gallows? You want to keep the conversation light and cheerful but, at the same time, you don't want to appear frivolous.

"How are things going at work?" asked Templeton, trying to restart the conversation after an awkward pause.

"Fine," the guys are all pulling for you," said Joubert, looking down at his hands.

"Good. Tell them I say thanks very much." He knew Joubert was lying. His former colleagues, especially the white policemen, believed Templeton betrayed them as well as the organisation they served.

In addition, he had killed one of their own. In general, most believed he deserved the rope.

The conversation ended abruptly again. Joubert drummed his slim fingers on the counter-top, not knowing what to say next.

Fuck! I wish I could just go, he thought. I knew this was going to be a mistake.

"What's the food like?" he asked.

"It's okay."

More silence except for the drumming of Joubert's fingers.

Templeton started to speak but had to clear his throat first.

"Jooba, let's clear the air and get this out in the open. I

know you do not approve of what I did but the fact is I did it and, faced with the same situation, would do it again. I had no choice but to save my son."

Joubert swallowed. Suddenly all the anger and resentment he had managed to keep bottled up for so long came bubbling out. His voice was cold.

"Yes!...and if I had been the first through that door you would have deprived my family of a father and husband! As it was, you took a son and brother away from another family. What gave you the right to play God?"

When he took a packet of cigarettes from his shirt pocket his hands were trembling.

"You could have handled it some other way!"

"I know," said Templeton. "You are absolutely right and I cannot even begin to tell you how sorry I am. All I could think of that moment was to save Roger. I don't expect you to forgive me, all I ask is you try to understand."

Joubert lit his cigarette and, with his hand still shaking, took a draw on it. He held the smoke in his lungs while he sat with his eyes closed. After a few moments he exhaled and felt a bit calmer.

"There are times when I look at my daughter and my wife and think, what would have become of them if I was the first through the door. You cannot believe how angry and sad it makes me.

"But what probably hurts more, is the fact that you would have shot me...after all we've been through together."

Templeton hung his head.

"I am ashamed," he said. "All I can do is beg that you may one day find it in your heart to forgive me."

Joubert slammed his fist down onto the counter-top. He stood up abruptly and began pacing around the room with his right hand on the back of his head.

"Jesus!" he said, "what a fuck up this is."

"I'm sorry, Jooba. I wish I could change this but I can't and I will die with this regret. All I can do is thank you for being such a good friend and for all you have done for my family.

"I can only imagine what it has already cost you and the price you will pay for your kindness in the future."

Joubert sat down again but avoided eye-contact with Templeton. Ngubane was right. He was paying a price. At work no-one said anything but he knew many people believed his association and support of Templeton had left him contaminated. Any prospect of promotion was now dead and buried. Long memories lurked in the corridors of power at the SAP. (South African Police)

When he looked at Ngubane he nodded. Yes, he would pay the price but he figured he owed Templeton. He was thinking about the time Templeton saved his life.

"I now consider my debt fully settled," he said. He stubbed out his cigarette in the stainless steel ashtray that was bolted to the counter-top, got up and walked out without looking back.

Chapter 65

Templeton was playing poker in his cell with a new inmate when Joe Koertzen appeared in the doorway.

The mood on Death Row was once again grim. It was the third week in February and the hangings were back in full swing. Just that week, seven guests of the Pot completed their appointment with Chris Barnard, a Warrant Officer in the police, who moonlighted as a hangman. *Oom** Barries, as he was known to the warders, personally saw off around 1 500 people on their journey to the other side.

When Koertzen arrived, Templeton was well ahead in his poker game – something that surprised him as his mind was elsewhere. Today was the last day of his appeal hearing and his stomach felt as though he had swallowed a handful of hot coals.

He was on edge, angry, frustrated and scared, all at the same time.

In Bloemfontein, at the Supreme Court of Appeals, a bunch of old white men were going over the evidence of his case and deciding whether he lived or died and there was not a thing he could do to influence their decision.

"There's a visitor for you," said Koertzen.

"Who is it?" Templeton asked, as he folded his hand and tossed it onto the bed.

"It's your advocate."

Templeton's heart skipped a beat. Naidoo must have flown back from Bloemfontein. That must mean it's good news.

"Let's go," he said, following Koertzen down the passageway. The nearer he got to the interview room, the more nervous and excited he became.

Oh, Dear God, please let it be good news! he prayed silently.

Koertzen unlocked a grey steel door using one of the

keys from the bunch that hung on his belt. He let Templeton enter then locked the door behind him, leaving him alone in the room with his advocate.

Like the rest of the prison cell-block it was painted in battleship grey but, as it also served as a place where ecclesiastics sometimes counselled inmates, there were some religious posters pasted on one of the walls.

There were three tables and some chairs in the room. On the table furthest from the door lay Naidoo's open, burgundy, leather briefcase. The advocate sat on the corner of one of the other tables.

He stood up as Templeton approached.

“Well?” asked Templeton but he did not really need an answer, Naidoo's expression said it all.

He shook his head, his lips tightly clenched.

“I'm sorry Templeton,” he said in a grave voice, “we lost, they turned us down.”

Ngubane sank down on to one of the chairs.

“How is that possible? You said we would win on appeal.” His voice was remarkably level and emotionless.

“I truly believed we would but I think some important people are determined to throw you to the wolves. They want to send a message.” Naidoo's voice was deflated. This was a long, hard, fight that he really thought he would win but it appeared powerful forces had stacked the decks against them.

Templeton's head spun. So this was it. After 17 years of faithful service he would be sacrificed because it was good politics? Unfucking believable!

In a strange way he was relieved. The waiting and hoping and not knowing was sometimes more than he could bear.

“What's next?” he asked.

“We can petition the State President for clemency.” Naidoo sighed. “But I must be honest, Templeton, after today, I doubt we will be successful. The call for your head has come from far up the ladder.”

Templeton stood up, walked to the door and banged on it.

"Do it if you want to," he said. "I'm done with this."

"Don't lose heart, there is still hope."

"Yeah, right!" said Templeton as Koertzen opened the door so he could return to his cell.

* *Oom – Uncle*

Chapter 66

Time passes very quickly when you don't have much of it left.

"When?" asked Templeton, as he followed Joe Koertzen back to his cell.

It was a question the warder had been asked many times yet he still did not know how to answer it properly.

You'd think by now...he thought.

"I honestly don't know," he said, shrugging his shoulders. "A month, six months, a year, I don't know. The decision is made by the Department of Justice. Maybe they'll just keep you here and use you as a bargaining chip somewhere down the road."

Templeton was silent as they walked down the passage, past the cells. He considered his lot with a sense of profound resignation.

There comes a time when every man must die, he thought. The only thing different for me, is I have an idea when my time will be.

Chapter 67

Ellen tried really hard to maintain a brave face but she just couldn't. No matter how hard she tried she still wept every time she saw Templeton.

She prayed every night that somehow God would perform a miracle and save her husband.

Through her church, Marie Joubert arranged for a social worker to call on Ellen in an effort to help her come to terms with her situation.

"All he did was try to save my son," she said over and over, during one of the social worker's visits.

"Surely they shouldn't kill him for being a good father."

"But my dear," said the social worker, a small bird-like woman who was much more comfortable dealing with the problems of the aged and destitute, "he killed another man and under the law he will have to pay for that."

"Are you a mother?" Ellen suddenly asked.

"Yes."

"Would you not have done the same for your child?"

The social worker did not answer.

Chapter 68

"We just have to be strong and keep believing the petition to the State President will be successful," said Ellen. The speaking-tube seemed to be distorting their words today. "We can't give up believing. That's all we have and I am told P.W. Botha is a regular church-goer and is a merciful man.

"We must cling to hope!"

Her eyes were moist and bloodshot but she was all cried out now. The tears had flowed freely on the drive from Johannesburg. So much so that, at one point, she had to pull off the road. But as she pulled into the visitor's parking area at Pretoria Central Prison she dried her eyes and resolved to be strong for Templeton's sake. She was determined not to make this any more difficult than it already was.

A warder she did not know and assumed must be new, sat lounging in a white plastic chair, arms folded across his chest and turned slightly away from them, so as to give them a small measure of privacy.

"Did you speak to Naidoo, today?" he asked.

She nodded.

"Did he say anything about the petition?"

She cleared her throat before she spoke into the tube. "It was sent yesterday with a letter from Eric pleading your case. It's too early to know anything. Naidoo says it will be a week or two before we know."

She sat back and examined her husband through the armoured glass. He appeared stronger – both physically and emotionally – than the last time she saw him and she told him so.

"I guess I have resigned myself to the fact there are some things I cannot change and I just have to accept that," he said.

"I've made peace both with my conscience and my maker – whoever that might be. If I can die and still appear honourable in the eyes of my children then I will have achieved more than many men."

"Don't speak like that!" she said, sharply. "We have to keep believing. We have to believe everything will be okay!"

He sighed. She too had lost weight since the trial and the strain had taken its toll. Her eyes appeared constantly tired and the sparkle that was once there was gone. It looked as though ten years had been added to her age but to him, she was still beautiful.

"Ellen," he said softly, his voice soft as a cool summer breeze, "we don't have enough time left to continue pretending."

How he wanted to take her hand in his and hold it against his cheek. He felt a prickle of frustration scratch at the back of his neck but he quickly suppressed it. His life was too short to waste time on useless emotions.

"Everything is in order. I have drawn up a will that has been sent to Naidoo. There won't be any payout from the insurance policies – not if death is at the hands of the judicial authorities. But my pension fund contributions with some interest will be refunded – after seventeen years that should be worth something. I'm sorry, I wish I could have done more."

All her resolve crumbled and tears streamed down her face. She sobbed softly into a white handkerchief that she held to her face.

Templeton continued, speaking quickly as he feared, he too might be overcome by emotion.

"I want you and Thandi to return to Kwa Zulu – Natal or the Transkei. I feel very strongly that you get back to our roots. Give her back the values we seem to have lost."

He looked away and swallowed hard before removing a handkerchief from his pocket and loudly blowing his nose.

At the sound the warder looked up but immediately turned away again.

Templeton clenched his teeth. Today, more than ever he needed to be strong and leave her with a lasting impression of his strength and dignity.

When he had gathered himself, he continued.

"It has been the greatest privilege and joy in my life to be married to you and to be the father of your children. My only regret is that it was not longer."

He turned away so she would not see the quivering of his bottom lip.

Chapter 69

Louis le Grange, Minister of Law and Order, was at his desk in his study at his home in the Parliamentary compound, Bryntirion in Pretoria, when the telephone rang. Situated in a closed community, adjacent to the Union Buildings, Bryntirion was where Cabinet Ministers and senior officials, with homes in Cape Town, lived when Parliament was not in session.

In a strange historical quirk, South Africa had three capitals, Cape Town, the Administrative Capital, Bloemfontein, the Judicial Capital and Pretoria the Executive Capital. While some parliamentarians kept homes of their own in each city, many chose to own property in only one of the capitals or in other towns and to make use of assigned, government housing, when working away from their own homes.

Although Parliament was still in session, Le Grange was in Pretoria to attend meetings with the Commissioner of Police and other senior generals.

Le Grange's study boasted an impressive personal library and an equally imposing collection of hunting trophies that the tall, ramrod-straight, minister had harvested over the years.

On the floor, in front of an exquisite, dark wood, writing desk, was a beautifully tanned zebra skin.

In front of the desk were two, expensive, maroon, leather, wing-back chairs and an equally elegant chair on the other side of the desk.

Le Grange sat in one of the wing-back chairs, with a fine scotch in a crystal glass, topped with ice that was placed on a finely-carved, wooden, side table beside him. He was reading the evening newspaper, when the telephone rang.

He put down the newspaper, straightened his silk,

paisley, dressing gown and stretched out his long, pyjama-covered legs in front of him. On his feet he wore a handmade pair of brown, leather, Italian slippers.

"Le Grange," he spoke into the mouthpiece.

"Louis, it's PW. Sorry to call you so late but I'm still at the office and want to finalise a few things tonight."

When the phone rang Le Grange had a feeling it may be the State President – Botha was the most likely person to call in the evenings."

"No problem at all, Mr President. What can I do for you?"

"I have a petition for clemency here for one of your chaps...Ngubane...are you familiar with the case?"

"Yes, Mr President. I have been keeping a close eye on it and am completely up to date on it."

"Good," said Botha. He spoke from his office in Cape Town.

"I was wondering what you think I should do about this."

Le Grange took a sip of whisky and ran his fingertips over his immaculately-clipped, thin moustache, while he considered his response."

"I don't think he deserves clemency, Sir," he said. "He killed another policeman in cold-blood and did nothing to arrest known ANC members. If any crime, deserves the death sentence, this is it."

Botha was silent for a few moments.

"But what about the mitigating factors and his years of service in the police?"

"None of that is relevant, Mr President. The evidence is rock-solid and he confessed to the murder. If we don't see this through, the Government and the National Party will be seen as weak and who knows where that will lead. At times like this we have to be unshakeably firm."

On the other end of the telephone line Botha cleared his throat.

"So your recommendation is that I do not grant a reprieve. Is that right."

"Absolutely," replied Le Grange. "In my opinion it would be the wrong thing to do."

"Thank you, Louis. I appreciate your input and your time. Once again, I apologise for telephoning you this late. Good bye."

The line clicked and went dead before Le Grange could say anything else.

Chapter 70

"Baadjies en adres! Baadjies en adres!"

The Head Warder, Piet van Zyl rattled his bunch of keys against the security bars at the bottom of the passage. With him was the Sheriff with a clipboard under his arm. All down the corridors inmates returned to their cells. A few minutes later warders began locking them in.

Templeton lay on his bed on his back with his forearm over his tightly shut eyes. His clothes were neatly folded and his possessions packed at the bottom of his bed. On top of the spare, green prison shirt was a sheet of paper with Ellen's address written in his neat, school-teacher, hand-writing.

He'd written it five baadjie en adres occasions earlier, but each time the Sheriff and Piet van Zyl had passed by his cell.

As he lay there he tried hard to think of his family and happy times but he was too focused on listening for the rattle of a key in the cell door.

Somewhere down the passage he heard a key being inserted into a steel door and the squeak of it's opening followed by the voice of the Sheriff.

Then he heard it again. Nearer this time and an anguished cry after the door was opened. He heard the grating, double metallic snick of fastening handcuffs.

And then he heard footsteps.

One, two, three, four, five...oh thank God they were going past. But they weren't.

A key slid into the key-hole of his cell door. As the door was pulled open it sucked air out of the cell as though drawing the last bit of hope with it.

"I'm sorry, Ngubane," said van Zyl.

Templeton stood up and turned around with his hands behind his back so that he could be cuffed.

Once secured he turned around to face the Sheriff. Strangely he felt no fear at that moment. It was as though he had somehow stepped out of his physical body and was now dispassionately looking down at the proceedings as an interested observer.

Somewhere, in the far distance of his consciousness, he could hear a voice that he thought must be talking to him.

"...in accordance with the ruling...Rand Supreme Court...sentenced to death...accordingly the sentence will be carried out in seven days time on April 27..."

It was all so unreal, like watching a movie in a smoke-filled room with cotton-wool jammed in his ears.

Mentally reeling and still in a daze, Templeton was led down the passage past the last of the Death Row cells where a door, made of heavy steel bars, was first unlocked and then locked behind them.

A little way on they took Templeton into a room with a table against a wall and a single chair by it. In the centre of the room was a scale – like those found in pharmacy clinics or used to weigh in boxers with beam-balances on which the measuring weights were adjusted. Bolted to the wall, beside the table, was a wooden measuring-rule that measured to a height of 2.1 metres or seven foot in the old language

"Stand on the scale please," said the Sheriff.

Still not even really aware of what was happening, Templeton stepped onto the scale and the Sheriff slid the weights along the beam until it balanced. He noted Templeton's weight and jotted it down on a form attached to a clip board.

Then he measured Templeton's neck and noted that as well.

"Stand by the measuring stick, please."

Templeton stood against it and the Sheriff noted his height and signed the form before putting it at the bottom of the other forms on the clipboard. Now it was up to Oom

Barries to work out the final details and how long the rope would need to be but, from his experience, the Sheriff figured the drop would be around twelve feet, a fraction under 3,5 metres.

With the paper-work completed Piet van Zyl led Templeton to his new cell in the Pot. It was equipped in exactly the same manner as his previous cell.

He removed the handcuffs and Templeton flopped down onto the bed on his back and covered his face with this arms.

"I'm sorry, Ngubane," was all van Zyl said as he closed and locked the cell door.

Chapter 71

"I don't want you to come back," said Templeton to Ellen. They faced each other through the armoured glass of a much smaller visitors' room that was used only by inmates of the Pot.

"I don't think I could bear the pain of seeing you again."

The room was permeated with an atmosphere of sadness and hopelessness that seemed to be embedded like grime on the walls and ceiling. It overwhelmed visitors and inmates like an oily mist.

It was the saddest room in the country, a room where all hope was abandoned and where people said goodbye forever.

"Why, Temp?"

"I need time to prepare myself. I need to be able to die with dignity and seeing you, when I know I will never touch you again and seeing the anguish in your eyes, is more than I can bear. Every time I see you it intensifies the agony."

Ellen wept softly.

"Do not cry for me, my Darling," he said, pressing the palm of his hand firmly against the glass. "It'll soon be over and what is over is over. Look at me."

She looked up and looked into his eyes.

"I cannot stand the thought of leaving you but I am not afraid to die. Over the past few days I have spoken at length with Joe Koertzen about death and he has given me new perspective. I now believe death is simply a frightening journey to a new life. Like an unborn baby that must face the pain of a mother's contractions and the terror of leaving a warm, safe, familiar place, to pass into a new and unknown world via the horrifying experience of birth. The baby can have no idea of what is on the other side yet, once it has gone through the experience of birth, it finds itself in the loving arms of a mother, with possibilities and experiences beyond the capabilities of it's imagination.

"I truly, with my whole heart, believe we will meet again."

She nodded.

"So do I."

Chapter 72

Ellen ate almost no supper that night. The mood at the dinner-table was sombre. Little was said and those who were able to eat, picked at their food.

Both Ellen and Templeton's parents were with her, as was Thandi.

At dinner she pushed the food around her plate but, after two bites, she could eat no more.

“Why aren't you eating, Mama?” asked Thandi.

She smiled weakly at her daughter.

“I'm just not hungry, Sweetheart.”

“Is it because you are sad?”

Ellen clenched her teeth and nodded as tears glazed her eyes.

The little girl leapt down from her chair, jumped onto Ellen's lap and wrapped her arms around her mother's neck.

“Don't be sad, Mama. You always tell me everything will be okay.”

She held her daughter tightly against her and could feel her tiny heart beating against hers. She fought to control her emotions.

At the table everyone stopped eating. Ellen wiped her building tears and dabbed her eyes.

“Sweetheart I am sad because we haven't been able to save Papa and in a short while he is going to be with Jesus.” She held the little girl close to her again and her voice was soft as a mother's breath.

Thandi trembled and began to cry softly.

“Do you understand?” Ellen asked.

Thandi looked at her mother through her tears.

She nodded.

“Like Martha is with Jesus after the bad men threw her in the fire when they burned our house down?”

"Yes, like Martha. And when Papa gets to heaven tomorrow you can be sure the first thing he will do is find Martha and keep her safe so you'll have her when we one day get to heaven and see Papa again.

"And another thing I want you to know is, Papa will always be watching you. Although you won't be able to see him, he'll always be right there with you. You'll know he's there."

She held her daughter's face between her soft hands.

"Papa can't be with you now because they have him locked up. But when he's with Jesus, he'll be able to be with you all the time."

"I understand," the little girl answered softly. "I just wish I could have given him a big hug and kiss before he left."

Chapter 73

"It's time, " said Piet van Zyl to Templeton. "I am sorry but there has been no response to the application for a stay of execution."

Templeton sat on his bed. He nodded without saying anything. He hadn't slept at all because the singing of the other inmates had gone on unceasingly and, at times, he too joined in.

Although he took comfort and believed (or thought he did) all that Joe Koertzen had said about being reborn into a new, better after-life, he was still afraid. What if those were just the desperate thoughts of a man trying to find an imagined prick of light where, in truth, there was only darkness?

What if it was all a big lie?

The singing continued, louder now than at any time during the night.

He stood up, turned around and placed his hands behind his back so that Koertzen could cuff him. Two days earlier he asked that Joe Koertzen escort him to the gallows.

On the bed he had neatly placed his final, meagre possessions in a cardboard box. On top, written on a sheet of prison-issued note-paper that was now folded in half was a letter to his family.

My darling Wife, brave Son and beautiful Daughter

I love you more than life itself. I always have and even after I have gone, I still will.

We will meet again. Somewhere. I don't know when, where or how but I know it will happen.

Do not grieve for me. I have had a life that was full and complete because you were in it. Focus only on the good times we had together – and there were many. My greatest wish for you is that you embrace life, live it and enjoy it, for none of us knows how much time we have left. Have no regrets and be happy.

I love you.

Templeton.

When he stepped out of his cell, led by Koertzen, four other men stood similarly handcuffed, each with his own escort.

van Zyl and the Sheriff were waiting. When all five were lined up, the Head Warder nodded and the line of dead men walking shuffled the few metres down the passage and through the steel door that led to the steps of the gallows. As he passed the last cell Templeton looked through the grate on the door and caught a momentary glimpse of a thin, elderly, white man, curled up on his bed in the foetal position, with his hands tightly pressed over his ears and his eyes scrunched shut.

The door slammed shut behind them with a woosh that seemed to suck the last bit of their existence from the cells. They were led into a small room with a blackened desk against one of the walls. On it was an inked finger-printing pad, finger-print cards and five files. Beside the desk stood a finger-print technician.

With their hands still cuffed behind their backs, the technician inked each man's right thumb and took a print. Then, using a magnifying glass, he matched each print against a print already in the prisoner's file.

When he was done he signed each card and nodded to van Zyl.

"Thank you," said van Zyl.

That was the signal for the escorts to lead the men to the prayer room situated next door.

They sat next to each other on a wooden bench with their backs against a wall painted in apple-green enamel paint.

Koertzen glanced at his watch. 6 40 am. Right on time. A white church minister, dressed in black robes with a purple, satin sash hanging loosely around the back of his neck and draped down the front of his robe, waited until the men were seated.

"All we like sheep have gone astray but blessed are they that repent in the sight of the Lord and beg his mercy," said the Padre. "God is a vengeful God but He is also loving and forgiving. If you truly are sorry He will forgive you and, even though you are worthless sinners, His grace will be sufficient that you will enter His kingdom and enjoy everlasting life."

He paused while he cast his gaze over each of the seated men.

"Brothers, there is little time left. Repent, I beg you! So that your sins may be washed away and that you may have life-eternal."

The prisoners said nothing.

"Let us pray then," said the minister, resigned to the probability that their souls would not be saved. He closed his eyes, turned his face heavenwards and spread out his arms like an eagle.

"Oh gracious, loving and merciful Father, I bring before You these wretched sinners and beseech that You will envelope them in Your infinite wisdom." His voice was clear and strong.

"Forgive them Oh great Lord and give their souls rest."

He took a deep breath but before he could continue van Zyl touched him on the shoulder and pointed to his watch when he opened his eyes.

"Amen."

Templeton could feel the man sitting beside him on his right begin to tremble violently. The tremors caused a wave of terror to sweep over him.

"Stand up please," said the Sheriff to the still-seated men. They stood up compliantly. It was as though all life had already left them.

In his hand the Sheriff had a clipboard with a sheet of paper that listed the order in which the men would line up on the gallows because each length of rope was individually prepared. Templeton stood at position number three in the line.

6 50 am. Right on schedule!

When the proper order was achieved, each escort drew a white cotton hood from his pocket and placed it over the prisoner's head. The front of the hood had a long material flap that could be rolled back and draped over the back of the head, allowing the prisoner's face to be visible. Once the face-flaps were rolled back, van Zyl nodded and the condemned men and their escorts began the 52-step climb to the gallows.

Templeton gasped for air. For a moment his legs buckled and he thought he would collapse but Koertzen kept a firm grip on his arm.

At the top of the stairs they entered the death chamber.

In the centre of the room was a thick steel scaffold situated over two hydraulically operated steel trapdoors, each of which weighed three quarters of a ton. From the scaffold hung seven hessian ropes, at the end of which was a metal ring that allowed a loop to be made, in much the same way as a dog's choke chain. Unlike in the movies, there was no giant knot.

The trapdoors were straddled by seven sets of painted white footprints, all facing away from the door and, on each side, was a stout, wooden guard-rail. At the end of the right hand-side guard rail was a large lever that protruded from an enclosure in the floor and reached up to a little over waist-height. In a corner against the far wall was a table and on it was an old Bakelite telephone that would ring, if a last-minute stay of execution was granted. Above it was a large, wall-mounted electric clock.

Standing to one side, checking his notes was Oom Barries.

The escorts formed the five men into a line at the edge of the entrance onto trapdoors and the Sheriff checked that each man matched his file photograph.

"All correct," he said, before signing a form attached to his clipboard. He nodded to Oom Barries.

The escorts, moving in such a way that they stood behind the left hand guard-rail, led the condemned men onto the trapdoors and positioned their feet on the painted footprints. Starting at the back, with prisoner number one and operating from behind the guard-rail on the right, Oom Barries placed the noose over the prisoner's head and pulled it up tight under his chin. As soon as this was done the prisoner's escort pulled the hood face-flap down to cover his eyes.

Templeton stared straight ahead as he heard the hangman tighten the noose around the neck of prisoner number two and the soft rustle of the hood being lowered. One of the men ahead of him began to say the Lord's Prayer.

Then Oom Barries was beside him. He closed his eyes as the noose went over his head and was strangely aware of how cold the steel ring felt as as it was pulled up under his chin. He began to tremble violently as Koertzen lowered the face-flap on his hood.

"Courage," whispered Koertzen and he squeezed Templeton's shoulder tightly with his right hand.

"For thine is the kingdom," prayed the prisoner in front of him.

They were the last words Templeton Ngubane, husband, father and faithful policeman heard before he fell eleven and a half feet and his neck snapped.

When the face-flap on the hood of the last prisoner was lowered, Oom Barries pulled the lever and sent five men to their graves. It was said it took only 18 seconds from the time they stepped onto the trapdoors for Oom Barries to hang seven men. He was the best in the business.

Koertzen looked down at the five men twitching on the end of the ropes then he looked at the clock. 7 03 am on the 27th day of April.

Chapter 74

There was a row of gumtrees that lined the right hand-side of Potgieter Street, the multi-laned road that ran past Pretoria Central Prison. Just a block away was the old Defence Force Headquarters building and, on the next corner, a recruiting centre for the South African Air Force.

Seven o'clock in the morning was not yet peak-hour but traffic was nonetheless fairly heavy as Potgieter Street is one of Pretoria's main feeder roads.

A yellow, Nissan Skyline had been parked under the trees, opposite the prison entrance from before six o'clock. No-one took any notice of it or its occupant.

Not even when the thin, blue-black-haired man got out of the car at a quarter to seven and stood with his hands clasped behind his back and his face turned towards the early morning sun.

He stood, straining to hear singing from within the prison walls but could hear nothing other than the roar of cars and buses, as commuters made their way to work for just another ordinary day in their lives.

At exactly seven o'clock his electronic watch beeped and he lowered his head and, if anyone had taken the time to look, they would have seen his lips moving silently. He stood quietly like that for a few minutes with his head bowed.

At 7 02 he looked up, stood to attention and saluted. Then he turned his face towards the sun again and cocked his head so that he could better hear.

“I can hear them singing now,” he said out loud.

“Templeton! I can hear the singing of angels,” he screamed at the traffic.

It was 7 03 am.

Five minutes later Eric Joubert started the Nissan Skyline®, put it into gear and edged towards the road. If his vision had not been so blurred by the tears that filled his eyes, he would probably have seen the tall, handsome, young, black man, who looked uncannily like his former partner, standing on the opposite pavement.

As he turned onto the road he could have sworn he saw Roger Ngubane, but then he was swallowed up in the traffic and, when he looked back, the youngster was gone.

The End.

Hillbrow Heights Immorality

This book is a work of fiction and any resemblance to persons, living or dead, or places, events or locales is purely coincidental. The characters are productions of the author's imagination and used fictitiously.

Chapter 1

Miems was not sure, as she stood on the pavement looking up at the white, two-story building. If they decided to take it, this would be the first apartment they had lived in since the twins were born.

She wasn't sure they'd adapt as, aside from six weeks in a poky, horrible, police apartment in Pretoria, just after they'd got married, they always lived in a house. Many of the houses were terrible - little better than those blacks lived in - but there was always a yard where they could keep a dog, have a barbecue and see the sky.

There were many houses during the course of their nineteen year-long marriage, but whenever she thought they were finally settled, and she'd turned the house into a home, they were forced to pack up and move again. It seemed she never got to make friends or put down roots.

Miems sighed. It was the lot of a policeman's wife and family.

Perhaps the only good thing was she knew how to pack and unpack an entire household in a day.

Maybe I should open a moving business, she thought and a wry smile crossed her face.

"What do you think?"

Her husband's question interrupted her thoughts.

"It seems very loud," she said, as a large delivery truck engaged low gear and belching plumes of oily, blue smoke and shuddering from the effort, struggled up the hill towards where they stood, .

Danie van Staden frowned. He was hot and the Johannesburg sun caused beads of perspiration to form on the bald patch on the top of his head. His armpits were sticky. He rubbed his graying goatee while he attempted to curb his irritation.

"I meant the building!" he said, snapping at his wife.

"What do you think of the building?"

She paused to examine it again before giving her answer.

Hillbrow Heights looked nice. It was freshly-painted and appeared well-maintained.

Danie also noticed that.

It meant the owners cared for it and were probably strict with the tenants, which was a good thing. He mentally noted that particular observation as a 'positive' he would factor into his decision. He smiled. He was a cop - trained to notice things and think like that.

"It looks nice, I suppose," said Miems. She picked at an imaginary piece of fluff on the jacket of her blue and white slacks suit.

Danie turned to the twins who stood a little way away from their mother. In his left hand he held a scuffed, brown, imitation leather briefcase. His short, dumpy body, round belly that struggled to be contained by his white shirt, and jiggling jowls made him look like the Buddha turned door-to-door insurance salesman.

"What do you to think?" he asked.

The twins were nineteen years, six months and eleven days old, five months and eight days younger than their parent's marriage.

Sias, the boy, a tall, slim-hipped youngster with beautifully manicured finger nails, and who preferred people to call him Butch, was four minutes and forty seven seconds older than his sister Elizabeth, who was equally tall, with a long, pale neck and cascading blond hair.

Butch shrugged. He filed the nails on his left hand with an emery board.

"It's okay," he said, his disinterest obvious.

Danie turned to his daughter, fixed a stare on her and awaited her answer.

"It's close to university so that's good," she said.

"We probably won't be able to have a dog," said Miems.

"That's okay," said Butch.

He was glad. He and his sister did not want a dog. They did not even like dogs, and it was always their job to pick up the animal's shit and to feed the miserable creature. Butch shuddered at the thought.

Danie glanced at his watch. They were right on time for their appointment with the owner of *Hillbrow Heights*.

"Apart from my own flat, this is the only three-bedroomed apartment in the building," explained Brigadier Earl "Buck" Rogers. "The other four are either singles or two-roomers."

He peered at the family through the top portion of his gold-rimmed, bifocal spectacles, twitching his gray, handlebar mustache at the same time.

He would need to question them more before he finally made up his mind they were suitable tenants, but they looked okay. The parents appeared solid and the fact the father was in the police force was a plus - although during his many years in the South African Air Force, he had dealt with members of the South African Police Force whose characters left a lot to be desired.

Still, he reasoned, they were all on the same side.

He examined the youngsters who, he was told, were twins and at university.

He thought the boy looked a bit too much like a girl and disapproved of his long hair, although he knew it was the way kids wore it nowadays.

Nothing the army won't sort out, he thought. Conscription was a wonderful thing for white boys in South Africa.

The girl was beautiful in a scruffy sort of way, but she looked like trouble. The Brigadier did not know why he felt that about her, and would not have been able to articulate his reasons if he were asked. It was a sort of sixth sense he developed during all his years of dealing with thousands of people in the armed forces. There was just something about her and her mannerisms, but he could not put his finger on it.

"There is a basement parking spot for one car? Other vehicles must be parked in the street," said the Brigadier. He removed his glasses and put them into the top pocket of his shirt. He stood straight as a rifle cleaning-rod, his slender build making him appear even taller than his 6' 5".

"Do you have a car?"

Danie nodded.

"Yes. We only have one car."

He felt even more short and stout when he compared himself with the retired airman.

"We are renting a house in the suburbs at the moment, but because we only have one car that I must use, Miems and the twins find getting around difficult at times." Although his English was good, he spoke with a thick Afrikaans accent.

"Sometimes the buses are unreliable and then I get called to fetch and carry the family."

He cleared his throat.

"It's not that I mind or anything, it's just, in my job, I never know where I am going to be."

He wiped his forehead with a white handkerchief.

"What exactly do you do in the police force?" asked the Brigadier.

"I am a sergeant in the Vice Squad," said Danie. "I am based in Hillbrow."

Brigadier Earl "Buck" Rogers had heard of the Vice Squad, but was not sure what it did. The truth was, he believed the activities of the S.A. police were akin to arranging the deck chairs on the sinking Titanic, especially in these times, when South Africa faced a build-up of Cuban troops and communist insurgents in Angola, and South West Africa was under threat.

"I'm not sure what the Vice Squad does," he said.

"We enforce the moral values the country needs to survive and prosper," said Danie. He was only a sergeant and felt intimidated and out of his depth with a brigadier, even a retired brigadier... from the air force. He was delighted to have the opportunity to explain how he too made an important contribution to keeping South Africa great, and upholding Christian values.

He saw his daughter look at him and roll her eyes.

"It may be 1976, Missy," he said fixing his gaze upon her and praying the Brigadier had not noticed the look of contempt that flashed across her face, "but there are still some old fashioned values that need to be maintained. The rest of the world is completely messed up, exactly because those traditions were tossed out and ridiculed."

He waved a dismissive hand at her and turned back to the Brigadier.

"The Vice Squad works to keep drugs off the streets and protect our children by locking up the pushers. We also crack down hard on possessors of pornography, prostitutes, strippers and their pimps. We raid massage parlors, where we arrest the clients and the girls and..."

He paused and shuddered as he thought about what he was about to say.

"... and the men who sometimes work there as male prostitutes. It makes me sick to my stomach."

He wiped his forehead with his handkerchief once more.

"We also enforce the **Group Areas Act*, as well as the **Immorality Act*."

The Brigadier pursed his lips and stroked his mustache. Although he hated and opposed the idea of a black person renting and occupying one of his apartments, he believed the country faced more pressing issues, and having policemen sneak around hunting down white people having sex with black people, was just a waste of resources. Not that he would or had ever - even for one second - considered sleeping with a black woman.

"There is a lot of that going on in this area," said Danie. "I think it is why they transferred me to Hillbrow. If we are not vigilant and careful, this country will end up a race of coloreds!"

Elizabeth raised her eyebrows, drew in a breath and opened her mouth to speak, but decided against it and remained silent.

Her actions did not go unnoticed by the Brigadier.

Miems opened the French doors of the lounge and went onto the balcony. The view from the second floor looked down onto a busy, tree-lined street. She thought when the traffic quieted down at night, as she hoped it would, it'd be pleasant to sit there.

She liked the apartment. It was large and airy, built in an era when having enough space to live in was in vogue. It was also convenient.

Hillbrow was close enough to the city center, where she worked for a small firm of attorneys, to allow her to walk to work if there was ever a problem with the bus service. And more buses passed through Hillbrow, more often and more regularly than anywhere else in Johannesburg. It was also within walking distance of the University of the Witwatersrand.

The Hillbrow police station was a couple of blocks away but she doubted Danie would ever walk, though God knew, doing so would help control his weight and be good for his health. But her husband hated exercising.

"Are you the landlord or the real estate agent?" Miems asked.

"The landlord and the owner," replied the Brigadier. "I own the building. I bought it when I retired from the air force. I figured I needed to invest in something that will supplement my pension and produce an income, even after I am gone. I live in Number 4. It's a mirror image of this apartment."

"That's a very good idea," said Miems. "I wish we could

do something like that, I don't know how we are going to survive on Danie's police pension one day."

van Staden flashed his wife an angry look.

"It'll be okay," he said, the irritation in his voice obvious. "When I am promoted to warrant officer, I'll get a healthy bump in salary."

Miems bit her tongue. She'd heard that story for years. It seemed her husband was the only person who failed to realize he would never be promoted. His superiors long ago came to the conclusion Danie van Staden was simply not a leader of men. He was a good foot soldier, someone who performed well in the trenches, and that was where he belonged.

"What are the other residents like?" asked Danie, hoping to change the subject.

"They're mostly young," said the Brigadier. "There is a single mother and her son who is still in primary school, a young married couple in their twenties, a single guy who works for a magazine and an older lady who moved here from England.

The Brigadier glanced at his watch. In a quarter of an hour another family was due to arrive to view the flat.

"I am sorry to push you but I do have someone else coming to check out the apartment in a few minutes."

He removed his spectacles from his shirt pocket and polished them with a soft, white handkerchief.

"Are you interested?" he asked, as usual not prepared to beat about the bush. "If you would like a few moments to discuss it, I'll step outside onto the balcony to give you some privacy."

"Thank you, Brigadier," said Danie. "I would appreciate that."

When the landlord was gone he turned to his wife and the twins.

"What do you think?" he asked.

"I think we should take it," said Miems.

Butch shrugged his shoulders.

"Whatever," said Elizabeth.

As far as she was concerned, this was temporary and the sooner she could get away from her father, the happier she would be.

"That's settled then," said Danie. "This will be our new home."

**Group Areas Act was the title of three acts of the Parliament of South Africa enacted under the apartheid government of South Africa. The acts assigned racial groups to different residential and business sections in urban areas in a system of urban apartheid. An effect of the law was to exclude non-Whites from living in the most developed areas, which were restricted to Whites (e.g., Sea Point). It caused many non-Whites to have to commute large distances from their homes in order to be able to work. The law led to non-Whites being forcibly removed for living in the "wrong" areas. The non-white majority were given much smaller areas (e.g., Tongaat) to live in than the white minority who owned most of the country. Pass Laws required that non-Whites carry pass books, and later 'reference books' (similar to passports) to enter the 'white' parts of the country.*

The first Group Areas Act, the Group Areas Act, 1950 was promulgated on 7 July 1950, and it was implemented over a period of several years. It was amended by Parliament in 1952, 1955 (twice), 1956 and 1957. Later in 1957 it was repealed and re-enacted in consolidated form as the Group Areas Act, 1957, which was amended in 1961, 1962, and 1965. In 1966 this version was in turn repealed and re-enacted as the Group Areas Act, 1966, which was subsequently amended in 1969, 1972, 1974, 1975, 1977, 1978, 1979, 1982, and 1984. It was repealed (along with many other discriminatory laws) on 30 June 1991 by the Abolition of Racially Based Land Measures

Act, 1991. - Source Wikipedia

**Immorality Act - was the title of two acts of the Parliament of South Africa which prohibited, amongst other things, sexual relations between white people and people of other races. The first Immorality Act, of 1927, prohibited sex between whites and blacks, until amended in 1950 to prohibit sex between whites and all non-whites. The second Immorality Act, of 1957, continued this prohibition and also dealt with many other sex offenses. The ban on interracial sex was lifted in 1985, but certain sections of the 1957 act dealing with prostitution remain in force as the "Sexual Offenses Act, 1957".*

Chapter 2

Adrian von Pletzen stood on the pavement outside Hillbrow Heights and looked anxiously up and down the length of the pavement. Despite the afternoon heat, he had on a black nylon tracksuit to hide the tight, black yoga shorts and pale pink vest he wore.

Life was usually tough for an unsure twelve year-old boy, who'd just entered puberty but it was made even more so, because he possessed a mother who hated men and was determined to raise her son in a gender-neutral fashion.

Her outlook on parenting instantly set him up as a target for the other kids in the school, and the regular bullying he endured, came not only at the hands of boys. He was also singled out for attention by groups of girls, who ganged up on him, occasionally beat him up and took pleasure in tipping the contents of his school bag onto the ground.

Adrian loved his mother - at least he thought he did - but sometimes he wished was born into a normal family. On many occasions he tried to speak to her about how he felt but she refused to listen.

"I don't want you to grow up to be like your father," Tamarin von Pletzen told her son. "He is a boorish chauvinist who thinks men are superior. But anyone with half a brain knows it is men who are responsible for the current state of the world and the reason it is so screwed up."

Adrian was not sure what a 'boorish chauvinist' was, but he imagined it was not anything good. His mother never had anything good to say about his father.

Tamarin met and married Adrian's father when she was twenty and working as a typist in the typing pool at Anglo American, the world's largest mining corporation at the time. She wasn't sure why she fell for him, as they could not be more different.

She grew up in a politically liberal family, where her mother, a fervent animal rights activist, dominated her father, a man who preferred to avoid conflict. Buried so deep within Tamarin, even she did not even know it was there, was a withering contempt for her dad's weakness.

Perhaps it was the reason she was attracted to Adrian's father. He was a geologist who breezed through the office from time to time, always dressed in shorts, rugby socks rolled down to the tops of his dusty hiking boots so his powerful, tanned legs were obvious. His face and arms were sunburned and he possessed a rough-and-ready, devil-may-care presence that senior management, in the oak panel-lined corridors of head office, hated, but that set the hearts of the girls in the typing pool fluttering.

They all longed to type his reports so they had the chance to flirt with him.

Tamarin was surprised when he paid her attention. When she compared herself with the other girls working at Anglo American, she believed she was plain and unattractive. So when he asked her out on a date, she accepted but was unsure, shy and terrified.

He took her to a restaurant in Braamfontein where, because she was raised a vegetarian, she ordered a large green salad. Adrian's father ordered a rare steak, leaking watery blood when he cut it, and the sight of it left her feeling queasy.

"Have you never tasted meat," he asked, chewing on a slice of the tender beef.

"No."

"You don't know what you are missing!"

She told him about her mother and her work as an animal rights activist, and how she always said: 'meat is murder!'

Tamarin remembered clearly how he leaned across the

table and placed his hand on hers. She could still clearly recall how masculine his touch felt. His hands were rough from work with a prospecting hammer - so different from those of her father.

"But how will you know?" he asked in a voice soft enough to cause her to lean forward in order to hear him. Their faces were so close she could smell him, and he smelled of danger and freedom.

"Life is too short not to try new things," he said. "Aren't you afraid of dying and never knowing?"

Suddenly he took her face in his hands and kissed her softly on the lips. It was unexpected and thrilling.

"You must grab every opportunity that presents itself," he said, while her heart thumped violently against her ribs.

He was intoxicating. Trouble with a capital 'T' but she didn't care. She tasted meat that night, and though it had a strange texture she liked it.

They went dancing at a nearby club and she found herself completely under his spell. He held her close and stroked her neck. And back at his flat she surrendered her virginity. It was wild and exciting, urgent and rough and she loved it but then hated herself for losing control.

But when he called later the following day, her heart soared and all the promises she made to herself about not seeing him again were forgotten.

Adrian's father changed her life. Her new-found love of juicy beef burgers was surpassed only by the passion they had for each other. Three months later he proposed and she accepted.

Tamarin's mother hated him. Her father wished he could be more like him.

Almost a year after they were married, Adrian was born.

Because of his job, Adrian's father spent long periods away from home, prospecting for new mining opportunities. When he was back he let off steam playing rugby for his school's old boys third team. He dragged Tamarin and the baby to the rugby matches and post-game socializing. She hated it.

The first time he hit her was on a Sunday morning when Adrian was two years old. It was after breakfast during an argument about housework. Adrian was teething. Tamarin was exhausted. She wanted to sleep while Adrian's father swept and cleaned the flat. But he had other plans.

A simple discussion quickly escalated into a full-blown row.

"I work all week!" he yelled. "I'm damned if I'm coming home to do a woman's work on the weekend. That is your job!"

Something snapped in her. She slapped him in the face, as hard as she could.

For a moment everything stopped and time stood still in their kitchen, his face fixed with an expression of shock and surprise. Then his eyes widened with rage and he hit her on the side of her head. The blow sent her tumbling over a table onto the floor, and before she could recover he was at her side. He grabbed her arms, dragging her into the bedroom, where he flung her onto the unmade bed, ripped off her pajama bottoms and raped her to teach her who was boss. Adrian stood in the doorway watching.

Later that day, Tamarin packed her and Adrian's possessions into three large suitcases and left to move in with her parents.

Her mother contacted a lawyer, and divorce proceedings were put in motion. He appeared genuinely sorry for his actions and decided not to contest the divorce. In the end Tamarin got custody of their son, and Adrian's father got the right to have the youngster spend a weekend a month with him, as well as one holiday per year.

In addition, he had to pay maintenance, which he did religiously, never missing a single monthly payment.

A few months after the divorce, Tamarin moved into a two-bedroomed apartment at *Hillbrow Heights*.

She had no option but to leave her job at Anglo American, because Adrian's father still worked for the company, and seeing him there was too awkward.

Tamarin's mother moved in with her for two months to help her daughter get back on her feet while she looked for a new job.

She quickly realized how far her daughter had strayed. Tamarin ate meat and her mother believed her daughter still had feelings for Adrian's father.

"Eating animal flesh is causing your mind to fog," she told Tamarin when she found her quietly sobbing in her bedroom one evening. "You must cleanse yourself of the poison of murder."

They held hands and Tamarin swore no animal products of any sort would pass her or Adrian's lips again.

"Now you must realize and accept all men are shits. Without proper guidance from you, my grandson will grow up to be one too - like his father. It's in his genes but he is young and malleable, you can mold him the way you want."

A while later, they got news Tamarin's father died of a massive heart attack. When neighbors reported a strange smell coming from the house, paramedics broke open the door and found him dressed only in underpants, face-down and dead in a plate of greasy, fried bacon.

Tamarin interpreted it as a sign to remain vigilant. Her mother saw it as an omen she was free to marry a rich cattle farmer in Natal.

Tamarin decided to look for a job. She wanted to work for another large corporation where there would be medical and other benefits.

But typing pools had gone the way of dinosaurs, replaced by skilled and specially-trained secretaries operating dedicated word processing machines. Skills Tamarin did not have.

In the end she found work as a waitress at the *Green Junction*, a vegan restaurant in Kotze Street on Hillbrow's strip. It was an easy, ten-minute walk from their apartment, and although vegans were known to be poor tippers, customers liked her and she did quite well.

Tamarin enjoyed her job. She got to mingle with like-minded people who believed in and had the same values she did. In addition, they tended not to sit around, so most nights she was home by eight, in time to see Adrian before he went to bed.

She left for work at a quarter to eleven every weekday morning and only returned home in the evenings. It wasn't ideal, she knew that. She was aware her son was considered a latchkey kid returning to an empty apartment after school and having to take care of himself.

But she figured there was no alternative and it did the boy good. He had to learn many things she believed made him a better human being.

One Saturday morning, on her day off, she sat Adrian down at the kitchen table.

"You know how hard Mummy works, don't you, Darling?" she asked.

He didn't but he accepted she did.

"I need you to help me," she continued. "I am going to teach you how to wash and mop the floor, and how to iron your clothes. If you can do that, it'll be a great help to Mummy."

Adrian looked bemused. At school he noticed all the cleaning was done by black women, and men worked in the gardens and did repairs to the buildings.

He asked his mother about it.

"That's just silly, reactionary, nonsense," she said. "Only old fools still think women do particular jobs and men others. It is so..." She hunted for the appropriate words she sought.

"Old-fashioned," she said. "Modern men aren't handicapped by that sort of narrow-minded thinking."

She paused and swallowed, her eyes firmly fixed on the child.

"You are a modern man, aren't you, Adrian?"

He blinked. He wasn't sure what kind of a man he was, or even if he was a man. It did not feel like it. His mother refused to let him do things other boys routinely did. He was not allowed to play rugby or cricket, because she felt they were too rough and macho. And tennis was out of the question because there was a winner, and Tamarin didn't believe in competition, winners and losers.

"There should be no losers and only winners," she told him, when he asked permission to try out for the under-10 rugby teams.

He thought she was naive and did not understand the way the real world worked - the world he inhabited. But he did not argue. It would be fruitless. His mother never changed her mind.

But Tamarin was not totally unsympathetic. She realized Adrian needed outside activities to exercise his body and brain and had two activities in mind that fitted the bill perfectly - where there was no competition and no winners.

She signed him up for yoga and pottery classes.

And because Adrian von Pletzen was a smart boy and a quick learner, Tamarin encouraged him to take over the cleaning and ironing chores in their household.

Adrian hated yoga and pottery. He was the only boy in the classes, and more than anything, he wanted to quit.

Tamarin would have none of it.

"We are not quitters," she scolded. "It is wonderful you are the only boy there. You're learning to socialize with girls - and gender is irrelevant."

When it became known he was doing yoga and pottery rather than playing rugby or cricket, the bullying he experienced was ratcheted up a few notches and his life was made even more miserable.

Which was why he stood, carefully studying the people on the sidewalk outside *Hillbrow Heights*. His tormentors loved to wait there for him.

When he was sure the coast was clear, he set off at a jog, praying he'd complete the two and a half block journey without incident.

Chapter 3

Gary Hayden, set his towel on the bench that ran the length of the *Hillbrow Indoor Swimming Poo*l, in a spot where he was in their line of sight when they stopped to rest and removed their swimming goggles. He made sure it was near their swimming towels and kit bags.

There were three women swimming lengths in the pool, two wore navy blue one-piece bathing suits, the other a red bikini. So far he'd only seen their backs and the back of their legs as they swam freestyle strokes, and although the two in the single-piece costumes had better figures, he was more interested in the girl in the bikini.

After years of trawling for women, he knew girls who dressed in serious swim-training kit were there to train, and seldom interested in meeting and hooking up with guys.

But those in bikinis were very often at the indoor pool for other reasons. In many cases they were bored wives, or single girls new to the area, looking to make new connections and have a little fun. It was a fruitful hunting area for Hayden and he'd met many women who fell for his slick patter and were prepared to take it to the next level, either at their apartments or in a room hired by the hour at the *Summit Club*, situated above the *Hillbrow Indoor Swimming Poo*l.

He positioned himself on the bench so he was directly in her eye-line when she emerged from the water and tensed and released his muscles. He did thirty push-ups in the change room to get himself pumped and looking his best, and hoped the women would stop their swimming and see him while he still looked good.

He glanced at his black, waterproof diver's watch. It was a little before three in the afternoon, and if bikini girl stopped swimming soon he could strike up conversation with her, buy her a cup of coffee, maybe get lucky and still be home at *Hillbrow Heights* before supper, so he would not have to make up excuses to Cindy.

Not that he minded lying to her. He did it often enough it'd become second nature. He smiled. His wife was beautiful, hot, sexy - and gullible. Sometimes he could not believe how trusting she was. From when they were married three years ago, if he told her he had to work late, or had a meeting with a client at night, or over the weekend, she accepted it without question.

It was the ideal situation. He liked being married. He liked having a hot meal ready for him when he got home and a warm and ready-to-please attractive body pressed against him in bed at night. He even thought, in his own way, he loved her.

He never told her as such, but she had to realize one woman was never going to be enough for him.

He viewed himself as a virile, sexual being. It was the way he was born, how he was hard-wired and he truly believed his urges were beyond his control.

Not that he had any desire to control them. What possible harm were his many liaisons doing? It was not like he had any feelings for the women he hooked up with. They were pleasant. Soft and fragrant. A way to scratch an itch, but that was all. It was Cindy he went home to and mostly Cindy he woke up with.

If she ever found out about his extra-marital activities, he believed she should be pleased about them. His dalliances made him alive and vital. They ensured he took care of himself and motivated him to remain attractive, well-groomed and fit - to be a husband who looked good on her arm. One she could proudly display to her friends and family.

He glanced at his watch again. If the girls did not stop for a break soon he'd have to put Plan B into operation, where he swam beside them and accidentally bumped into them, causing them to stop. It was not what he wanted to do. It gave him an opportunity to strike up conversation, but trying to talk to and pick up women in a swimming pool was fraught with risk. There was always the possibility of snot on their faces, or ears filled with water so they could not hear him, or swimming goggles fogged so they could not see how magnificent he was.

He carefully watched the three girls. The two in one-piece suits were definitely swimmers. They glided through the water effortlessly, doing slick tumble-turns at the end of each length. Bikini Girl looked less assured. All three wore bathing caps, so he could not see the color or length of their hair.

Just as Hayden stood up, about to dive into the water so he could put Plan B into operation, Bikini Girl touched the pool wall and stopped. She removed her swimming goggles and placed her elbows and forearms on the tiled floor surrounding the pool. She sucked in large gulps of air as she tried to recover her breath, then rubbed her eyes.

She looked up and saw Gary on the bench directly in front of her, his already flat stomach sucked in even more. He nodded and smiled at her and she smiled in return.

Even before she attempted to lift herself out of the pool, he was there with an outstretched hand, offering assistance. She took his hand and he pulled her out of the pool, and with the palm of his right hand on the small of her back, led her dripping towards her towel.

It was a seduction technique he used many time before that he liked to think of as 'the canary in the mine' method. In days gone by, miners took caged canaries underground with them, as indicators of undetectable poisonous, methane gas. If the bird grew agitated they knew there was danger and they needed to get out of there. In Gary's case, if the woman, moved his hand off her back or was uncomfortable about it, he knew he should move on. It saved a lot of time.

Bikini Girl appeared to be perfectly comfortable. He held her towel for her and she allowed him to wrap it around her body. When she removed her rubber swimming cap she revealed short, black hair cut in a sort of pageboy style.

For the first time, Gary had the opportunity to examine her closely. She was probably twelve to fifteen years older than him. He guessed late thirties. She obviously took care of herself but her body was less ripped than that of an athlete or gym rat. But she oozed sexuality and promise.

"I'm Gary," he said, holding out his right hand.

She took his hand in both of hers and he immediately noticed her immaculately manicured, crimson nails. Her fingers were long and slim and a shudder of delicious anticipation was triggered deep within him.

"Elaine," she said.

For a moment he was disappointed. He was expecting her name to be Clarisse or Michelle, or something along those lines. Elaine was such a plain, unsexy name. But, as some dead writer once said: "A rose by any other name..."

She toweled herself off, then sat beside Gary on the bench. Their bare thighs touched.

For a little while they made small talk but both seemed anxious about the time and regularly glanced at their watches.

"Would you like to get out of here and have a cup of coffee?" he asked eventually.

"Why don't we just skip the coffee," said Elaine, gazing into his eyes. She put her hand on his lap.

Chapter 4

Norah Braithwaite-Smith made herself a cup of Earl Grey tea, put two chocolate, Romany Cream biscuits onto a white china plate and went onto the balcony of her two bedroom flat at *Hillbrow Heights*.

She set the tea and cookies on a white, wrought-iron table, adjusted her flowing caftan and sat on a matching chair. From a silver cigarette case on the table beside a steamy Harold Robbins novel she was busy reading, she took a cigarette and fitted it into a translucent, cigarette holder. She lit the cigarette with a gold-plated lighter, drew the smoke deep into her lungs and sighed.

Norah Braithwaite-Smith had just turned sixty two, and although she was in good health and in good shape, she looked older. Her face and neck were prematurely wrinkled and on her arms she had a few dark sun spots. Both were the result of endless days of lying in the baking sun on the beaches of Spain and Portugal, while smeared with coconut oil.

I'd do it differently if I could go back in time, she thought. But we didn't know. No-one told us about the dangers of the sun. Heck, if you were dark and tanned you were considered healthy! It was only in the last year or two sun creams that protect from ultra-violet rays came onto the market.

That morning, when she stood naked, tall and slim, in front of the full-length mirror in her bedroom, she took the time to carefully examine herself. The examination was the result of an article about skin cancer she read in a woman's magazine, and she carefully checked the sun spots and beauty marks on her body. It appeared none had grown darker or larger, and she breathed a sigh of relief. For a moment she considered canceling her subscription with the magazine, because every month it seemed to feature an article on health that scared the daylights out of her. But she decided against it, as she figured it was probably better to be aware than not.

After checking her skin for early signs of cancer she took the opportunity to examine the rest of her body. She studied her wrinkles and pulled the loose skin on her cheeks and neck towards her ears, so she could see what a face-lift would achieve.

It'd be a big improvement she decided, and made a mental note to make inquiries about prices and doctors. Then, with her face close to the mirror she inspected her hair.

She looked like her mother, she thought, and shuddered. The old lady always wore her gray hair, long and tied back in a simple ponytail, just as Norah did. She always thought it made her mother look ten years older than she really was, and here she was doing the same.

Without waiting a second longer and still naked, Norah used the telephone on a table in the dining room to book an appointment for the following day at the hairdressing salon located in the Highpoint building.

A face-lift would have to wait, but she darn well could get her hair cut and colored in the meantime. It would take a few years off her appearance.

Norah stubbed out her cigarette and picked up her teacup. She blew on the surface of the dark liquid.

South Africa is nice, she thought. But it's definitely not home. I miss England, I miss London and I miss the social life I had there.

She moved into *Hillbrow Heights* sixteen years ago - before the Brigadier bought the block of flats - after fleeing England and a scandal that was in all the papers and threatened to engulf and destroy her.

Norah Braithwaite-Smith, nee Blake, was the daughter of a struggling, scrap iron and steel merchant in Hartlepool, England. She completed high school, but a lack of money meant going to university was out of the question - not that she ever had intentions of enrolling at an institution of higher learning. In the 1930s, even the wealthy considered it a waste of time and money to send their daughters to university.

Norah knew her best chance of lasting success was to marry well. She realized her greatest asset was her good looks and shapely body, and she was happy to use both however she could to get her nearer her goal.

Soon after leaving school she deliberately took a job as a cocktail waitress at a club, a short walking distance from the Houses of Parliament in London. It was an establishment frequented by the men who ran England. The job required her to wear a short satin skirt and tight top that showed off her figure, and she was instantly a hit with the male-only patrons.

The pay and tips were good, as were the lavish gifts showered upon her by randy benefactors. It was fun and she did well but Norah Blake held a long term view - she was looking for a husband.

She quickly realized setting her sights on marrying a Cabinet Minister or senior party member was a waste of time and effort. Those men were happy to engage in a bit of *rumpy-pumpy* with her but it would always be as far as they went. Most were married and would never leave their wives, and those who weren't, moved in upper-crust social circles that would neither tolerate nor accept a "bit of fluff from Hartlepool."

When it came to finding a husband, she needed to home in on back-benchers not in the limelight, but who had ambition and were likely to go places in politics. That was where she needed to hitch her star.

In the end it was her husband who found her. He was a junior Labour Party Member of Parliament for Bexhill and Battle in East Sussex, the location of the 1066 Battle of Hastings. Other party members told her he was a rising star in the Labour Party.

He was divorced, twenty two years older than her, and smitten the moment he laid eyes upon her. He wooed her, she seduced him and six months later, Norah Blake became Mrs Randolph "Randy" Braithwaite-Smith. Neither party in the marriage was interested in having children.

Randy did not want his wife to work, and certainly not in the club where they met. They bought a house in the country where Norah spent her days keeping the home and its secluded garden ship-shape, as well as making sure she remained attractive and available to her husband.

It was while they were on holiday in Spain, celebrating their second wedding anniversary, that Norah discovered Randy's dark side. After a shopping trip she returned to their hotel room earlier than expected and walked in on Randy lying spread-eagled on the bed, blindfolded and dressed in her panties, stockings, suspenders and bra.

He hadn't heard her come into the room, and for a while she stood in the doorway, watching and allowing him to finish.

Then she cleared her throat. Randy almost wet himself.

"I just like the feel of them on my skin," he stammered, trying desperately to wrap himself in the bed covers.

He was crimson, and for a moment she thought he might puke on the bed.

"I've never done this before," he lied.

She sat on the bed beside him, gently touching his face with the back of her hand.

"It's okay, I don't mind," she whispered. "But you're stretching and soiling my underwear. If you're going to do this you should get your own."

"I'm sorry, I should have asked your permission," he said, in a girly voice. "I've been a bad boy, you should punish me. You could use your hairbrush."

Norah was taken aback. But she'd figured, if that was

how he wanted to play, then she would play along. For the next half hour she swatted his backside with her wooden, paddle-shaped hairbrush until his cheeks glowed like fire and he could take it no more.

He was so aroused he eventually rolled her onto her back on the bed and took her more urgently than she could ever remember.

Randy was living a part of his life in secret, but once he let Norah take a peek into it and found she was fascinated rather than disgusted, he opened the door wide and invited her in.

Norah always fancied herself as modern and enlightened, and happily ventured where Randy led.

He and his ex-wife were members of an exclusive swingers and fetish group. It was the reason they eventually divorced. It wasn't something she wanted to be part of, but he coerced her and she resented that. Although desperately jealous, she gritted her teeth and tolerated seeing him with other women - and men.

What finally ended the marriage for her was Randy was not jealous or upset at all when she was with other people.

If he was not even a tiny bit jealous it proved he did not love her, she reasoned. She was right.

The divorce was quick. He gave her everything she asked for, so she would keep quiet about his activities and tastes.

Norah had no such reservations. She knew the way to ensure he would love her forever was to embrace and become part of his hidden world.

She took to and participated in it with gusto and enthusiasm, and the fact she shared his darkest secrets made him dote on her even more.

It gave him peace and produced the tranquility he required to focus on his position in the political party that was taking notice of him. He was asked to join a number of committees, and a few years later selected to chair a committee tasked with studying defense expenditure. His star rose and shone brightly. There was even talk of a Cabinet position one day.

But then everything came unraveled. On a Thursday morning in June in 1958, a hotel cleaning maid opened the door to room 416 of a hotel in London's Soho district, despite the *Do not Disturb* sign attached to the handle. She knocked a few times and after getting no answer decided she needed to get in and clean the room.

There she found the Honorable Randolph Braithwaite-Smith, dressed in women's underwear, with some sort of device jammed into his backside, blindfolded, with a ball-gag in his mouth and his hands handcuffed behind his back. He dangled limp and dead from a rope expertly tied in a noose around his neck and secured to a sturdy overhead shower rail in the bathroom. From the police photographs taken at the scene, and the stains on the front of the nylon stockings he wore, it appeared he died happy.

Because of Randy's position on the Defense Revenue Committee it was first suspected he was murdered. There was speculation the Russians were involved. But an autopsy revealed a heart attack was the cause of Randy's untimely and embarrassing death.

It did not take much for the police and tabloid newspapers to dig up the truth. Randy and another MP who was part of their fetish group, booked the hotel room and hired two professional dominatrices specializing in breath-suppression and erotic strangulation play. It was a fetish area Randy was exploring, where breath is cut off, almost and sometimes to the point of unconsciousness, at the moment of ejaculation. According to practitioners, orgasm truly does become what the French call "the little death!" Except in the Honorable Randolph Braithwaite-Smith's case it was the big death.

When he could not be roused, the others panicked and bolted but were quickly rounded up by the police and subjected to hours of unrelenting, hostile questioning by British Counter Intelligence authorities. Names were named, the press published photographs and the rats ratted on the other rats.

The scale of the sexual network was staggering and included politicians, industry leaders, senior police officers and even an arch bishop. It was Britain's biggest ever sex scandal, and intelligence agencies in Britain and the USA scrambled, in desperate efforts to establish if the country and its allies' secrets were compromised.

In an off-the-cuff comment, not meant to be heard by the press, the Chief Constable said: "It's easy to blackmail a cabinet minister when you 'ave a photo of 'im wi' another man's cock up his bum and 'is wife's bra jammed in 'is mouth."

Norah's name and involvement was soon known and the press descended upon her like a pack of frenzied dogs. They followed her, photographed her, camped outside her home, harassed her, and dug up every tiny detail of her life and past they could.

Soon there was nowhere to hide and, as long as she lived in Britain, no matter how long that was, it would always be true.

One night she evaded the press and escaped in a friend's car. At Heathrow she bought a plane ticket to Johannesburg and fled to South Africa.

She made her way to Hillbrow, where she contacted a friend of one of the members of the fetish club, who put her up in her flat and allowed her to stay out of sight for a few months, until the Press grew tired of looking for her.

Randy was well insured, and although the insurance companies tried to repudiate the claim, submitting it was a case of suicide, the court ruled his death the result of natural causes. There was enough money in the estate to allow Norah to live comfortably, if not extravagantly, for the rest of her life.

A couple of months after arriving in Johannesburg, when it appeared she'd successfully avoided the press, and they focused their attentions elsewhere, she decided she needed to find a place of her own to live.

In the meantime she reverted to her maiden name.

Hillbrow Heights, at the beginning of 1960, was the ideal place for her, as Hillbrow was a tiny enclave of liberal, modern thought and progressive attitudes, in a South Africa that was becoming increasingly **verkrampt* and nationalistic.

It was claimed to be the most densely populated square mile in Africa, with a cosmopolitan set of white, foreign immigrants, students and old people who'd occupied their flats for most of their lives.

Norah was forty six years-old when she moved into *Hillbrow Heights*. She was still an attractive woman. She made friends easily and took a lover. Over the years other lovers passed through her life, and she received three different marriage proposals that she turned down.

As she sat on the balcony of her flat that afternoon, slowly sipping her Earl Grey tea and watching the afternoon traffic gradually build, she wondered if she made a mistake refusing those proposals of marriage.

The thought of growing old and dying alone terrified her.

She sighed.

I should have married Martin, she thought. I'd not only have a companion, but also be the Lady of the Manor of a Cape wine farm.

Martin was a director and shareholder at Anglo American Corporation. Their love affair was wild and exciting and he was smitten by her. He was devastated when he proposed and she rejected him.

He never spoke to her again, refusing to take her calls, cutting her out of his life. The last she heard, he was retired to his wine farm near Stellenbosch in the Cape.

Friends told her years later he was seeing a woman, but still thought about her.

I was a fool, she thought.

She finished her tea and lit another cigarette.

Shouts from the sidewalk, near the top of the block, caught her attention and she leaned over the balcony's guard rail to see what the commotion was about.

It was the von Pletzen kid from Number 2, running wailing and screaming down the pavement, while five youngsters, including a girl, chased him.

**Verkrampt - ultra conservative and restrictive*

Chapter 5

"Whoa!" yelled Dave Marais. "Slow down! You'll do yourself and someone else an injury."

He put out his hands to stop Adrian von Pletzen, who barreled through the entrance doors at *Hillbrow Heights.*

A second or two later, a group of puffing kids came racing in behind him.

"Help!" gasped Adrian, his face crimson, his lungs screaming for air. He scuttled in behind Dave, using him as a shield against his pursuers.

The chasing youngsters skidded to a halt, stopped by Dave's size, and the fact he was an adult.

"What's the problem?" he asked.

"They're trying to beat me up," panted, Adrian. He desperately tried to get air into his burning lungs.

They were waiting for him when he left his yoga class, hiding in the doorway of an adjacent shop. But he saw them and the chase was on. For three and a half city blocks he ran as fast as he could, dodging pedestrians, parking meters and cars. On previous occasions the bullies gave up the chase after a block, but this time they were determined to catch him.

"Is that true?" asked Dave, moving into the entrance doorway to block their escape.

"Naah!" sneered one of the youngsters, a boy who looked older and was bigger than Adrian, and who wore his baseball cap backwards. "It's just a bit of fun, a game. He's just acting like a baby."

The others nodded.

Dave had often seen these youngsters hanging around the streets and in video game arcades. He guessed they probably all went to the same school, lived nearby and liked to pretend they were tough, little, hoodlums.

"It doesn't look like he's having fun or enjoying your

game," he said, pointing at Adrian with his chin.

He did not know Adrian's name but had seen him around *Hillbrow Heights*, knew where he lived and who is mother was - and thought she was sexy, in an unusual sort of way.

Dave was a big guy. In the army he played lock in the regiment's rugby team and most of his life he took part in karate, where he held a third dan black belt. While at Rhodes University where he studied for a degree in journalism, he worked as a nightclub bouncer on weekends to help pay off his student loan.

He looked intimidating, and a crooked nose, the result of it being broken and not properly set, did little to soften the impression.

"I know where you little turds live and where you go to school and if I hear you've been picking on this young man - or anyone else - you'll have to answer to me," he said, his voice raised and harsh.

"Do we understand each other?"

They nodded reluctantly.

"I didn't hear you!" he snapped, bending forward so he could stick his nose into the face of the kid with the reversed baseball cap.

"Yes," they said.

"Now get out of here and don't let me see you around here again."

He stood aside so they could exit in single file, one person at a time, and fixed a hostile stare on each of them in turn.

When they were gone he turned to Adrian. The boy's face was tear-stained.

"Thank you," said the child softly.

"You are welcome. I'm Dave," he said and stuck out a hand. Adrian shook it and Dave could not but help notice how soft the kid's hand was. "Why were they picking on you?"

Suddenly Adrian's eyes blazed.

"Because my stupid mother makes me go to stupid yoga and pottery classes!" he said angrily. "They think I am a sissy because she won't let me play rugby or cricket. They pick on me because she makes me different!"

Dave could see the kid was close to tears and the frustration in his voice was palpable.

"Is your mother home now?" asked Dave.

"No, she works in a restaurant and only gets home later, at night."

"So you're on your own most of the time?"

"Yes and I hate it," he said.

Dave looked at the kid. He looked so small, weedy and pathetic, and he felt immensely sorry for him.

It must be really tough growing up without a father, he thought.

It was his father who taught him much of what he needed to survive. He remembered how, when he came back from primary school one day, crying because a bully roughed him up, his father said: "It's time for you to learn how to look after yourself as I won't always be around to protect you."

The old man signed him up with a boxing club and after getting over the initial fear of being hit in the face, Dave found he enjoyed the activity and was good at it.

Soon afterwards he dished out a severe beating to the bully, and after that no-one ever looked for trouble with him again. Later he gave up boxing and switched to karate.

Someone needed to teach this kid a few tricks to help him take care of himself, and that certainly won't be his mother, he thought.

"I've got some cold Coke® upstairs," said Dave. "Would you like a can?"

Adrian looked hesitant. His mother often warned him about evil men who preyed on little boys.

"Mommy said I shouldn't go with strangers," he said.

"I'm not a stranger," replied Dave. "I live in the same block of flats. You know where I live, we see each other every day."

Adrian thought about it for a while. What Dave said was true. He wasn't a stranger and he was very thirsty, and all there was to drink in his apartment was herbal tea or water - his mother disapproved of Coca Cola®, alcohol or anything not natural and healthy. The thought of a cold Coke® was irresistible.

"I suppose it will be okay," he said, his voice still unsure. "But I can't stay very long."

Dave's one bedroomed flat was on the top floor, and the first thing Adrian noticed was the punching bag attached to a metal frame in the corner of the lounge area. Beside it was a set of dumbbells.

While Dave got them each a Coke® from the refrigerator in the kitchen, Adrian examined the framed photographs on the walls. Some looked a lot like photographs he saw in the newspapers and there were pictures of boxers and rugby players, but there were also a lot of photographs of pretty ladies who wore no tops - not even a bra.

Adrian gasped and his heart beat faster. On a few occasions he'd seen his mother naked when he looked into her room after she came out of the bathroom. Once she saw him standing in the doorway, his eyes wide, and she scolded him and left him feeling ashamed. Another time he saw a magazine one of the kids brought to school and they all looked at it in the boys' toilets, while someone kept a lookout for teachers or prefects.

"My dad smuggled it in when he came back from overseas," explained the boy who brought it to school. "He hid it inside a shirt in his luggage. If they found it at the airport, or the police saw it, he would go to jail. He hid it under his mattress but I know he keeps his dirty books and pictures there."

The incident was confusing, naughty and exciting to Adrian and he experienced strange feelings and emotions he'd never had before.

The photographs on Dave's wall weren't naughty like those in the magazine but they still caused Adrian to have those funny feelings in his tummy again.

When Dave returned with the Cokes®, Adrian quickly turned away, but his face was crimson with embarrassment. Dave noticed but said nothing. He handed the kid a frosty red and white can and gestured to him to take a seat.

Adrian took a large gulp of soda, the icy liquid burning his throat. If his mother saw him now, she would definitely be angry.

For a while they sat quietly until the silence became awkward.

"Are those your girlfriends?" stammered Adrian, suddenly and pointed at the photographs on the walls.

Dave laughed.

"I wish!" he said. "No they are girls we photographed for the magazine where I work."

He rifled through a pile of magazines on a table beside the worn couch, found what he was looking for, and tossed it to Adrian.

"I am the Johannesburg editor of *Rogue* magazine," he said. "It's a magazine for men and things men like, like women, cars, guns and fishing."

Adrian paged through the glossy magazine. He recognized one of the girls - the center spread - from one of the photographs he'd seen on the wall; only this time she had stars on her nipples.

There was also an article about the war in Vietnam and another about South African soldiers in South West Africa.

He'd seen copies of *Rogue* magazine for sale at the café and convenience store owned by a Greek couple in Kotze Street but he never paged through one.

"So you are a reporter?" he asked. "Did you go to Vietnam to write this story?"

"Yes I am a reporter but I do more than that. And no, I didn't write that story, we bought it from overseas."

"So people write stories and then sell them?" asked Adrian. It sounded like a fun job he might like to do when he was grown up.

"Yes."

The kid sipped his Coca Cola®, enjoying the rare, forbidden treat.

"Do the other kids bully you a lot?" asked Dave, crumpling his empty soda tin and putting it on the table beside his chair.

Adrian nodded.

"Why do you think that is?"

He sighed.

"Because my mother won't allow me to be like them. She won't allow me to play sports at school because she doesn't want me to grow up to be a male...," he struggled to find the word Tamarin always used. "A male something pig. I can't remember what she calls it."

"Chauvinist?" offered Dave.

Adrian nodded.

"Yes, that's right. She doesn't want me to grow up to be one of them and she says playing sports will make me one. She is still very cross with my dad and I don't think she likes men. I am sure she would have been happier if I was a girl."

He looked away so Dave would not see the tears making his eyes shine.

"I could teach you a few tricks to use against the bullies," said Dave.

Adrian looked at him and smiled broadly so his wire braces showed.

"Would you?"

"Sure! Let's see how you punch on the punching bag."

Adrian put down his unfinished can of soda and went to stand in front of the red, leather punching bag. He drew back his fist, ready to punch, but Dave stopped him.

"Wait!" he instructed. "If you punch with your thumb placed inside your other fingers, you will break it. Before you can hit anyone, you need to make a proper fist."

He showed the youngster how to first curl his fingers tightly into the palm of his hand and then wrap his thumb around them.

"You want to strike with the first two knuckles, because that puts them in a straight line with your forearm," Marais explained. "Also use your hips and legs to generate more power in the punch."

He demonstrated exactly what he meant on the punching bag by stepping forward and smacking it with a blow that caused it to swing on the chain and that cracked like a gunshot.

It was so fast and unexpected Adrian was startled by it.

"When you decide you must fight, your opponent must not even see the blow coming," said Dave. "It must be unexpected, a complete surprise to him and delivered so hard all the fight is knocked out of him. Put everything into that one shot, so it is over right then and you are the one who walks away the winner."

Adrian nodded.

"But what happens if he hits you first?" he asked.

"Sometimes you are going to get hit," replied Dave. "That is just the way life is. You have to be a man and decide to suck it up and then teach your attacker a lesson he'll never forget. But luckily almost all attacks start the same way. It's called a right hook and if you know what to do, it is easy to block and land a counter-punch before he even knows what hit him. Let me show you."

He demonstrated to the kid what a right hook was, then showed him how to parry it with his left arm and hand, and how to deliver a counter-strike with his right hand.

"Wow!" cried Adrian, beaming broadly. "That's awesome!"

"Let's practice a bit," said Dave. "I'll be the attacker. I'll go slowly so you can get it right."

For the next quarter of an hour, Adrian rehearsed the drill and quickly gained confidence and dexterity as Marais sped up the simulated attack. In the end, one of his counter-punches clipped Dave on the lip and split it.

"Good shot!" said Dave as a thin line of blood dribbled down his chin.

Adrian was devastated.

"I'm sorry, I'm sorry!" he cried. "It was an accident. I didn't mean to."

His eyes filled with tears.

Dave put a hand on his shoulder.

"It's okay," he said softly. "It's what you were supposed to do. It's just a little cut and I won't die, but I'll certainly be careful of your fists in the future."

The youngster smiled.

"You did good," said Dave. "Do you see now that you can handle a bully?"

"I guess so," said Adrian, "but it usually does not start like that."

He explained how it always began with his tie being grabbed or being jabbed or pushed in the chest.

"That's even easier to handle," said Dave.

He showed him how to instantly break the grip and apply an arm-bar that dropped an opponent to his knees.

"If you do it quickly you can break his wrist or fingers, but mostly you just want to get him down and make him surrender. If he refuses to give up, you have him at your mercy and can punch him on the side or back of his head."

They practiced the technique and Adrian found, to his surprise, if he was quick and decisive enough he could take Dave down to his knees.

Marais glanced at his watch. It was running towards supper time and he had an appointment to meet a girl for drinks and dinner.

"You'd better get on home," he said to Adrian. "But remember, what I've taught you today is for you to use to protect yourself, it's not meant to turn you into a bully."

"Thank you, Dave," he said. He wrapped his arms around Marais' waist and hugged him.

Chapter 6

"Darling! I'm home!" called Tamarin, opening the door of their flat. She could hear the television in the new tenants' apartment. She hadn't met them but Norah told her the man was a policeman, news that left her ill at ease.

Tamarin's only vice was she occasionally smoked marijuana, or *dagga*, as it was called on the streets of South Africa. There were times all she wanted to do was relax, and dagga allowed her to do that. She bought small amounts from Norah, who got her supply from a black taxi driver plying his trade outside the nearby Hillbrow Hospital.

It's a natural herb put on earth for our use by the *Mother Creator*, Tamarin reasoned.

But with a cop now living in the complex, she'd have to be extra careful. They all would.

Although it was not loud, the sound of the television annoyed her. The country last year got television broadcasts for the first time, and the novelty of being able to stare at a glowing box and watch what the rest of the world had seen for decades, completely captivated those who could afford it. Social activities and invitations were arranged to take into consideration the TV programs being broadcast.

Tamarin did not have a television set. She figured it would be too distracting for Adrian and adversely affect his school work and other activities.

Adrian came out of his bedroom and hugged his mother. She smelled of vegetables. He was practicing the techniques Dave taught him and his T-shirt was damp with sweat.

"How was your day?" she asked, kissing him on his forehead. He was sticky, tasted salty and appeared out of breath.

"What on earth have you been up to?" she asked, wiping her lips with the back of her hand.

"Just practicing yoga, he lied. He could not tell her the truth because she was opposed to all forms of violence and he knew she would instantly put on her 'disapproving face', and for the next two weeks he'd have to listen to her telling him how much he disappointed her and how she worried he would turn out just like his father.

She put her woven grass basket, that she used instead of a leather handbag, on the dining room table.

"So yoga was good then?"

Adrian nodded.

"Have you eaten?"

"I had an apple and a banana earlier," he replied.

"There are frozen soy burgers in the freezer. I can make you one, if you like?"

Adrian pursed his lips and thought about the offer for a moment. Then he shook his head.

"No thank you, could I rather just have a sandwich, please?"

"With peanut butter?"

He nodded.

Tamarin tossed her nylon windbreaker over the back of one of the dining room chairs and went to the kitchen. Adrian followed.

"Have you done your homework?" she asked, spreading a thin layer of margarine onto two slices of wholewheat bread.

"Yes," he said. But there was a math exercise he had not completed. He hadn't had time because he was occupied with self defense practice, and also reading a copy of *Rogue* magazine he asked Dave if he could borrow. The publication was now well hidden under the mattress on his bed.

Tamarin handed her son a plate with his sandwich.

"When you're done eating, you must bath and go to bed," she said. She poured a glass of iced, herbal tea for him.

"Yes, Mommy," he said.

It was a tough day at the restaurant. Tips were poor and the asparagus, a core ingredient in many of their signature dishes, was not delivered. And customers somehow seemed more difficult and picky than usual. In addition, the busboy spilled most of the contents of a mug of black coffee down the front of her skirt, and it would have to be sent for dry cleaning.

She really needed a smoke. Normally she waited for Adrian to fall asleep, then sat on the balcony and smoked a joint. She was pretty sure the Brigadier and his wife did not know the smell of weed, and Gary and Cindy used, so they were no problem, and she assumed the big guy who was a journalist would have no issues with it.

But a cop, he would know. She would have to be very careful.

While she waited for Adrian to finish in the bathroom and go to bed, she prepared his school lunch, then ironed a clean school shirt for him, as well as a set of clothes she planned to wear the next day.

"Good night, Mommy! Sleep well and sweet dreams!" Adrian called from his bedroom.

"You too, Darling!"

A half an hour later she finished the ironing and tidied the kitchen. She tiptoed to the open door of Adrian's bedroom and stood quietly listening. His breathing was slow and even. He was asleep.

In her bedroom, she retrieved a cigar box she kept hidden behind her sweaters on the top shelf of her cupboard. Inside was a small, clear, plastic bank bag, half-filled with *dagga*. There was also a pack of cigarette papers and a disposable lighter.

She sat at her dressing table and rolled a joint. When she

was done, she packed the paraphernalia back into the cigar box, scooped up the lighter and went onto the balcony where she stood listening to the sounds of the night for a few moments.

With some trepidation, Tamarin lit the joint and sucked a great gulp of smoke into her lungs, where she held it until she could no longer, then exhaled.

Almost instantly she felt more relaxed and unwound.

She sat back on a plastic chair, her legs stretched out before her, her head back, her eyes closed.

She sucked on the joint again, enjoying its soothing effects. Truly a gift from the *Mother Creator*!

She blew a long stream of smoke through her nose and mouth, allowing the soft evening breeze to waft it upwards towards the open windows of the flat above. That of Danie van Staden, sergeant in the Vice Squad of the South African Police Force.

Chapter 7

Elizabeth van Staden, or Liza, as her friends called her, sat at her desk by the window of her bedroom. She struggled to finish a university assignment requiring discussion of *The role and importance - or not - of Tribal Law in the South African judicial process.*

She was barely half way through her first year of legal studies at Wits University and the growing volume of work was more than anything she ever imagined.

She sighed. It was going to be another late night.

I should have chosen to study drama, like Butch, she thought. All they seem to do is rehearse for stage plays and go to parties.

Liza planned to become a human rights lawyer when she graduated in three years time. She planned to defend the kind of people her father arrested and oppressed. Things were wrong and unjust in South Africa and she was determined to be a part of the process that would turn the country on its head.

She leaned back and rocked on the hind legs of her chair, her fingers interlocked and her hands behind her head. A wry smile crossed her face as she once again thought of the irony. She was at university because, as the child of a policeman, she qualified for a government bursary and the reason she was at university was to gain the skills needed to overthrow the organization that was paying for her to be there.

Butch was in his bedroom, with the door closed, listening to his *Walkman*. Miems, her mother, was in the bathroom, and she had no idea where her father was. Undoubtedly out harassing people again!

She despised her father, and with every day that passed, her contempt for him grew. In her eyes, he was the symbol of all wrong and evil in the country. He was a fat, not very clever Afrikaner, who by virtue of the color of the skin he was born into, and his lowly position in an authoritarian government organization, was a legalized bully.

She hated his old-fashioned, so-called, Christian values and his unwavering beliefs and attitudes.

It wasn't always like that.

There was a time when she was his little girl and loved to sit on his lap. When he was her hero.

But that started to change when she left primary school and went to high school. Her mother insisted they go to an English high school, something her father was against.

"We come from a long line of Boers and Afrikaners," he said. "The English burned our farms, and killed our women and children in concentration camps during the Boer War. Why would you have our children become one of them?"

"I am not trying to make the kids English. They will always be Afrikaners," Miems countered. "But no matter what you think, South Africa is not the whole world, and learning to speak English properly is important."

"They teach English at Afrikaans schools," Danie said.

"Not very well," Miems retorted. She steadfastly refused to be swayed and eventually got her way.

High school was an eye-opener for the twins. The institution was known for encouraging free thinking and liberal values. Their history teacher was the nephew of a prominent, Jewish Communist activist serving a twenty year prison sentence on Robben Island. And although Mr Berkowitz never admitted any connections to the banned SA Communist Party or the African National Congress, it was obvious where his sympathies lay.

He gave his students glimpses into a version of the history of their country that they did not know existed. He mocked the government and ridiculed what he fervently believed were unjust laws. He toppled holy cows, and the kids in his classes loved it. They embraced what he said.

It was exciting and dangerous, in a time where simply quoting an ANC leader, or having a picture of the movement's logo, or a photograph of Nelson Mandela, could earn a person a three year-long jail term for 'furthering the aims of a banned organization'.

After a while, Liza began to question some of the things her father said. She argued and asked difficult questions he struggled to answer.

One evening, at the dinner table, on the day Berkowitz gave a lesson about the **Pass Laws* in South Africa, Liza tackled her father.

"Do you think it is right that people, who are born in a country should have to carry passports to be allowed to move around in their own country?" she asked.

Danie knew what was coming. This was not the first time his daughter raised political issues, and it irked him.

"If we didn't have the pass laws we would have blacks flooding into our cities and overrunning us," he said, his temper immediately flaring. "They don't need to be here. The government has created homelands for them where they can live peacefully and rule themselves!"

"But there is no work, no industry and no infrastructure in those homelands, and the people living there didn't ask for them. They were forced upon them. Do you think it is right they should not be allowed to travel freely to look for work and live anywhere they want in their own country?" she countered.

"This is not their country," Danie snapped. He emphasized the word 'not'. "This is our country. We white men built it. The homeland is their country. Let them build that themselves - but they never will, because they are too damn stupid and lazy!"

Liza looked across the table at her father's crimson face and bulging eyes.

"Not true!" she hissed. "It was built on the sweat of black men and women who must carry a passbook to move around in the land of their birth. And it not right that you - the police - murdered sixty nine of them in Sharpeville because they objected to that unjust law!"

Miems thought her husband would suffer a heart attack or stroke right there. His face was almost purple and swollen veins throbbed in his temples.

When he finally spoke, he sputtered and tiny beads of spit exploded from his mouth.

"Where are you learning this garbage?" he raged.

"At school in history class," said Butch, spooning a second helping of mashed potatoes onto his plate.

"Who is your history teacher?" Danie asked. He forced himself to calm down and take deep breaths to slow his racing heart and pounding blood.

"Mr Berkowitz," said Butch.

Danie leaned over the table and fixed a sharp, icy stare on his daughter.

"You tell Mr Berkowitz he is teaching you kids dangerous rubbish and he'd better watch himself!" He pushed his plate away and left the table in a huff.

Two weeks later, Berkowitz stopped coming to school and a substitute teacher, who was much more interested in teaching the history of the Boers, took over.

The students never knew for sure, but a story did the rounds that Berkowitz's home was raided and he was charged with, and convicted of furthering the aims of a banned organization.

Liza rubbed her temples and yawned. The assignment was excruciatingly boring. She slid her chair back and went to the window where she suddenly smelled the unmistakable, sweet, fragrant aroma of *dagga*. She sniffed the air like a dog, then quietly stuck her head out of the window. On the balcony below their flat she saw the orange glow of a joint and could just make out the face of the mother of the weedy-looking boy she'd seen hanging around *Hillbrow Heights*.

Liza smiled.
I need to have a chat with you, she thought.

**Pass Laws.*

In South Africa, pass laws were a form of internal passport system that was designed to segregate the population, manage urbanization, and allocate migrant labor. The pass laws severely limited the movements of black African citizens by requiring them to carry pass books when outside their homelands or designated areas.

It was compulsory for all black South Africans over the age of 16 to carry the "pass book" at all times within white areas. The law stipulated where, when, and for how long a person could remain in an area. No black person could stay in an urban area for more than 72 hours unless allowed to by Section 10.

The document was similar to an internal passport, containing details of the bearer, such as their fingerprints, photograph, the name of his/her employer, his/her address, how long the bearer had been employed, as well as other identification information. Employers often entered a behavioral evaluation on the conduct of the pass holder.

Before the 1950s, this legislation largely applied to African men, and attempts to apply it to women in the 1910s and 1950s were met with significant protests. The hated laws were the spark that ignited the Sharpeville Massacre on March 21, 1960

Pass laws would be one of the dominant features of the country's apartheid system, until it was effectively ended in 1986.

(Source Wikipedia)

Chapter 8

Sias, who preferred to be called Butch, but looked anything but when seen from behind, was more often than not mistaken for a girl. A slim, shapely girl. He was meticulous about his personal grooming and skin care routine, and twice a day made sure he used a moisturizer on his face neck, forearms and the back of his hands.

He put a tablespoon of baby oil into his bath water every night and dabbed, rather than rubbed, his face dry with a soft towel. He wore his blond hair long and had it cut and styled at a ladies' hairdressing salon. He adored fashion and art and loved the feel of lacy panties on his skin.

He had to keep all of this a secret from the rest of his family, although he suspected Liza knew, but presumed she did not care.

If his father found out it would be the end of the world - for both of them. The only thing his father hated more than cheeky blacks, was gays - or as he and his cop mates called them: *effing *moffies*!

Butch always knew he was different. As a little boy he loved wearing his mother's high-heeled shoes, and enjoyed it when Liza dressed and made him up to look like a girl.

He was convinced he was gay but hadn't yet crossed the physical line that would finally prove it.

He was in his first year of drama studies at Wits University and loved every moment of it. He could imagine himself performing in a big musical production on Broadway, and at night when he lay in his bed he dreamed about the day he'd stand in the spotlight, a huge bouquet of flowers clutched to his chest and answer curtain call after curtain call.

His father was fiercely opposed to the field his son chose to study. The truth was, he was ashamed of it. When his police buddies asked what his son was doing at university, he lied and said he was studying accounting.

Accounting! Pu..leaze! thought Butch.

But, lately he struggled to concentrate on his studies and began to turn in sub-standard work.

He couldn't focus, as his mind was constantly on his new crush. Butch became infatuated with a husky boy in his class who loved wearing vests that showed off his muscular frame. His name was Jarrod and he looked like a rugby player. He wore his dark hair shaved on the sides but kept the fringe long. To Butch, he was the yummiest creature he'd ever seen.

From the moment he first saw him, Butch could not take his eyes off Jarrod, but was too afraid to approach him or strike up a conversation. Something about Jarrod said he was gay, but he couldn't be sure.

What if he isn't and beats the crap out of me? agonized Butch.

His instincts turned out to be right when Jarrod made the first move.

It wasn't the slickest pick-up line ever used, but it didn't matter.

One Friday afternoon, after their last lecture, Jarrod chased after Butch who was on his way to collect his bicycle and head for home.

"Are you enjoying the course?" he stammered, grasping Butch's shoulder. He was almost as nervous about making contact as Butch was.

"Err... yeah... I guess so," answered Sias, taken aback, his voice uncertain. "It's good."

"Do you want to get a milkshake... or a beer? We can discuss the play," Jarrod asked, blushing to his roots.

"Yes, that would be nice. When?"

"Now?"

"Okay."

They went to an ice cream shop a block away, off

campus. There, for the first ten minutes they made small, insignificant talk until Jarrod blurted out:

"Look, I really like you and would like to take you out... on a date."

He looked around anxiously, making sure no-one was looking, then put his hand on Butch's.

Sias's heart skipped. For a moment he thought he would faint.

"I would like that," he said. "I've never been out with a guy before but I'd like it."

He quickly withdrew his hand when he saw a guy and his girlfriend, sitting at a nearby table, checking them out. Moffie-bashing was a common event and seemed condoned rather than condemned by the police.

"Where will we go?" he asked.

"I think a movie to start. That would be the safest. It's dark and no-one will see us."

Butch nodded. His heart pounding in his chest, his well-moisturized hands clammy.

"When?"

"Tomorrow night?"

"That sounds wonderful."

"Let's meet at the movie house and get there early so we can get a seat in the back row, out of the way."

Butch licked his dry lips.

"Okay," he said.

~ ~ ~

The date went well. Better than well. They found seats in the far back corner of a theater showing a movie almost no-one wanted to see. As a result, the nearest patron was seated in front of them, two rows and ten seats away.

When Butch felt Jarrod take his hand and interlink their fingers he thought he would die, and a short while later, when he leaned in and kissed him passionately, he was sure he had, and was now in heaven.

For the rest of the evening they kissed, made out and fondled each other, and when the house lights eventually came on, at the end of the movie, Butch rose, flushed and unsteady to his feet. Love was a dizzy, heady feeling.

Jarrod lived in the suburbs with his parents. His mother was a stay-at-home mom. He caught a bus to and from university, and on weekends borrowed his parents car when he went out. He longed to get a flat of his own where he would have some privacy.

They stood on the pavement, outside the movie theater, both in a swoon.

"Can we go to your place?" whispered Jarrod.

Butch shook his head.

"What about your house?" he asked, still feeling light-headed.

"No. My parents and brother are there."

"Where do people like us go?"

Like us?

It was the first time Butch acknowledged his sexual persuasion.

"I don't know. I've never done this before. I'll ask someone I know, on Monday."

Sias desperately wanted to take Jarrod's hand and hold it to his heart, but it was too public and there were too many people around.

"I don't know if I can wait until Monday," he said, with tears in his eyes.

**Moffie - derogatory South African word used to describe a male homosexual.*

Chapter 9

Sergeant Danie van Staden glanced at his watch. It was a little before nine in the evening and he was parked in an unmarked police vehicle in the street on the side of the Chelsea Hotel. His partner, Constable Dirk Visser, who was almost young enough to be van Staden's son, cleaned his nails with a pocket knife.

Their source told them the show would start at ten and there'd be at least five hookers to take care of the needs of the juiced up men at the end of the performance.

Both policemen were dressed casually in jeans and loose shirts that hung over their belts, so they could hide the pistols tucked into their waistbands. Visser could almost pull off the plain clothes disguise but it was much more difficult for Danie, and he hoped in the dim light he'd be mistaken for just another, horny, middle-aged, loser.

He wondered who the strippers would be. He hoped one was the girl with the python called Henry. The things she did with that snake and the places Henry got to see were mind blowing, and got Danie's motor running. He also hoped Bobby St Claire, a trans-gendered she-male would be performing. He found the sight of a 'chick with a dick' both disgusting and exciting at the same time - like stopping to look at a fatal car accident.

The Vice Squad cops knew most of the strippers, hookers, pimps and drug dealers. Sometimes they arrested them, sometimes they shook them down and let them go and sometimes they screwed them. Sometimes it was difficult tell the difference between the cops and the criminals.

The plan tonight was to attend the illegal sex show, posing as patrons. The performance was set to take place in an upstairs room in the Chelsea Hotel that did duty as a discotheque on weekends. They planned to wait until the very last moment and then, with the help of the bouncer at the door, who owed them a favor, slip in and watch the show from the back. At the appropriate moment they would turn on the lights and arrest everyone in the room.

van Staden and Visser had discussed what the 'appropriate moment' was. By rights it was as soon as a nipple was exposed but they agreed it'd be better to let the performance run right through to the end - it was simply good police work to gather as much evidence as possible.

"There are going to be plenty of unhappy men and pissed off wives tonight," said van Staden. Patrons who attended illegal sex and strip shows were considered as guilty of an offense as the performers and were arrested and prosecuted.

There were many cases of guys losing their jobs, or having their wives divorce them, after they appeared in court and their names were published in the newspapers.

It was harsh punishment for what many considered a trivial offense, but Danie felt no sympathy at all for those men. What they were doing was illegal and immoral and watching something like that led to moral corruption and the decaying of Christian values.

It is right there are such laws, he thought. A morally corrupt nation is a weak nation, and it was all the communists and Soviet Union needed to conquer South Africa.

It was different for Danie. He was not there because he found the shows titillating. It was a job and he'd taught himself to be immune to the sight of young, naked, flesh and the smells and sounds of unfettered lust. His *raisson d' être* was noble and in the national interest.

He wondered who they'd scoop up tonight. Usually it was just a bunch of ordinary, working-class Joes but every now and then they landed a whale and ended up arresting a powerful captain of industry. Invariably they did not charge and prosecute the big fish. Those men were always so afraid their reputation and social standing would be ruined that they begged and pleaded, and made offers of generous gifts.

The Vice Squad cops figured the whales were far more valuable that way, and they then had a hold over powerful and influential people. They scared the crap out of them, took photos and details that could be useful in the future, then cut them loose, but only after reminding them the cops now held their marker.

But sometimes things turned out badly. Eighteen months ago, the Moderator of one of the country's largest churches was arrested at a strip show, and rather than face the coming shame and humiliation, he snatched a pistol from the holster of the cop interviewing him and shot himself in the head.

van Staden checked his watch again. Still half an hour to go. He longed for a smoke but was trying to give up.

Moving into a flat, after living in a house with a yard, was an adjustment for the family but now that they were settled, it appeared they made the right decision. It was convenient for all of them and getting to and from work was quicker and easier.

There was also a lot more for the twins to do, although he worried about the lure of the bright lights and dangers of Hillbrow.

Miems appeared irritated and distant lately, but he figured it was the result of the stress of moving house. Or maybe it was that time of the month. He didn't know.

Perhaps it was a woman thing, because his daughter also seemed to have caught it, but worse. She was incapable of speaking to him politely and always moody and irritable.

And Sias? He didn't know what was going on with the boy. He hoped it was simply a phase.

"Time to go," said Visser, snapping closed his knife and

putting it into his pocket.

When they reached the top of the dimly-lit stairs on the second floor of the Chelsea Hotel, the doors to the discotheque were already closed and manned by a chunky bouncer with no neck. He stepped forward to stop them, then recognized the two cops and moved aside.

"Everyone in?" asked van Staden.

"Yep." The bouncer nodded.

"Who are the performers?" asked Danie.

"Dunno."

Inside, they could hear someone on a microphone revving up the crowd, and a few minutes later a song Danie recognized from other strip shows, but did not know the name of, began to blare.

"That's our cue," he said.

The bouncer opened the door and the two cops slipped in. The room was dark, a single spotlight and a couple of colored foot lights illuminated only the small dance area that also served as a stage. Guys sat at tables carefully arranged to give them the best view of the performance area.

Sitting in the light, on a chair, was a girl with a blond wig. She was dressed in a school uniform a size too small, wore thick, dark-rimmed, schoolmarmish glasses and seductively sucked on a lollipop. Unusual for a stripper, she was a little chubby, which worked well with the look she was going for. She did indeed look like a schoolgirl carrying a bit of puppy fat.

Her act left Danie dabbing his bald spot and forehead with his handkerchief. He could see how such things would corrupt a man, and was grateful he was a seasoned professional. Were that not the case...

He thought of Miems.

The second performance was indeed by Bobby St Claire. She did things that staggered him, and at one point Danie had to lean against the wall to steady himself, as he felt dizzy.

He wanted to get home to Miems. It wasn't right she was always on her own.

"Visser," he whispered, as Bobby St Claire began building up to the money shot. "I think we should consider tonight reconnaissance. Now that we know how it works we can plan better for next time."

Visser was confused. All they had to do was turn on the lights, announce their presence and they could sweep up everyone.

He started to protest by Danie cut him off.

"This is a big one. I don't want to mess this up because we went off half-cocked. Let's go back and plan and then come back another time."

Visser nodded. It was not his place to argue with the sergeant. If that's what his superior wanted, then that is what they would do.

But he wondered if he could stay behind and get the lollipop stripper's phone number.

Danie was lucky. He found a parking spot for the unmarked police car on the same block as *Hillbrow Heights*, a little way down from the entrance. It was close to midnight and the area was quiet.

Miems pretended to be asleep when he entered their bedroom, but not before he made sure each of the twins' bedroom doors was closed.

He closed his bedroom door softly and turned the key to lock it, kicked off a pair of running shoes, slid his jeans down his hairy legs and tossed his shirt onto a chair in the corner. Wearing just a pair of white socks and a baggy pair of cotton underpants, he crawled into bed and rolled Miems onto her back.

"No," she protested, but he put a meaty hand over her mouth to quiet her.

Outside their bedroom, Liza who got up to get herself a glass of water, stopped to listen. She heard her father grunt like a rutting pig, pursed her lips and furrowed her brow in disgust.

Gross! she thought.

Chapter 10

It was just past seven thirty in the evening and Liza stood on the sidewalk, leaning against the wall beside the entrance to *Hillbrow Heights*. She was waiting for Tamarin.

For the last few days she watched to see what time Adrian's mother got home.

It was a balmy evening and she wore a pair of cutoff shorts, a white spaghetti-strapped T-shirt and no bra. Her brother was out and her mother was heating up her father's dinner, as he phoned a short while ago to say he was on his way home.

Silently she prayed she would get to see Tamarin before her father returned and saw her waiting on the pavement.

Her mind drifted to her university work. She had not yet got back her marked paper on *The role and importance - or not - of Tribal Law in the South African Judicial Process* but she wasn't optimistic about how well she'd done. She suspected poorly but hoped she'd at least done enough to scrape through.

She was so deep in thought she did not notice a white sedan stop in front of her.

"How much for a blow job in the car, Darling?" yelled the driver, winding down the passenger window. He was a fifty-somethingish man with a bald spot in the center of his head and reminded her of her father.

His shout disturbed her reverie and for a few moments she did not realize he was calling to her.

"You talking to me?" she asked.

"Who else? How much to suck my dick in the car?"

At first she did not grasp what he was saying. Then it dawned upon her he thought she was a street whore.

"Fuck off!" she yelled at him, "before I cut your balls off and call the cops!"

He flashed his middle finger at her and took off, tires

squealing.

She glanced at her watch, growing increasingly concerned her father would soon be home and see her there. It would certainly result in a raft of unwanted questions and another screaming session.

Come on lady! Where are you? Where are you? she thought, fidgeting anxiously.

Then she saw Tamarin round the corner at the end of the block and she breathed a sigh of relief.

Tamarin had a cotton, messenger-style bag slung over her neck and shoulders, and Liza set off down the sidewalk towards her.

"Hello," she said, stopping in front of her. "I'm Liza. I live in the flat above yours."

Tamarin was taken aback. Why had this girl, the daughter of a policeman stopped her?

"Err... yes?" she stammered.

"I saw you smoking on your balcony the other night," said Liza, figuring she should get right to the point. "I'm new and looking for someone who can supply me with weed when I need it."

Tamarin was instantly on her guard. Her stomach knotted.

"I can't help you. I occasionally smoke a normal cigarette. That must have been what you saw."

Liza smiled hoping it would ease the other woman's mistrust.

"I know what I smelled. I've been smoking *zol* since I was fourteen. I'm not trying to trap you. I just need to know where I can get some around here."

Tamarin was edgy and not convinced.

"I know your father is a cop. I think the two of you have a plot to somehow entrap me."

Liza frowned. She grew irritated. Her father was due home at any moment.

"I hardly ever speak to my father," she said, her voice

more strident. "He and I don't agree on anything and I despise him, but I know what I saw, and if you won't help me perhaps I'll tell him what I saw and smelled the other night."

An icy shiver ran through Tamarin's body.

The bitch is blackmailing me, she thought.

"To prove I'm telling the truth, leave a joint in our mailbox in the foyer, and I'll come to your apartment and smoke it. That way, I'll be guilty of committing a crime and you can phone the cops, have me arrested and nothing will lead to you," said Liza.

Tamarin was quiet for a while as she considered what the girl said. If she was prepared to do that, she appeared legitimate.

"I'll make some inquiries and see what I can do," she said. "I think I may know someone who knows someone... you know what I mean."

Liza took Tamarin's right hand and gave it a squeeze. It was a gesture that appeared to be warm, genuine and sincere.

"Thank you," she said. "You are a rock star!"

Tamarin nodded and stared into Liza's eyes.

"I'm going to trust you," she said, "probably against my better judgment, but remember, karma can be a bitch!"

"I promise you I'm on the level," said Liza. She hesitated. "Do you think you could leave something in my letterbox this evening so I can smoke it later tonight? I have money."

"I can do that and you don't have to pay for it. Consider it a gesture of good faith."

Chapter 11

Miems was frustrated. Her life was not going the way she wanted and she was bored. She realized married life inevitably became mundane but had hoped the move to Hillbrow would bring with it more excitement. There was so much to do, so many places to visit. She heard the nightlife was fantastic.

But Danie wasn't interested.

"I get more than enough thrills at work," he said. "When I get home I want to relax."

Her husband spent three hours, most afternoons and evenings, drinking with his police colleagues. When he got home, always a little drunk, he ate his supper in front of the television then fell asleep on the couch. When he stumbled to bed, sweaty and stinking of booze, he was always awake enough to quickly fuck his wife.

It was a ritual Miems hated. She wasn't against sex - she enjoyed the idea of the act but wished she could do it more passionately, and not with her husband. She resented the fat clown and regretted being married to him. How she wished she could go back in time and have a 'do over'.

All it took was a moment of weakness almost twenty years ago, when fresh out of school she went to a party, drank too much and allowed a baby-faced police constable to talk his way into her pants. She surrendered her virginity to Danie van Staden in the back seat of a car and two weeks later she missed her period.

Their parents insisted they get married, as it was the right thing to do to avoid bringing shame to their families.

Their honeymoon was three days at the hot springs in Warmbaths, north of Pretoria. Danie qualified for a special discount as a member of the South African Police Force .

He made love to her twice a day and could not get

enough of her, making her worry in the future she'd not be able to keep up with his sexual appetite. But his ardor soon waned and he became more interested in drinking and hanging out with his cop buddies. She was glad he wasn't a drunkard or womanizer, but wished he would pay more attention to her and the twins.

When the children started school she found a mornings-only job. Danie was not happy about it, but they needed the money. Promotion had not come as rapidly as he hoped and it was almost impossible to survive on a low-ranking policeman's salary.

Miems had no special work skills but she was pretty, friendly and had a talent for organization. She found a job as a receptionist and filing clerk with a firm of lawyers, and for once the van Stadens stayed in one place for a few years without Danie being transferred. This gave her the opportunity to properly learn the administrative operations of a law firm. She was exceptional at her job, and when Danie was transferred again, the firm gave her a glowing testimonial.

When they moved to Johannesburg she was offered a position with a large firm of attorneys that occupied five floors of a building near the Supreme Court in the city.

She'd never worked for a company like that before. The senior partners were English-speaking and the fifty two lawyers and associates under them were all young. They believed in working and playing hard. It was like a breath of fresh air to her and she tossed out her conservative, dark, monotone skirts and high, frill-necked blouses and replaced them with slim, short, brightly-colored pencil skirts and tight tops that flattered her figure.

She swapped sensible shoes for tall, peep-toed stilettos and ankle-high boots that showed off her shapely legs. She cut her hair in a modern, sexy style and felt young and vibrant again. The truth was, she was young. Her kids were the same age she was when she got married. In two years she'd celebrate her fortieth birthday.

Danie hated the way Miems changed. In his opinion the outfits she wore to work were too provocative. She should dress like a respectable Afrikaner woman.

Miems made herself a cup of tea before bed, sighed deeply and stepped onto the balcony outside the lounge, wearing her dressing gown. Her husband stifled her.

She felt like a kid, destined to stand outside the display window of a sweet shop but never permitted to enter and taste. What she desperately needed was a dose of excitement in her life and she knew Danie would not provide it.

For a moment she allowed her mind to wander. She still turned men's heads, and though she was fifteen years older than some of the young lawyers at the firm, many were sexually attracted to her. She found the whole idea of young men (not much older than Sias) being turned on by her strange, but also exciting. It was delicious and dangerous.

It was fun to be the object of a crush. To gaze into lust-filled, puppy eyes and see the fierce competition between them for her affections. To fantasize.

When Miems stepped through the doors of her workplace she became a different person. Confident, playful, professional and alluring - all traits she suppressed when around Danie, who was secretly frightened by women like that.

One attorney in particular was especially taken with Miems. Dane McDonald was twenty seven years old and strikingly good looking. Tall with blond hair and icy blue eyes, he was smitten with Mrs Miems van Staden and determined to get her into his bed and make her fall in love with him.

He found every excuse possible to stop by the reception desk to chat with her. He knew about her family, her frustrations and her dreams. Twice he asked her out for an after-work drink and both times she refused, touching his hand softly and kissing him on the cheek.

"You are very sweet and adorable," she said. "But it would not be right. I am a married woman."

"It's just a drink!" he said, his voice pinched and in obvious agony.

"I know, but someone might see us."

That night, after Miems went to bed, she lay on her back in the dark and allowed her mind to wander. Danie was not home, and when he phoned earlier in the evening said he was not sure what time he'd be back. They had a tip about a white man living with a colored woman in Highpoint and were going to raid the apartment, but had to wait until they were sure the guilty couple were in bed together.

The twins were in their rooms with the doors shut, and as Miems lay in the dark she thought about Dane McDonald and slipped her hand beneath her nightgown. She was surprised how wet she was, as she never got wet with Danie.

"Oh my God!" she gasped out loud, biting on her bottom lip and arching her back - then immediately she felt guilty for taking the Lord's name in vain.

"Fuck me Dane! Fuck me with your big, young cock!" she whispered.

The mental image pushed Miems over the edge and a jolt of high-voltage electricity coursed down her spine and arced in an explosion of sensational energy and pleasure in her hips. Her orgasm consumed every cell of her body. Her brain was enveloped in swirling orange colors that spiraled on the inside of her tightly-shut eyelids and continuing jolts on her sensitive pubic bone triggered more orgasms that came in shivering aftershocks.

Finally her climax subsided and she lay on her back trembling and completely spent.

For a long while she could think of nothing, happy to

simply enjoy the contented sensations of satisfaction.

As she drifted into a peaceful sleep she thought of Dane and imagined how wonderful it would feel with him spooned against her back, his arms wrapped around her.

Chapter 12

It was a Wednesday morning and Tamarin was helping set out the plates and prepare tables in the restaurant, to be ready for the lunchtime diners who'd start arriving in around half an hour.

For some unknown reason they were never able to figure out, Wednesday lunchtimes were always busy.

"Maybe it's the day for a mid-week cleanse," speculated Kerishnee, the Indian cook who grew up in Durban. She checked a tall saucepan of lentils simmering on a gas-burner, and stirred them with a wooden spoon.

Tamarin pursed her lips. It was a discussion they had many times before and one day, perhaps they would come up with the answer.

"I still think by Wednesday people are sick of eating packed lunches and want a change. It also gives them a chance to get out of the office," said Tamarin, holding a spoon to the light to check it was properly clean.

She thought about Adrian a lot that day. Over the past few weeks the boy had changed. He was more confident. No longer so timid. He was also evasive about what he did in the afternoons. When she asked him, he brushed her off with answers and explanations she knew were not true. And she could no longer brow-beat him to get him to tell the truth. She shuddered and silently prayed he was not turning into his father.

I must go home early and unexpected one afternoon, she thought. It's the only way I'll find out what's really going on.

She folded starched, crisp, white, linen napkins so they looked like miniature swans and carefully placed them on the side-plates. In the center of each table she arranged a small vase of flowers bought from a flower vendor on the sidewalk.

She was just about to fill the glass pitchers with water when Anita, the restaurant owner, called to her, pointing to the phone at the reception counter.

Tamarin frowned. Who was calling her now? She hoped it wasn't her mother.

"Who is it?" she asked Anita.

"They didn't say."

She wiped her hands on the front of her apron before picking up the telephone receiver.

"Tamarin," she said.

"Mrs von Pletzen?" asked a voice on the other end of the line.

"Yes."

"This is Mrs Nel."

She did not recognize the name.

"Yes," she said tentatively.

"I am the head mistress at Adrian's school."

A surge of panic hit Tamarin like a freight train.

"Adrian!" she gasped. "Is Adrian okay? What's happened?" Her voice was strident, laced with anxiety.

"He is fine," said Mrs Nel. "He is absolutely okay... unfortunately I cannot say the same about the other boy."

Tamarin's mind whirled, struggling to understand what the woman said. Other boy? What other boy?

"Adrian was involved in an altercation with another pupil, an older boy," said Mrs Nel. "Unfortunately he injured the other child quite badly."

"Adrian?" said Tamarin, her surprise obvious. "My Adrian? Are you sure? Adrian has never had a fight in his life. He's a gentle boy who hates violence. Are you sure you have the right child?"

"I'm afraid so. He's here in my office. The other boy was taken to hospital. I think it best if you get down here as soon as possible."

Tamarin hung up the phone, her head spinning.

Chapter 13

Liza was worked up. The South African government was beating its chest and threatening to send more troops into Angola.

She was outraged that Pretoria was eager to interfere in the affairs of another country, just at the time it freed itself, from what she believed, was the yoke of colonialism. She was not the only one upset. Students at Wits University organized a lunchtime protest meeting in the open-air amphitheater located across the courtyard, opposite the steps of the *Great Hall*.

The meeting drew a capacity crowd of irate youngsters, many carrying placards condemning the South African Defense Force, calling for the fall of the government and demanding the release of jailed African National Congress leader, Nelson Mandela.

It was the sort of gathering that terrified the security authorities, and a large squad of riot policemen was assembled to monitor proceedings.

Liza found a spot near the front, close to the speakers' podium. She carried a placard that read FREE NELSON MANDELA. Beside her was a fellow law student with a poster on which was written: UNBAN THE ANC!

They knew they were committing a crime by displaying those slogans. Both placards could land them in jail, but they did not care. If spending time in prison meant they contributed to the fall of an unjust system, it was a price they would pay.

The first speaker was the chairman of the Students' Representative Council, a fiery, red-bearded, anthropology graduate busy with his honors degree.

"Are we going to let old white racists send us to war against people we don't know, to prop up a regime we don't support?" He bellowed into a megaphone.

"No!" they responded.

"Are we?" he screamed again.

"No! No!"

This time louder.

About fifty yards away, the assembled policemen fidgeted. Each carried either a **sjambok* or a long baton. Fingers curled and uncurled around the handles of the instruments. Many of the cops were the same age as the protesters. They trembled, excited and pumped by the prospect of cracking the heads of liberal long-hairs.

"Look at the pigs. How they dare invade our campus and intimidate us!" yelled the SRC chairman. "The fuckers are spoiling for a fight!"

On the top of the steps of the amphitheater a student wearing a red T-shirt, with the image of Che Guevara on the front, stood and turned to face the police. He stretched out his right arm, his middle finger raised.

"There is no doubt, we want you out!" he began to chant, urging the other students to join him.

The crowd rose, copying his gesture and chanting: "There is no doubt. We want you out!"

They advanced towards the line of policemen, maintaining the chant and gesture, stamping their feet in time.

Liza was in the middle of the pack, her face contorted, veins in her temples bulging as she hurled abuse at the cops. If it was the last thing she did in her life, she was going to be part of the struggle to bring down the government.

Sjamboks and batons were clasped, knuckles white, cops swallowed nervously, coiled and waiting for the order to charge and break up the gathering.

A police captain, his face slick with sweat, his armpits wet, hollered at the approaching phalanx through a megaphone, his Afrikaans accent apparent.

"This is an illegal gathering. You must disperse!"

His instructions were met with jeers and derision from the students.

"We have no doubt! We want you out! We have no doubt! We want you out!"

Suddenly an empty bottle arced through the air and shattered at the feet of one of the police officers, showering him in shards of flying glass.

The reaction of the cops was instant. Teargas cannisters were fired and then they charged, sjamboks and batons raised above their heads.

Blows rained like a summer hail storm on the students. Panic and pandemonium followed. They scattered in all directions, the cops after them, like greyhounds hunting rabbits. Liza watched horrified, as a burly policeman chased a girl with an UNBAN THE ANC placard and smacked her across the back of her head with his baton.

She collapsed in a heap, blood staining her blond hair. The cop did not break stride or slow down as she fell, his stare fixed on his next target.

Liza's eyes and throat burned. She gasped and coughed as a wave of teargas wafted over her. She ran blindly, terrified, unsighted and unaware of where she was going. All she could focus on was getting away.

Her body was aflame with the chemical sting of the teargas, and she stumbled blindly, vaguely conscious of the screams of fellow students and the sounds of the dull thuds of striking batons and sjamboks.

She kept expecting to have a blow land on head. She braced herself for it and wondered if she could bear the pain.

Unimaginable terror gripped her. She thought of her father, how he'd disapprove of her then, and hated him even more.

Behind her she heard the thump of boots on the brick paving and instinctively swerved right. The sudden and swift change of direction made her lose her footing and she fell heavily, grazing her hands and skinning her right elbow. The tumble knocked the wind out of her and she lay gulping on her side. Through watery eyes she saw cops wailing away at fallen students, then dragging them to vans parked along the edge of the courtyard.

Get up! she screamed inwardly but the messages sent by her brain refused to reach her body and limbs. Her body burned, agonizingly hot.

They were coming! The cops worked their way towards her and she knew she was going to spend the night in a holding cell at the Hillbrow Police Station.

She couldn't help it, she didn't want to, but she began to sob.

In the clutter of her thoughts, jumbled with the noise of the dying battle, she did not hear him at first.

"Take my hand!" he said, louder and more urgently this time.

Her eyes refused to focus.

"Hurry!" he yelled. "Take my hand, let me get you out of here."

A black youngster she'd seen on campus, stood over, his hand reached out to her.

His other hand held his T-shirt tightly over his nose and mouth.

She reached out and he pulled her to her feet, and with her arm around his shoulders so she would not fall, dragged her away from the melee. He guided her into a passage, leading from a door on the side of the *Great Hall* and into a male toilet designated: *Staff Only*.

Fleeing made Liza cough uncontrollably. Snot leaked in strings from her nose, her eyes watered so badly it was impossible to see.

Trembling violently, she grasped the edge of a wash-basin and threw up. Painful spasms wracked her body as she retched.

When she was done she collapsed onto her knees on the

tiled floor. The young, black man who rescued her, soaked his T-shirt in cold water in a basin, went to where she sat with her back against the wall, and washed her face.

"This will help," he said, squeezing water onto her head. It cascaded down her forehead, across her cheeks and onto her neck and chest. The relief it brought was indescribable.

"Thank you," she said softly, almost too exhausted to speak. "I think you may have saved my life."

He sat on the floor beside her and softly dabbed her face.

"If that's true I guess you owe me," he said, his face breaking into a broad smile that showed his white teeth.

She rubbed her eyes, and for the first time in a while they focused properly. She ran her gaze over his bare torso, immediately aware of how muscular he was. Like a polished statue.

Her heart skipped a beat and she had to clear her throat before she could speak.

"I guess I do," Liza said softly.

**The sjambok or litupa is a heavy leather whip. It is traditionally made from an adult hippopotamus (or rhinoceros) hide, but is also commonly made out of plastic.*

A strip of the animal's hide is cut and carved into a strip 0.9 to 1.5 meters (3 to 5 ft) long, tapering from about 25 mm (1 in) thick at the handle to about 10 mm (3⁄8 in) at the tip. This strip is then rolled until reaching a tapered-cylindrical form. The resulting whip is both flexible and durable. A plastic version was made for the South African Police Service, and effectively used for riot control.

The sjambok had a variety of uses, with the most obvious being cattle driving. It was heavily used by the Voortrekkers driving their oxen while migrating from the Cape of Good Hope. Even today, the sjambok is used by herdsmen to drive cattle. They are widely available in South Africa from informal traders to regular stores from a variety of materials, lengths and thicknesses. They are an effective weapon to kill snakes and ward off dogs and other attackers and are still carried in public by many black South Africans for self-defense. Many South African households keep a sjambok. - Source Wikipedia.org

Chapter 14

Tamarin was sweating and out of breath when she mounted the steps of Adrian's, school two at a time. She ran all ten blocks from the restaurant, stopping only when forced to do so by a red traffic light.

When she stopped at the reception window of the administration office she panted so fiercely she could not speak and stood bent over struggling for air. She waved a hand towards the receptionist, indicating the woman should give her a few moments to compose herself.

The headmistress's office was diagonally across from the reception hatch and Mrs Nel got up from behind her desk and came out when she heard Tamarin.

"Mrs von Pletzen?" she asked, putting a hand on the shoulder of the bent over woman.

"Yes," Tamarin squeaked, trying desperately to fill her lungs and calm her pounding heart.

"Please come into my office," Mrs Nel said, gently maneuvering Adrian's mother towards the door. She turned to the receptionist.

"Marge, please bring Mrs von Pletzen a glass of cold water. I'm sure she needs it."

Tamarin nodded and entered the office. Immediately she saw Adrian sitting on a couch in a corner of the room, beneath a color photograph of the country's Prime Minister. Her son had specks of blood on the front of his white shirt and it was apparent someone had yanked his school tie, as the knot was compressed, tiny and tight.

Tamarin hoped they would be able to loosen it and not have to cut it off his neck.

"Mom," he said, standing up to go to her.

"Sit down and keep quiet," she snapped at him. Her breath had returned and with it her seething anger.

He sat down, his hands in his lap, refusing to look at her

while he picked at his fingernails.

Mrs Nel indicated to Tamarin to take a seat on either of the chairs in front of her desk. She rocked back on her swivel chair, her fingers interlocked and her hands clasped and resting on her belly.

"What happened?" asked Tamarin, anxious to get straight to the point.

Marge, appeared with a tall glass of cold water balanced on a white dinner plate. She handed it to Tamarin.

"Thank you," Tamarin said, after first gulping down two thirds of the cool liquid.

When Marge left the office, Mrs Nel spoke.

"It appears one of the older boys, a senior, Nico Grobbelaar, was harassing Adrian. The boy is a renowned trouble-maker and bully."

"He grabbed my tie and slammed me against the wall," interrupted Adrian. "I wasn't doing anything but he started choking me and calling me a faggot. I reacted just like Dave taught me and the next thing I knew he was on the ground, crying and screaming."

"I told you to be quiet!" said Tamarin, glaring at her son, her voice pinched.

Adrian snapped his mouth shut.

"Is that what happened?" asked Tamarin, turning back to the headmistress.

"Yes, it would appear so. The other boy definitely started it."

"You said he was taken to hospital?"

"Yes, seems Adrian broke his arm."

Tamarin frowned. She touched her dry lips with the tip of her tongue, then drained the rest of her glass of water.

"I don't condone violence in any circumstances whatsoever," she said. "I've raised Adrian to solve confrontations through dialog and negotiation."

A wry smile briefly crossed Mrs Nel's face but it was gone in a flash.

"To be honest, I don't think he'd have much chance getting that right with Nico Grobbelaar," she said. "He's not really much of a reasoner or negotiator."

She was secretly glad the school bully was dealt a lesson by the most unlikely of victims.

"Be that as it may," said Tamarin, "I still disapprove. What will happen next? Will my son be expelled from the school?"

"I doubt it. There will be an internal inquiry and if Adrian's version of events is accurate, he'll be given a warning."

Tamarin sighed with relief.

"Will the parents press charges?"

"I believe it very unlikely," said Mrs Nel. She leaned forward with her forearms resting on the desk.

"The boy's father puts great stock in his son being the toughest kid on the block. Like father like son, if you get my meaning. Bringing charges will make the whole incident public. People will know your son handed Nico a beating, and I don't think Mr Grobbelaar senior could bear the shame of that."

Tamarin nodded. The last thing she could afford right now was an expensive legal battle.

"Take Adrian home and send him back to school tomorrow. I will keep you appraised of developments but I honestly don't think you should worry."

She showed Adrian and Tamarin to the steps of the school and said goodbye to them, before turning on her heel and heading back to her office.

As soon as they stepped onto the sidewalk and were out of view from the office, Tamarin's temper exploded and she slapped Adrian across the side of his head.

The blow took him by surprise and stars danced before his eyes.

"What have I told you about using violence to solve problems?" railed his mother, and he had to duck to avoid another swat she aimed at him.

Chapter 15

Back home Tamarin sat Adrian down at the kitchen table and read him the *Riot Act*. She knew she should get back to work, because every minute she was away she lost income, but she figured it was more important to give Adrian a stern talking to.

She noticed changes in the boy over the last few weeks. He seemed more confident and sure of himself, like his father, and for a moment she shuddered.

Even now he was different. In the past he would have cowered and apologized sheepishly when scolded, but now he seemed unaffected, defiant even.

"Do you understand you did something terrible and wrong?" she asked, pulling out a chair so she could sit and face him. She leaned forward with her forearms on the table, fixing a penetrating stare on him.

Unusually, he held her gaze and did not blink.

"I asked you a question, Young Man and I expect an answer! Do not defy me, or I will punish you." She emphasized the word 'will'.

"Yes," he replied.

"Yes what?" Tamarin snapped.

"Yes I realize I have done something you think is wrong," he said, his voice firm.

"So you don't think it was wrong?"

"No. I'm tired of being bullied. Maybe now they'll leave me alone."

"You know I don't condone violence. It is the weak way of handling things," she said.

"I bet Nico Grobbelaar and his friends don't think I'm weak any more," he said. He folded his little arms and set his jaw.

"The way to have handled would've been to talk to him, to tell him how sad it made you feel."

Adrian rolled his eyes and snorted.

"I tried that and it just made it worse. This is your fault for not allowing me to be a normal kid."

Tamarin sat up as though her son slapped her in the face.

"What do you mean by that?" the surprise in her voice genuine.

"You won't let me do what other boys do. I can't play cricket or rugby or be part of the running races. You make me go to stupid yoga and pottery and it makes me look like a sissy."

Tamarin was flabbergasted.

"But you love yoga and pottery!" she cried. "You told me so!"

"I just said that to make you happy," Adrian mumbled. "I hate it... them."

For a few minutes neither spoke a word, each absorbed in their own thoughts.

Tamarin tapped her fingers on the table while Adrian traced patterns on the surface with his.

He was concerned about the punishment his mother would dish out, but glad he did what he had to. He was also pleased he told her how he felt about pottery and yoga.

Tamarin tried to process the events and what her son said. She struggled to gather her thoughts and think coherently. It was a bitter to pill to swallow. She truly believed she was doing a good job raising Adrian, and was a good mother.

Tears welled in her eyes and she looked away hoping he would not see them.

It took her a while to bring her emotions in check.

"Where did you learn to fight like that?" Her voice was soft, her hands clasped on the table in front of her.

"Dave showed me," he replied.

She cocked an eyebrow. There was no-one at the school

called Dave that Adrian had ever spoken about.

"Is he a new kid in your class?" she asked.

Adrian smiled.

"He's not a kid. He's the guy who lives upstairs. He's a journalist and an editor or something. You must see the cool photos he has."

Tamarin knew exactly who he was. They had greeted each other on many occasions, and though he seemed keen to strike up conversation, she made sure she always remained cool and aloof. Norah told her he worked for a girly magazine, and that alone was enough to make her decide she wanted nothing to do with him.

She despised those magazines and the people who worked for them, but even more she despised the girls who posed for them. They were willingly permitting themselves to be exploited, and setting back the liberation of women - and the fight to be recognized as equal - by years. Tamarin viewed them as traitors to a cause to which she was deeply committed.

"I know who he is," she said, her voice cold. "I told you I don't want you talking to strangers."

"He's not a stranger," said Adrian defiantly. "He lives in *Hillbrow Heights*. He is our neighbor."

"All the same, we know nothing about him. For all you know, he could be an ax-murderer or someone who does bad things to little boys."

"He's not an ax-murderer or anything bad," said Adrian, his voice strident as he grew offended. "He's a nice guy. He's my friend. He saved me when the bullies chased me after yoga and wanted to beat me up. He stopped them and chased them away. I would have thought you'd be glad about that, Mommy."

"Of course I am," said Tamarin. "I just don't think it right for a boy of your age to be friends with a grown man - especially that man. I think what he does for a living is wrong and you are young and impressionable. I don't want you to learn bad things."

Adrian's bottom lip trembled. Once again his mother was interfering in his life. He liked Dave. He reminded him of his dad and he missed his father. He wished his family could be normal like most of the other kids at school.

"He's not like that at all," wailed Adrian, growing increasingly anxious. "You don't even know him. You always tell me not to judge people until I know them, but now you are doing it."

It was like a slap in the face with a wet towel to Tamarin. Her son was right. She had taught him that. She had no counter argument to offer.

She sighed.

"You are quite correct," she said. "I don't know him. I will make a plan to meet him and then decide if it's appropriate for you to be friends with him."

The truth was, she had already decided, and was simply going through the motions to appease her son.

"But until we know for sure, I don't want you to see him. I think that is fair. I'm doing it to keep you safe."

Adrian pouted and looked at his hands.

"Do we have a deal?" asked Tamarin.

"Yes," muttered Adrian reluctantly. "When will you go and see him?"

"Soon."

"You promise?'

"I promise?"

Chapter 16

"Thank you for your help," said Liza. "I think you may have saved my life!"

She looked better than she did half an hour ago, but knew she still looked terrible. She washed off the black eye-shadow streaking her cheeks - the result of the teargas. Her hair was wet, stringy and clung to her forehead, and her face and eyes were still puffy and blotched.

She sniffed and searched in her nylon backpack for a tissue.

"I'm sorry, I hope I've not ruined your T-shirt," she said, fixing her gaze upon him.

He was tall, muscular and coffee-colored. More Nescafe® with cream than Mocca Java .

"Nothing that won't wash out," he said.

His accent was different. More English. Caribbean? She wasn't sure. The only Caribbean accents Liza had heard were in movies.

He held out his hand.

"I'm Kofi," he said.

She shook his hand. His grip was strong, his skin warm. She shivered involuntarily.

"Elizabeth... Liza," she said.

He held her hand in his for longer than he should have, but she did not mind. She liked it. He had, after all, saved her.

"Wait here," Kofi said. "I'll check if it's safe to leave."

She nodded.

A while later he returned and Liza could not help but notice how his wet T-shirt clung to his chiseled body.

"If we slip out of the back of the *Great Hall* we'll be okay," he said. "The cops have rounded up a bunch of people by the amphitheater and are loading them into police vans."

"Pigs!" spat Liza, hating her father even more.

"They're probably also waiting off campus, so maybe we should lie low for a bit," said Kofi.

For the first time he was able to study the girl. He'd seen her around campus and took note of her because she was so beautiful. She wasn't in any of his engineering classes and he figured she was a freshman.

"Why don't we get a cup of coffee at the canteen while we wait for the heat to die down," he suggested. "I'll buy you a burger if you like."

Liza blushed. The tips of her ears and cheeks burned, and for a moment she was pleased her emotions were concealed by the ruddy blotches on her face.

"Thank you," she whispered, avoiding his gaze. "I'd like that."

It was around a five minute walk to the new canteen, located in a tall, unpainted concrete building. Neither of them spoke. Liza dearly wanted to take his hand but fought the urge. Doing so was illegal and could land her in trouble.

Screw this fucked up country! she thought, suddenly seething. She gritted her teeth, more resolved than ever to destroy the system and be part of creating something better.

The canteen was filled with students, nosily recounting the stories of confrontations with the police. The majority of youngsters were firmly anti-government, but on one side of the huge room, occupying three tables, was a group of students who were ex-servicemen and they held an opposing view. They eyed the others, spoiling for a fight.

"See if you can find somewhere to sit," said Kofi. "I'll get us something to eat and drink."

For the briefest of moments he touched her forearm.

Liza scanned the room. Every table was occupied and

she thought they may have to take their food and eat it outside. But then a group of four diners, at a table right by where she stood, got up and left without clearing away and disposing of their trays and paper cups. Liza claimed the table before anyone else got the chance.

She shoved the used plastic trays, food wrappers and paper cups into a pile, to make space.

A few minutes later Kofi arrived, precariously balancing a tray in his hands.

"For you," he said, handing her a polystyrene container with a burger and chips, as well as a waxed paper mug of steaming coffee.

"Sugar?"

She nodded and he tossed a small, white, sealed packet to her. She ripped it open, emptied the contents into the coffee and stirred it with a disposable, wooden stick.

Her heart beat fast, her breath was short and she could not understand why she was so nervous.

The truth was, she knew. This was her knight in shining armor, the savior of damsels in distress, her man on a white horse.

She sipped her coffee and picked at her food, not sure what to say, avoiding his gaze because she was terrified she'd blush like a silly schoolgirl.

"What are you studying?" he asked, finally breaking the awkward silence.

"Law. I plan to be a human rights lawyer one day."

He nodded. That explained why she was at the protest rally.

"First year?"

She nodded.

"You?"

"Engineering. Third year."

"Where are you from? Your accent does not sound local."

He smiled.

"Originally from Nigeria but I've lived in different places

around the world. My father is a diplomat. He is the ambassador in Lesotho."

Liza raised her eyebrows. She was impressed. The highest ranking government official she ever met was a police colonel - her father's boss... and the brigadier who owned *Hillbrow Heights*.

"Why did you choose to study here?" she asked. "Surely you could have gone to a university in England instead of in this shithole country."

He smiled, his teeth white and perfect.

"I could have, but my mother wanted me close by. It's only a few hours drive to Lesotho. Maseru is right by the border."

"But don't you feel uncomfortable here? I mean there aren't a lot of...," she hesitated, trying to find the right word.

"Blacks," he said. "It's okay, you can say it. It's not an offensive term."

She felt herself blush. Liza guessed there were less than a hundred black students at Wits University. There were universities for blacks in the homelands, and that was where the government wanted them to go.

"Do I feel uncomfortable?" He shrugged his shoulders. "Sure... sometimes... but I ignore it. I figure there is nothing I can do about other people's ignorance."

He dipped a potato wedge into a puddle of crimson ketchup and popped it into his mouth.

"And after the difficulties I faced in getting admitted to the university, I'm certainly not going to allow anyone to spoil my experience."

"What sort of difficulties?" asked Liza. She held the hamburger in both hands and took a healthy bite, sauce running down her chin. It was greasy, juicy and delicious.

Kofi leaned across the table and wiped her chin with a paper napkin.

"Thank you," she mumbled, her mouth full of food.

"Because I am black - actually I am only half black, my mother is white but that doesn't count with the South African government - I had to apply for special exemption to attend a white university. At first the government refused. They said there were black universities I could go to. In the end my father had to pull a few strings and I think the British Ambassador to South Africa whispered in a few of the right ears."

Liza shook her head.

"That's terrible," she whispered. She wanted to reach across the table and take his hand, but stopped herself when she realized the group of military veterans was watching.

He shrugged.

"You learn to live with these things. I'm a lot more privileged than millions of people who were born here." His voice was sombre but suddenly he smiled. "But things are changing in this country, faster than many realize. I know a lot of brave people working to overthrow the regime and create something better."

"It can't happen soon enough for me," said Liza.

Kofi dumped the contents of a packet of sugar into his coffee and stirred it.

"Enough about me, tell me about you," he said.

For a moment Liza felt a stab of panic.

"There really isn't much to tell," she said. "Next to yours, my life is plain and boring."

"I don't believe you for one second," he said, his voice chocolaty. "Someone as beautiful as you must have a life filled with adventure."

Liza's heart skipped a beat. This guy certainly knew the moves.

"If you believe being the daughter of an asshole policeman is an adventure, then yes, I guess my life is filled with excitement."

She thought she should get what her father did, out and

on the table as quickly as possible. She studied Kofi's face, half expecting him to get up and leave.

When he reached for the salt shaker he briefly and gently touched her hand with the tips of his fingers.

"I can imagine," he said softly. "I don't always see eye-to-eye with my father."

She released the breath she held trapped in her lungs, exhaling slowly, an immense feeling of relief wafting over her.

"I like you and thought you might run screaming when I told you that," she said, her hand trembling, her eyes locked on his.

He smiled tenderly.

"I learned long ago not to judge people by the beliefs of their parents or the color of their skin."

His voice was soft and Liza's heart turned to goo.

"I saw how you conducted yourself today and that told me all I need to know."

"I'd like to see you again," Liza blurted out. She hoped she didn't appear too forward or eager."

"I would like that but it won't be easy, and you know you are putting yourself at risk. A white woman with a black man will draw instant attention and could get you arrested."

He paused while he drained the last of his coffee.

"And I don't think your father would approve," he added.

"Fuck him!" she spat. "He's an asshole."

"We can't meet around here," he said, meaning in a white area. "It would have to be in Soweto, and even there will be dangerous. But I have friends there."

A thrill of excitement blasted through Liza, starting in her belly and radiating outwards until it felt as though every cell in her body tingled.

Soweto, a giant black city right on Johannesburg's doorstep few whites knew anything about or had ventured into. Just the thought of it - and the horror stories her father told of it - made her shiver deliciously.

"Cool!" she said trying to appear nonchalant and worldly.

Kofi glanced at his watch.

"I need to get going, I have plans for the weekend. Let's meet here again on Monday at lunchtime when we can take it further."

Liza was disappointed. She wanted to spend more time with this caramel god. She wanted to talk to him more, and Oh God, how she wanted to take his face in her hands and kiss those sweet lips!

"Monday," she said. "Lunchtime. I look forward to it."

Chapter 17

"Get a grip on yourself!" Tamarin scolded herself out loud.

It was the third time she went to her front door with the intention of marching to that gutter journalist's flat to tell him to stay away from Adrian - and it was the third time she chickened out.

She couldn't figure why she was so nervous. Normally she had no problems tearing men a new one. But there was something about this guy that intimidated her. Not that she thought he might turn violent or anything like that, but he was strong and self-assured and she was convinced he would not be intimidated by her.

She was used to men withering and crumbling before her, but she didn't believe Dave Marais would. More likely he'd find her amusing and laugh in her face, and Tamarin did not know how she'd handle that.

For a moment she considered putting it off until sometime in the future, but Adrian was on her case about keeping her promise.

And she needed to get to work. Saturday lunches at the restaurant were usually busy and profitable.

She already decided she wasn't going to like Dave and would declare him unsuitable to Adrian, forbidding her son to have anything to do with him. She was simply doing this for the sake of appearances.

Adrian was going to be furious. She knew that and braced herself for his anger - especially now he was so much more assured and self-confident. She hated causing her son hurt, but sometimes a mother knew best. One day he'd thank her and be pleased she kept him safe from people who could make him like his father. Of course he would not see it now, but she hoped he'd understand she did it because she loved him and one day, sometime in the future, thank her.

The Green Junction closed for the weekend after lunch on Saturday, and Tamarin thought they might go to a movie that night. She planned to get a newspaper to see if anything suitable was showing and tomorrow she thought they could have a picnic on the lawns at Zoo Lake.

She hoped Adrian would like that and that it would calm his anticipated anger.

Tamarin took a deep breath and sighed. She gathered up her grass basket, locked the door behind her and headed upstairs to Dave's apartment.

When she got to his front door she again had to gather her courage, and after giving herself a stern talking to, she knocked loudly on the door. For a long while there was no response and just when she decided no-one was home and was about to leave, someone slid back a deadbolt on the door.

It swung open and Dave Marais stood there, dressed only in a pair of white cotton briefs that did little to hid his package. Instinctively Tamarin glanced at his crotch but instantly looked away, feeling guilty. She felt the tips of her ears burn hot, and ran her tongue over her dry lips. South of her belly-button a warm, long-forgotten glow flickered.

She hated men, but even more, she hated that she missed sex with a man. It was one of the few good things in her marriage.

Dave's hair was disheveled and he rubbed his eyes. It was obvious he was sleeping when she knocked.

"Hello," he said, stifling a yawn. "You're from downstairs, Adrian's mother."

"Yes, I need to talk to you about Adrian." She hesitated. "But I can come back some other time when you're... dressed."

He followed her gaze to his briefs.

"Yes, sorry about that. Don't be silly. Come in. Let me

have a pee and I'll put some pants on."

He turned around and headed back into the apartment, expecting her to follow. For a moment she watched him.

Wow! He's built! she thought.

She immediately tried to change her train of thought. After all, she despised powerful, alpha males who thought their role in life was to protect and dominate women.

Is that what he believed? She didn't know him and knew she should not make judgments without evidence, but decided he did. Why else would he have a punching bag in his lounge?

She could hear him in the bathroom and took the opportunity to examine the lounge. For a single guy, living alone, it was remarkably neat and tidy.

When she saw the photographs on the wall she gasped. Her mind was now definitely made up! The man was a pervert and she did not want her son to have anything to do with him.

She would ban Adrian from even talking to him. She found a chair where she did not have to look at the photographs of topless women, and sat, tightly crossing her legs and arms.

A while later Dave returned. He wore a pair of navy shorts and a white T-shirt with a cartoon of Snoopy seated at a typewriter on the front of it.

"Coffee," he said, setting out two mugs on the kitchen counter. "I can't talk without it. I have a deadline looming so I worked 'til late last night."

"I must talk to you about your relationship with my son," she said, her mouth dry as powder, her voice wavering.

"Sure, but first coffee." He spooned a heaped teaspoon of coffee powder into each mug. "I've only got instant, sorry."

"Instant is fine," said Tamarin, growing flustered. She wanted to dictate the way the conversation went.

"You work at that vegetarian restaurant near the

hospital, eh? I saw you there when I walked past."

"Vegan," she corrected.

"I'll stop in sometime. Never really seen the attraction. I figure vegetarian meals must be incredibly bland and boring but maybe you'll convince me otherwise."

The kettle boiled and he poured boiling water into the two mugs.

"Milk?"

She shook her head.

"Of course," he said. "Sorry, Adrian told me you are vegan. I forgot. Sugar?"

"Two please."

He stirred her mug and handed it to her and she clasped it in both hands.

"Would you like a **rusk*?" he asked opening a cake tin with a picture of a dog on it.

"No thank you. I already had breakfast and this is not a social call."

He sat on the couch opposite her, dunking his rusk in his coffee.

"Sounds serious, what's on your mind?"

Tamarin took a sip of coffee and drew in a breath.

"It seems you and my son have developed something of a relationship and I am not sure I like it."

"I'm not sure I'd call it a relationship. He stops by sometimes and I've shown him a few ways to protect himself from bullies."

"Exactly... and I don't approve of your teaching him violence. It's not the way I want him to grow up. I want him to know there is a better way than using his fists."

"Which is?"

"Negotiation and reasoned discussion."

Dave raised his eyebrows and pursed his lips.

"That didn't seem to work for him. It got his ass kicked and made his life miserable. He tells me, since putting that bully in his place he's had no further problems and has new friends. Sometimes a boy has to man up and take charge if he wants his life to be better."

"You may believe that but I don't and it's not the way I want my son to grow up. In addition, I don't want him around this filth."

She pointed at the photographs on the lounge wall.

"You mean the pictures of naked women?" asked Dave.

"Yes. They are objectionable and exploit women."

Dave smiled.

"They're just titties," he said. "Like you and every other woman has." He made a point of looking at her chest. "And not one of these women was exploited. Every single one asked to be photographed and each was very well paid."

This wasn't going the way Tamarin planned it. She normally dominated conversations and intimidated men.

Dave set his empty coffee mug on a small table beside the couch. He leaned back and stretched out his legs causing his shorts to pull taut in his lap.

Oh my God! thought Tamarin. His dick was clearly outlined.

"I don't want Adrian seeing you," she stammered, quickly standing up. "I will tell him today."

"I'm sorry you say that. I like the little guy," said Dave. He escorted her to the front door. "But I'm still going to stop by the restaurant sometime."

He ushered her out and closed the door behind her.

Tamarin stood in the passage outside Dave's apartment, her mind racing.

All she could think about was how pissed Adrian was going to be... and the image of the outline of Dave's penis that was burned into her brain!

**rusk - a hard, dry biscuit or a twice-baked bread. It is very popular in South Africa.*

Chapter 18

Gary Hayden's wife, Cindy, was a nurse at the old Johannesburg Hospital and worked the day shift that Sunday.

She left their apartment in *Hillbrow Heights* at a quarter past six to make the three block walk to the hospital. It would give her plenty of time to gulp down a cup of coffee and a sandwich, and get herself organized before she started her shift.

Gary was irritated and sulking. He woke when she stepped out of the shower and figured it would be a good time to have sex.

Cindy liked a fuck as much as anyone else - just not when she was trying to get ready for work!

There was nothing she could do about his petulant disappointment, he'd just have to get over it!

After Cindy left, Gary made himself a cup of coffee and went back to bed. He was horny and frustrated. He needed to call someone and hook up. But who?

Almost all the women he knew were either married or in serious relationships. It was how he wanted it. The last thing he needed was some girl falling in love with him, with ideas of one day getting married and living happily ever after.

With married women he knew where they stood. All they wanted was little excitement on the side, and someone to do the things their husbands stopped doing.

It was a wonderful arrangement with only one down side - weekends were spent with husbands and boyfriends.

While Gary drank his coffee he wracked his brains. In the end he got up and got a little leather-bound address book he kept concealed in his work briefcase.

It listed all the women he had or could hook up with, and he was immensely proud to have passed sixty just last week. Of the sixty one names in the book there had to be one who could meet on a Sunday.

He started at the "*As*".

Anthea... no

Adrianna... uhuh

Britanny... moved to Cape Town.

Methodically he checked the names off , discounting all of them until he came to Elaine.

At first he wasn't sure who she was, but the note: *Hillbrow pool, red bikini, big tits, great fuck*, jogged his memory.

Yeah, he remembered her! It was an afternoon liaison. They went to her flat in Highpoint. She was an energetic poke. Why hadn't he called her back?

He recalled she said her husband owned or managed a nightclub - which meant he probably slept most of Sunday. Perhaps she could slip out.

Gary Hayden's one rule was he never brought women to his flat. The risk of being seen was simply too great and he certainly did not want them to know where he lived, and chance having one of them come knocking on his front door when Cindy was there.

If they could not meet at her place, he booked a room at the *Summit Club*, if he had money. The problem was, right now, he did not have money, as it was a lean month at work.

But he was horny and unless he scratched it, this itch was not going away. And he was pissed at Cindy. Screwing someone in their bed would serve her right.

He rolled across the double bed so he could reach the phone on the nightstand on Cindy's side of the bed and dialed Elaine's number.

She answered on the third ring.

"Hello."

"Elaine?"

"Yes."

"It's Gary. We met at the Hillbrow pool a while back. Do you remember?"

The line went silent for a few moments before she spoke, and when she did her voice was soft and it was obvious she held her hand over the receiver.

"Yes I remember very well. I was wondering when you were going to call, like you promised."

"I'm sorry about that. I had to go overseas on urgent business unexpectedly," he lied. "But I'm back now and I'd love to see you again. Can we get together?"

"When?"

"Today."

"My husband is here. He's sleeping."

"Can you slip out and come to me?"

She hesitated. This guy knew what he was doing in bed. He took her to places she never knew existed. He knew exactly what strings to pluck.

And lately that cupboard was pretty bare with her husband.

"An hour... two at the most," she whispered. "I'll leave a note saying I've gone to have coffee with my girlfriend."

"When can you be here?" asked Gary.

"An hour?"

"Excellent."

He gave her the address and directions.

It would give him just enough time to shower and make the bed.

~ ~ ~

A little over two hours later, Elaine, freshly showered and sexually satisfied, kissed Gary passionately in the open doorway of his apartment. She rubbed the palm of her hand over the front of his shorts.

"I'll call you soon," she said, before she kissed him once again and left.

She was euphoric and contented, stars in her eyes, and never saw the nurse leaning against a car parked on the other side of the road across from the entrance to *Hillbrow Heights*, carefully watching her.

Elaine glanced at her watch.

Shit! I'd better get home before Paulo becomes suspicious, she thought, quickening her pace.

Fifty yards behind her, on the other side of the road, the nurse did the same, her eyes firmly fixed on Elaine.

Chapter 19

When Butch saw Jarrod at university on Monday morning, his heart beat faster. He spent the whole weekend thinking of him. He could think of nothing else.

He was convinced he was in love, and the feeling left him dizzy and light-headed.

They found seats next to each other in the lecture hall and sat so the outsides of their thighs touched. It was electric. They ached to hold hands.

"I missed you," whispered Jarrod.

"Me too. You were all I thought about."

"I couldn't sleep. I wanted to call you."

"Why didn't you?"

"I was afraid after what you told me about your dad."

Sias nodded.

He could not believe how beautiful Jarrod was in his tight T-shirt and skin-tight black jeans.

"When can we get together?" he asked, suddenly lowering his voice when a girl sitting in the row in front of them turned around.

"Let's talk at lunchtime."

Butch nodded.

The lecture was on *Victorian Theater Practices* but Butch heard none of it and instead of taking notes, he doodled, drawing mostly hearts. The lunch break was more than two hours away and he wasn't sure if he could stand the wait.

~ ~ ~

They found a vacant table easily in the new canteen. Butch placed the plastic tray on the table and handed a grease-soaked packet containing a toasted cheese sandwich to Jarrod, as well as a Tab®. He ripped open a similar packet for himself and popped open a can of Fanta Grape®.

They sat across from each other, gazing into the each other's eyes. Butch dabbed the corners of his mouth with a paper napkin.

"I spoke to my friend about where we can go," said Jarrod. "There is a gay nightclub called the *Blue Bayou* he suggests."

Butch nodded. He knew where it was - inside a seedy-looking hotel he walked past quite often.

The words 'gay nightclub' disturbed him. Was he finally able to admit, even to himself, he was gay? An ordinary nightclub, where there were some gay people, still seemed normal, but once he went to a 'gay' nightclub, he crossed the line, nailed his colors to the mast and quite probably could never go back.

But perhaps it was the final push he needed.

"Do you want to go?" asked Jarrod.

When Butch spoke his mouth was dry.

"Yes," he whispered.

~ ~ ~

Butch saw his sister and the black guy come into in the canteen a few minutes after they sat down. He nodded to her and she returned the greeting. They found a table on the other side of the room.

The canteen was filling up.

"How was your weekend?" asked Liza, her eyes firmly fixed on Kofi's face.

"Good. I hung out with some friends in Soweto but it would've been better if you were there."

She blushed.

"Maybe sometime," she said.

"How about this weekend? I'm planning a get together with some friends I think you'll like."

Liza was quiet for a while. She wanted to say 'yes' but the fact was, she was scared. For most of her life her father fed her stories of terrible things that happened in black townships - and Soweto was the worst! According to her father, it was the murder and rape capital of the world, more dangerous than even war zones, and no white person stood a hope of coming out alive.

And a white woman!... the thought was too terrible to contemplate.

"You'll be safe, I promise," said Kofi, as though reading her mind. "You'll have a great time."

Finally Liza nodded.

"Okay. How will we get there?"

"I have a car. I can fetch you."

"Not at my home!"

Kofi smiled.

"Of course. I forgot. I have an apartment not far away from the university, we can go there and head on to Soweto later."

"You have an apartment... here?" Her voice was filled with surprise. It was illegal for blacks to live in white areas.

Kofi laughed.

"There are some advantages to having a father who is a diplomat. We enjoy some privileges. I think, for residence purposes, I am classified an 'honorary white'."

"So you can eat at white restaurants and go to movies in white areas?"

"Yes, in theory, but I don't. When a bunch of white farm boys is kicking the crap out of you because they figure you're a cheeky **kaffir*, a piece of paper with a government stamp on it doesn't mean much."

Liza gasped.

"Has that ever happened to you?"

"Not to me but to people I know."

Suddenly Liza felt ashamed. Ashamed of her father,

ashamed she was an Afrikaner and ashamed she was white.

Things had to change in this fucking country!

**kaffir - The word kaffir is a term used in South Africa to refer to a black person. Now widely considered an offensive ethnic slur, it was formerly considered by whites to be a neutral term for South African blacks.*

The word is derived from the Arabic term kafir (meaning "disbeliever"), which originally had the meaning "one without religion" (Wikipaedia)

Chapter 20

"Milk?" asked Norah.

Tamarin shook her head.

They sat in Norah's lounge with the glass doors leading to the balcony, open.

"I keep forgetting," said Norah. She handed Tamarin a cup of tea on a saucer and offered her a plate of biscuits, deliberately not mentioning they contained milk and butter. The poor thing could do with getting a bit of real food into her - and that wasn't the only thing she needed getting into her.

Norah Braithwaite-Smith's outlook on life, and how to solve its problems was simple. There was nothing much in life that couldn't be fixed by good marijuana, good food, strong booze and an energetic fuck - and that, she figured was what this girl lacked.

Tamarin took a chocolate biscuit and set it on the saucer beside the delicate china teacup.

"Take a few so I don't have to keep getting up," urged Norah.

Tamarin took two more biscuits.

She felt out of sorts that day and called in sick at the restaurant. After seeing Adrian off to school she took a hot, herb-infused bath then decided to visit Norah.

The woman was a tonic, but she also needed to buy more dope for her and Liza. But mostly she needed someone to talk to.

After her visit to Dave, and forbidding her son to see him, things turned unpleasant at home. As she expected, Adrian was furious and sulked. He refused to speak to his mother and did everything possible to avoid her. She figured he'd get over it in a day or two and things would return to normal, but they didn't. If anything, Adrian grew increasingly distant, and when he had no option but to speak to her, he was rude and snippy.

By keeping him away from the man she feared would influence him to become like his father, she was making him become like his father.

She sipped her tea and nibbled on a biscuit.

Norah sat across from her, dressed in a yellow and purple, tie-dyed caftan. Her new hairstyle made her look ten years younger. She stretched out her legs, displaying her bare feet.

"A penny for your thoughts," she said.

Tamarin sighed.

"I'm afraid it'll take more than a penny."

Norah leaned forward and patted Tamarin's knee.

"Tell me. It'll make you feel better."

"It's Adrian, he hates me."

"I'm sure he doesn't. All boys his age get angry with their mothers from time to time."

Tamarin set her teacup on a table beside her chair.

"I know, but this time it's different. I have never seen him so angry before. It's been days now and he refuses to talk to me or even be with me."

Norah dipped a biscuit into her tea and swore softly under her breath when the soggy half broke off and fell into the hot liquid.

"What brought this about?" she asked.

Tamarin told her about Dave and how he taught her son to protect himself, the encounter with the bully and how humiliated she was when summoned to the school.

"Adrian idolizes the man," said Tamarin.

"How is that a problem?" asked Norah. "I've got to know Dave and I think he's a nice guy."

"He reminds me too much of Adrian's father. All strong and macho. I don't want my boy to grow up to be like that."

"Why not? It seems to me far too many men are pussies nowadays. Sometimes it's nice to have someone to protect you, and let's be honest, being dominated in bed can be fun."

A naughty smile crossed her face and she chuckled.

Tamarin blushed as the image of Dave's dick crossed her mind. She made a point of not commenting.

Norah refilled her cup.

"Every boy needs a hero," she said. "Be careful about taking your son's away from him."

Tamarin avoided Norah's gaze. In her heart she knew it was the truth. But still, it went against so many firmly-held beliefs.

"But what about his job?... and those photographs on the wall! What will happen if Adrian sees them."

Norah threw her head back and laughed throatily.

"He's already seen them and the sky hasn't fallen in. And as Dave said; they're just titties. You don't think your son hasn't figured you have a pair? At his age and his likely raging hormones, he probably spies on you in the shower."

"That's just gross!" said Tamarin, but she knew it was probably true.

"Don't teach the boy a woman's body is dirty, should be hidden, not admired and not adored. It'll fuck him up and turn him into the person you don't want."

"Maybe you're right," said Tamarin.

"You know I am."

Chapter 21

It was just Danie and Miems at the dinner table.

Sias said he and some kid called Jarrod were going to the movies and then had to work on a university project at Jarrod's house.

"We've got a lot of ground to cover so I'll sleep at his home," lied Sias.

Liza was in a mood again and did not want to be around her parents, so she went to a book shop in Wolmarans street and figured she'd also play a few games of pinball at the amusement arcade nearby. She was worn out from the weight of university work and looked forward to the varsity vacations in a couple of weeks.

She was excited about her visit to Soweto on Friday and the chance to spend time alone with Kofi.

"Would you like more mashed potatoes?" asked Miems.

Danie nodded, his mouth full.

It was the first night in almost two weeks he was home early and he was glad the kids weren't around. Sometimes it was nice to spend time alone with his wife.

But Miems was not as enthusiastic. Of late she felt she had less and less in common with her husband. He lived in a cocoon woven from the strands of his work and life in the South African Police. He appeared interested in nothing else.

She, on the other hand, found stimulation at work, where people talked about movies, politics, fashion and travel. And they valued her opinion and took her seriously.

They were concerned about the increasingly militaristic and belligerent position the South African government took in South West Africa and the political pronouncements they about Angola.

"Mark my words, they are going to send our all sons to war," said one of the senior partners.

Miems shuddered when she considered the prospect of Sias being sent to fight in a foreign country.

She tried to talk to Danie about it, but he dismissed her concerns, saying everyone had a duty to fight to preserve Christian values and standards. She was thankful, as long as her son was at university, he was exempted from military training.

"How was your day?" asked Danie, spooning an additional heap of mash onto his plate.

"Good," said Miems. "Good, and yours?"

"Busy. You know how it is. It getting to be an increasingly perverted world out there and this area is a whore's nest. It's like Sodom and Gomorrah. You wouldn't believe if I told you, how many whores, druggies and **moffies* there are. Sometimes I think I'm gonna puke!"

He became so agitated he had to take a gulp of his brandy and Coke®.

"And *meid naaiers*, it's like a bloody epidemic. Seems sleeping with black women is now a national sport!"

van Staden was going to use the word 'kaffir' but stopped himself, because he knew Miems hated the term, and he wasn't in the mood for an argument.

"We got a tip a white man is living with a black woman in a block of flats not far from the police station. And not a young man, a middle aged guy with money. Makes you wonder what the hell is wrong with him that he can't find a real woman."

He took another mouthful of his drink and swirled the ice in the glass with the tip of a pudgy finger.

"But he's going to shit. We know exactly where he is and we have a raid planned later this week. We'll have them in jail so fast they won't have time to blink."

"What harm are they doing to anyone?" asked Miems, trying to keep her voice even and not provoke a row. "What people do in private hurts no-one else, why should anyone care."

Danie glowered at her. First his daughter and now his wife spouting liberal garbage. He figured working for lawyers - the lowest profession possible - affected her mind and he vowed when he was promoted to Warrant Officer and got a bump in salary he would force her to give up her job and stay at home. Where a good, Afrikaner woman was supposed to be.

He drew in his breath and puffed out his chest, and when he spoke it was as a schoolteacher talking to a particularly slow child.

"What harm? I can't believe you even ask that! First of all it's against the law and secondly, what happens when they have a child? Do you want a nation of coloreds? We're already being overrun by non-whites. If we don't hold the line we'll be overwhelmed and there'll be no future anymore for a white man. And the Bible is also clear about not mixing water and wine."

Miems wiped her mouth with a pale, blue, linen napkin.

"One day we are going to have to accommodate the blacks and find a way to all live in peace. Perhaps it's better to do it now, rather than wait until it's too late."

"We've already found a way," said Danie, using the same patronizing tone. "It's a beautiful solution. It's called *apartheid*. Where they have their own homelands to do whatever they want, and we live and rule in our country."

"But what about the people who were born and grew up here and have no connection with some faraway, rural piece of land and no allegiance to the man appointed chief."

Danie grew irritated.

"I don't know where you heard the communist crap you're speaking, but if you are black, no matter where you now live or were born, you are part of a tribe and your homeland is where that tribe is based. That's where you have rights, not in my country. Here you are a guest."

His voice grew strident, his face red, a vein pulsed on his

forehead and Miems knew it was best to shut up then. Her husband was a narrow-minded bonehead and trying to have a rational, adult conversation was a waste of time and breath. If it was debate she wanted, she'd have to seek it at work.

She clamped her lips into a thin, white line and began clearing the dishes from the table.

Danie took his plate of food and went to the lounge so he could watch the evening television news. He figured he'd finish the bottle of brandy he opened, because he wasn't going to get lucky tonight.

**moffie - derogatory South African term for a gay man.*

Chapter 22

Sias stood a little way up the road from the *Palms Hotel* while he waited for Jarrod to arrive. His parents believed he was meeting a friend and afterwards going to work on a university project.

He took his time getting dressed and primping himself. After a long soak in a tub infused with fragrant bath oils, he plucked his eyebrows, applied moisturizer liberally to his body and dabbed aftershave on his face and groin. He checked his nails were neatly clipped, and after brushing and flossing, gargled and rinsed with a peppermint-flavored mouthwash.

In the pocket of the figure-hugging jeans he struggled into, was a box of spearmint chewing gum. He wore a white, semi-transparent T-shirt. When he examined himself in the mirror, he was pleased.

"You look gooood," he said out loud and growled at his image.

He saw Jarrod make a u-turn in the road and reverse into a vacant parking spot a little way up the road. His heart pounded.

Jarrod wore a black fishnet vest and tight white trousers.

"Hi," said Butch. His hands were clammy and his lips dry. "You look nice."

"So do you," said Jarrod.

He put a hand behind Butch's head and drew him closer so he could kiss him.

For a moment Sias's instinct was to pull away, afraid people would see, but when Jarrod's lips touched his he relented. He returned the kiss passionately, pressing his tongue into Jarrod's open mouth. It felt so good, so liberating.

"How are you feeling?" asked Jarrod.

"Nervous as hell."

"Me too but it'll be fine. These are our people."

They walked hand-in-hand to the entrance of the *Palms Hotel*.

The *Blue Bayou* nightclub was situated in the cellar of the hotel and accessed by a narrow flight of concrete steps. Music pounded through a set of impressive speakers, colored strobes flashed and a ceiling-mounted mirror-ball slowly turned.

It seemed shiny, black leather was the most popular outfit. Leather caps and riveted collars were also big. The DJ wore a set of leather chaps that showed his bare ass cheeks. Studded straps criss-crossed his sweating chest, as he thrust his hips and gyrated to the music.

A number of couples were on the dance floor, locked together at the hips and lips.

"Do you want a drink?" asked Jarrod, his mouth close to Sias's ear so he could be heard above the throbbing music.

Butch nodded. He needed a drink, that was certain. He was a little overwhelmed by the situation.

"What?" yelled Jarrod.

"Cinzano® and lemonade. Make it a double Cinzano®."

He reached for his wallet but Jarrod waved his hand indicating he should put it away.

"On me, tonight," he said.

The bar was set up in a corner at the back of the room and business was brisk. It was going to take Jarrod a while to work his way to the front of the line.

Sias stood on one side of the room, away from the DJ, his arms crossed, while he watched the dancers. His head spun and he felt slightly dizzy. He was not sure if it was the result of nervousness or excitement. Probably a combination.

He was so engrossed watching the dance floor that he was unaware of a huge, bearded, man beside him, until a meaty hand clamped onto his butt cheeks.

He jerked with fright.

"Fresh meat!" said a gravely voice from behind the reddish beard. "Nice!"

Sias backed away from the man who reminded him of a bear.

"Haven't seen you here before," said the bear.

A wave of panic washed over Sias.

"No, first time," he said in a squeaky voice. "I'm here with someone."

"Doesn't matter. We're all friends."

Suddenly Butch knew exactly what it meant when people talked about being a rabbit trapped in the headlights of a speeding Peterbilt®. He looked around the room, desperately looking for some way to escape the bear.

Help came from an unexpected source.

"Quit scaring the virgins, Bruno," scolded a middle-aged woman, who appeared to have stepped off the set of an Adams Family movie. She put her hands on the bear's huge chest and pushed him away. "Fuck off and go get yourself a drink."

The giant's head drooped. He mumbled something and shuffled away.

She turned to Sias.

"Don't worry about him, he's mostly harmless."

She parted her black lips and smiled, and Butch felt better.

"Sit with us."

She indicated he should join her girlfriend at their table.

"I'm Elle and this is Helen," she said.

"Hello, I am Butch."

"You don't look it," snorted Helen.

Elle rolled her eyes.

"She thinks she's comedienne. Welcome Butch, are you here with someone?"

"My friend over there," said Sias, pointing to Jarrod, who appeared to have made little progress in reaching the bar counter.

"Your first time?"

He nodded and she smiled.

"It can be a little overwhelming in the beginning. Best advice I can give is keep an open mind and go with the flow. You've entered a new, exciting world. People come here because they don't fit in out there. In here they can lose their inhibitions and be totally free, without being judged. Embrace that."

They chatted for a few minutes while Butch waited for Jarrod to return with their drinks. He learned Elle knew she was a lesbian before she was a teenager and worked as a mid-level manager at an insurance company in the city.

Helen was married, bisexual and her husband was comfortable with her lifestyle.

Finally Jarrod returned and Butch thanked them for their company and excused himself.

They found a spot in an arched alcove where they could set their drinks on a waist-high shelf attached to the wall.

Jarrod slipped an arm around Butch's waist.

"What do you think?" he asked.

"Different and kinda scary," replied Butch. He laced his fingers into Jarrod's hand and kissed him. "But at least I can do this without being afraid."

Jarrod slid his hands down Butch's back and cupped his backside. He returned the kiss passionately while he pulled Sias's hips against his.

"Oh my God!" Butch moaned. His dick stirred.

For a few minutes they kissed and ground their hips together and were in heaven.

"Let's dance," said Butch, breaking away from their kiss. He was afraid he would ejaculate in his pants. He took Jarrod by the hand, and swaying his hips in time to the beat of the music, sashayed to the dance floor.

They danced until their faces glistened with sweat.

"I need a pee," yelled Jarrod.

"Me too. I could also do with another drink, I'm absolutely parched."

They maneuvered through the sweaty, mostly leather-clad dancers and headed up the concrete steps to the toilets on the first floor.

When Sias, pushed through the swing door, grimy and sticky, and stepped into the bathroom, he gasped and stopped in his tracks.

"Jesus!" he whispered.

A man was bent over one of the white, enamel basins, his trousers pooled around his ankles. Behind him, his chaps also down, was the bear, rhythmically thrusting his hips, as he fucked the man's ass.

The two youngsters stood rooted to the spot, their eyes stretched wide.

"Wassa matter?" said the bear, spit pooled in the corners of his mouth. "You never seen anyone get fucked before?"

The truth was, Sias had not.

He opened his mouth but no words would come out of it.

From the moans of pleasure of the guy with the bear's cock up his butt, it appeared he was enjoying the experience, and Sias could not help but see his penis was erect and angry.

"Let's just pee and get out of here," whispered Jarrod, his voice dry and hoarse.

Sias nodded, still unable to speak.

They relieved themselves at a large, cracked porcelain urinal, situated in front of a row of toilet stalls.

When Sias zipped himself up and turned around, he had a clear view of one of the open toilet stalls, where a guy in a leather cap was on his knees sucking the cock of a man seated on the toilet.

He was unable to pull his eyes away from the scene, until Jarrod took his hand and led him out of the restroom. As the door swung shut behind him, he heard the bear roar.

~ ~ ~

The boys were shell-shocked when they left the *Blue Bayou* and the *Palms Hotel*. Sias struggled to process what he saw. In a strange, perverse way it excited him - but it also disgusted him. The raw, uninhibited, unashamed, animal-like lust he observed was both liberating and exciting, but a universe away from what he imagined he had with Jarrod.

Their feelings were pure and gentle... beautiful, he thought. He couldn't imagine they'd ever be reduced to rutting like dogs in heat, not caring who saw them. But still, the groans of pleasure coming from the participants continued to ring loud in his head and refused to leave.

"I'll give you a lift home," said Jarrod.

They stood by his car, facing each other, their fingers interlocked. Jarrod leaned in and kissed Sias tenderly.

That's nice, thought Sias, as his world exploded when someone hit him on the back of the head with a wooden baton.

"Fucking scum, moffies!" was the last thing he heard through a storm of blows and kicks delivered by three large men who stepped out of the shadows.

Just before the darkness overtook him, Sias caught a glimpse of Jarrod on the pavement beside him.

He looked very dead.

Chapter 23

"What the hell!" said Danie. He turned on the bedside lamp on his nightstand, blinking as he struggled to get his eyes focused.

It took a while for the banging on the front door to wake him, and a few moments to overcome his confusion.

Miems sat up in bed beside him, her face etched with concern. When someone knocks on your door at 3:53 a.m. it can only mean trouble. She instantly knew something had happened to Sias.

"I'm coming!" yelled Danie, pulling on a pair of shorts and a T-shirt.

Miems followed him, and Liza came out of her room, rubbing her eyes.

"What is it?" she asked.

The hammering on the door continued.

"Okay! Okay! I'm here!" shouted Danie.

He unlocked the door and swung it open.

A young, white police constable he recognized from the Hillbrow police station stood there. He held something in his hand, but Danie could not make out what it was.

"Mr van Staden?" asked the constable.

"Sergeant van Staden," corrected Danie.

"Yes...er... sorry, Sergeant. Is your son..." he hesitated while he opened and looked inside what Danie now saw was a leather wallet he recognized. "Is your son Sias Jacobus van Staden?"

"Oh my God!" wailed Miems. "I knew it. Sias is dead!"

It felt as though iced water was suddenly poured over her and she was convinced she would vomit. Her legs felt rubbery as overcooked spaghetti, and Liza, ashen-faced, had to help her to a chair.

"Sias is not dead, Ma'am but he was injured tonight."

"You'd better come in," said Danie, his voice wavering.

His heart pounded and he suddenly felt cold.

He gestured to the constable to take a seat.

"What happened?"

"Your son and another youngster were attacked outside the *Palms Hotel* tonight, Sir. It seems they'd just left the *Blue Bayou* nightclub when three men attacked them."

Danie's breath was trapped in his throat.

Sweet Jesus! *The Blue Bayou*! He knew that place. A famous moffie hangout. There had to be a mistake. The shame!

"That can't be right," said Miems. "Sias went to study at his friend's house tonight."

"Do you know the friend's name?" asked the policeman.

"Jarrod. That's all Sias said."

"Jarrod McKenzie?" asked the cop.

"I don't know his surname. What has this got to do with my son?"

She was rapidly becoming frantic.

"Unfortunately the youngster he was with was killed in the attack. His name was Jarrod McKenzie."

"Oh my God!" whispered Liza.

"How is my son? Where is he? Is he going to be okay?" snapped Danie. His hands trembled.

"The ambulance took him to Jo'burg Gen. He was unconscious but the paramedics believe he will recover completely."

"Thank God," said Miems. "We need to be with him!"

"The *Blue Bayou*," said Danie. "You're absolutely sure about that?"

"Yes, Sir. We questioned people there and they confirmed the two boys were there."

He avoided Danie's gaze.

"And the attackers?"

"You know how it is in these kind of attacks. No one saw anything definite. There were three of them. Big guys who hated moffies."

Danie's face turned purple and a vein twitched in his neck. He balled his fists and fought to control his anger at the constable.

For a few moments he was so enraged he could not speak.

"Thank you, Constable. You can fuck off out of my house now," he hissed through clenched teeth.

~ ~ ~

The Johannesburg General Hospital, situated on a ridge in Parktown that gives occupants magnificent views of Johannesburg's northern suburbs, is an enormous, gray concrete structure with miles of corridors.

As a result, it took the van Staden's a while to track down the ward Sias was in. When they found him he was conscious but groggy. His head was swathed in white bandages, as the blow from the baton cracked his skull, and his face was bruised and swollen. His lips were cut and puffy and a tear in his right ear was stitched.

His ribs and back were bruised from the kicking he took, it was painful to breathe, and his testicles felt as large and swollen as oranges.

A doctor was with him when the family arrived.

"How is he?" asked Miems. "Is he going to be all right?"

The doctor, a first year resident, nodded.

"He took a bad beating, there's no denying that. His skull is cracked and he has two broken ribs, but we've done x-rays and there are no serious internal injuries. He'll be fine in a couple of weeks."

"Thank God!" said Miems.

She leaned over the bed and kissed her son but he winced in pain.

"He needs to rest," said the doctor, "but I'll give you a few minutes with him."

When the doctor was gone Danie drew close to his son.

"Is it true?" he asked. "The *Blue Bayou*!"

Sias turned his face away so he could see his mother.

"Jarrod?" he rasped through broken lips.

Miems shook her head.

"I'm sorry," she said softly.

A moment later she leaned forward and gently wiped away the tears streaming down her son's bruised cheeks.

Chapter 24

It was a little before nine in the evening when Dave knocked on Tamarin's front door. He saw her come home a little earlier and figured he'd give her time to tend to Adrian and grab a bite to eat before he called.

After a few moments he knocked again, a little louder this time.

Tamarin opened the door. She was dressed in gray sweatpants, baggy white T-shirt and bunny-rabbit slippers. Dave ran his eyes over the length of her slim body and smiled before he spoke.

"Adrian left this at my place a while ago," he said, holding up a red sweater.

"Thank you," said Tamarin.

She reached for it.

"Dave!" squealed Adrian, skidding into the room on a pair of white socks. He'd heard Marais' voice from his bedroom. "You came to visit."

He pushed past his mother and wrapped his arms around Dave's waist.

"He's not visiting, he just returned your sweater," said Tamarin.

Adrian turned to face her, his eyes moist.

"Please Mom, can he come in?" he pleaded. "I've missed him."

"I'm sure he doesn't want to waste his evening with us." She struggled to find a graceful way to get rid of Marais but not upset Adrian. She hoped Dave would help her out. "He's probably on his way out."

"Nope," said Dave, shaking his head. "I've got nothing to do. I'd love to visit."

"See, Mom!" said Adrian.

Tamarin glared at Marais.

"Fine. But only for a few minutes. You have school

tomorrow."

She stepped aside as her son took Dave by the hand and led him into the small lounge.

"What do you want to drink? We've got herbal tea," said Adrian, twisting his lips as though he'd just sucked on a lemon, "and fresh apple juice. Sorry, no Coke®."

"I think I might try some of that herbal tea," said Dave. "I've heard it's good for you."

Adrian frowned.

"Are you sure?"

Dave nodded.

"What do you want to drink, Mom?"

"Tea, please." There was a chill in her voice.

She sat on a white faux leather couch opposite Dave, her legs curled beneath her, her arms tightly folded across her chest.

When Adrian left, the silence in the room was thick and awkward.

"He's a great kid," said Dave finally. "You should be very proud of him."

"I am," replied Tamarin. "I only want the best for him."

"I know you do and he knows that too. He told me."

She raised an eyebrow and looked surprised.

"He did? I thought he hated me."

Dave smiled.

"Only sometimes. All children his age hate their parents at times. I'm sure you did too."

Tamarin smiled.

"Not just at his age. My mother still drives me nuts. There are times I could happily strangle her."

"I think I know the feeling. Parents don't know when to let go."

Tamarin was not sure if he was talking about his parents, her parents, or her.

Adrian returned from the kitchen with a tray containing three glasses. He offered his mother her drink first, then went to Dave.

"I still think you'd have preferred the apple juice," he said.

He sat on the couch beside Tamarin, his eyes alive and bright with excitement, a broad grin on his face.

"Are you writing any exciting stories?" he asked.

Dave pursed his lips and rolled his eyes as he contemplated the question.

"Yes."

There was silence while Adrian waited for an answer.

"What?"

"It's so secret, if I told you I'd have to kill you."

For a few moments Adrian was not sure if Dave was serious or not.

"Aw, you're teasing me," he said when he saw Marais could no longer suppress a smile. "Tell me, I promise I won't tell anyone."

"First you have to swear the sacred journalist's oath."

"But I'm not a journalist."

Dave placed his right hand on his heart.

"By the powers of the *Most Noble Ancient Order of Ink and Writers* I hereby appoint you, Adrian von Pletzen, temporary journalist," he said. "Do you accept this appointment and swear you will never reveal your sources, on pain of having to drink only fermented prune juice for the rest of your days?"

Adrian stood up, snapped to attention and saluted Dave.

"I do," he giggled.

Tamarin also laughed. She had to admit it was the happiest she'd seen her son in more than a week.

"Now you can tell me," said Adrian.

"We're investigating a syndicate of doctors and workers at pharmaceutical companies selling drugs to dealers. It is going to be a huge story that will cause ripples in high places."

"Cool," said Adrian.

Tamarin was confused.

"I thought the magazine you work for is all about naked women."

"Have you ever seen a copy of *Rogue*?" asked Dave.

"Of course not!"

"You should take a look. It's true we feature beautiful women, but are also a very serious news and investigative publication."

Adrian was about to offer to fetch the copy he had hidden under his mattress so she could see, but quickly thought better of it.

"For example, this particular expose will likely result in government introducing new laws to control medicine distribution. It'll also see three recent, high-profile murders solved."

"Wow!" said Adrian, his eyes wide. "So you are sort of like a detective solving crimes."

Dave smiled.

"Sometimes it works out that way, but that's not my job. I have to get the news to the people who read the magazine."

"Yeah but you're still solving crimes, kinda like a superhero. I can't wait to tell my friends at school!"

Dave wagged a finger at him.

"Do you want to drink fermented prune juice for the rest of your life?"

Adrian gulped.

"Oops! Sorry, I forgot," he said, pretending to zip his lips.

Tamarin studied her son while he spoke.

It was obvious he admired and adored this man. Was that really such a bad thing? Though she hated to admit it, he seemed a genuinely nice guy - just as Norah said.

She glanced at her watch.

"Time for bed, Adrian. School tomorrow."

"Aw, Mom!"

"No arguments young man!"

He pouted for a moment.
“Can Dave come visit us again?” he asked.
The question took Tamarin by surprise and she hesitated.
“If he wants to... I... suppose he can,” she stammered.

Chapter 25

Cindy was cold and aloof, and Gary could not figure why. Since Sunday she virtually ignored him and spurned all his sexual advances.

He wondered if something happened at work to upset her. It would be just like a woman to take out her frustrations on him. For the briefest of moments he wondered if she'd discovered one of his dalliances but instantly dismissed the idea. He was an old hand, made sure his ass was always covered and made no mistakes. It had to be something else. Or maybe it was just that time of the month.

But Cindy Hayden was seriously pissed. For a while she suspected her husband might be having an affair. There were no obvious signs. More like intuition. Nothing she could put her finger on, but somehow she knew.

On Sunday she took a day's leave but did not tell Gary and pretended to go to work. But instead of going to work, she waited across the road from where she had a clear view of the entrance to *Hillbrow Heights* and, if she went through the entrance to the apartments' garages, she could see the door of her flat.

She waited almost two hours, and was about to give up, when she saw the woman enter the block of flats. Somehow Cindy knew exactly where she was headed and later, when she stood hidden in the courtyard at the back and watched Gary kiss her goodbye in the doorway, she was not in the least bit surprised.

Deep inside her a seething anger she did not know she was capable of began to bubble. Her first instinct was to run, screaming and yelling and confront them, but she forced herself to control her surging emotions.

She thought about contacting a divorce lawyer the next day, but decided the associated pain and humiliation would be too much to bear.

Keeping a safe distance, she followed the woman to her home, three blocks away.

Convenient, she thought. Just a ten minute walk to fuck my husband!

She couldn't get a close look at her, but from what she could see, the slut looked old enough to be her mother - and that made her furious. Gary had her, young, beautiful and willing; why the fuck was he interested in a woman that age? Granted, she obviously took care of herself but...

She simply couldn't understand it.

She spent the rest of the day sitting in the *Florian Cafe*, sipping strong, black coffee, while she tried to figure out what she would do.

One thing she knew for certain: Gary was going to pay!

Chapter 26

Sias only spent a day in hospital. The doctors figured what he most needed was rest and he could get that at home, so they issued him with a packet of pain pills and discharged him.

Miems took time off work to fetch him because Danie said he was too busy working on a case, but the truth was he was disgusted by his son and didn't think he could look him in the eyes.

The attack and murder was common knowledge at the Hillbrow Police Station, but after a few shallow proclamations of sympathy, his colleagues avoided talking about it.

Jarrod's death was being investigated by the Brixton Murder and Robbery Squad, a notorious unit situated in another part of Johannesburg, and Danie was not interested in the progress being made.

He wanted to run and hide and never be seen again. The shame was more than he thought he could bear.

He was glad the other youngster was dead, as he was sure it was he who led Sias astray. The world was better off with one less, filthy *moffie*!

He was convinced his colleagues and superiors were looking at him and talking behind his back, chalking him down as the father of a queer, debating what he'd done to make his son gay.

Miems needed the car to fetch Butch, so she dropped Danie at work, then drove to the Johannesburg General Hospital.

The rectangular building, with its black smokestacks, reminded her of a huge and ominous warship. She found parking near the entrance and made her way to the reception area where Sias sat, waiting in a wheelchair. He looked better than when she saw him the previous night -

the swelling around his eyes was down - but he appeared forlorn and mentally broken.

After hearing the news about Jarrod he was overwhelmed by an immense sense of sadness and loss. He figured he lost the only person in the world who truly knew and understood him.

He withdrew mentally, answering questions robotically, speaking only when asked something. He wished he too was killed, so he could be with Jarrod.

Miems bent down so she could kiss him softly on the forehead.

"You're looking much better," she said.

He stared at her with blank eyes but said nothing.

"I'm quickly going to sign the discharge papers and then we'll go home. The doctor says it won't be long before you're well enough to go back to university."

When she got no response, she left him and went to the reception desk, where she signed three sets of documents. A black, hospital porter helped her wheel Sias to the car.

"Can you manage to get into the car on your own?" she asked.

He nodded and stood up shakily. The porter opened the car door and helped him slide into the passenger seat.

Back home at *Hillbrow Heights* Miems needed to support Sias by holding his arms when he climbed the steps. She assisted him to his room and helped him change into set of clean pajamas. He sank back onto the bed, his eyes closed, exhausted.

"Would you like something to eat, perhaps a cup of tea?" asked Miems.

He shook his head, his eyes still closed.

"I'll let you sleep."

She closed the door behind her and went to the telephone. She dialed a number and waited for someone at the Hillbrow Vice Squad to answer.

It rang for a long time and she was about to hang up when someone picked up.

"Vice."

"Can I speak to Sergeant van Staden, please."

"Hold on."

She heard Danie's name being called, and a few moments later he was on the phone.

"van Staden."

"It's me, Liefie. Sias is home and I thought you'd like to know how he's doing."

"If he's home I know he's okay," snapped Danie. "Don't interrupt me at work with stuff that's not important."

The line went dead as he hung up.

Chapter 27

Liza was excited and in a good mood. Sias was doing better, but still seemed unable to shake the depression hanging over him. But he was on the mend, and she was going to be with Kofi in a few minutes.

She stood fidgeting at the base of the steps to the *Great Hall*, where they agreed to meet.

Butterflies flew in formation in her stomach and she silently prayed he'd not stand her up. She didn't sleep much last night, her mind occupied with thoughts of being with Kofi and going to Soweto.

She glanced at her watch for the umpteenth time.

Shit! Where is he? she thought.

She licked her dry lips. Her throat was dry as dust.

And then she saw him, and her heart soared.

He had a nylon backpack slung over his shoulder and wore a baseball cap.

"Hi," he said. "Been waiting long?"

She shook her head.

"Are you ready for your adventure?"

"It's all I've been thinking about."

He smiled, showing his perfect white teeth.

"Let's go to my apartment. It's only a short walk and I'll make us a sandwich."

"Okay," said Liza. How she wished she could take his hand.

It was a five-block walk, up the hill through Braamfontein, towards the Johannesburg Civic Center.

Kofi's apartment was in a tall, circular building that looked expensive. They took the escalator to the tenth floor. His flat was on the south side, with views of Johannesburg's central business district.

"Make yourself at home," he said, tossing his backpack beside a small writing desk near the window.

He opened the balcony doors and a warm breeze filled the room.

"Welcome to my humble abode," he said, silhouetted against the city's skyline.

"It's lovely," said Liza, resolving to get her own place just as soon as she could.

"Can I offer you the grand tour?"

She nodded and he held out a hand to her.

"This, as you can see, is the lounge, dining room, study, chill-room and whatever else it needs to be," he said. "And if you'll follow me, this is the master bedroom and guest bedroom... the only bedroom actually."

His grip was firm, his touch cool.

"This is the bathroom and over there is the kitchen."

He smiled at her. "I guess the tour wasn't all that grand after all."

"I'd give my eye-teeth to live here," said Liza.

"Then maybe you should marry me," he laughed.

She squeezed his hand and blushed.

"About that sandwich you promised...," she said.

She followed him to the kitchen where he opened the refrigerator, handed her a can of Tab® and removed a tub of margarine and a block of cheese.

He opened a Tab® for himself and took a long draft, before slicing a loaf of bread.

"That's what I like to see," said Liza. She leaned against a kitchen counter, watching him. "A man who can cook is so damn sexy."

He laughed and handed her a cheese sandwich on a white plate.

"I'm afraid you have just witnessed my entire cooking repertoire," he said.

They sat side by side on the couch, munching on their sandwiches and sipping their drinks - and when Kofi's thigh brushed against hers, Liza trembled.

She felt like a twelve year-old schoolgirl with a crush on

the football team captain. A tiny rivulet of sweat ran down her back and her hands were moist. When she was done eating, she put her empty plate on the small table beside the couch.

Kofi turned to her.

"You have crumbs on your chin," he said. "Let me get them for you."

Gently he brushed her chin and lips with the tips of his fingers.

Liza closed her eyes and trembled.

She felt his warm breath on her face and his soft lips touch hers. She sighed and wrapped her arms around his neck.

He kissed her tenderly and then with increasing passion and she responded, snaking her tongue into his mouth. A little ball of fire ignited and radiated in her belly.

He cupped her face in his hands and kissed her ears, nipping the lobes so she gasped with pleasure.

"Oh my God you are so beautiful!" he groaned.

She dug her fingers into his back, her breasts heaving, her nipples hard as granite pebbles. His hands cupped her breasts over her T-shirt.

"Oh sweet Jesus!" she moaned.

Suddenly he let her go and scooped her up into his arms. He carried her to the bedroom and dropped her on her back on the bed. For a few moments he stood beside the bed and gazed at her. Her face was flushed, her breathing short. Then he straddled her, a knee on either side of her body. He kissed her neck and mouth a few times, then pulled her into a sitting position so he could remove her T-shirt. Liza raised her arms to make it easier for him, then she lay back on the bed.

She wore a white bra that showed off her small breasts. Her nipples poked through the fabric.

Kofi began to kiss her neck, slowly tracing a wet line with the tip of his tongue down her chest. When he reached her breasts he used his hands to pull aside the cups of her bra so he could suck her nipples.

Liza thrust her hips against him. Her eyes were closed, her mouth open, her lips drawn back to bare her teeth.

She reached down and rubbed the front of his trousers with the palm of her hand and felt him grow. He bit his bottom lip and groaned.

"Make love to me," she whispered, her breath hot on his neck.

~ ~ ~

They lay side by side on their backs, their young bodies slick with perspiration, staring at the ceiling.

"That was incredible," said Liza softly. She'd only ever been with two other guys, and Kofi was way better than either of them.

"It was," he said, turning to nuzzle her bare neck. "Thank you."

They held hands, enjoying the receding magic of the moment.

Suddenly Kofi rolled over and opened a draw on his nightstand. He took a marijuana joint from a square, tin can and lit it with a disposable lighter, drawing and holding the smoke deep in his lungs. Then he handed the **zol* to Liza and she took a deep and satisfying drag.

Could it get any better than this? she wondered.

For a while they swapped the *zol* without speaking, until Liza finally giggled.

"If my father saw us now, we'd spend the rest of our lives in jail."

**zol - South African slang for marijuana cigarette*

Chapter 28

Soweto was nothing like Liza imagined it would be. People appeared to be going about their business normally and peacefully - completely unlike the mayhem described by her father and his colleagues.

There was life on the streets. Kids kicked soccer balls in the dim pools of light thrown by the streetlights, and in the front yards of the identical little block houses, people sat around burning braziers, barbecuing meat and drinking beer.

Pavement hawkers plied their trade near bus stops and taxi ranks.

"What do you think?" asked Kofi. They were in his car.

"It's nothing at all like I expected," replied Liza. "White people have been lied to forever!"

Kofi laughed.

"We live side by side but in different worlds," he said.

She nodded.

"That's the truth."

Kofi turned into the dusty driveway of a house with a green corrugated iron roof.

"We're here," he said.

Loud music throbbed from inside the house.

He took Liza's hand and led her through the front door. Inside were three young black men and four black women, all in their early twenties.

A table by the wall was littered with empty, quart-sized beer bottles.

"Guys!" yelled Kofi.

Someone turned down the music to a level where they could hear themselves speak.

"This is my girlfriend, Liza," he said, introducing her.

Her heart skipped. Was that what she was? His girlfriend?

Some of them waved to her.

He introduced them all to her but, because she was overwhelmed by the situation, she could only remember the names of two of the people: Thabo and Lerato.

"Sit," said Kofi.

They made space for her on a tatty couch. Someone filled a glass with beer and handed it to her.

"Thank you," she said, feeling awkward.

"How do you two know each other?" asked Lerato, a woman around her age.

"We met at university. We got teargassed together at a protest rally."

They nodded in approval.

"She's studying to be a human rights lawyer."

One of the guys leaned forward and clinked glasses with her.

"Good, we need plenty of them."

The sound system was tuned to a black station and suddenly a lively tune began to play.

"Turn it up," said Kofi. "Let's dance!"

He took Liza by the hand and pulled her into the center of the room. He spun her around and began to dance with her. The volume was cranked up and the other's joined them on the floor. And soon it was a party!

Liza loved it. It was so free and uninhibited. No-one cared about anything except having fun.

After an hour of enthusiastic dancing they were all wet with sweat and exhausted, all awkwardness evaporated.

"Time for **chesa nyama*," declared one of the guys.

They trooped outside into the backyard, where a cut-off steel drum with holes punched in the sides, did duty as a cooking brazier.

They grilled meat, drank beer, talked like old friends and when, a little after midnight, Kofi said it was time to go home, Liza was disappointed.

She hugged them each in turn and they made her promise she would visit again soon.

On the drive back to the city she rested her hand on the inside of his thigh.

"Did you mean what you said about me being your girlfriend?" she asked suddenly.

He turned his face towards her.

"If that's okay with you."

She was silent for a while. Then she squeezed his leg.

"I like the sound of that," she said.

**chesa nyama - hot, barbecued meat*

Chapter 29

Dave decided to stop in at the *Green Junction*. He wasn't hungry and did not really like the idea of eating vegan, rabbit food but he wanted to see Tamarin.

He couldn't figure why he was so attracted to a geeky woman with views and beliefs completely opposite to his. Heck, he could date any number of beautiful woman who'd do just about anything to be photographed for *Rogue* magazine.

But perhaps that was exactly why. They always had an agenda. Tamarin wanted nothing from him. Her opinions were at odds with his, but at least she had opinions, and was prepared to argue and defend them.

And, he figured, under the hippy-styled, loose-fitting clothing she seemed to always wear, lurked a hot body.

The lunch-sitting was over when he got to the restaurant and Tamarin and the rest of the staff were completing the final clear-away. As he expected, the place was almost empty, other than for a guy with grimy dreadlocks who sat at a table near the door, sipping a glass of something thick and green, while writing in a notebook.

She saw Dave when he walked in and experienced a strange, inexplicable surge of excitement.

"Hi," he said, wondering whether he should shake her hand or hug her. In the end he did neither.

"I was in the area and thirsty," he lied. "So I figured I'd stop in for a cup of coffee. You do, do coffee?"

"Sure but not with milk. If you want it white we have a palm-oil creamer."

Dave frowned for a second.

"I'll give it a try," he said. "Can I buy you one?"

Instinctively Tamarin was about to refuse his invitation but she stopped herself. It was the quietest time in the restaurant and she figured it'd be more awkward standing around than if she joined him.

"Thanks, I'll get them," she said.

He took a table by the window where he could watch people passing in the street. While he waited, he scanned the room. The walls were decorated with posters of fruit and vegetables, in addition to framed photographs of sludge-like beverages.

Tamarin returned carrying two, steaming, large, white mugs. She put one on the table in front of Dave and took a seat opposite him.

He picked up the mug and sniffed. It was coffee, normal percolated coffee. He saw her watching him.

"Just checking," he said, and smiled.

She returned the smile. She had to admit, he was very good looking, and Adrian adored him - and since allowing her son to see him again, the boy's attitude had improved enormously. Perhaps she was wrong about him before and he was good for her child.

Dave spooned three spoons of sticky, brown sugar into the cup.

"How are you?" he asked.

"Good. Adrian is doing well and there were no repercussions about the incident at school. You can go ahead and say: 'I told you so' but he is much happier. He's made new friends who previously would not have given him the time of day, and the bullying has stopped. His school marks are also improving."

She smiled.

"I'm a little embarrassed to say this, but I suppose I should thank you."

Their eyes met for a moment and she blushed.

"But I still think violence is wrong," she added quickly.

"You are welcome and I won't say: 'I told you so'," he said. He reached across the table and put his hand on hers, expecting her to pull away but she didn't.

For a while they made awkward small talk. It was fun.

Eventually Dave glanced at his watch.

"I'd better be going," he said. "I have a meeting at the office."

He gulped down the remainder of the his third mug of coffee.

"There is a car show next weekend. I'm sure Adrian will enjoy it. Would you both care to join me?"

He thought the pitch of his voice was higher than normal and there was a strange knot in his belly.

Jesus! Why did he feel so nervous asking this woman to a frigging car show?

"It'll have to be Sunday," she said, and his heart skipped.

"Sunday's perfect. Can I knock on your door at ten?"

"Ten is good," she said. "We'll be waiting."

After Dave left, she remained seated at the table, hardly able to believe she agreed to go on a date.

Was it a date? Of course not. It was just an outing with her son. Nothing more.

She wiped her clammy palms on her apron and took a deep breath.

Chapter 30

Danie woke up with a hangover and a headache that felt as though a ton of bricks fell on his head. He knew he was drinking more than he should, but booze was the only thing that dulled the pain and shame.

He got no support from his family - Miems was cold towards him, Liza barely spoke to him and was away every opportunity she got, and Sias... he couldn't bare to even look at Sias. His son was the cause of his anxiety and humiliation.

He knew his family was falling apart and he had to do something, but he had no idea how to fix it.

God knew, he and Miems tried to bring the kids up with strong Christian principles. They drummed those values into them. But somewhere he failed. Even Miems appeared to be wavering in the fight against the advancing forces of evil. Perhaps it was a symptom of the growing assault against the values and standards that made South Africa great. Things that attempted to shake the foundations of the country - mixing of the races, communism, black nationalism, drugs, immoral behavior, pornography, loose women. When he thought about such things, it made him shudder.

He realized he was one of the last soldiers in a thin line in the fight to save the country and the whites, and it was a responsibility he took very seriously. He saw his job as a sacred calling, that needed to be done no matter how painful, if there was to be any hope of creating a future for his children.

One day they would thank him, he was absolutely convinced of that.

But right now he was worried. His children were out of control. Liza was evasive and shifty and it was obvious, to a highly trained investigator like himself, she was constantly lying.

She was vague when he asked her where she was going and who she'd be with and he intended to do something about that soon.

But right now his problem was Sias, and he needed to solve that. He needed expert help and figured he'd get that from his pastor.

The van Stadens were members of the *Fundamental Soldiers of Christ Church*, a small, but growing group of people who broke away from mainstream churches because they believed those denominations were too liberal and permissive.

The FSCC was on the far right of conservative.

Danie rubbed his eyes, groaned and picked up his watch on the nightstand beside his bed. He needed to get a move on if he was going to get showered, ready and be at church on time.

He tapped Miems on the shoulder.

"Better get up, we're going to be late for church."

She opened an eye and peered at him from beneath her hair.

"I'm not going."

"Why not?"

"I just don't want to."

He was about to argue with her but figured it wasn't worth the effort, and his head hurt too much anyway.

"Suit yourself," he said, swinging his legs out of bed.

While he ran the shower allowing the water to get hot, he opened the medicine cupboard on the wall, found a bottle of aspirin and washed down three tablets with a mouthful of water.

He stood in the glass shower cubicle, allowing the scalding water to wash over his body. After a while the pounding in his head eased.

~ ~ ~

Pastor Albert Mostert was a few years older than Danie. He ruled his congregation with an iron fist. For him, everything in the bible was either black or white - there was simply no room for any shade of gray.

Danie waited for the Sunday morning service to end and for all the other congregates to leave.

"Pastor, I need to speak to you on a matter of urgency," he said, his voice trembling. He feared condemnation for failing to keep his son on the Path of Righteousness.

"Let's go to my office," said Pastor Mostert. He had a thick Afrikaans accent but spoke English perfectly.

He gestured to Danie to take a seat on a chair by his desk. He drummed his fingers unconsciously on the desk pad in front of him.

"I see something is troubling you. What is on your heart?"

Danie took a deep breath. He felt nauseous and his stomach fluttered. A bead of sweat rolled down the back of his neck.

"I don't know how to say this," he said, his voice trembling.

"Draw strength from the Lord and speak," said Mostert, lacing together the long, thin fingers of his hands. His angular features and beak-like nose reminded Danie of a vulture waiting to pounce upon a dying animal and rip its flesh from its bones.

"I've failed! My son is a homosexual!" He spat the words out as quickly as he could and experienced a sense of relief once they left his mouth.

Mostert frowned and pursed his lips.

"I am afraid, if we don't do something he will suffer eternal damnation."

Mostert drummed his finger tips on the table once again.

"You are right to be worried," he said. "The Holy Book is very specific that homosexuality is an abomination."

He reached for a thick, leather-bound copy of the Bible on his desk, opened it and flicked through the pages.

"Leviticus 18:22: 'You shall not lie with a male as one lies with a female; it is an abomination', and Leviticus 20:13: 'If there is a man who lies with a male as those who lie with a woman, both of them have committed a detestable act; they shall surely be put to death. Their bloodguiltness is upon them.' I think it is very clear."

Danie shuddered.

"There are many more references in the Bible," said Mostert, beginning to turn pages yet again.

Danie raised a hand to stop him.

"I know what the book says," he said. "What do I do about it?"

Mostert rubbed his sharp chin for a few moments.

"It requires an intervention," he said. "The church has a program to de-gay sinners. I suggest Sias be enrolled in that. It lasts two weeks and is run at a retreat in the Magaliesburg mountains, about forty minutes drive from here. It is tough for the participants, but we have had good success. I am confident we can de-gay your boy."

An intense wave of relief washed over Danie. There was an answer... a way out of this nightmare for him.

"How does it work?" he asked.

"It is a combination of sexual stimulus, reward and punishment. We break them down and build them up again, but this time in the image God wants. It's not easy for them and you'll have to sign a waiver."

"Of course. All I care about is that it works and my son stops being a moffie."

Mostert smiled.

"The next program starts in two days time. It is quite expensive as we have costs that must be met."

"I don't care about the price," said Danie, his eyes shining. "I have a little money saved that I'll happily spend if it will cure my son."

"Good," said Mostert.

He opened a desk drawer, removed a cardboard folder and handed a set of forms to Danie to fill in.

"It might be a good idea not to tell him where he is going. Say you're taking him for a drive in the country or something. When you get to the facility, we'll take care of everything."

Danie nodded.

"I'll have him there," he said.

Chapter 31

Danie packed a small back with toiletries, underwear and a change of clothes for Sias and stowed it in the car the night before. At dinner he told his son he'd taken the day off, and the next day they were going for a drive in the country, because he thought it would do them both good.

Sias shrugged his shoulders. He didn't care one way or the other. The truth was, he didn't care much about anything. Jarrod, and what happened, was constantly on his mind and he played the scene in his thoughts over and over.

Could he have done anything? Why had he not suggested they go somewhere else? Rationally he knew none of it was his fault but he still felt guilty and could not shake the gloom that hung over him like a cloud of stale, blue, cigarette smoke.

Danie woke him shortly after sunup. He got dressed, combed his hair and for a few moments, considered shaving but quickly dismissed the idea.

He peered at his face in the mirror. His complexion was sallow, his skin appeared leathery and there were dark rings under his eyes. He had not used a moisturizer for almost two weeks and it showed.

In the past he would not have dreamed of going out with that face, but now it was simply too much trouble to do anything about it.

He shrugged and went to the kitchen where he made himself a cup of instant coffee. Danie had four slices in the toaster.

"Do you want some breakfast?" he asked. His voice founded different. Nervous somehow.

Sias shook his head. He knew he should eat but was not hungry.

He thought this whole father - son bonding thing today

was strange and out of character for Danie. Especially since his father made it obvious he was ashamed of him.

He'd hardly spoken a word to Sias from the time he saw him in hospital, and suddenly he wanted them to spend the day together? It didn't make sense. But then little did, when it came to his father.

After Danie wolfed down three slices of toast they headed out of Hillbrow, traveling west in the car.

Neither spoke and eventually Sias spent the time peering out of the passenger-seat window but not seeing anything.

The FSCC rehabilitation camp was situated high up in the Magaliesberg mountains on a farm where a bloody battle was fought between British soldiers and Boer fighters, almost seventy five years before.

It was accessed by a long, winding gravel road, lined on either side by Bluegum and Black Wattle trees - both species imported from Australia in the last century that were now taking over.

Sias's first realization something was not right was when he saw a tall wooden cross perched on the ridge of the mountain.

"Where are we going?" he asked, his voice anxious.

Danie ignored him.

"Where are you taking me?" Sias screamed.

"To a church rehabilitation center where you can be cured."

"Jesus! Cured of what?"

"Homosexuality. It's a satanic disease."

"Oh Christ! You can't be fucking serious!"

"Don't use that language with me!" snapped Danie. "This is for your own good. One day you'll thank me."

Sias's stomach knotted and he thought he might piss himself. He broke into a cold sweat, his shirt clung to his chest and back.

"Please!" he pleaded. "Don't send me there. I won't

survive!"

"You will. And you'll come home stronger - and a man."

His father's jaw was set. It was a look Sias had seen many times before, when Danie made his mind up and nothing would change it.

"It's decided," said Danie. He looked resolutely ahead as he navigated the car along the twisting road.

Sias's mind swirled as jumbled thoughts of panic bounced around in his brain.

He'd heard of places like this, and they sounded little more than medieval torture facilities. People sometimes killed themselves there, or were fucked up for the rest of their lives.

He doubted he would come out alive. He had to do something - and fast!

They approached a right-hand hairpin bend where the road wound its way through a cutting in the mountainside. The ground fell away steeply on the left. Sias knew the car would be traveling slowly there, and it was the only opportunity he would likely have to escape.

Danie changed down to first gear when they entered the bend.

He was still saying something when Sias flung open the passenger door and leaped out of the slow-moving car. He landed awkwardly and fell face down in the dirt, but was unhurt and in an instant was on his feet.

He went down the slope, kicking up dust and small rocks as he slid on his backside. He heard his father screaming at him to come back but then he was in the trees and running as though the devil was snapping at his heels.

Danie started down the hillside after Sias, but quickly realized it was useless and he struggled, sweating and gasping back up the cutting to his car.

He knew people in the Police Dog Squad and needed to find a phone to get a tracker dog out here. When he reached the car he was both exhausted and dirty from the effort. Slick with sweat, moist, caked dust ringed his armpits.

He opened the car door and slid in behind the steering wheel, wheezing and gasping.

Finally he had the strength to scream: “Fuck!”

Chapter 32

Cindy was working the night shift. Normally when she did, she got home before Gary left for work. But that day she hung around at the hospital until she knew her husband was gone.

She was convinced he was cheating on her regularly and sure she could smell other women on him - but maybe it was the stink of deception.

She took a shower and got into bed. It'd been a long, busy night but she couldn't sleep. Finally, after tossing and turning and wrestling with her pillow, she got up. The bedside clock told her it was ten past eleven. She pulled on a pair of jeans and a T-shirt, closed the front door behind her and went to Norah's flat.

Norah opened the door almost immediately after Cindy knocked. She wore a silk, floral nightgown and had a cup of coffee in one hand and a cigarette in the other.

"Come in, Darling," she said airily. "You're just in time for a cup of coffee. There's a fresh pot."

She ushered Cindy into the kitchen and poured a mug of thick, black coffee.

"Cream and sugar?"

Cindy nodded.

"Two please."

"This is a nice surprise. I haven't seen you for ages," said Norah, handing her the mug. "How are you keeping?"

"Okay thanks. I've been busy, working a lot."

"And how is that handsome husband of yours?"

Cindy cupped the hot mug in both hands and sighed.

"That's why I am here. I think he's cheating on me."

"Oh dear. Maybe we should go sit in the lounge and you can tell me all."

Cindy followed Norah to the lounge and took a chair with her back to the balcony door.

Norah sat on the couch, coiling her legs beneath her.

"Tell me," she said.

Cindy told her about Elaine and how she followed her. Norah clucked sympathetically. Even though her sex life was once colorful and exotic, she could not abide the idea of cheating and dishonesty. If both parties agreed it was okay to fuck other people, that was fine, but going behind the other's back was simply not acceptable.

"I'm sure there are many more women," said Cindy. "There were plenty of signs but I guess I chose to ignore them. I never imagined Gary would cheat on me."

"Don't beat yourself up," said Norah. "Love has a way of blinding you, especially when you are young."

"I guess."

"Did you confront him?"

"No. I don't want him to know I know. I haven't yet decided what I want to do. All I know is, he hurt me badly and I want him to pay."

"I can understand that. How can I help?"

"I need to be sure he's still screwing around. I think he sometimes brings women to our apartment and fucks them in our bed. It makes my skin crawl!"

She shivered.

Norah went to Cindy and wrapped her arms around her.

"I know you are at home a lot," Cindy continued. "I'd like you to keep an eye out and let me know what you see."

"You want me to spy on your husband?"

Cindy swallowed nervously.

"Yes."

"Consider it done," smiled Norah. "Let's catch us a rat!"

Chapter 33

Sias ran until he could run no more. When he stopped in a grove of trees, a long way down the mountain and far from the road, he vomited then sank, gasping, with his back against a tree.

His lungs screamed, there were little lines of blood on his arms and face, scratches from forcing his way through thorny bushes, and he was more thirsty than he had ever been in his life.

He drew his knees to his chest and buried his face in his hands. Without any warning, he began to sob, tremors pulsing through his body.

The outpouring of emotions was accompanied by an intense sense of relief and the fuzz in his head slowly cleared. Gradually his feelings of panic receded, replaced by the knowledge he needed to formulate a plan and implement it as quickly as possible. His father would come looking for him, most likely with his police buddies, and when they caught him they would take him to the church rehabilitation facility - only this time in handcuffs.

But first he had to do something about his thirst. He remembered reading somewhere travelers in the desert sucked on a pebble for relief. He found little white stone and put it into his dry mouth. As he sucked, saliva began to flow and he experienced a measure of relief.

He had his wallet and some money in the back pocket of his jeans. It wasn't a lot but enough to pay for a ride back to Johannesburg if he caught a black, minibus taxi.

While he recovered his strength, he considered his options. He knew he could not go home. He also knew his father would... could... never give up the hunt. And deep down he knew there'd be no acceptance of the way he was in South Africa.

No chance of a relationship where he did not always

have to look over his shoulder, worrying about having his head smashed in.

If he was ever going to find true freedom and happiness, it would be in another country.

At home he had a passport, and there was a savings account in his name containing almost R10 000 - the proceeds of an insurance police his parents signed up for when he was born, to pay for his university education.

With it, he could catch a plane to England that night, and from there make his way to a gay-friendly country like Holland. Suddenly it was all clear and a great weight lifted off his shoulders.

But then he had doubts. His father would know he had to go home and most likely be waiting for him. Or would he? Shit! He didn't know. He had no option but to enlist Liza's help, but worried he'd not be able to reach her, as she was always out. And what, if when he managed to call home, his father answered?

A new panic-ball developed in the pit of his stomach and he forced himself to calm down and think.

The immediate priority was to get back to Hillbrow. Then he could figure out how to reach his sister. If he could hitch a lift quickly, maybe he could still find her on campus.

He struggled to his feet, dusting off the seat of his pants. Then he set off in the direction of the road, praying when he got there he would not run into his father and his goons.

~ ~ ~

Sias remained hidden in the bushes watching the paved road. A few pickup trucks passed but he stayed out of sight. A few minutes later he saw what he waited for - a *Toyota Hi Ace* minibus driven by a black driver.

He stepped into the road, waving for the driver to stop.

The battered vehicle veered to the side of the road, one of it's shock absorbers sheared, its muffler holed, exhaust pipe belching blue smoke.

The wreck was empty except for the driver, who wore a knitted cap and was in his mid forties.

"I need to get to Johannesburg urgently," said Sias, standing by the driver's door. "How much?"

The driver raised his eyebrows. Whites almost never used black taxis.

"R150."

Sias knew the price was outrageous.

"That's ridiculous. I'll give you a hundred."

The taxi driver shrugged and engaged the clattering transmission. He slipped the clutch so the vehicle edged forward.

"R150 or you can walk."

Sias went around to the passenger side, opened the door and slid in beside the driver.

"If you're going to rob me you should wear a mask."

"Money first," said the taxi driver.

~ ~ ~

Danie was worried. By the next morning there was still no sign of Sias. He managed to get a tracker dog to the spot his son fled the car, and the animal followed the scent for a couple of miles until it was lost at the road. He figured his son got into a car there.

He was sure he'd make his way home, and assigned two police constables to watch *Hillbrow Heights* but there was no sign of Sias. All they reported was Liza coming home and leaving soon after with a backpack. She returned shortly before Miems served dinner.

Supper was a strained affair. When Miems asked how the day went with Sias and where he was, Danie lied to her.

"I dropped him off at a church recovery center. I figured

he needed to relax and reflect, in order to get better."

"How long will he be gone?"

"A week or two, three at the most."

Miems thought she saw Liza roll her eyes and smile wryly.

"I hope he'll be okay," said Miems. She took a sip of water from a glass on the table in front of her.

"He'll be fine, you'll see."

Danie hoped they'd find his son in the morning. Perhaps the boy's friends would know where he was but then he realized he had no idea who his son hung out with. Liza might know, but he'd have to talk to her on her own. If Miems found out what really happened, that Sias was missing... he shuddered. The fallout was too terrible to contemplate.

Liza dabbed her mouth with a pink, linen napkin, folded it neatly, glanced at her watch, and stood up from the table.

"I'm going out. Don't wait up," she said.

"Where are you going?" asked Danie. He really needed to talk to her.

"Out. To study with a friend."

"Who?"

She rolled her eyes.

"You don't know her."

"What's her name and where does she stay?"

"Sarah Cormack. Braamfontein. See, you don't know her. I'm late. I don't have time for this shit."

She knew Kofi was already waiting in his car, parked up the road.

"I need to talk to you," he said.

"Tomorrow at breakfast."

She scooped up her backpack and breezed out of the apartment, slamming the door behind her.

~ ~ ~

It was the early hours of the morning when Liza returned. Danie couldn't sleep and was in bed but still awake. For a few moments he considered getting up and confronting her, but dismissed the idea - the last thing he needed was a screaming match and getting Miems involved.

When Liza came to the kitchen for breakfast, it was obvious she'd had a late night. Although she used more makeup than usual she wasn't able to completely hide the dark rings under her eyes and the two love bites on her neck.

She smiled. Kofi was a fucking machine!

"You got in late last night," said Danie. "Must have been a heavy study session. I hope you learned something."

"Uh-huh," she mumbled.

She tried not to smile. If only her idiot father knew. Kofi certainly taught her a few things last night! More than once! Three times!

"I still need to talk to you," said Danie.

Liza glanced at her watch. Seven thirty.

"I'll save you the time," she said. "In a few minutes from now, Sias will be landing in London. He asked me to give you a heartfelt message. He said: 'Fuck you!'"

~ ~ ~

Danie never felt so alone as that night when he unpacked his small suitcase in a room at the *Parkview*, a flea-pit of a hotel in Joubert Park. After Liza delivered the news about Sias, he and Miems had the worst fight of their married life. In the end she gave him an ultimatum; move out until she could stand to look at him again, or she would leave and never come back. He'd never before seen such resolve in her eyes, so he packed a few changes of clothing, as well as his toiletries, and left for work.

From there he called the airline desk at the airport and

they confirmed his son boarded the flight to London the night before.

He lay on his back on the worn, velvet bed cover, watching a cockroach scuttle up the grimy wall and disappear into a crack behind the mirror.

He unscrewed the cap on a half-jack of brandy and gulped down a mouthful, the bottle still in a brown paper bag. The smoky liquid seared his throat and made him feel better, so he took another slug.

He thought about what happened and decided it was his fault, because he had not kept a tight rein on Sias. There was nothing he could do about that, but he could make sure he did not make the same mistake with Liza.

There was something going on with that girl, and he intended to find out what it was.

Chapter 34

Dave knocked on Tamarin's door at precisely ten o'clock and Adrian opened it immediately. He flung his arms around Marais and hugged him.

Dave ruffled the youngster's hair.

"Looking forward to today?" he asked.

"You bet! I couldn't sleep last night!"

Dave laughed. He did not want to admit he'd had the same problem. He could not understand why Tamarin had such an effect on him. He felt like a schoolboy about to go to the prom with the head cheerleader.

"Hi," said Tamarin, coming out of her bedroom, where she applied the final touches to her makeup. She too had a restless night.

Dave gasped. He'd only ever seen her without makeup and dressed in loose, baggy clothing, but today she wore a pair of skinny jeans that looked like they were spray-painted onto her, and a spaghetti-strapped white T-shirt, under which Dave could see the outline of a lacy bra.

"Wow! You look nice, Mom," said Adrian. He couldn't remember ever seeing his mother dressed like that or wearing makeup.

"Double wow!" said Dave.

He always figured, beneath the dowdy clothing Tamarin was so fond of, was the body of a goddess.

He ran his eyes over her. Her legs were long and shapely, her waist slim, her hips round. Her breasts were the size of grapefruits.

She smiled.

"Thank you, gentlemen," she said, secretly delighted by their reaction.

"You ready?" asked Dave, still unable to pull his eyes off her.

She nodded, scooping up a backpack containing vegan

food she prepared for her and Adrian.

~ ~ ~

The annual car show was held at the National Exhibition Center on the outskirts of Johannesburg and was a huge event. It was the opportunity for manufacturers and dealers to show their wares and strut their stuff. It was also a chance for the many vintage car and motorcycle clubs, based throughout South Africa to display their collections.

Sunday was the busiest day, and they had to park some distance from the entrance, leaving them a fifteen minute walk.

Dave slipped the backpack over his shoulders and led the way. It rained earlier in the week and there were still puddles and muddy patches on the ground. As Tamarin attempted to negotiate a wet spot, she slipped and grabbed Dave's hand. She hung on as they picked their way through the slippery terrain, and when they reached the pavement she did not let go.

They walked, hand-in-hand towards the entrance, neither saying anything, but both their hearts beating wildly.

"Do you think they'll have racing cars?" asked Adrian.

"I think so," replied Dave, his voice trembling.

They stopped to buy tickets at the entrance and Dave had no option but to release her hand. She reached for her purse but he stopped her.

"I invited you, it's my treat."

He paid for three tickets and they slipped through the turnstiles. It was still early but the place was buzzing, and by lunchtime it would be swarming with people.

"House rules first," said Dave. "We stick together, but if we get separated we all make our way to that tower and wait for the others to arrive."

He pointed to a tall concrete structure on top of which, a

flag fluttered in the breeze.

"Understood?"

Adrian saluted.

"Yes, Captain."

"Aye aye, Skipper," giggled Tamarin.

It was the first time Dave heard her laugh and it was intoxicating.

"Can we go see the cars now... please?" said Adrian, tugging at Dave's arm.

Adrian skipped on ahead.

"Not too far!" called Dave.

Tamarin smiled at the way Marais fussed over her son, and when he reached for her hand, she laced her fingers between his.

~ ~ ~

By lunchtime their feet were sore, and they were tired. They looked for a place to sit, finding an open spot on a patch of grass, under a tree, outside one of the pavilions. Tamarin dug in the backpack and produced a plastic container. She handed a sandwich, with a filling Dave could not identify, to Adrian and offered one to Dave.

He shook his head.

"If you don't mind, I'm going to go and get a burger and Coke®. Can I get you anything to drink?"

"Fruit juice, if they have, please," said Tamarin.

A few minutes later Dave returned, carrying two cartons of orange juice and a packet with a cheeseburger, chips and a Coke®.

He stretched his legs in front of him on the grass, reclined on one elbow and took a bite of his burger.

"Help yourself to chips, if you like," he said.

Adrian glanced at his mother, who smiled and nodded. He took two large fries and stuffed them into his mouth.

The burger smelled and looked delicious, and he noticed

how Tamarin carefully watched as he took a bite.

"You never eaten meat?" he asked.

"I have, when I was married."

"Did you like it?"

She nodded.

"I hate to admit it but I did."

"Why did you stop?"

"I was brought up a vegan, and after the divorce my mother convinced me it was best to become one again."

She watched him take another bite.

"Do you want a taste?"

She hesitated, her gaze locked on Adrian.

"Just a little one?"

He handed her the burger.

She took a bite and closed her eyes while she chewed. Oh yes! I've missed you. Come to Mama.

When she opened her eyes Adrian was staring at her.

"Don't you say a word about this to Grandma!" she said, wiping sauce from the corner of her mouth.

"Only if I can also have a bite," he said.

"Why don't I just get you each a burger?" said Dave. "That way I'll end up having some lunch myself."

He smiled.

Tamarin studied her son's face then shrugged.

"Screw it! Why not?"

Adrian whooped, making Tamarin realize her kid was not a burger virgin.

Dave struggled to his feet.

"I'll come with you," said Adrian.

"Remember, not a word to your grandmother," said Tamarin.

~ ~ ~

Adrian was exhausted and fell asleep in the car on the way home. When Dave parked in the garage at *Hillbrow*

Heights, Tamarin wanted to wake her son but he stopped her.

"I'll carry him," he said.

He scooped the youngster up in his arms, holding him to his chest, and made his way to Tamarin's flat.

"Put him in his bed. I'll wake him early so he can bath tomorrow, before he goes to school," she said.

She drew back the blankets and helped Dave remove Adrian's shoes. Then she covered him and kissed him softly on his forehead, before turning out the light.

"He... we... had a wonderful day," she said softly. "Thank you."

"You are welcome," he said, touching her forearm. "So did I."

He followed her to the lounge.

"I'm sorry I don't have any alcohol..." She hesitated, unsure of whether to continue. "But I do have some very good weed."

Dave smiled.

"I could do some of that."

She went to her bedroom and got the cigar box from behind her sweaters. She took a thick, pre-rolled joint and found a lighter.

"On the balcony," she said, taking Dave by the hand.

She was right. It was good shit and soon they both had a good buzz going as they shared the joint. Tamarin started giggling and soon Dave followed suit. And the more they laughed the funnier they thought the situation.

When the joint was burned down so much they could no longer hold it, Dave flicked it over the balcony onto the pavement.

"Do you know a cop lives directly above me?" snorted Tamarin, trying unsuccessfully to contain her laughter.

"I know," said Dave, suddenly concerned about the noise they were making. "Maybe we should take this party inside."

He took her hand and led her into the lounge where she plopped down on the couch. When he sat on a chair opposite her, she patted the sofa cushion beside her.

"Over here, Buster!"

She was baked as a tin of choc chip cookies.

He sat beside her and she rested a hand gently on his thigh.

"You're a very bad influence, Dave Marais," she said, turning to face him, her mouth close to his. "But I think I like it."

She burst into peals of laughter.

He put the tip of his index finger to her lips to quiet her, afraid she'd wake Adrian. She opened her mouth and wrapped her wet lips around his finger. Instantly he felt a stirring in his groin.

She looked deeply into his eyes, holding his gaze. The image of the outline of Dave's penis she once saw, was vivid in her mind and a ball of fire ignited in her belly. She grew moist and her nipples hardened like steel rivets, pressing against the inside of her bra.

His hand cupped her breast over the outside of her T-shirt. She shuddered, wrapped her arms around his neck and kissed him. He returned the kiss with urgency and passion, their lust for each other exploding.

He slid the straps of her T-shirt off her shoulders, rolling the fabric tube to her waist. For a few moments he simply looked at her, her perfect breasts heaving in her white, lacy bra, as she gasped, her lips wet.

Then he pulled one of the bra cups aside and planted his mouth on her breasts, his lips sucking at her nipple. She threw her head back, her mouth open, her teeth bared, her eyes closed.

"Oh sweet Jesus!" she murmured, while she struggled to undo the belt of his trousers.

He lifted his backside to make it easier for her, and she slid his pants and boxer shorts to his ankles in a single movement. He was already erect and hard as iron, and she wrapped her slim fingers around his shaft.

He unclipped her bra, slipped it off her shoulders and arms and tossed it onto the floor. He cupped her mound in his hand and she shuddered as she experienced a mini orgasm.

"Let's go to the bedroom," he whispered.

Adrian coughed in his sleep.

It was like a bucket of ice water emptied over Tamarin.

"Jesus! What am I doing?" she said, suddenly pushing Dave away. "I can't do this!"

She wriggled out from beneath him, pulling up her T-shirt to cover her breasts.

"I'm not ready for this. My life is the way I want it. I don't need complications and that's what you'll be," she said, standing on the other side of the room.

Dave appeared shell-shocked. His erection subsided.

"What is it? What have I done?"

"It's not you. I'm just not ready to let anyone else into my life."

A tear rolled down her cheek and she brushed it away.

"I had a lovely time today, and I'm sorry if I led you on, I really am. But it's probably best if you go now."

He opened his mouth to speak but she stopped him.

"Please go," she whispered, struggling to hold back her tears. "It's best."

"Can we talk tomorrow?" he asked.

"I don't think so."

She ushered him out of her apartment and closed the door behind him.

What the fuck just happened? thought Dave.

Chapter 35

When Miems went to work she wore sunglasses to hide her red, puffy eyes. For the past few days she couldn't stop crying, bursting into tears without warning, and it was affecting her performance at work.

It was half an hour before the close of business, and Miems was in the little office kitchen making a cup of coffee when Dane McDonald, a young lawyer intensely attracted to her came in and put a hand on her shoulder.

"Something is wrong," he said softly. "Everyone in the office can see it and the partners are becoming concerned. What has upset you so badly? Are there problems at home?"

She turned to face him, instinctively about to say all was fine, but before she could say anything she was sobbing.

She buried her face against his chest and clung to him, her body heaving. He held her and stroked her hair. A junior clerk entered the kitchen but Dane waved her away.

After a while Miems managed to compose herself and stepped away from him, sniffing. He handed her his handkerchief and she blew her nose vigorously.

Dark lines ran down her cheeks where her mascara smudged.

"I'm sorry, I've dirtied your shirt," she whimpered, trying to smile. She dabbed her eyes with his handkerchief.

"That's okay. I'm sure it'll wash out."

He took her hand in his.

"Get your things. You look like you could use a drink and need to talk."

She squeezed his hand.

"Thank you," she whispered.

~ ~ ~

Danie waited on the sidewalk outside the building where Miems worked. He tried to call her a few times but she either refused to take the call or hung up. He figured he'd catch her when she finished work and was on her way to the bus stop. He had a large bunch of flowers in his hand and shuffled about uneasily, embarrassed when people stared at him.

He wondered what they thought. He didn't look like a flower-toting romantic, and reckoned they'd guess he was in shit with a woman. He could not remember when he last bought flowers for his wife - or if he ever had.

He glanced at his watch as he fidgeted. Cars were exiting the underground parking garage and turning into the street. Suits on their way home. God! How he hated them and their fancy cars!

The worker drones followed, flooding out of the building, on their way to catch buses or trains. He watched anxiously for Miems. Then he saw her, in a fancy car, driven by a suit, exiting the garage.

It took a few moments for his mind to process what he saw and by then it was too late. The car turned left and was swept away by the flow of traffic.

His heart pounded, he gasped for breath, his head was about to burst. A vein throbbed in his temple and he thought he was having a heart attack or stroke. His legs were over-cooked spaghetti strings, and he had to sit before they collapsed beneath him.

He sank onto the steps at the entrance of the building, unaware of people rushing past him.

Danie wasn't sure how long he sat there. He did not look at his watch. When he finally struggled to his feet, the streets were quiet and it was getting dark.

He tossed the flowers into a trashcan and trudged back to where he parked his car. His family was disintegrating around him and it was all because he was too lenient and had let things slide.

He wasn't going to let that happen with his daughter.

~ ~ ~

Dane McDonald turned off the M1 and headed north to *Sunnyside Park Hotel* in Parktown. He parked, took Miems's hand and led her to the terrace, where they found an empty table. The evening air was warm and sticky, the surroundings pleasant.

The hotel was one of the original Randlord homes, built in 1896 for a mining magnate and used by Lord Milner during the Anglo-Boer War.

"Are you comfortable?" asked Dane, gesturing to a black waiter standing nearby.

Miems nodded.

"I'm feeling much better, thank you."

When the waiter arrived, Dane did not ask what Miems wanted to drink. He ordered an expensive bottle of South African cabernet and asked for dinner menus.

"Have you been here before?" He leaned across the table and put his hand on hers.

She shook her head. This place was way out of her league.

"It's lovely," she said.

The wine arrived soon after and they ordered dinner - steak, rare for Dane, grilled fish for Miems. Under a canopy, near the pool, a man dressed in a tuxedo softly tinkled the keys of a baby grand piano.

This was a world foreign to Miems, but she liked it.

"Tell me what's going on with you?" said Dane softly, peering at her over the rim of his wine glass.

She sighed, took a gulp of wine and launched into the sordid details of her marriage and family travails.

Dane listened intently, nodding occasionally but not interrupting. It was just what she needed. A chance to unload her emotions, and when she was done a huge weight was lifted off her chest. She could breathe again.

When their food arrived, they ate in silence for a while, until she reached forward to place her hand on his forearm.

"Thank you," she said softly, her eyes shining.

"For what? I've done nothing."

"For listening and being a friend."

He placed his hand on hers and smiled.

"You are welcome but now let's talk of more pleasant things. Tell me about Miems van Staden and what she wants from life. A beautiful woman like you should have her dreams come true."

She knew he was trying to seduce her, but did not mind. It was wonderful to finally be told she was beautiful and sexy. It was a long time since she heard those words, and she allowed them to wash over and leave her feeling giddy and light-headed.

They chatted and flirted, and for a while Miems forgot her troubles.

When their meal was done, Dane shifted his chair around the table so he could sit beside her. He ordered a Cape brandy for each of them and sat with his arm around her shoulders while they sipped their drinks. The smooth alcohol washed away her cares and she rested her head on his shoulder, more contented than she'd been in years.

When he gently turned her face so he could kiss her lips, she offered no resistance. They kissed like teenagers making out in the backseat of a car at a drive-in theater.

She held his hand, her fingers interlaced with his.

"I can get us a room," he whispered, his breath hot on her cheek.

She shook her head and kissed his tenderly.

"I want to," she said. "But I can't. Not until things are settled at home. Until then, can you just be my friend?"

"Sure," said Dane, but he did not sound convincing.

Chapter 36

"Visser, get over here!" Danie yelled at the constable who was his partner.

He'd hardly slept and was in a foul mood. All night long visions of his wife with another man tormented him.

Visser arrived with two chipped mugs of what was claimed to be coffee.

"Sergeant."

"Sit down."

Visser pulled up a chair on which the vinyl cushion covering was torn.

"I have something you need to do but you must keep quiet about it. No-one - and I mean no-one - is to know."

The constable nodded.

"I want you to follow my daughter. I think she's up to something and I want to know what it is."

"I understand."

~ ~ ~

Visser kept his distance as he followed Liza from the university campus. She crossed Jan Smuts Avenue and headed up the hill towards the Civic Center, before turning to a circular block of flats. He quickened his pace, as he knew if she went into an apartment block he'd need to ride the elevator with her.

He wore a blue baseball cap, sunglasses, a black T-shirt and jeans, and hoped he looked like any other student, but deep down knew he didn't. He had 'cop' written all over him and could only hope she would be too involved in her own thoughts to take notice of him.

She was already standing, waiting at the elevator doors, along with two other people, when he caught up to her. He carefully avoided making eye contact with her. When the elevator arrived they all got in. Visser waited to see which button she pressed. When she pressed '10' he pressed '9'.

A man got off carrying two plastic grocery packets at the sixth floor. The next stop was '9' and Visser exited. He urgently searched for the fire escape and saw the doorway at the end of the passage. He took off at a sprint, climbing the steps two at a time. When he opened the fire escape door on the next floor, making sure he was not seen, Liza had just left the elevator and walked in his direction. He closed the door and ducked behind the glass panel. She stopped at an apartment near by and tapped on the door. A few moments later it swung open.

"Fuck!" Visser swore under his breath, as Kofi passionately kissed Liza, before pulling her into the flat and closing the door. "The Sergeant is going to shit his pants!"

Chapter 37

"I absolutely hate to tell you this," said Norah. She poured a glass of white wine and handed it to Cindy. "I'm afraid your suspicions were right. Your husband is cheating on you."

Cindy expected the worst, but the news still came as a shock. She took a large gulp of wine. It was mid morning, she was working the night shift and they sat in Norah's kitchen.

"I've seen him with three different women, but one more often than the others. They spend a couple of hours in the apartment and he always walks them out."

"Do you think they could be clients?"

Cindy clutched at straws.

Norah shook her head.

"No-one says 'goodbye' to clients like that."

When Cindy set her glass on the kitchen table her hand shook. Her eyes were slick with tears.

"I'm so sorry, Love," said Norah. She put an arm around Cindy's shoulders and hugged her. "But you knew it."

Cindy sniffed.

"I know. I guess I was hoping it was a one time thing."

She sobbed softly. The probability of her marriage ending was now a reality, and though she knew it was best that way, it still cut at her heart.

Norah tore off a piece of roller towel from a holder attached to the wall and handed it to her. Cindy dabbed her eyes and wiped her nose.

"None of this is your fault. You are a beautiful, sexy young woman who married a stray dog. He'll never change."

"I always tried to make him happy. I don't know what I did wrong. I never refused him anything."

"You did nothing wrong. There was nothing more you

could have done. It's the nature of the beast. Some men are like that."

She filled Cindy's glass and topped up her own.

"Drink up. There's lots more where that came from - and a large tub of chocolate ice cream in the freezer. I think it's time you teach the cheating rat a lesson he'll never forget, and I have a few ideas how you can do it."

Chapter 38

Danie was shaken to his core by the news Visser gave him. Could his life be any more screwed up? First Sias and now his daughter with a black man!

He was disgusted.

It was almost more than he could take, and for a brief moment he considered taking a drive into the middle of nowhere and shoving the barrel of his police-issued pistol into his mouth.

But suicide was a mortal sin for which there was no forgiveness and he was afraid of spending eternity burning in the fires of hell.

"Not a word about this," he warned Visser, "or I swear I will put a bullet in your head."

Visser placed his hand on his heart.

"No-one will ever hear me say anything. I can understand how you feel."

Danie knew he could not, but said nothing.

"What are you going to do?"

It was a question Danie asked himself many times. He had a plan but he was not yet prepared to share it with his partner.

"I need you to find out everything you can about that little *kaffir*," he said. "Who he is, where he comes from, how he gets to be living in a white area, how many times a day he takes a shit and anything else you can. Drop everything else you are doing now. If the captain asks, I'll tell him you're checking out a tip concerning the breaking of the Immorality Act."

"Okay, Sarge. I'll get to it right away."

"I'll make a few calls, but I'm going to have to be careful. Jesus! Can you imagine what people will say if they find out about my daughter?"

"I can," said Visser. His boss looked like he'd aged ten

years in the last week. His skin was sallow and wrinkled, his eyes outlined by dark rings.

Danie picked up the phone on his desk.

"Why the fuck are you still here?" he asked Visser.

~ ~ ~

It did not take Constable Dirk Visser long to get the information he sought. By late that afternoon he pretty well knew all there was to know about Kofi Okafor.

He called Danie, who was still at the office, from a pay phone in Braamfontein.

"I got what you want. Shall I come to the office, or do you want to meet somewhere else?"

"I'll see you in the bar at the Chelsea Hotel in thirty minutes."

"Okay," said Visser and hung up.

It was a tough day for Danie. All sorts of disgusting images filled his brain and he grew increasingly angry and frustrated. By the time he met Visser he was more angry than he could ever remember being.

"Brandy and Coke® - double!" he snapped at the black barman. "What are you having?"

Visser ordered a beer. When the drinks arrived, the two men found a booth away from the bar counter.

"Tell me," ordered Danie.

Visser took a notebook from his pocket and opened it to the place he'd made notes.

He told his boss how the boy was the son of an ambassador - which explained why he was able to live in Braamfontein and attend Wits University, that he was studying engineering, appeared to be a bright student, had connections with the ANC underground, and was involved with Liza for a few weeks now. He knew Kofi's car registration number, his telephone number and had a list of the youngster's friends, some of whom were being watched by the Security Police.

Danie was impressed. One day Visser was going to make one hell of a detective, but right now they needed to figure what to do with his information.

He gestured to a waiter to bring them another round of drinks.

"Are you going to arrest the little shit?" asked Visser. "He's broken the law so there won't be a problem having him deported."

Danie use the tip of his finger to trace a wet pattern on the table while he thought.

He shook his head.

"If I do that, Liza's name will become known and will bring more shame on me."

He drummed his fingers on the varnished table top.

"I'm going to have to handle this myself," he said, waiting until the waiter who brought their drinks left.

"What do you have in mind?"

Visser peered at his boss and saw something in his eyes he'd not seen before.

"I'm going to make him disappear off the face of the earth – forever!"

Chapter 39

Kofi turned his car into the underground parking garage at his apartment block and headed down the concrete ramp. His parking bay was on the second level, some distance from the elevator.

Liza was coming to visit later, and he planned to cook dinner for her. He really liked her, as she was a kindred spirit. They planned to go to Soweto again on the weekend, where the gang would introduce her to some political activists they knew. Big changes were coming in South Africa. Youngsters were planning an uprising, and the banned African National Congress was hard at work, mobilizing people in the townships.

At first Liza was regarded with suspicion. They thought it possible she was a police spy, but with time they grew to believe her beliefs were genuine and saw her as a supporter of their cause. She became involved in campus politics and was beginning to catch the eye of the Security Police.

As Kofi maneuvered into his parking spot he noticed the lights were not working and there were shards of broken glass on the ground. Someone had smashed the light bulbs.

Probably the kids on the fourteenth floor, he thought. They were obnoxious hooligans. He made a mental note to report it to the building supervisor.

It was still early in the afternoon and most of the parking bays were empty, although there was strange car parked in the bay beside his.

He wondered if his neighbors had changed their car.

He parked his car, locked the doors and opened the trunk to retrieve his backpack and two packets of groceries he needed for their dinner.

"Kofi Okafor?" asked a voice from behind.

He turned to face a middle-aged, man with a bald spot on the top of his head and a gray goatee.

"Who wants to know?"

"Are you Kofi Okafor?" the man asked again, his voice aggressive.

"Yes."

Suddenly a black, canvas hood was pulled over his head from behind him and he was kicked brutally in the balls. He doubled over in excruciating agony, trying to scream but had no breath and vomited into the hood.

As he collapsed, his hands were yanked behind his back and handcuffed, then he was dragged to his feet, strong hands beneath each armpit, and frog-marched to the car parked beside his. He heard the trunk opened and was bundled into it.

"Shout or scream and I'll put a bullet in your head," said the voice Kofi recognized as that of the man with the goatee.

The trunk lid slammed shut.

With squealing tires, the car backed out of the parking bay, turned right and headed up the ramp out of the parking garage.

In the trunk, Kofi Okafor, sobbed, never more terrified in his life.

~ ~ ~

The drive was short, no more than a few blocks, and from the way the car crested a steep hill, went down the other side then turned right, Kofi believed they were somewhere in Hillbrow. After two more turns they stopped and the ignition shut off. He heard the car door open and began to tremble, as waves of panic surged over him. He began to pray.

They opened the trunk and dragged him out of the car, grazing his shins as they did so.

"Walk!" a new voice commanded.

Hands gripped each of his upper arms and roughly guided him along a paved pathway and through a door that slammed shut behind him. He was forced to sit on a cold, metal chair, his ankles shackled to a steel ring embedded in the concrete floor.

He blinked when the hood was removed, his eyes struggling to adjust to the light. His chin and shirt was caked with drying vomit.

Slowly he focused on his surroundings. The windows in the room were blacked out, the concrete floor had a drain outlet by the steel chair. Placed nearby, was a table against a wall, on which was an electric cattle prod. Beside it was a leather bag with a wooden handle attached to it. At the far end of the room was a faucet above a large concrete laundry sink and three steel water buckets on the floor.

The man with the gray goatee held a water bucket in his hands.

"Welcome to my world, fuckwad!" he said and dumped the contents of the bucket over Kofi. "Looks like you could do with a shower, you piece of filth."

Kofi spluttered and gasped.

"What is it? What do you want?" he cried.

He watched in horror, as the other man, much younger, about the same age as he was, picked up the cattle prod. Kofi strained against his restraints as the man brought the instrument towards him and pressed it against his wet chest.

Jesus! This is going to hurt!

Visser flicked the switch on the handle. He only gave Kofi a one-second jolt but the effect was instantaneous and spectacular.

His head snapped back, his eyes rolled in his head, his hips rose from the chair and the veins in his neck felt as though they were about to pop.

He slumped in his chair, his head sagging against his chest.

Visser took a handful of Kofi's hair so he could lift his face.

"You like to fuck white girls, 'huh?" he snarled. "See where it gets you?"

So this was what it's about! Kofi thought.

He figured the man with the goatee was Liza's father.

"We like each other... a lot," he said weakly, his tongue thick.

Danie took the prod from Visser and zapped Kofi again.

"Don't you ever fucking talk to me about my daughter," he said.

Kofi said nothing. His mouth hung open and a stream of saliva ran from it.

Visser flung another bucket of water into Kofi's face.

Danie seethed, his fury barely contained. He planned to teach this kid a lesson, then take him out somewhere and kill him. Bury him in the middle of nowhere, where his stinking corpse would never be found. It was what he deserved and when they picked Kofi up he had two shovels stowed in the back of his car.

But Visser talked him out of it.

"This is not some ordinary coon, where his disappearance and investigation can be swept under the rug, Sarge," he said. "His father is an ambassador. There'll be a proper investigation. They'll find out about your daughter and eventually suspect you are involved."

Danie knew his partner was right.

"So what do I do?"

"Teach him a lesson that'll scare the shit out of him and keep him away from Liza."

~ ~ ~

They took turns beating Kofi with the leather bag filled

with lead shot. It was designed to inflict internal damage but leave no visible external marks.

Finally Danie knelt in front of the broken youngster. He drew his pistol from its holster, cocked it and pressed the muzzle against Kofi's forehead.

"Do you believe I will happily blow your brains out?"

Kofi nodded. It was too painful to speak.

"Today is your lucky day. I'm going to let you go, but there are conditions. You walk away from my daughter and never see her again. Can you do that?"

He lifted the boy's chin with the barrel of the pistol, so he could look into his eyes.

"I asked, can you do that?"

Kofi nodded.

"And if you mention a word of our time together today, to anyone, especially my daughter..." His voice trailed off. "If you think this was bad... and then you'll die."

Kofi peered at him through bloodshot eyes.

"Do we understand each other," said Danie, his voice soft and laced with menace.

"Yes," whispered Kofi.

Danie got to his feet and turned to Visser.

"Take him home," he said.

Chapter 40

When Liza knocked on Kofi's door that evening, there was no response. She thought she heard movement inside, but eventually she gave up when there was no answer, and went home. She was pissed. She hated being stood up, but on top of that she faced a walk in the dark, past the Civic Center, back to Hillbrow - and it made her nervous.

The only scrap of paper she could find in her purse was a crumpled cash receipt, and she scribbled a harsh note to Kofi on the back of it. When she was done, she slid it under the door and left. While she walked home she tried to figure out why Kofi stood her up. It was not like him. He was always a perfect gentleman, a caring and concerned boyfriend, and she was in love with him.

Sometimes she day-dreamed about being married to him - he a successful engineer, she a human rights lawyer and champion of the underdog. Of course it'd have to be in another country. England, most likely.

It was a twenty five minute walk, and by the time she got home Liza had cooled off considerably. Kofi must have had a good reason. Perhaps something urgent came up.

Miems was in the kitchen frying an egg for her supper. Liza saw her mother was crying. Her eyes were puffy, her face blotched.

"What is it? What's wrong?"

Miems pointed to a postcard on the kitchen table.

"It's from Sias."

Liza read it.

Dear Mom and Liza

I hope you are well. I am in London and have found a place to live. I have a temporary job in an Italian restaurant, where I do whatever is needed.

I'm planning to move to Holland. Amsterdam most likely,

where people like me are accepted as normal. Do not worry about me, I am fine. I will send you my postal address when I am properly settled.

Love Sias.

Liza dropped the postcard onto the table and gazed at her mother.

"I miss him so much," said Miems, trying hard not to sob.

Liza wrapped her arms around her mother.

"I know you do but he's fine. He is better off away from here... away from Dad."

Miems sniffed.

"I know but it's still hard."

Liza opened the refrigerator and poured herself a glass of milk.

"Have you heard from Dad?"

"He tries to phone every day but I refuse to speak to him."

"It's probably best. Do you still love him?"

Miems considered her answer for a while.

"Right now I don't. Perhaps it'll change in the future, but I can't say for sure."

She lifted the egg from the pan and slid it onto a plate.

"Why are you back? I thought you had another study date."

Liza shrugged and sighed.

"It got canceled at the last moment."

"I'm sorry about that. Do you want something to eat?"

"I'll have an egg, too," said Liza.

Miems slid her plate across the kitchen table to her daughter.

"Take this one, I'll fry another."

~ ~ ~

After they finished their supper Miems went to her bedroom and closed the door. She didn't feel like talking and wanted time to herself. She figured her daughter felt the same.

Liza rolled a joint and went onto the balcony for a few puffs. She needed something to mellow her.

She watched the traffic in the street below and thought of Sias. Maybe one day she and Kofi would live overseas and they'd visit, perhaps tour and travel together. She missed her brother. After he left there was a void in her life that Kofi managed to partly fill. She did not think she could survive without Kofi.

Soon she had a nice buzz going and sat on a folding, canvas, camping chair. She closed her eyes, giving herself permission to relax and enjoy the sensation. All around her she heard sounds of life in Hillbrow. Televisions tuned to the only station broadcast in South Africa, people talking in the street below, and a dog barking far away. In the distance an ambulance wailed and she figured it was on its way to the Hillbrow Hospital.

A while later she got up and went inside. Her mother's bedroom door was closed and she heard the radio softly playing inside.

There was a telephone extension in the entrance hall on a small table. Liza dialed Kofi's number. The phone rang for a long time and she was about to hang up when he answered.

"Hello."

It was him, but his voice sounded different - as though he were drunk or ill.

"Kofi."

He recognized her voice instantly and wanted to hang up but didn't.

"Where were you? I knocked and left a note."

"I know. I'm sorry. Something came up."

"Are you okay? You sound like something's wrong. Your voice is strange."

"I'm fine."

"So where were you?"

"I can't discuss it now."

A tiny tremor of panic fluttered in Liza's belly. Was there another girl?

"We had an arrangement. I think you owe me an explanation."

Silence.

"If there's a problem, you need to tell me."

She heard him take in a gulp of air.

"I don't want to see you anymore," he said. "I don't think it's working out. It's best we end it now."

It took a few moments for his words to sink in, but when they did they hit Liza like a kick in the gut.

Her blood turned to ice and she broke into a cold sweat. She struggled to breathe.

"But why?" she was finally able to ask. "Things are going so well."

"It can never work. We come from different worlds."

"That's bullshit and you know it," she growled, suddenly filled with fury. "It is working! Be a fucking man and tell me the real reason!"

When he spoke, his voice was hesitant, and it was obvious he was lying.

"I think I'll be better off with a black woman. She'll understand my culture. You were simply a novelty and I don't want to see you anymore. Please leave me alone."

"Fuck you!" screamed Liza and slammed down the phone.

"Goodbye," murmured Kofi, tears streaming down his cheeks.

Chapter 41

Dave did his best to put Tamarin out of his mind, but couldn't. He stopped by the *Green Junction* twice, but she was cold and stand-offish. Whenever he saw her in the entrance hall or corridors at *Hillbrow Heights*, she was polite but did her best to avoid him and hurried away. But she did not stop Adrian from visiting Dave.

Dave taught him more karate techniques and they worked out on the punching bag.

"What's with your mother?" he asked one day. They sat in his lounge sipping iced water after a training session. "What have I done that she doesn't like me anymore?"

Adrian set his glass on the floor beside his feet and fixed his gaze on Dave.

"She does like you but I think she is scared. She says my father hurt her badly and doesn't want that to happen again."

"Then why does she treat me like a dick?"

The boy sighed. When he spoke it was like a teacher speaking to a slow child.

"It's what girls do when they like a boy. I see it at school. I think they want to force the boys to try harder so then they know they really like them."

Dave smiled.

"When did you get so smart, Midget?"

"I know these things."

"So what do you suggest I do about your mother?"

"Keep trying. Eventually she'll give in."

"Aye aye, Captain Love," said Dave, saluting the boy.

Chapter 42

Liza looked terrible when she woke. After her phone call to Kofi she cried herself to sleep, but woke a little while later and tossed and turned for the rest of the night.

She could not process or accept what happened and, for the first time in her life she understood what heartbreak was.

Now she comprehended how Sias felt about Jarrod and wished her brother were home, or that there was some way to contact him. She couldn't face her mother, so she left early while Miems was still in the shower. She was determined to see Kofi and get the truth out of him.

She knew he had an early lecture and planned to ambush him at the entrance to the lecture hall when he was not surrounded by friends.

The early morning air was crisp but the thirty minute-long walk warmed her. When she got to Wits she had forty minutes to wait before the start of the lecture, so she bought a cup of coffee and sat drinking it on the steps of the *Great Hall*. She mentally rehearsed the speech she had planned, but knew when she confronted Kofi she'd probably remember none of it.

She prayed he changed his mind during the night, and they'd be able to resume their relationship where they left off, because she couldn't imagine living without him.

Liza had just finished her coffee when she saw him approaching on the paved walkway. He saw her and stopped, his first impulse to turn and head in the opposite direction.

Kofi too, had a terrible night. The reality was, he'd fallen for this girl in a big way. He wanted to be with her and saw a future with her, but her father made it more than clear that was impossible. He had no doubt Danie van Staden would kill him next time. He struggled to get out of bed that morning. Every inch in his body ached, and the pain killers he swallowed throughout the night had no effect.

When he passed water, his stream was tinged crimson, and the associated agony was like peeing molten steel. But there were no external marks on his body. No outward evidence, other than a few small burn marks from the cattle prod.

Liza waved a hand tentatively and he made his way to her. He grimaced as he climbed the steps and sat beside her.

"Hi," she said softly.

She reached for his hand but he pulled away. Her father may have someone watching and reporting back.

"Hi."

"Are you all right? You look as though you were run over by a bus."

He nodded.

His eyes were puffy and she wondered if he'd been crying.

"Why?" she asked, her voice trembling.

"It's complicated. There are things you don't know."

"Tell me, so I can understand."

"I can't.

"Can't or won't?"

"Can't."

Suddenly Liza became angry.

"You owe me an explanation!" she snapped. "I gave myself to you. I fell in love with you. I took a risk. You owe me!"

His eyes were moist when he looked at her. His heart ached.

"I'm sorry, I truly am. But I can't tell you. Maybe one day, then you'll understand. When there is a new, better world."

He sniffed and fished a handkerchief out of his pocket so

he could wipe his nose.

"I love you, and this is for the best," he said. "I promise. Please don't make this more difficult. Stay away from me."

He struggled to his feet, took her face in his hands and kissed her softly on the lips. Then he turned and walked away.

Chapter 43

Miems was not sure why, but when Danie phoned that morning and begged her to meet him for lunch, she agreed. Perhaps it was because she wanted to bring their situation to some sort of resolution. The truth was, she no longer knew how she felt about her husband, and figured seeing him in the flesh might help clarify her feelings toward him.

But maybe it was because he sounded so desperate and lonely. It was true, he was not the fairytale prince on a white horse she dreamed she'd marry, but in his own misguided way, he cared for his family and honestly believed his actions were in their best interests.

She was however torn by her association with Dane. He was exciting and dangerous. He made her heart pound. Her breathe grew short and her hands were clammy when he was near. Seeing Danie might help her decide what to do on that front.

They arranged to meet at a small Italian restaurant about a block away from the building where Miems worked. Danie hated Italian food, as he figured it was too much like the food he ate at home, but it was Miems's favorite.

He was already waiting when Miems arrived, and she noticed he had a haircut and his goatee was neatly trimmed. It was only a little over a week since she last saw him, but he appeared older, with a sadness that hung over him like a gray rain cloud.

Danie got to his feet awkwardly when he saw his wife enter the restaurant. He was not sure how he should greet her. Hug her? Kiss her? Miem's gave him no clue, so he shook her hand. To anyone looking in from the outside, they could simply be two people at a business meeting - which, in a way, they were.

He pulled out a chair for her, something she could not remember him ever doing before.

"You look lovely," he said. A few beads of sweat glistened on the bald spot on the top of his head.

"Thank you."

She placed her hands in her lap.

A waiter with a grubby towel draped over his arm sidled up to them. He used the towel to wipe the table while they examined the menu.

"I'll have lasagna and rooibos tea to drink," said Miems.

Danie ordered a pizza with salami and a Coke®.

"I've missed you."

She nodded but said nothing.

He wanted to reach across the table and take her hands in his, but she kept them in her lap.

Finally he took a deep breath and said: "Please let me come home. I promise I've changed. I know I've made a lot of mistakes, but I'm different now I've had time to think."

What struck Miems more than her husband's words was how sad his voice was. She'd never heard that before. For a moment she felt sorry for him, but realized it'd take more than words to convince her. In the end it would be his actions that would change her feelings about him.

Can a leopard really change its spots? She did not know. But if it wasn't given the chance, it never would.

"You sleep on the couch," she said. "Everyone deserves a second chance. You don't get a third."

"Thank you," he whispered, tears in his eyes.

Chapter 44

It was almost a month since Dave last saw Tamarin. She successfully managed to avoid him, and his work schedule was hectic.

In South Africa's black townships a simmering discontent grew and there was a sense it was only a matter of time before the pressure cooker blew its lid. Journalists tried to understand what sources in the security and intelligence communities predicted was coming.

But the news occupying the minds of white Johannesburgers was that a serial rapist was at work in the city's apartment complexes. During the past three weeks, seven women living on their own, or with young children, were attacked and raped in their flats. The modus operandi was always the same - the rapist gained access to their apartments by breaking a window or levering a door open with a crowbar. He raped the women with a knife held to their throats.

So far he'd not killed any victims but each was beaten, and the level of violence was turned up with each incident. The cops figured it was only a matter of time before he added 'murder' to his C.V.

They knew almost nothing about him, except he always wore a balaclava cap pulled down over his face and rubber gloves. The press dubbed him the *Rubber Glove Rapist*. They knew he was white, believed he was in his twenties and physically strong.

But little else. He was smart, left no clues, and seemed able to disappear into thin air.

Dave worked on a feature article about the case and spent much of his time tracking down and trying to persuade female victims to talk to him. It was good, old-fashioned, pound-the-pavements, grunt work, journalism. The police were reluctant to talk to him, but his persistence paid off and a powerful story began to emerge.

He thought about Tamarin and what Adrian said about her liking him, and that he should not give up. He wanted to see her, but his workload prevented it.

He arrived home after ten that night and saw the lights in her apartment were still on. He considered knocking on her door but decided it was late and likely not a good time. Perhaps tomorrow he would drop in, after Adrian went to school, and before she left for work.

But Adrian was away. It was school holidays - which Dave did not realize - and the youngster was spending a week with his father.

When she got home from work Tamarin changed into a short, white, cotton nightdress, made herself supper, and when she was finished, rolled a joint and sat on the balcony. Behind her, the lights in the lounge burned. She sucked the smoke down her throat and held it in her lungs, giving it time to take effect.

She thought about Dave. She knew for certain she really liked him, but that was not enough. He would change her life and it frightened her. He'd already changed their lives. They now ate meat regularly, although she still felt guilty and kept it a secret from her mother. She also drank wine, and though she'd never admit it, she read a few issues of *Rogue Magazine* and was impressed by the quality of the articles.

But she reminded herself of how Adrian's father was when they first met. Charming, dashing and a little dangerous. But then he changed. What if Dave was the same? She did not think she could bear it.

She flicked the remnants of the *zol* over the balcony railings, got up and stood in the doorway of the lounge, completely unaware of how the lights from inside made her nightgown transparent and showed off her shapely silhouette.

Across the road, hidden in the shadows, a man with a balaclava in one jacket pocket, and a pair of rubber gloves in the other, licked his lips.

Chapter 45

It was after midnight and Dave was still working - dressed only in boxer shorts - when he realized he left a cassette tape in the car that needed transcribing. He pulled on a baggy, white T-shirt grabbed his car keys and headed down the corridor to the steps leading to the underground parking garage.

It took him a while to find the tape, because it'd slipped out of his bag and fallen between the seats. He locked the car and jogged up the stairs, his bare feet silent on the floor.

When he stepped into the corridor he stopped in his tracks. The dark figure of a man kneeling outside Tamarin's front door was visible in the dim, overhead lights in the passage.

He wore a balaclava and yellow rubber gloves... and he was in the process of prying open her door with a yard-long, steel crowbar.

"Hey!" Dave yelled, sprinting towards the crouched figure.

The man sprang to his feet, crowbar held high above his head, ready to shatter Dave's skull. But Dave kept coming.

"I'm going to fucking kill you, asshole," Marais hissed, not slowing down at all.

It wasn't response *the Rubber Glove Rapist* expected and he turned and fled. But Dave's approach blocked the path to the steps and exit of *Hillbrow Heights*, and the only way he could flee was up.

With Marais closing in on him he reached the corridor on the top floor and discovered he had nowhere to escape, unless he could leap across a ten foot-wide gap to a balcony on an adjoining block of apartments.

He scrambled onto the concrete railing.

"Don't do it!" yelled Dave. "You'll never make it!"

The Rubber Glove Rapist hesitated for the briefest of seconds then turned and leaped, still holding the crowbar in his right hand.

He didn't come close to making the jump and tumbled towards the asphalt below. At the last moment he let go the crowbar but it still pointed upwards when he landed on it with his thigh. The inch-thick length of steel shattered the femur and ripped his femoral artery, spewing blood in a dense mist. His forehead cracked against the ground and he rolled onto his back, arms splayed wide, rapidly bleed to death.

His last breath was a sigh he made just as Dave reached him.

Some of the *Hillbrow Heights* residents heard Dave's yelling and came out of their apartments onto the corridor, trying to figure out what was going on.

"Call the cops and an ambulance!" yelled Dave.

First to arrive was Cindy. She lifted the balaclava, revealing the face of a white man she guessed was in his mid thirties. Then she touched *the Rubber Glove Rapist's* neck with the tips of her fingers and shook her head.

"He's dead."

The others gathered around, shocked and trying to avoid stepping in the growing stream of blood leaking from the body."

"What happened?" asked Brigadier Earl "Buck" Rogers. He wore a satin, paisley dressing gown and Italian leather slippers.

Liza though she would puke and had to move away.

In the dim lights of the courtyard, Dave's face appeared ashen.

"I went to the car to fetch something and when I came back I saw him trying to break into Tamarin's apartment. He took off when I tried to tackle him, and I guess thought he could escape by jumping to the next building."

"Jesus!" Tamarin gasped. The realization of what could have happened struck her, and she was overcome by a bout of uncontrollable trembling.

"Good riddance to the piece of shit," said Norah, wrapping her arms around Tamarin.

"I called the station and the flying squad is on the way. Also an ambulance, although it seems it won't be needed," said Danie. He prodded the corpse with his foot. "They'll be here in a couple of minutes."

"Do you think he is... was... the rapist?" asked Cindy.

Dave nodded.

"You were very lucky," Danie said to Tamarin.

Miems returned from her apartment with a glass of sugar water she handed to Tamarin.

"Drink it. It'll help for the shock," she said.

Tamarin drained the glass in a single gulp, but the tremors continued. She clung to Norah, finding it hard to breathe.

In the distance they heard the wail of approaching sirens. Danie went to the entrance hall to meet the cops and paramedics.

"It's a bad business," he said to the two cops, who were based at Brixton, but known to him. "I've got a wife and daughter who could been victims. I don't know what this country is coming to. A white man is no longer safe in his own home - not even from his own kind!"

When the paramedics from the Johannesburg Emergency Services confirmed the rapist was dead, the cops from the flying squad returned to their vehicle to use the radio. It was a now a case for the detectives.

"The CID guys will be along sometime, but until then no-one is to touch anything or move any evidence. I've called for uniformed guys to monitor the situation until the detectives get here," said the senior member.

He locked eyes with Danie.

"Until then, I'm sure the sergeant will keep an eye on

things. We can't hang around, we've just got a call about an armed robbery in progress."

Danie nodded.

"Go! I know the procedure."

~ ~ ~

It was almost sunrise when the body was finally removed and the crime scene investigators left. They said they'd be back with follow up questions, but from what they could see, everything happened exactly as Dave reported. There was no doubt the dead man was *the Rubber Glove Rapist*.

They sat in Tamarin's lounge after completing their examination of the marks on her door frame, taking photographs and dusting for fingerprints.

"I think you owe this man a dinner," said the lead investigator, a lieutenant with a nicotine-stained mustache and over twenty years experience. "If he hadn't come along and confronted the rapist when he did, this would have turned out very badly for you."

"I know," whispered Tamarin. "I do owe him - and more than a dinner."

When she looked at Dave, her eyes were wet.

The lieutenant made a final note, then snapped his notebook closed, put it into his shirt pocket and stood up.

"I think we have all we need for now. If there is anything else I'll call you. If you remember anything else, give me a call."

He handed Tamarin his business card and another to Dave.

Tamarin closed the door behind him. Suddenly she was exhausted. Her legs were rubbery and she stumbled. Dave caught her and held her, her body trembling, her heart pounding.

"You should lie down before you fall down," he said,

scooping her up in his arms, as though she were constructed of goose down.

He carried her to her bedroom and gently laid her on her bed, covering her with the comforter.

"Don't go," she said, as he turned to leave. She held out her hand. "Please stay with me."

She pulled back the comforter so he could slide in beside her.

"Are you sure?"

"Yes."

He kicked off his running shoes and slipped into bed with her.

She wrapped her arms around him, clinging to him while he held her.

"I'm sorry," she whispered, her breath warm and soft on his cheek.

"For what?"

"For treating you so badly. Ever since my ex-husband..."

He touched her lips with his fingertips to shush her.

"I am not him. I know he hurt you but I will never do that. I promise."

She kissed him softly and reached into his shorts.

"Make love to me," she murmured, her voice pleading.

Chapter 46

Cindy was working the day shift but took time off work to go shopping that afternoon. There were a few things she needed to get for what she planned for her husband that night.

There'd been no change in his behavior. According to reports from Norah he was entertaining women in their apartment regularly.

"So cheap he doesn't have to class to take them to a hotel," she muttered, while she scribbled a list of everything she needed.

Tonight Gary was going to be fucked - in a couple of ways!

~ ~ ~

When Gary walked into the apartment after work he was greeted by the smell of chicken roasting in the oven. The table was set for two. Tall wine glasses, candles and their best cutlery and crockery was set out. In the refrigerator two bottles of wine chilled and his favorite chocolate pudding was in a bowl.

He had no idea what the occasion was. Had he forgotten something? Their anniversary? No, next month. Cindy's birthday? Two months ago.

"Cindy!" he called.

She came out of the bedroom wearing a short black, silk robe and red, peep-toe stilettos with heels so high she thought her nose may bleed. Gary had a thing for heels.

"Fuck!" he gasped.

"You like?"

"I like!"

"Wait 'til you see what's under."

He made a grab for her but she evaded him.

"Later," she said, laughing. "All good things come to those who wait."

"What's this? What's the occasion?" he asked.

"I figured we've not spent much time together lately. I want to give us both a night we'll never forget!"

He smiled.

"Sounds good!"

Cindy popped the cork on a bottle of white wine and poured him a glass.

"Go take a relaxing bath while I finish preparing the meal."

"You're too good for me," he said, sipping the wine.

"I know," she replied.

~ ~ ~

After they finished their meal, Cindy took Gary's hand and led him to their bedroom. She kissed him passionately, pressing her tongue into his mouth, grinding her hips against him, while she dug her nails into his butt cheeks.

She pushed him onto his back on the bed and slid his boxer shorts off his legs. He was already hard and she stroked him a few times while she kissed him. Suddenly she broke away.

"I'm going to freshen our drinks. Keep yourself going. I'll be back in a moment."

In the kitchen she refilled their wine glasses. She opened her purse and took out a small plastic container with white tablets.

"*Rohypnol*, Darling," she whispered to herself. "It's what we give patients to make them sleep."

She dropped two into the wine and stirred with a teaspoon until they were dissolved.

Cindy sashayed into the bedroom and handed Gary his drink.

"Ready for your unforgettable night?"

"Oh yeah, Baby! Bring it on!"

His voice was thick with lust.

She undid the sash holding her silk robe closed, and allowed it to slip from her shoulders and puddle in a fabric ring on the floor. Beneath it she wore a set of crotchless red panties, cut high on the sides of her hips, and a matching bra with holes her nipples poked through.

Gary could see she shaved for him, something she always refused to do.

"Oh Fuck!" he groaned, his penis bobbing in the air.

She stood with her legs and arms splayed wide.

"Finish your drink, then come grab a mouthful of this," she said.

He gulped down his wine. His heart pounded, his mouth dry, his dick so hard he thought it would split.

"Get over here!" he growled, shucking off the rest of his clothes.

Cindy slithered onto the bed beside him, planting tiny, wet kisses on his chest, nipping softly at his erect nipples.

He threw his head back and groaned, his teeth bared.

He'd never felt like this before. Chilled. Sailing on a cloud of sexual intoxication. He could feel his wife working her magic on his dick but it was as though he was detached and floating above his physical body.

Fuck! This was so weird.

~ ~ ~

When Gary awoke it was mid morning. He had to pee so badly his tonsils were drowning. He also needed to take a dump. He could remember nothing about last night.

He shook his head and slowly the fog lifted.

Then he began to scream.

Chapter 47

Liza woke feeling ill but she struggled out of bed and got dressed. She needed to speak to Kofi that day, no matter how he felt, and thought her best opportunity was in the canteen during the lunch break. But first she had to struggle through two early morning lectures.

The situation at home was odd. Her father still slept on the couch, as her mother still would not allow him back into her bed. But even Liza had to admit, Danie was trying to change, although she guessed it was not a real change of heart but rather alteration of a pattern of behavior to worm his way back into their lives.

Whatever, she didn't care. She still hated him and everything he represented.

When she was dressed she went to the kitchen and made herself a cup of coffee. Danie was there frying eggs and making toast.

"Can I do you a couple?" he asked.

She shook her head. The thought of eggs made her want to throw up.

"How are you?" he asked.

She shrugged.

"I'm fine I guess."

"If there's anything you ever want to talk about, you know I am here," he said.

Yeah like that's ever going to happen!

"I don't have anything I want to talk about."

"Okay. But if you do..."

"I don't!" she cut him off.

~ ~ ~

She found Kofi at a table in the canteen where he sat with his engineering classmates.

He did not see her approach, but when she put her hand on his shoulder he turned around.

"Can we talk, please? I have something important to tell you."

"Sure."

"In private?"

He nodded.

"I'll be back in a moment," he said to his friends.

They found a vacant table.

"How are you?" he asked. She looked tired and sad.

Liza shrugged.

"All right, under the circumstances, I guess. I've missed you."

"Me too."

"Then why did you toss me aside like a piece of garbage."

"I told you. It's complicated. It simply would not have worked out."

"That's bullshit! And you know it!"

"Is that what you dragged me away to tell me?"

She shook her head.

"I have something to tell you that'll change your life, but before I can, I need to know the truth about us."

"Jesus! I've told you."

"And I know you are lying! For once be a man and tell the truth. If you're going to be a coward I'm going to walk away and you'll never know!"

Kofi's anger suddenly exploded.

"If you must know, your father and one of his goons beat me almost to death, then he stuck a gun against my head and said if I didn't walk away from you he'd come back and blow my brains out."

He sucked in his breath, trembling.

"And do you know what? I fucking believed him - and I still do!"

Liza was aghast. She struggled to understand what Kofi

told her. Icy tremors ran all the way down to the soles of her feet, her heart race, her stomach knotted. She couldn't breathe.

But one thing she knew for certain was, today, Wednesday 16 June 1976, as far as she was concerned, her father was dead to her. She would never forgive him and do everything in her power to see him rot in hell.

"I am so sorry," she whispered. "I had no idea." She reached across the table and took his hand in hers, not giving a damn who saw them.

He squeezed her hand while they both choked back tears, neither speaking for fear of breaking down completely.

Finally he swallowed and asked: "What is it you need to tell me?"

She held his hand tightly and took a deep breath, but before she could speak a student with long red hair and scraggly beard raced into the canteen screaming.

"The cops are shooting school kids in Soweto!" he screeched. "They say the whole fucking place is at war! And the riot police are outside the *Great Hall*!"

~ ~ ~

In the melee to get outside and see what was happening, Liza and Kofi got separated. It was the last she saw of him, as the security authorities embarked on a campaign to round up political activists and sympathizers of the ANC.

Kofi was scooped up in the dragnet on campus, and after rigorous questioning at *John Vorster Square,* taken to the Lesotho border and deported.

Liza was frantic when he disappeared. Finally she found someone who knew what happened.

It was the final straw. She could no longer stand around idly while her father and those of his ilk jammed their boots on the throats of an oppressed people. Waving placards and singing protest songs was no longer enough. She wanted to get her hands dirty. Become a soldier. Take up arms. Be a real part of the inevitable struggle, and play a meaningful part in the destruction of the system.

But how? Kofi's friends in Soweto would know but there was no way a white girl would get into a black township unnoticed by the cops. The townships would be locked down tighter than a bank vault. She had no way of contacting them.

Then she remembered someone she once met with Kofi. They stopped outside a chicken restaurant in Hillbrow where a black waiter came outside to chat on the sidewalk. Kofi introduced Liza to John, but while the two men talked she grew bored and wandered along, peering into shop windows. After a few minutes later Kofi caught up with her.

"Who is he?" Liza asked.

Kofi smiled wryly.

"He looks like a lowly waiter but he's an **MK* operative. He got military training in Angola and Russia and now he's back, recruiting mostly I think."

Liza was impressed but thought no more of it.

Until now.

John would know. If he had military training he'd be able to arrange for her to do the same, she thought.

She prayed he still worked at the chicken restaurant and was not in Soweto, or worse, picked up by the Security Police.

**MK - uMkhonto we Sizwe (abbreviated as MK, Zulu for "Spear of the Nation") was the armed wing of the African National Congress (ANC), co-founded by Nelson Mandela in the wake of the Sharpeville massacre. Its founding represented the conviction in the face of the massacre that the ANC could no longer limit itself to nonviolent* *protest; its mission was to fight against the South African government. After warning the South African government in June 1961 of its intent to resist further acts of terror if the government did not take steps toward constitutional reform and increase political rights, MK launched its first attacks against government installations on 16 December 1961. It was subsequently classified as a terrorist organization by the South African government and the United States, and banned. - Source Wikipedia*

Chapter 48

When Norah heard Gary's screams she rushed to the apartment. Cindy deliberately left the door unlocked. She knew when she left for work her husband would holler like a stabbed pig when he woke, and she wanted him to be discovered. It was the plan - to humiliate him as publicly as possible.

"Oh my goodness but you're in a spot of bother," said Norah, doing her best not to shriek with laughter. "I suppose I'd better call for an ambulance."

"Please hurry," said Gary, his face pale. "I'm in agony. And cover me with a blanket."

But Norah had already left to make the phone call, giggling uncontrollably as she did.

~ ~ ~

"Doctor, I think you'd better get down here and take a look at this," said the Duty Sister at the Casualty Department of the Johannesburg General Hospital. She was on the telephone to the Emergency Services Doctor. "I guarantee you won't have seen anything like this before."

He thought he heard her snort.

"What is it?"

He figured he'd seen everything possible that there was to see, after ten years in emergency rooms around the country.

"Come and see for yourself. I don't want to spoil the surprise."

She giggled as she hung up.

Dr Phillip Ostron was intrigued. If the sister had not hung up so quickly he would have taken a bet with her that whatever it was, he would have seen it before.

It was a good thing he did not, as he would have lost.

In the emergency room stood Gary Hayden. His penis was glued to his stomach with *Krazy Glue®*, his ass cheeks similarly pasted together and the palms of his hands stuck to them.

Written on his chest in thick, black permanent marker, were the words: *I'm a lying cheater!*

Chapter 49

The chicken restaurant where John Ngoza worked was only two blocks from *Hillbrow Heights*. Liza pressed her face against the window, peering in to see if he was there.

He saw her, recognized her, and gestured for her to come in.

"I need to speak to you urgently," she whispered, her voice hoarse.

"I heard about Kofi. I'm sorry. This thing in Soweto is going to blow up, but it's for the best. People are angry."

Liza glanced around to see if anyone was in earshot. There was only a couple seated at a table, and the owner was in the back, in the kitchen.

"I'm also angry," she said. "I want to do something. Can you help me get out of the country to get military training?"

He raised his eyebrows.

Was this a trap? Was she a plant?

"I dunno. Maybe. I'll have to see if I can find anyone who knows about those things."

Liza knew he was stalling.

"Kofi told me who you are," she said, grasping his forearm. "I want to do something. I want to help."

John was quiet for a few moments while he thought about the white girl's request. Kofi told him on previous occasions she was solid and committed to their cause. But he also told him her father was a cop, and what he did to Kofi.

"Your father is a policeman, 'eh?"

She nodded and it was obvious she was ashamed about that.

"I hate him," she said.

"I'll ask around," said John. "But you may be more valuable to us here, on the inside."

Liza looked confused.

"How?"

"If you can get information from your father that is useful to us, it would be a huge contribution."

Suddenly she understood.

"Like a spy?"

He nodded.

"But he is in the vice squad, he's not a security policeman."

"Cops from all departments hang out and socialize together. They talk about things to each other. They love to brag. Your old man will hear things, know about operations. I need you to find a way to get him to tell you those things."

"I understand. But I don't see how. He knows how I feel about him. We barely speak to each other."

John smiled.

"Make up with him. Win his confidence. Become his little girl again. That way, when you plunge the dagger into his heart it will be even more sweet. Can you do that?"

"Yes," replied Liza.

Chapter 50

Danie got home a little after eight that night. The student uprising in Soweto saw all police personnel placed on standby and all leave canceled, as the unrest quickly spread to other areas.

Shops and delivery vehicles were attacked, looted and burned. Schools torched and black officials working for government departments fled, as they became the targets of enraged youngsters.

The government feared the situation would swiftly become uncontrollable. The country stood on the brink of civil war and they responded with an iron fist, by throwing an armored cordon around black townships.

"You look tired," said Liza.

He nodded.

"Yes. You've heard about Soweto, I imagine."

"Sure. It's been on the television news and in all the newspapers. It's all anyone's talking about at university."

"We're running around like chickens without heads and it's going to be worse tomorrow. I'm on standby, so they could call me out tonight."

"It's terrible," said Liza. "I can understand some of their unhappiness, but when they behave like savages, looting and burning, I'm completely against that."

She put her hand on his forearm - the first time she'd touched him in more than a year.

"I hate to admit it," she said, her voice soft, her eyes gazing into his. "But you were right. Blacks are different. Maybe in a thousand years they'll reach our level."

He took her hand in his, his heart soaring.

"I just want what is best for our family," he said. "You know that?"

"I do now."

It took the start of a revolution to change his daughter's

mind, and a great weight was lifted off his chest.

"Can I pour you a drink?" she asked.

He nodded, unable to speak because of the emotion that welled inside him. There were tears in his eyes when he looked at his little girl who'd finally returned to the fold.

Liza smiled while she poured her father's drink. The feeling of satisfaction was heady and intoxicating.

And while she stood there, enjoying the moment, although she knew it was way too early, she was sure she felt Kofi's baby kick in her belly.

The End

Another book by Hilton Hamann you will enjoy:

Queen of Hearts - a deadly battle of wits with an unlikely serial killer

Lieutenant - formerly Captain - Mickey Kruger was banished to the equivalent of 'Cop Siberia', where all he wants is keep his head down, his nose clean, and hang on until he can retire and quietly disappear.

Every year, for the past twenty three years, he calls Lucinda Blake on the anniversary of the day her parents were brutally murdered when she was only sixteen. And every year it's the same: he tells her he has not forgotten his promise to hunt down the 'King of Hearts' killer - though they both know, it's not going to happen.

It's that day again. Time for Kruger, once considered the best detective on the force, to pick up the phone, call Lucinda, and tell her he is no closer to catching the murderer than he was over twenty years ago. The day he hates most of all in his crappy life.

But today will be different. A package addressed to Kruger arrives containing a playing card and a chess piece, the same as the calling cards left by the 'King of Hearts' killer all those years ago.

Written across the front of the card are the words: "Let's play!"

Mickey is convinced the serial killer is back, about to resume a deadly game with his erstwhile opponent. It's a chance for Kruger to finally find redemption and absolution. But his boss believes he is delusional, a has-been clutching at straws, who long ago should've been put out to pasture.

What follows is a deadly battle of wits between Mickey and the killer. A game of chess, where bodies stack up and the serial killer appears to know every move Mickey will make.

Can Mickey Kruger overcome the odds stacked against him, not just by the killer, but also by colleagues out to sabotage him? Can he keep his promise to Lucinda? Can he face the truth when he finds it, or will he hesitate, and die?

Queen of Hearts is a fast-paced, action-thriller that will keep you guessing, and on the edge of your seat, deep into the night.

ABOUT THE AUTHOR

Hilton Hamann is an award-winning, journalist and author based in South Africa. He was Bureau Chief and military correspondent of South Africa's largest newspaper, the Sunday Times and "Special Investigations Editor" of Living Africa Magazine. He has had hundreds of articles and photographs published in newspapers and magazines in over 55 countries.

Hilton married to Joy and has two adult sons and is now a full time novelist.

Other interests include motorcycling, photography, shooting and spending time in the veld with his dog, Andy.

Contact him at: hiltonh@ymail.com

Printed in Great Britain
by Amazon